PREPARE TO BE DAZZLED
BY CLOSE ENCOUNTERS
OF THE MYSTERIOUS KIND

Isaac Asimov's *The Singing Bell* features a lunar murderer with an uncanny ability to avoid prosecution—and a scientist with enough expertise to finally put him away. . . .

In *The Winner* by Donald Westlake, a very different sort of criminal in a very ominous sort of future has a run-in with a very ugly sort of correctional instrument—called the "Guardian." . . .

In *Time Exposures*, Wilson Tucker takes us to a near future where guns are prohibited—and cops like Sergeant Tabbot operate cameras capable of taking extraordinary pictures. . . .

Philip K. Dick's *War Game* tells the story of a few Earthlings who must crack the meaning behind a mysterious object from Ganymede— before *it* cracks the meaning behind *them*. . . .

And others!

SCI-FI PRIVATE EYE

SCI-FI PRIVATE EYE

Edited by

Charles G. Waugh

and

Martin H. Greenberg

A ROC BOOK

ROC
Published by the Penguin Group
Penguin Books USA Inc., 375 Hudson Street,
New York, New York 10014, U.S.A.
Penguin Books Ltd, 27 Wrights Lane,
London W8 5TZ, England
Penguin Books Australia Ltd, Ringwood,
Victoria, Australia
Penguin Books Canada Ltd, 10 Alcorn Avenue,
Toronto, Ontario, Canada M4V 3B2
Penguin Books (N.Z.) Ltd, 182–190 Wairau Road,
Auckland 10, New Zealand

Penguin Books Ltd, Registered Offices:
Harmondsworth, Middlesex, England

First published by Roc, an imprint of Dutton Signet,
a division of Penguin Books USA Inc.

First Printing, March, 1997
10 9 8 7 6 5 4 3 2 1

"The Singing Bell" by Isaac Asimov. Copyright © 1954 by Fantasy House, Inc. From *The
Complete Stories of Isaac Asimov, Vol. II.* Used by permission of Doubleday, a division
of Bantam Doubleday Dell Publishing Group, Inc.
"The Martian Crown Jewels" by Poul Anderson. Copyright © 1972 by Poul Anderson.
Reprinted by permission of the author and Ted Chichak, SCG Inc., 381 Park Avenue
South, New York City, New York 10016.
"A Scarletin Study" by Philip José Farmer. Copyright © 1975 by Mercury Press, Inc. First
published in *The Magazine of Fantasy & Science Fiction.* Reprinted by permission of
the author.
"The Winner" by Donald Westlake. Copyright © 1970 by Harry Harrison. First published
in *Nova 1.* Reprinted by permission of the author.
"The Detweiler Boy" by Tom Reamy. Copyright © 1977 by the Estate of Tom Reamy.
First published in *The Magazine of Fantasy & Science Fiction.* Reprinted by permission
of the Estate and the Estate's agent, Virginia Kidd.
"Time Exposures" by Wilson Tucker. Copyright © 1971 by Terry Carr. First published in
Universe 1. Reprinted by permission of the author.
"Getting Across" by Robert Silverberg. Copyright © 1973 by Agberg, Ltd. Reprinted by
permission of the author and Agberg, Ltd.
"War Game" by Philip K. Dick. Copyright © 1959 by the Galaxy Publishing Corporation.
Reprinted by permission of the author's agent, Russ Galen, SCG Inc., 381 Park Avenue
South, New York City, New York, 10016.
"ARM" by Larry Niven. Copyright © 1975, 1976 by Larry Niven. Reprinted by permission
of the author and his agents, Spectrum Literary Agency.

 REGISTERED TRADEMARK—MARCA REGISTRADA

Printed in the United States of America

Contents

Introduction

Crime and fiction have gone hand in hand for years, back to what is widely considered to be the first detective story, "The Murders in the Rue Morgue" by Edgar Allan Poe. In fact, a case could be made that this classic tale is also the first speculative crime fiction piece as well. During the investigation of the locked-room murders, the reader is convinced that whatever killed those two women could not have been human. Therefore, what was it? The revelation of the killer (and no, we're not going to spoil it for those out there who haven't read the story) is almost anticlimactic when one thinks of what *could* have been in the room with the victims.

Of course, this is not to say that all science-fiction crime deals with bug-eyed monsters. Often, it is man himself who is more distant and alien than anything from another planet.

Regardless, speculative crime fiction has existed for many years, as imaginative writers try to extrapolate how the crimes of the future will be committed and also how these criminals will be caught. With the invention of not-yet-existing technology, the writer can make it easier for either the criminal, as in Robert Silverberg's tale of social terrorism, "Getting Across," or the detective, as seen in Wilson Tucker's police procedural, "Time Exposures." Still, no matter how advanced the society, nothing takes the place of good, old-fashioned deductive reasoning, and no one made this point better than grand master Isaac Asimov in "The Singing Bell."

We've assembled some of today's finest science fiction and crime writers' stories on the future of crime and detection. So turn the page and catch a glimpse of the criminals of the future and the men and women (and aliens) who catch them.

—*The Editors*

The Singing Bell

ISAAC ASIMOV

Isaac Asimov (1920–1992) is probably the most well-known science-fiction writer in the world. His *Foundation* trilogy is considered a classic of socio-political science fiction, examining the decline and fall of a galactic empire set thousands of years in the future. He also wrote many nonfiction articles on the theories of science itself, as well as hundreds of fantasy, science fiction, and mystery short stories. His most famous short story, "Nightfall," about a planet's civilization which descends into anarchy when they experience the setting of their suns for the first time, was adapted into a novel with fellow author Robert Silverberg.

Louis Peyton never discussed publicly the methods by which he had bested the police of Earth in a dozen duels of wits and bluff, with the psychoprobe always waiting and always foiled. He would have been foolish to do so, of course, but in his more complacent moments, he fondled the notion of leaving a testament to be opened only after his death, one in which his unbroken success could clearly be seen to be due to ability and not to luck.

In such a testament he would say, "No false pattern can be created to cover a crime without bearing upon it some trace of its creator. It is better, then, to seek in events some pattern that already exists and then adjust your actions to it."

It was with that principle in mind that Peyton planned the murder of Albert Cornwell.

Cornwell, that small-time retailer of stolen things, first approached Peyton at the latter's usual table-for-one at Grinnell's. Cornwell's blue suit seemed to have a special shine, his lined face a special grin, and his faded mustache a special bristle.

"Mr. Peyton," he said, greeting his future murderer with no fourth-dimensional qualm, "it is so nice to see you. I'd almost given up, sir, almost given up."

Peyton, who disliked being approached over his newspaper and dessert at Grinnell's, said, "If you have business with me, Cornwell, you know where you can reach me." Peyton was past forty and his hair was past its earlier blackness, but his back was rigid, his bearing youthful, his eyes dark, and his voice could cut the more sharply for long practice.

"Not for this, Mr. Peyton," said Cornwell, "not for this. I know of a cache, sir, a cache of . . . you know, sir." The forefinger of his right hand moved gently, as though it were a clapper striking invisible substance, and his left hand momentarily cupped his ear.

Peyton turned a page of the paper, still somewhat damp from its tele-dispenser, folded it flat and said, "Singing Bells?"

"Oh, hush, Mr. Peyton," said Cornwell in whispered agony.

Peyton said, "Come with me."

They walked through the park. It was another Peyton axiom that to be reasonably secret there was nothing like a low-voiced discussion out of doors.

Cornwell whispered, "A cache of Singing Bells; an accumulated cache of Singing Bells. Unpolished, but such beauties, Mr. Peyton."

"Have you seen them?"

"No, sir, but I have spoken with one who has. He had proofs enough to convince me. There is enough there to enable you and me to retire in affluence. In absolute affluence, sir."

"Who was this other man?"

A look of cunning lit Cornwell's face like a smoking torch, obscuring more than it showed and lending it a repulsive oiliness. "The man was a lunar grubstaker who had a method for locating the Bells in the crater sides. I don't know his method; he never told me that. But he has gathered dozens, hidden them on the Moon, and come to Earth to arrange the disposing of them."

"He died, I suppose?"

"Yes. A most shocking accident, Mr. Peyton. A fall from a height. Very sad. Of course, his activities on the Moon were quite illegal. The Dominion is very strict about unauthorized Bell-mining. So perhaps it was a judgment upon him after all. . . . In any case, I have his map."

Peyton said, a look of calm indifference on his face, "I don't want any of the details of your little transaction. What I want to know is why you've come to me."

Cornwell said, "Well, now, there's enough for both of us, Mr. Peyton, and we can both do our bit. For my part, I know where the cache is located and I can get a spaceship. You . . ."

"Yes?"

"You can pilot a spaceship, and you have such excellent contacts for disposing of the Bells. It is a very fair division of labor, Mr. Peyton. Wouldn't you say so, now?"

Peyton considered the pattern of his life—the pattern that already existed—and matters seemed to fit.

He said, "We will leave for the Moon on August the tenth."

Cornwell stopped walking and said, "Mr. Peyton! It's only April now."

Peyton maintained an even gait and Cornwell had to hurry to catch up. "Do you hear me, Mr. Peyton?"

Peyton said, "August the tenth. I will get in touch with you at the proper time, tell you where to bring your ship. Make no attempt to see me personally till then. Good-bye, Cornwell."

Cornwell said, "Fifty-fifty?"

"Quite," said Peyton. "Good-bye."

Peyton continued his walk alone and considered the pattern of his life again. At the age of twenty-seven, he had bought a tract of land in the Rockies on which some past owner had built a house designed as refuge against the threatened atomic wars of two centuries back, the ones that had never come to pass after all. The house remained, however, a monument to a frightened drive for self-sufficiency.

It was of steel and concrete in as isolated a spot as could well be found on Earth, set high above sea level and protected on nearly all sides by mountain peaks that reached higher still. It had its self-contained power unit, its water supply fed by mountain streams, its freezers in which ten sides of beef could hang comfortably, its cellar outfitted like a fortress with an arsenal of weapons designed to stave off hungry, panicked hordes that never came. It had its air-conditioning unit that could scrub and scrub the air until anything *but* radioactivity (alas for human frailty) could be scrubbed out of it.

In that house of survival, Peyton passed the month of August every subsequent year of his perennially bachelor life. He took out the communicators, the television, the newspaper tele-dispenser. He built a force-field fence about his property and left a short-distance signal mechanism to the house from the point where the fence crossed the one trail winding through the mountains.

For one month each year, he could be thoroughly alone. No one saw him, no one could reach him. In absolute solitude, he could have the only vacation he valued after eleven months of contact with a humanity for which he could feel only a cold contempt.

Even the police—and Peyton smiled—knew of his rigid regard for August. He had once jumped bail and risked the psychoprobe rather than forego his August.

Peyton considered another aphorism for possible inclusion in his testament: There is nothing so conducive to an appearance of innocence as the triumphant lack of an alibi.

On July 30, as on July 30 of every year, Louis Peyton took the 9:15 A.M. non-grav stratojet at New York and arrived in Denver at 12:30 P.M. There he lunched and took the 1:45 P.M. semi-grav bus to Hump's Point, from which Sam Leibman took him by ancient ground-car—full grav!—up the trail to the boundaries of his property. Sam Leibman gravely accepted the ten-dollar tip that he always received, touched his hat as he had done on July 30 for fifteen years.

On July 31, as on July 31 of every year, Louis Peyton returned to Hump's Point in his non-grav aeroflitter and placed an order through the Hump's Point general store for such supplies as he needed for the coming month. There was nothing unusual about the order. It was virtually the duplicate of previous such orders.

MacIntyre, manager of the store, checked gravely over the list, put it through to Central Warehouse, Mountain District, in Denver, and the whole of it came pushing over the mass-transference beam within the hour. Peyton loaded the supplies onto his aeroflitter with MacIntyre's help, left his usual ten-dollar tip and returned to his house.

On August 1, at 12:01 A.M., the force field that surrounded his property was set to full power and Peyton was isolated.

And now the pattern changed. Deliberately he had left himself eight days. In that time he slowly and meticulously destroyed just enough of his supplies to account for all of August. He used the dusting chambers which served the house as a garbage-disposal unit. They were of an advanced model capable of reducing all matter up to and including metals and silicates to an impalpable and undetectable molecular dust. The excess energy formed in the process was carried away by the mountain stream that ran through his property. It ran five degrees warmer than normal for a week.

On August 9 his aeroflitter carried him to a spot in Wyoming where Albert Cornwell and a spaceship waited. The spaceship, itself, was a weak point, of course, since there were men who had sold it, men who had transported it and helped prepare it for flight. All those men, however, led only as far as Cornwell, and Cornwell, Peyton thought—with the trace of a smile on his cold lips—would be a dead end. A very dead end.

On August 10 the spaceship, with Peyton at the controls and Cornwell—and his map—as passenger, left the surface of Earth. Its non-grav field was excellent. At full power, the ship's weight was reduced to less than an ounce. The micropiles fed energy efficiently and noiselessly, and without flame or sound the ship rose through the atmosphere, shrank to a point, and was gone.

It was very unlikely that there would be witnesses to the flight, or that in these weak, piping times of peace there would be a radar watch as in days of yore. In point of fact, there was none.

Two days in space; now two weeks on the Moon. Almost instinctively Peyton had allowed for those two weeks from the first. He was under no illusions as to the value of homemade maps by non-cartographers. Useful they might be to the designer himself, who had the help of memory. To a stranger, they could be nothing more than a cryptogram.

Cornwell showed Peyton the map for the first time only after takeoff. He smiled obsequiously. "After all, sir, this was my only trump."

"Have you checked this against the lunar charts?"

"I would scarcely know how, Mr. Peyton. I depend upon you."

Peyton stared at him coldly as he returned the map. The one certain thing upon it was Tycho Crater, the site of the buried Luna City.

In one respect, at least, astronomy was on their side. Tycho was on the daylight side of the Moon at the moment. It meant that patrol ships were less likely to be out, they themselves less likely to be observed.

Peyton brought the ship down in a riskily quick non-grav landing within the safe, cold darkness of the inner shadow of a crater. The sun was past zenith and the shadow would grow no shorter.

Cornwell drew a long face. "Dear, dear, Mr. Peyton. We can scarcely go prospecting in the lunar day."

"The lunar day doesn't last forever," said Peyton shortly. "There are about a hundred hours of sun left. We can use that time for acclimating ourselves and for working out the map."

The answer came quickly, but it was plural. Peyton studied the lunar charts over and over, taking meticulous measurements, and trying to find the pattern of craters shown on the homemade scrawl that was the key to—what?

Finally Peyton said, "The crater we want could be any one of three: GC-3, GC-5, or MT-10."

"What do we do, Mr. Peyton?" asked Cornwell anxiously.

"We try them all," said Peyton, "beginning with the nearest."

The terminator passed and they were in the night shadow. After that, they spent increasing periods on the lunar surface, getting used to the eternal silence and blackness, the harsh points of the stars and the crack of light that was the Earth peeping over the rim of the crater above. They left hollow, featureless footprints in the dry dust that did not stir or change. Peyton noted them first when they climbed out of the crater into the full light of the gibbous Earth. That was on the eighth day after their arrival on the Moon.

The lunar cold put a limit to how long they could remain outside their ship at any one time. Each day, however, they managed for longer. By the eleventh day after arrival they had eliminated GC-5 as the container of the Singing Bells.

By the fifteenth day, Peyton's cold spirit had grown warm with desperation. It would have to be GC-3. MT-10 was too far away. They would not have time to reach it and explore it and still allow for a return to Earth by August 31.

On that same fifteenth day, however, despair was laid to rest forever when they discovered the Bells.

They were not beautiful. They were merely irregular masses of gray rock, as large as a double fist, vacuum-filled and feather-light in the moon's gravity. There were two dozen of them and each one, after proper polishing, could be sold for a hundred thousand dollars at least.

Carefully, in double handfuls, they carried the Bells to the ship, bedded them in excelsior, and returned for more. Three times they made the trip both ways over ground that would have worn them out on Earth but which, under the Moon's lilliputian gravity, was scarcely a barrier.

Cornwell passed the last of the Bells up to Peyton, who placed them carefully within the outer lock.

"Keep them clear, Mr. Peyton," he said, his radioed voice sounding harshly in the other's ear. "I'm coming up."

He crouched for the slow high leap against lunar gravity, looked up, and froze in panic. His face, clearly visible through the hard carved lusilite of his helmet, froze in a last grimace of terror. "No, Mr. Peyton. Don't—"

Peyton's fist tightened on the grip of the blaster he held. It fired. There was an unbearably brilliant flash and Cornwell was a dead fragment of a man, sprawled amid remnants of a spacesuit and flecked with freezing blood.

Peyton paused to stare somberly at the dead man, but only for a second. Then he transferred the last of the Bells to their prepared containers, removed his suit, activated first the non-grav field, then the micropiles, and, potentially a million or two richer than he had been two weeks earlier, set off on the return trip to Earth.

On the twenty-ninth of August, Peyton's ship descended silently, stern bottomward, to the spot in Wyoming from which it had taken off on August

10. The care with which Peyton had chosen the spot was not wasted. His aeroflitter was still there, drawn within the protection of an enclosing wrinkle of the rocky, tortuous countryside.

He moved the Singing Bells once again, in their containers, into the deepest recess of the wrinkle, covering them, loosely and sparsely, with earth. He returned to the ship once more to set the controls and make last adjustments. He climbed out again and two minutes later the ship's automatics took over.

Silently hurrying, the ship bounded upward and up, veering to westward somewhat as the Earth rotated beneath it. Peyton watched, shading his narrow eyes, and at the extreme edge of vision there was a tiny gleam of light and a dot of cloud against the blue sky.

Peyton's mouth twitched into a smile. He had judged well. With the cadmium safety-rods bent back into uselessness, the micropiles had plunged past the unit-sustaining safety level and the ship had vanished in the heat of the nuclear explosion that had followed.

Twenty minutes later, he was back on his property. He was tired and his muscles ached under Earth's gravity. He slept well.

Twelve hours later, in the earliest dawn, the police came.

The man who opened the door placed his crossed hands over his paunch and ducked his smiling head two or three times in greeting. The man who entered, H. Seton Davenport of the Terrestrial Bureau of Investigation, looked about uncomfortably.

The room he had entered was large and in semi-darkness except for the brilliant viewing lamp focused over a combination armchair-desk. Rows of book-films covered the walls. A suspension of Galactic charts occupied one corner of the room and a Galactic Lens gleamed softly on a stand in another corner.

"You are Dr. Wendell Urth?" asked Davenport, in a tone that suggested he found it hard to believe. Davenport was a stocky man with black hair, a thin and prominent nose, and a star-shaped scar on one cheek which marked permanently the place where a neuronic whip had once struck him at too close a range.

"I am," said Dr. Urth in a thin, tenor voice. "And you are Inspector Davenport."

The Inspector presented his credentials and said, "The University recommended you to me as an extraterrologist."

"So you said when you called me half an hour ago," said Urth agreeably. His features were thick, his nose was a snubby button, and over his somewhat protuberant eyes there were thick glasses.

"I shall get to the point, Dr. Urth. I presume you have visited the Moon . . ."

Dr. Urth, who had brought out a bottle of ruddy liquid and two glasses, just a little the worse for dust, from behind a straggling pile of book-films, said with sudden brusqueness, "I have never visited the Moon, Inspector. I never intend to! Space travel is foolishness. I don't believe in it." Then, in softer tones, "Sit down, sir, sit down. Have a drink."

Inspector Davenport did as he was told and said, "But you're an . . ."

"Extraterrologist. Yes. I'm interested in other worlds, but it doesn't mean I have to go there. Good lord, I don't have to be a time traveler to qualify as a historian, do I?" He sat down, and a broad smile impressed itself upon his round face once more as he said, "Now tell me what's on your mind."

"I have come," said the Inspector, frowning, "to consult you in a case of murder."

"Murder? What have I to do with murder?"

"This murder, Dr. Urth, was on the Moon."

"Astonishing."

"It's more than astonishing. It's unprecedented, Dr. Urth. In the fifty years since the Lunar Dominion has been established, ships have blown up and spacesuits have sprung leaks. Men have boiled to death on sun-side, frozen on dark-side, and suffocated on both sides. There have even been deaths by falls, which, considering lunar gravity, is quite a trick. But in all that time, not one man has been killed on the Moon as the result of another man's deliberate act of violence—till now."

Dr. Urth said, "How was it done?"

"A blaster. The authorities were on the scene within the hour through a fortunate set of circumstances. A patrol ship observed a flash of light against the Moon's surface. You know how far a flash can be seen against the night-side. The pilot notified Luna City and landed. In the process of circling back, he swears that he just managed to see by Earthlight what looked like a ship taking off. Upon landing, he discovered a blasted corpse and footprints."

"The flash of light," said Dr. Urth, "you suppose to be the firing blaster."

"That's certain. The corpse was fresh. Interior portions of the body had not yet frozen. The footprints belonged to two people. Careful measurements showed that the depressions fell into two groups of somewhat different diameters, indicating differently sized spaceboots. In the main, they led to craters GC-3 and GC-5, a pair of—"

"I am acquainted with the official code for naming lunar craters," said Dr. Urth pleasantly.

"Umm. In any case, GC-3 contained footprints that led to a rift in the crater wall, within which scraps of hardened pumice were found. X-ray diffraction patterns showed—"

"Singing Bells," put in the extraterrologist in great excitement. "Don't tell me this murder of yours involves Singing Bells!"

"What if it does?" demanded Davenport blankly.

"I have one. A University expedition uncovered it and presented it to me in return for— Come, Inspector, I must show it to you."

Dr. Urth jumped up and pattered across the room, beckoning the other to follow as he did. Davenport, annoyed, followed.

They entered a second room, larger than the first, dimmer, considerably more cluttered. Davenport stared with astonishment at the heterogeneous mass of material that was jumbled together in no pretense at order.

He made out a small lump of "blue glaze" from Mars, the sort of thing some romantics considered to be an artifact of long-extinct Martians, a small meteorite, a model of an early spaceship, a sealed bottle of nothing scrawlingly labeled "Venusian atmosphere."

Dr. Urth said happily, "I've made a museum of my whole house. It's one of the advantages of being a bachelor. Of course, I haven't quite got things organized. Someday, when I have a spare week or so . . ."

For a moment he looked about, puzzled; then, remembering, he pushed aside a chart showing the evolutionary scheme of development of the marine invertebrates that were the highest life forms on Barnard's Planet and said, "Here it is. It's flawed, I'm afraid."

The Bell hung suspended from a slender wire, soldered delicately onto it. That it was flawed was obvious. It had a constriction line running halfway about it that made it seem like two small globes, firmly but imperfectly squashed together. Despite that, it had been lovingly polished to a dull luster, softly gray, velvety smooth, and faintly pock-marked in a way that laboratories, in their futile efforts to prepare synthetic Bells, had found impossible to duplicate.

Dr. Urth said, "I experimented a good deal before I found a decent stroker. A flawed Bell is temperamental. But bone works. I have one here" — and he held up something that looked like a short thick spoon made of a gray-white substance— "which I had made out of the femur of an ox. Listen."

With surprising delicacy, his pudgy fingers maneuvered the Bell, feeling for one best spot. He adjusted it, steadying it daintily. Then, letting the Bell swing free, he brought down the thick end of the bone spoon and stroked the Bell softly.

It was as though a million harps had sounded a mile away. It swelled and faded and returned. It came from no particular direction. It sounded inside the head, incredibly sweet and pathetic and tremulous all at once.

It died away lingeringly and both men were silent for a full minute.

Dr. Urth said, "Not bad, eh?" and with a flick of his hand set the Bell to swinging on its wire.

Davenport stirred restlessly. "Careful! Don't break it." The fragility of a good Singing Bell was proverbial.

Dr. Urth said, "Geologists say the Bells are only pressure-hardened pumice, enclosing a vacuum in which small beads of rock rattle freely. That's what they *say*. But if that's all it is, why can't we reproduce one? Now a flawless Bell would make this one sound like a child's harmonica."

"Exactly," said Davenport, "and there aren't a dozen people on Earth who own a flawless one, and there are a hundred people and institutions who would buy one at any price, no questions asked. A supply of Bells would be worth murder."

The extraterrologist turned to Davenport and pushed his spectacles back on his inconsequential nose with a stubby forefinger. "I haven't forgotten your murder case. Please go on."

"That can be done in a sentence. I know the identity of the murderer."

They had returned to the chairs in the library and Dr. Urth clasped his hands over his ample abdomen. "Indeed? Then surely you have no problem, Inspector."

"Knowing and proving are not the same, Dr. Urth. Unfortunately he has no alibi."

"You mean, unfortunately he *has,* don't you?"

"I mean what I say. If he had an alibi, I could crack it somehow, because it would be a false one. If there were witnesses who claimed they had seen him on Earth at the time of the murder, their stories could be broken down. If he had documentary proof, it could be exposed as a forgery or some sort of trickery. Unfortunately he has none of it."

"What does he have?"

Carefully Inspector Davenport described the Peyton estate in Colorado. He concluded, "He has spent every August there in the strictest isolation. Even the T.B.I. would have to testify to that. Any jury would have to presume that he was on his estate this August as well, unless we could present definite proof that he was on the Moon."

"What makes you think he *was* on the Moon? Perhaps he is innocent."

"No!" Davenport was almost violent. "For fifteen years I've been trying to collect sufficient evidence against him and I've never succeeded. But I can *smell* a Peyton crime now. I tell you that no one but Peyton, no one on Earth, would have the impudence or, for that matter, the practical business contacts to attempt disposal of smuggled Singing Bells. He is known to be an expert space pilot. He is known to have had contact with the murdered man, though admittedly not for some months. Unfortunately none of that is proof."

Dr. Urth said, "Wouldn't it be simple to use the psychoprobe, now that its use has been legalized?"

Davenport scowled, and the scar on his cheek turned livid. "Have you read the Konski-Hiakawa law, Dr. Urth?"

"No."

"I think no one has. The right to mental privacy, the government says, is fundamental. All right, but what follows? The man who is psychoprobed and proves innocent of the crime for which he was psychoprobed is entitled to as much compensation as he can persuade the courts to give him. In a recent case a bank cashier was awarded twenty-five thousand dollars for having been psychoprobed on inaccurate suspicion of theft. It seems that the circumstantial evidence which seemed to point to theft actually pointed to a small spot of adultery. His claim that he lost his job, was threatened by the husband in question and put in bodily fear, and finally was held up to ridicule and contumely because a news-strip man had learned the results of the probe held good in court."

"I can see the man's point."

"So can we all. That's the trouble. One more item to remember: Any man who has been psychoprobed once for any reason can never be psychoprobed again for any reason. No one man, the law says, shall be placed in mental jeopardy twice in his lifetime."

"Inconvenient."

"Exactly. In the two years since the psychoprobe has been legitimized, I couldn't count the number of crooks and chiselers who've tried to get themselves psychoprobed for purse-snatching so that they could play the rackets safely afterward. So you see the Department will not allow Peyton to be psychoprobed until they have firm evidence of his guilt. Not legal evidence, maybe, but evidence that is strong enough to convince my boss. The worst of it, Dr. Urth, is that if we come into court without a psychoprobe record, we can't win. In a case as serious as murder, not to have used the psychoprobe is proof enough to the dumbest juror that the prosecution isn't sure of its ground."

"Now what do you want of me?"

"Proof that he was on the Moon sometime in August. It's got to be done quickly. I can't hold him on suspicion much longer. And if news of the murder gets out, the world press will blow up like an asteroid striking Jupiter's atmosphere. A glamorous crime, you know—first murder on the Moon."

"Exactly when was the murder committed?" asked Urth, in a sudden transition to brisk cross-examination.

"August twenty-seventh."

"And the arrest was made when?"

"Yesterday, August thirtieth."

"Then if Peyton were the murderer, he would have had time to return to Earth."

"Barely. Just barely." Davenport's lips thinned. "If I had been a day sooner— If I had found his place empty—"

"And how long do you suppose the two, the murdered man and the murderer, were on the Moon altogether?"

"Judging by the ground covered by the footprints, a number of days. A week, at the minimum."

"Has the ship they used been located?"

"No, and it probably never will. About ten hours ago, the University of Denver reported a rise in background radioactivity beginning day before yesterday at 6 P.M. and persisting for a number of hours. It's an easy thing, Dr. Urth, to set a ship's controls so as to allow it to blast off without crew and blow up, fifty miles high, in a micropile short."

"If I had been Peyton," said Dr. Urth thoughtfully, "I would have killed the man on board ship and blown up corpse and ship together."

"You don't know Peyton," said Davenport grimly. "He enjoys his victories over the law. He values them. Leaving the corpse on the Moon is his challenge to us."

"I see." Dr. Urth patted his stomach with a rotary motion and said, "Well, there is a chance."

"That you'll be able to prove he was on the Moon?"

"That I'll be able to give you my opinion."

"Now?"

"The sooner the better. If, of course, I get a chance to interview Mr. Peyton."

"That can be arranged. I have a non-grav jet waiting. We can be in Washington in twenty minutes."

But a look of the deepest alarm passed over the plump extraterrologist's face. He rose to his feet and pattered away from the T.B.I. agent toward the duskiest corner of the cluttered room.

"No!"

"What's wrong, Dr. Urth?"

"I won't use a non-grav jet. I don't believe in them."

Davenport stared confusedly at Dr. Urth. He stammered, "Would you prefer a monorail?"

Dr. Urth snapped, "I mistrust all forms of transportation. I don't believe in them. Except walking. I don't mind walking." He was suddenly eager. "Couldn't you bring Mr. Peyton to this city, somewhere within walking distance? To City Hall, perhaps? I've often walked to City Hall."

Davenport looked helplessly about the room. He looked at the myriad volumes of lore about the light-years. He could see through the open door into the room beyond, with its tokens of the worlds beyond the sky. And he looked at Dr. Urth, pale at the thought of non-grav jet, and shrugged his shoulders.

"I'll bring Peyton here. Right to this room. Will that satisfy you?"

Dr. Urth puffed out his breath in a deep sigh. "Quite."

"I hope you can deliver, Dr. Urth."

"I will do my best, Mr. Davenport."

Louis Peyton stared with distaste at his surroundings and with contempt at the fat man who bobbed his head in greeting. He glanced at the seat offered him and brushed it with his hand before sitting down. Davenport took a seat next to him, with his blaster holster in clear view.

The fat man was smiling as he sat down and patted his round abdomen as though he had just finished a good meal and were intent on letting the world know about it.

He said, "Good evening, Mr. Peyton. I am Dr. Wendell Urth, extraterrologist."

Peyton looked at him again. "And what do you want with me?"

"I want to know if you were on the Moon at any time in the month of August."

"I was not."

"Yet no man saw you on Earth between the days of August first and August thirtieth."

"I lived my normal life in August. I am never seen during that month. Let him tell you." And he jerked his head in the direction of Davenport.

Dr. Urth chuckled. "How nice if we could test this matter. If there were only some physical manner in which we could differentiate Moon from Earth. If, for instance, we could analyze the dust in your hair and say, 'Aha, Moon rock.' Unfortunately we can't. Moon rock is much the same as Earth rock. Even if it weren't, there wouldn't be any in your hair unless you stepped onto the lunar surface without a spacesuit, which is unlikely."

Peyton remained impassive.

Dr. Urth went on, smiling benevolently, and lifting a hand to steady the glasses perched precariously on the bulb of his nose. "A man traveling in space or on the Moon breathes Earth air, eats Earth food. He carries Earth environment next to his skin whether he's in his ship or in his spacesuit. We are looking for a man who spent two days in space going to the Moon, at least a week on the Moon, and two days coming back from the Moon. In all that time he carried Earth next to his skin, which makes it difficult."

"I'd suggest," said Peyton, "that you can make

it less difficult by releasing me and looking for the real murderer."

"It may come to that," said Dr. Urth. "Have you ever seen anything like this?" His hand pushed its pudgy way to the ground beside his chair and came up with a gray sphere that sent back subdued highlights.

Peyton smiled. "It looks like a Singing Bell to me."

"It *is* a Singing Bell. The murder was committed for the sake of Singing Bells. What do you think of this one?"

"I think it is badly flawed."

"Ah, but inspect it," said Dr. Urth, and with a quick motion of his hand, he tossed it through six feet of air to Peyton.

Davenport cried out and half-rose from his chair. Peyton brought up his arms with an effort, but so quickly that he managed to catch the Bell.

Peyton said, "You damned fool. Don't throw it around that way."

"You respect Singing Bells, do you?"

"Too much to break one. That's no crime, at least." Peyton stroked the Bell gently, then lifted it to his ear and shook it slowly, listening to the soft clicks of the Lunoliths, those small pumice particles, as they rattled in vacuum.

Then, holding the Bell up by the length of steel wire still attached to it, he ran a thumbnail over its surface with an expert, curving motion. It twanged! The note was very mellow, very flutelike, holding with a slight *vibrato* that faded lingeringly and conjured up pictures of a summer twilight.

For a short moment, all three men were lost in the sound.

And then Dr. Urth said, "Throw it back, Mr. Peyton. Toss it here!" and held out his hand in peremptory gesture.

Automatically Louis Peyton tossed the Bell. It traveled its short arc one-third of the way to Dr. Urth's waiting hand, curved downward and shattered with a heartbroken, sighing discord on the floor.

Davenport and Peyton stared at the gray slivers with equal wordlessness and Dr. Urth's calm voice went almost unheard as he said, "When the criminal's cache of crude Bells is located, I'll ask that a flawless one, properly polished, be given to me, as replacement and fee."

"A fee? For what?" demanded Davenport irritably.

"Surely the matter is now obvious. Despite my little speech of a moment ago, there is one piece of Earth's environment that no space traveler carries with him and that is *Earth's surface gravity*. The fact that Mr. Peyton could so egregiously misjudge the toss of an object he obviously valued so highly could mean only that his muscles are not yet readjusted to the pull of Earthly gravity. It is my professional opinion, Mr. Davenport, that your prisoner has, in the last few days, been away from Earth. He has either been in space or on some planetary object considerably smaller in size than the Earth—as, for example, the Moon."

Davenport rose triumphantly to his feet. "Let me have your opinion in writing," he said, hand on blaster, "and that will be good enough to get me permission to use a psychoprobe."

Louis Peyton, dazed and unresisting, had only the numb realization that any testament he could now leave would have to include the fact of ultimate failure.

The Martian Crown Jewels

POUL ANDERSON

Poul Anderson is a seven-time winner of the Hugo award and three-time winner of the Nebula award. He has written in all genres and styles from hard science fiction to high fantasy and everything in between. His novels and stories are richly textured examinations of life, whether it be human or alien. Through his well-drawn, fully realized characters, he chronicles man's struggle to live in worlds, whether they be past, present, or future, that are ever changing.

The signal was picked up when the ship was still a quarter million miles away, and recorded voices summoned the technicians. There was no haste, for the ZX28749, otherwise called the *Jane Brackney*, was right on schedule; but landing an unmanned spaceship is always a delicate operation. Men and machines prepared to receive her as she came down, but the control crew had the first order of business.

Yamagata, Steinmann, and Ramanowitz were in the GCA tower, with Hollyday standing by for an emergency. If the circuits *should* fail—they never had, but a thousand tons of cargo and nuclear-powered vessel, crashing into the port, could empty Phobos of human life. So Hollyday watched over a set of spare assemblies, ready to plug in whatever might be required.

Yamagata's thin fingers danced over the radar dials. His eyes were intent on the screen. "Got her," he said. Steinmann made a distance reading and Ramanowitz took the velocity off the Dopplerscope. A brief session with a computer showed the figures to be almost as predicted.

"Might as well relax," said Yamagata, taking out a cigarette. "She won't be in control range for a while yet."

His eyes roved over the crowded room and out its window. From the tower he had a view of the spaceport: unimpressive, most of its shops and sheds and living quarters being underground. The smooth concrete field was chopped off by the curvature of the tiny satellite. It always faced Mars, and the station was on the far side, but he could remember how the planet hung enormous over the opposite hemisphere, soft ruddy disc blurred with thin air, hazy greenish-brown mottlings of heath and farmland. Though Phobos was clothed in vacuum, you couldn't see the hard stars of space: the sun and the floodlamps were too bright.

There was a knock on the door. Hollyday went over, almost drifting in the ghostly gravity, and opened it. "Nobody allowed in here during a landing," he said. Hollyday was a stocky blond man with a pleasant, open countenance, and his tone was less peremptory than his words.

"Police." The newcomer, muscular, round-faced, and earnest, was in plain clothes, tunic and pajama pants, which was expected; everyone in the tiny settlement knew Inspector Gregg. But he was packing a gun, which was not usual, and looked harried.

Yamagata peered out again and saw the port's four constables down on the field in official spacesuits, watching the ground crew. They carried weapons. "What's the matter?" he asked.

"Nothing . . . I hope." Gregg came in and tried to smile. "But the *Jane* has a very unusual cargo this trip."

"Hm?" Ramanowitz's eyes lit up in his broad plump visage. "Why weren't we told?"

"That was deliberate. Secrecy. The Martian crown jewels are aboard." Gregg fumbled a cigarette from his tunic.

Hollyday and Steinmann nodded at each other. Yamagata whistled. "On a robot ship?" he asked.

"Uh-huh. A robot ship is the one form of transportation from which they could not be stolen. There were three attempts made when they went to Earth on a regular liner, and I hate to think how many while they were at the British Museum. One guard lost his life. Now my boys are going to remove them before anyone else touches that ship and scoot 'em right down to Sabaeus."

"How much are they worth?" wondered Ramanowitz.

"Oh . . . they could be fenced on Earth for maybe half a billion UN dollars," said Gregg. "But the thief would do better to make the Martians pay to get them back . . . no, Earth would have to, I suppose, since it's our responsibility." He blew nervous clouds. "The jewels were secretly put on the *Jane,* last thing before she left on her regular run.

I wasn't even told till a special messenger on this week's liner gave me the word. Not a chance for any thief to know they're here, till they're safely back on Mars. And that'll be *safe!*"

Ramanowitz shuddered. All the planets knew what guarded the vaults at Sabaeus.

"Some people did know, all along," said Yamagata thoughtfully. "I mean the loading crew back at Earth."

"Uh-huh, there is that." Gregg smiled. "Several of them have quit since then, the messenger said, but of course, there's always a big turnover among spacejacks—they're a restless bunch." His gaze drifted across Steinmann and Hollyday, both of whom had last worked at Earth Station and come to Mars a few ships back. The liners went on a hyperbolic path and arrived in a couple of weeks; the robot ships followed the more leisurely and economical Hohmann A orbit and needed 258 days. A man who knew what ship was carrying the jewels could leave Earth, get to Mars well ahead of the cargo, and snap up a job here—Phobos was always shorthanded.

"Don't look at me!" said Steinmann, laughing. "Chuck and I knew about this—of course—but we were under security restrictions. Haven't told a soul."

"Yeah. I'd have known it if you had," nodded Gregg. "Gossip travels fast here. Don't resent this, please, but I'm here to see that none of you boys leaves this tower till the jewels are aboard our own boat."

"Oh, well. It'll mean overtime pay."

"If I want to get rich fast, I'll stick to prospecting," added Hollyday.

"When are you going to quit running around with that Geiger in your free time?" asked Yamagata. "Phobos is nothing but iron and granite."

"I have my own ideas about that," said Hollyday stoutly.

"Hell, everybody needs a hobby on this Godforsaken clod," declared Ramanowitz. "I might try for those sparklers myself, just for the excitement—" He stopped abruptly, aware of Gregg's eyes.

"All right," snapped Yamagata. "Here we go. Inspector, please stand back out of the way, and for your life's sake don't interrupt us."

The *Jane* was drifting in, her velocity on the carefully precalculated orbit almost identical with that of Phobos. Almost, but not quite—there had been the inevitable small disturbing factors, for which the remote-controlled jets had to compensate, and then there was the business of landing her. The team got a fix and were frantically busy.

In free fall, the *Jane* approached within a thousand miles of Phobos—a spheroid 500 feet in radius, big and massive, but lost against the incredible bulk of the satellite. And yet Phobos is an insignificant airless pill, negligible even beside its seventh-rate planet. Astronomical magnitudes are simply and literally incomprehensible.

When the ship was close enough, the radio directed her gyros to rotate her, very, very gently, until her pickup antenna was pointing directly at the field. Then her jets were cut in, a mere whisper of thrust. She was nearly above the spaceport, her path tangential to the moon's curvature. After a moment Yamagata slapped the keys hard, and the rockets blasted furiously, a visible red streak up in the sky. He cut them again, checked his data, and gave a milder blast.

"Okay," he grunted. "Let's bring her in."

Her velocity relative to Phobos's orbit and rotation was now zero, and she was falling. Yamagata slewed her around till the jets were pointing vertically down. Then he sat back and mopped his face while Ramanowitz took over; the job was too nerve-stretching for one man to perform in its entirety. Ramanowitz sweated the awkward mass to within a few yards of the cradle. Steinmann finished the task, easing her into the berth like an egg into a cup. He cut the jets and there was silence.

"Whew! Chuck, how about a drink?" Yamagata held out unsteady fingers and regarded them with an impersonal stare.

Hollyday smiled and fetched a bottle. It went happily around. Gregg declined. His eyes were locked to the field, where a technician was checking for radioactivity. The verdict was clean, and he saw his constables come soaring over the concrete, to surround the great ship with guns. One of them went up, opened the manhatch, and slipped inside.

It seemed a very long while before he emerged. Then he came running. Gregg cursed and thumbed the tower's radio board. "Hey, there! Ybarra! What's the matter?"

The helmet set shuddered a reply: "Señor . . . Señor Inspector. . . . the crown jewels are gone."

*   *   *

Sabaeus is, of course, a purely human name for the old city nestled in the Martian tropics, at the juncture of the "canals" Phison and Euphrates. Terrestrial mouths simply cannot form the syllables of High Chlannach, though rough approximations are possible. Nor did humans ever build a town exclusively of towers broader at the top than the base, or inhabit one for twenty thousand years. If they had, though, they would have encouraged an eager tourist influx; but Martians prefer more dignified ways of making a dollar, even if their parsimonious fame has long replaced that of Scotchmen. The result is that though interplanetary trade is brisk and Phobos a treaty port, a human is still a rare sight in Sabaeus.

Hurrying down the avenues between the stone mushrooms, Gregg felt conspicuous. He was glad the airsuit muffled him. Not that the grave Martians stared; they varkled, which is worse.

The Street of Those Who Prepare Nourishment in Ovens is a quiet one, given over to handicrafters, philosophers, and residential apartments. You won't see a courtship dance or a parade of the Lesser Halberdiers on it: nothing more exciting than a continuous four-day argument on the relativistic nature of the null class or an occasional gunfight. The latter are due to the planet's most renowned private detective, who nests here.

Gregg always found it eerie to be on Mars, under the cold deep-blue sky and the shrunken sun, among noises muffled by the thin oxygen-deficient air. But for Syaloch he had a good deal of affection, and when he had gone up the ladder and shaken the rattle outside the second-floor apartment and had been admitted, it was like escaping from nightmare.

"Ah, Krech!" The investigator laid down the stringed instrument on which he had been playing and towered gauntly over his visitor. "An unexbectet bleassure to see hyou. Come in, my tear chab, to come in." He was proud of his English—but simple misspellings will not convey the whistling, clicking Martian accent. Gregg had long ago fallen into the habit of translating it into a human pronunciation as he listened.

The Inspector felt a cautious way into the high, narrow room. The glowsnakes which illuminated it after dark were coiled asleep on the stone floor, in a litter of papers, specimens, and weapons; rusty sand covered the sills of the Gothic windows. Syaloch was not neat except in his own person. In one corner was a small chemical laboratory. The rest of the walls were taken up with shelves, the criminological literature of three planets—Martian books, Terrestrial micros, Venusian talking stones. At one place, patriotically, the glyphs representing the reigning Nestmother had been punched out with bullets. An Earthling could not sit on the trapezelike native furniture, but Syaloch had courteously provided chairs and tubs as well; his clientèle was also triplanetary. Gregg found a scarred Duncan Phyfe and lowered himself, breathing heavily into his oxygen tubes.

"I take it you are here on official but confidential business." Syaloch got out a big-bowled pipe. Martians have happily adopted tobacco, though in their atmosphere it must include potassium permanganate. Gregg was thankful he didn't have to breathe the blue fog.

He started. "How the hell do you know that?"

"Elementary, my dear fellow. Your manner is most agitated, and I know nothing but a crisis in your profession would cause that in a good stolid bachelor. Yet you come to me rather than the Homeostatic Corps . . . so it must be a delicate affair."

Gregg laughed wryly. He himself could not read any Martian's expression—what corresponds to a smile or a snarl on a totally nonhuman face? But this overgrown stork—

No. To compare the species of different planets is merely to betray the limitations of language. Syaloch was a seven-foot biped of vaguely storklike appearance. But the lean, crested, red-beaked head at the end of the sinuous neck was too large, the yellow eyes too deep; the white feathers were more like a penguin's than a flying bird's, save at the blue-plumed tail; instead of wings there were skinny red arms ending in four-fingered hands. And the overall posture was too erect for a bird.

Gregg jerked back to awareness. God in Heaven! The city lay gray and quiet; the sun was slipping westward over the farmlands of Sinus Sabaeus and the desert of the Aeria; he could just make out the rumble of a treadmill cart passing beneath the windows—and he sat here with a story which could blow the Solar System apart!

His hands, gloved against the chill, twisted together. "Yes, it's confidential, all right. If you can solve this case, you can just about name your own fee." The gleam in Syaloch's eyes made him regret that, but he stumbled on: "One thing, though. Just how do you feel about us Earthlings?"

"I have no prejudices. It is the brain that counts, not whether it is covered by feathers or hair or bony plates."

"No, I realize that. But some Martians resent us. We do disrupt an old way of life—we can't help it, if we're to trade with you—"

"*K'teh.* The trade is on the whole beneficial. Your fuel and machinery—and tobacco, yesss—for our kantz and snull. Also, we were getting too . . . stale. And of course space travel has added a whole new dimension to criminology. Yes, I favor Earth."

"Then you'll help us? And keep quiet about something which could provoke your planetary federation into kicking us off Phobos?"

The third eyelids closed, making the long-beaked face a mask. "I give no promises yet, Gregg."

"Well . . . damn it, all right, I'll have to take the chance." The policeman swallowed hard. "You know about your crown jewels, of course."

"They were lent to Earth for exhibit and scientific study."

"After years of negotiation. There's no more priceless relic on all Mars—and you were an old civilization when we were hunting mammoths. All right. They've been stolen."

Syaloch opened his eyes, but his only other movement was to nod.

"They were put on a robot ship at Earth Station. They were gone when that ship reached Phobos. We've damn near ripped the boat apart trying to find them—we did take the other cargo to pieces, bit by bit—and they aren't there!"

Syaloch rekindled his pipe, an elaborate flint-and-steel process on a world where matches won't burn. Only when it was drawing well did he suggest: "Is it possible the ship was boarded en route?"

"No. It isn't possible. Every spacecraft in the System is registered, and its whereabouts are known at any time. Furthermore, imagine trying to find a speck in hundreds of millions of cubic miles, and match velocities with it . . . no vessel ever built could carry that much fuel. And mind you, it was never announced that the jewels were going back this way. Only the UN police and the Earth Station crew *could* know till the ship had actually left—by which time it'd be too late to catch her."

"Most interesting." Syaloch puffed hard.

"If word of this gets out," said Gregg miserably, "you can guess the results. I suppose we'd still have a few friends left in your Parliament—"

"In the House of Actives, yesss . . . a few. Not in the House of Philosophers, which is of course the upper chamber."

"It could mean a twenty-year hiatus in Earth-Mars traffic—maybe a permanent breaking off of relations. Damn it, Syaloch, you've *got* to find those stones!"

"Hm-m-m. I pray your pardon. This requires thought." The Martian picked up his crooked instrument and plucked a few tentative chords. Gregg sighed and attempted to relax. He knew the Chlannach temperament; he'd have to listen to an hour of minor-key caterwauling.

The colorless sunset was past, night had fallen with the unnerving Martian swiftness, and the glowsnakes were emitting blue radiance when Syaloch put down the demifiddle.

"I fear I shall have to visit Phobos in person," he said. "There are too many unknowns for analysis, and it is never well to theorize before all the data have been gathered." A bony hand clapped Gregg's shoulder. "Come, come, old chap. I am really most grateful to you. Life was becoming infernally dull. Now, as my famous Terrestrial predecessor would say, the game's afoot . . . and a very big game indeed!"

A Martian in an Earthlike atmosphere is not much hampered, needing only an hour in a compression chamber and a filter on his beak to eliminate excess oxygen and moisture. Syaloch walked freely about the port clad in filter, pipe, and *tirstokr* cap, grumbling to himself at the heat and humidity. He noticed that all the humans but Gregg were reserved, almost fearful, as they watched him—they were sitting on a secret which could unleash red murder.

He donned a spacesuit and went out to inspect the *Jane Brackney*. The vessel had been shunted aside to make room for later arrivals, and stood by a raw crag at the edge of the field, glimmering in the hard spatial sunlight. Gregg and Yamagata were with him.

"I say, you *have* been thorough," remarked the detective. "The outer skin is quite stripped off."

The spheroid resembled an egg which had tangled with a waffle iron: an intersecting grid of girders and braces above a thin aluminum hide. The jets, hatches, and radio mast were the only breaks in the checkerboard pattern, whose depth was

about a foot and whose squares were a yard across
at the "equator."

Yamagata laughed in a strained fashion. "No, the
cops fluoroscoped every inch of her, but that's the
way these cargo ships always look. They never land
on Earth, you know, or any place where there's air,
so streamlining would be unnecessary. And since
nobody is aboard in transit, we don't have to worry
about insulation or airtightness. Perishables are
stowed in sealed compartments."

"I see. Now where were the crown jewels kept?"

"They were supposed to be in a cupboard near
the gyros," said Gregg. "They were in a locked
box, about six inches high, six inches wide, and a
foot long." He shook his head, finding it hard to
believe that so small a box could contain so much
potential death.

"Ah . . . but *were* they placed there?"

"I radioed Earth and got a full account," said
Gregg. "The ship was loaded as usual at the satellite station, then shoved a quarter mile away till it
was time for her to leave—to get her out of the
way, you understand. She was still in the same free-
fall orbit, attached by a light cable—perfectly standard practice. At the last minute, without anyone
being told beforehand, the crown jewels were
brought up from Earth and stashed aboard."

"By a special policeman, I presume?"

"No. Only licensed technicians are allowed to
board a ship in orbit, unless there's a life-and-death
emergency. One of the regular station crew—fellow
named Carter—was told where to put them. He
was watched by the cops as he pulled himself along
the cable and in through the manhatch." Gregg

pointed to a small door near the radio mast. "He came out, closed it, and returned on the cable. The police immediately searched him and his spacesuit, just in case, and he positively did not have the jewels. There was no reason to suspect him of anything—good steady worker—though I'll admit he's disappeared since then. The *Jane* blasted a few minutes late and her jets were watched till they cut off and she went into free fall. And that's the last anyone saw of her till she got here—without the jewels."

"And right on orbit," added Yamagata. "If by some freak she had been boarded, it would have thrown her off enough for us to notice as she came in. Transference of momentum between her and the other ship."

"I see." Behind his faceplate, Syaloch's beak cut a sharp black curve across heaven. "Now then, Gregg, were the jewels actually in the box when it was delivered?"

"At Earth Station, you mean? Oh, yes. There are four UN Chief Inspectors involved, and HQ says they're absolutely above suspicion. When I sent back word of the theft, they insisted on having their own quarters and so on searched, and went under scop voluntarily."

"And your own constables on Phobos?"

"Same thing," said the policeman grimly. "I've slapped on an embargo—nobody but me has left this settlement since the loss was discovered. I've had every room and tunnel and warehouse searched." He tried to scratch his head, a frustrating attempt when one is in a spacesuit. "I can't maintain those restrictions much longer. Ships are coming in and the consignees want their freight."

"*Hnachla*. That puts us under a time limit, then." Syaloch nodded to himself. "Do you know, this is a fascinating variation of the old locked room problem. A robot ship in transit is a locked room in the most classic sense." He drifted off into a reverie.

Gregg stared bleakly across the savage horizon, naked rock tumbling away under his feet, and then back over the field. Odd how tricky your vision became in airlessness, even when you had bright lights. That fellow crossing the field there, under the full glare of sun and floodlamps, was merely a stipple of shadow and luminance . . . what the devil was he doing, tying a shoe of all things? No, he was walking quite normally—

"I'd like to put everyone on Phobos under scop," said Gregg with a violent note, "but the law won't allow it unless the suspect volunteers—and only my own men have volunteered."

"Quite rightly, my dear fellow," said Syaloch. "One should at least have the privilege of privacy in his own skull. And it would make the investigation unbearably crude."

"I don't give a fertilizing damn how crude it is," snapped Gregg. "I just want that box with the crown jewels safe inside."

"Tut-tut! Impatience has been the ruin of many a promising young police officer, as I seem to recall my spiritual ancestor of Earth pointing out to a Scotland Yard man who—hm—may even have been a physical ancestor of yours, Gregg. It seems we must try another approach. Are there any people on Phobos who might have known the jewels were aboard this ship?"

"Yes. Two men only. I've pretty well established that they never broke security and told anyone else till the secret was out."

"And who are they?"

"Technicians, Hollyday and Steinmann. They were working at Earth Station when the *Jane* was loaded. They quit soon after—not at the same time—and came here by liner and got jobs. You can bet that *their* quarters have been searched!"

"Perhaps," murmured Syaloch, "it would be worthwhile to interview the gentlemen in question."

Steinmann, a thin redhead, wore truculence like a mantle; Hollyday merely looked worried. It was no evidence of guilt—everyone had been rubbed raw of late. They sat in the police office, with Gregg behind the desk and Syaloch leaning against the wall, smoking and regarding them with unreadable yellow eyes.

"Damn it, I've told this over and over till I'm sick of it!" Steinmann knotted his fists and gave the Martian a bloodshot stare. "I never touched the things and I don't know who did. Hasn't any man a right to change jobs?"

"Please," said the detective mildly. "The better you help the sooner we can finish this work. I take it you were acquainted with the man who actually put the box aboard the ship?"

"Sure. Everybody knew John Carter. Everybody knows everybody else on a satellite station." The Earthman stuck out his jaw. "That's why none of us'll take scop. We won't blab out all our thoughts to guys we see fifty times a day. We'd go nuts!"

"I never made such a request," said Syaloch.

"Carter was quite a good friend of mine," volunteered Hollyday.

"Uh-huh," grunted Gregg. "And he quit too, about the same time you fellows did, and went Earthside and hasn't been seen since. HQ told me you and he were thick. What'd you talk about?"

"The usual." Hollyday shrugged. "Wine, women, and song. I haven't heard from him since I left Earth."

"Who says Carter stole the box?" demanded Steinmann. "He just got tired of living in space and quit his job. He *couldn't* have stolen the jewels— he was searched, remember?"

"Could he have hidden it somewhere for a friend to get at this end?" inquired Syaloch.

"Hidden it? Where? Those ships don't have secret compartments." Steinmann spoke wearily. "And he was only aboard the *Jane* a few minutes, just long enough to put the box where he was supposed to." His eyes smoldered at Gregg. "Let's face it: the only people anywhere along the line who ever had a chance to lift it were our own dear cops."

The Inspector reddened and half rose. "Look here, you—"

"We've got *your* word that you're innocent," growled Steinmann. "Why should it be any better than mine?"

Syaloch waved both men back. "If you please. Brawls are unphilosophic." His beak opened and clattered, the Martian equivalent of a smile. "Has either of you, perhaps, a theory? I am open to all ideas."

There was a stillness. Then Hollyday mumbled: "Yes. I have one."

Syaloch hooded his eyes and puffed quietly, waiting.

Hollyday's grin was shaky. "Only if I'm right, you'll never see those jewels again."

Gregg sputtered.

"I've been around the Solar System a lot," said Hollyday. "It gets lonesome out in space. You never know how big and lonesome it is till you've been there, all by yourself. And I've done just that—I'm an amateur uranium prospector, not a lucky one so far. I can't believe we know everything about the universe, or that there's only vacuum between the planets."

"Are you talking about the cobblies?" snorted Gregg.

"Go ahead and call it superstition. But if you're in space long enough . . . well, somehow, you *know*. There are beings out there—gas beings, radiation beings, whatever you want to imagine, there's *something* living in space."

"And what use would a box of jewels be to a cobbly?"

Hollyday spread his hands. "How can I tell? Maybe we bother them, scooting through their own dark kingdom with our little rockets. Stealing the crown jewels would be a good way to disrupt the Mars trade, wouldn't it?"

Only Syaloch's pipe broke the inward-pressing silence. But its burbling seemed quite irreverent.

"Well—" Gregg rumbled helplessly with a meteoric paperweight. "Well, Mr. Syaloch, do you want to ask any more questions?"

"Only one." The third lids rolled back, and coldness looked out at Steinmann. "If you please, my good man, what is your hobby?"

"Huh? Chess. I play chess. What's it to you?" Steinmann lowered his head and glared sullenly.

"Nothing else?"

"What else is there?"

Syaloch glanced at the Inspector, who nodded confirmation, and then replied gently:

"I see. Thank you. Perhaps we can have a game sometime. I have some small skill of my own. That is all for now, gentlemen."

They left, moving like things of dream through the low gravity.

"Well?" Gregg's eyes pleaded with Syaloch. "What next?"

"Very little. I think . . . yesss, while I am here I should like to watch the technicians at work. In my profession, one needs a broad knowledge of all occupations."

Gregg sighed.

Ramanowitz showed the guest around. The *Kim Brackney* was in and being unloaded. They threaded through a hive of spacesuited men.

"The cops are going to have to raise that embargo soon," said Ramanowitz. "Either that or admit why they've clamped it on. Our warehouses are busting."

"It would be politic to do so," nodded Syaloch. "Ah, tell me . . . is this equipment standard for all stations?"

"Oh, you mean what the boys are wearing and carrying around? Sure. Same issue everywhere."

"May I inspect it more closely?"

"Hm?" *Lord, deliver me from visiting firemen!* thought Ramanowitz. He waved a mechanic over to him. "Mr. Syaloch would like you to explain your outfit," he said with ponderous sarcasm.

"Sure. Regular spacesuit here, reinforced at the seams." The gauntleted hands moved about, pointing. "Heating coils powered from this capacitance battery. Ten-hour air supply in the tanks. These buckles, you snap your tools into them, so they won't drift around in free fall. This little can at my belt holds paint that I spray out through this nozzle."

"Why must spaceships be painted?" asked Syaloch. "There is nothing to corrode the metal."

"Well, sir, we just call it paint. It's really gunk, to seal any leaks in the hull till we can install a new plate, or to mark any other kind of damage. Meteor punctures and so on." The mechanic pressed a trigger and a thin, almost invisible stream jetted out, solidifying as it hit the ground.

"But it cannot readily be seen, can it?" objected the Martian. "I, at least, find it difficult to see clearly in airlessness."

"That's right, Light doesn't diffuse, so . . . well, anyhow, the stuff is radioactive—not enough to be dangerous, just enough so that the repair crew can spot the place with a Geiger counter."

"I understand. What is the halflife?"

"Oh, I'm not sure. Six months, maybe? It's supposed to remain detectable for a year."

"Thank you." Syaloch stalked off. Ramanowitz had to jump to keep up with those long legs.

"Do you think Carter may have hid the box in his paint can?" suggested the human.

"No, hardly. The can is too small, and I assume he was searched thoroughly." Syaloch stopped and bowed. "You have been very kind and patient, Mr. Ramanowitz. I am finished now, and can find the Inspector myself."

"What for?"

"To tell him he can lift the embargo, of course." Syaloch made a harsh sibilance. "And then I must get the next boat to Mars. If I hurry, I can attend the concert in Sabaeus tonight." His voice grew dreamy. "They will be premiering Hanyech's *Variations on a Theme by Mendelssohn,* transcribed to the Royal Chlannach scale. It should be most unusual."

It was three days afterward that the letter came. Syaloch excused himself and kept an illustrious client squatting while he read it. Then he nodded to the other Martian. "You will be interested to know, sir, that the Estimable Diadems have arrived at Phobos and are being returned at this moment."

The client, a Cabinet Minister from the House of Actives, blinked. "Pardon, Freehatched Syaloch, but what have you to do with that?"

"Oh . . . I am a friend of the Featherless police chief. He thought I might like to know."

"*Hraa.* Were you not on Phobos recently?"

"A minor case." The detective folded the letter carefully, sprinkled it with salt, and ate it. Martians are fond of paper, especially official Earth stationery with high rag content. "Now, sir, you were saying—?"

The parliamentarian responded absently. He would not dream of violating privacy—no, never—but if he had X-ray vision he would have read:

"Dear Syaloch,

"You were absolutely right. Your locked room problem is solved. We've got the jewels back, everything is in fine shape, and the same boat which brings you this letter will deliver them to the vaults. It's too bad the public can never know the facts—two planets ought to be grateful to you—but I'll supply that much thanks all by myself, and insist that any bill you care to send be paid in full. Even if the Assembly had to make a special appropriation, which I'm afraid it will.

"I admit your idea of lifting the embargo at once looked pretty wild to me, but it worked. I had our boys out, of course, scouring Phobos with Geigers, but Hollyday found the box before we did. Which saved us a lot of trouble, to be sure. I arrested him as he came back into the settlement, and he had the box among his ore samples. He has confessed, and you were right all along the line.

"What was that thing you quoted at me, the saying of that Earthman you admire so much? 'When you have eliminated the impossible, whatever remains, however improbable, must be true.' Something like that. It certainly applies to this case.

"As you decided, the box must have been taken to the ship at Earth Station and left there—no other possibility existed. Carter figured it out in half a minute when he was ordered to take the thing out and put it aboard the *Jane*. He went inside, all right, but still had the box when he emerged. In that uncertain light nobody saw him put it 'down' between four girders right next to the hatch. Or as you remarked, if the jewels are not *in* the ship, and yet not *away* from the ship, they must be *on* the ship. Gravitation would hold them in place. When the *Jane* blasted off, acceleration pressure slid the box back, but of course the waffle-iron pattern kept it from being lost; it fetched up against the after rib and stayed there. All the way to Mars! But the ship's gravity held it securely enough even in free fall, since both were on the same orbit.

"Hollyday says that Carter told him all about it. Carter couldn't go to Mars himself without being suspected and watched every minute once the jewels were discovered missing. He needed a confederate. Hollyday went to Phobos and took up prospecting as a cover for the search he'd later be making for the jewels.

"As you showed me, when the ship was within a thousand miles of this dock, Phobos gravity would be stronger than her own. Every spacejack knows that the robot ships don't start decelerating till they're quite close; that they are then almost straight above the surface; and that the side with the radio mast and manhatch—the side on which Carter had placed the box—is rotated around to face the station. The centrifugal force of rotation threw the box away from the ship, and was in a direction toward Phobos rather than away from it. Carter knew that this rotation is slow and easy, so the force wasn't enough to accelerate the box to escape velocity and lose it in space. It would have to fall down toward the satellite. Phobos Station being on the side opposite Mars, there was no danger that the loot would keep going till it hit the planet.

"So the crown jewels tumbled onto Phobos, just as you deduced. Of course Carter had given the box a quick radioactive spray as he laid it in place, and Hollyday used that to track it down among all those rocks and crevices. In point of fact, its path curved clear around this moon, so it landed about five miles from the station.

"Steinmann has been after me to know why you quizzed him about his hobby. You forgot to tell me that, but I figured it out for myself and told him. He or Hollyday had to be involved, since nobody else knew about the cargo, and the guilty person had to have some excuse to go out and look for the box. Chess playing doesn't furnish that kind of alibi. Am I right? At least, my deduction proves I've been studying the same canon you go by. Incidentally, Steinmann asks if you'd care to take him on the next time he has planet leave.

"Hollyday knows where Carter is hiding, and we've radioed the information back to Earth. Trouble is, we can't prosecute either of them without admitting the facts. Oh, well, there are such things as blacklists.

"Will have to close this now to make the boat. I'll be seeing you soon—not professionally, I hope!"

Admiring regards,
Inspector Gregg

But as it happened, the Cabinet minister did not possess X-ray eyes. He dismissed unprofitable speculation and outlined his problem. Somebody, somewhere in Sabaeus, was farniking the krats, and there was an alarming zaksnautry among the hyukus. It sounded to Syaloch like an interesting case.

A Scarletin Study

Jonathan Swift Somers III
(Philip José Farmer)

Philip José Farmer has written more than fifty novels and numerous short stories in the past five decades, garnering three Hugo awards along the way. His stories are always thought provoking, speculating on alien reproduction, religion, and the transformation of mankind under any and all conditions, from the horrors of vampires and werewolves to reincarnation and the afterlife. In "A Scarletin Study" he turns his formidable talent to the detective story, with his usual unpredictable results.

BEING A REPRINT FROM THE REMINISCENCES OF JOHANN H. WEISSTEIN, DR. MED., LATE OF THE AUTOBAHN PATROL MEDICAL DEPARTMENT.

Foreword

Ralph von Wau Wau's first case as a private investigator is not his most complicated or curious. It does, however, illustrate remarkably well my colleague's peculiar talents. And it is, after all, his first case, and one should proceed chronologically in these chronicles. It is also the only case I know of in which not the painting but the painter was stolen. And it is, to me, most memorable because through it I met the woman who will always be for me *the woman*.

Consider this scene. Von Wau Wau; his enemy, Detective-Lieutenant Strasse; myself; and the lovely Lisa Scarletin, all standing before a large painting in a room in a Hamburg police station. Von Wau Wau studies the painting while we wonder if he's right in his contention that it is not only a work of art but a map. Its canvas bears, among other things, the images of Sherlock Holmes in lederhosen, Sir Francis Bacon, a green horse, a mirror, Christ coming from the tomb, Tarzan, a waistcoat, the Wizard of Oz in a balloon, an ancient king of Babylon with a dietary problem, and a banana tree.

But let me begin at the beginning.

Chapter I
Herr Ralph Von Wau Wau

In the year 1978 I took my degree of Doctor of Medicine of the University of Cologne and proceeded to Hamburg to go through the course prescribed for surgeons in the Autobahn Patrol. Having completed my studies there, I was duly attached to the Fifth North-Rhine Westphalia Anti-Oiljackers as assistant surgeon. The campaign against the notorious Rottenfranzer Gang brought honors and promotions to many, but for me it was nothing but misfortune and disaster. At the fatal battle of the Emmerich Off-Ramp, I was struck on the shoulder by a missile which shattered the bone. I should have fallen into the hands of the murderous Rottenfranzer himself but for the devotion and courage shown by Morgen, my paramedic aide, who threw me across a Volkswagen and succeeded in driving safely across the Patrol lines.

At the base hospital at Hamburg (and it really is base), I seemed on the road to recovery when I was struck down with an extremely rare malady. At least, I have read of only one case similar to mine. This was, peculiarly, the affliction of another doctor, though he was an Englishman and suffered his wounds a hundred years before on another continent. My case was written up in medical journals and then in general periodicals all over the world. The affliction itself became known popularly as "the peregrinating pain," though the scientific name, which I prefer for understandable reasons, was "Weisstein's Syndrome." The popular name arose from the fact that the occasional suffering it caused me did not remain at the site of the original wound. At times, the pain traveled downward and lodged in my leg. This was a cause célèbre, scientifically speaking, nor was the mystery solved until some years later. (In *The Wonder of the Wandering Wound,* not yet published.)

However, I rallied and had improved enough to be able to walk or limp about the wards, and even to bask a little on the veranda when smog or fog permitted, when I was struck down by *Weltschmerz,* that curse of Central Europe. For months my mind was despaired of, and when at last I came to myself, six months had passed. With my health perhaps not irretrievably ruined, but all ability to wield the knife as a surgeon vanished, I was discharged by a paternal government with permission to spend the rest of my life improving it. (The health, not the life, I mean.) I had neither kith nor kin nor kinder and was therefore as free as the air, which, given my small social security and disability pension, seemed to be what I was expected to eat. Within a few months the state of my finances had become so alarming that I was forced to completely alter my life style. I decided to look around for some considerably less pretentious and expensive domicile than the Hamburg Hilton.

On the very day I'd come to this conclusion, I was standing at the Kennzeichen Bar when someone tapped me on the shoulder. Wincing (it was the wounded shoulder), I turned around. I recognized young blonde Stampfert, who had been an anesthetist under me at the Neustadt Hospital. (I've had a broad experience of women in many nations and on three continents, so much so in fact that I'd considered entering gynecology.) Stampfert had a beautiful body but a drab personality. I was lonely, however, and I hailed her enthusiastically. She, in turn, seemed glad to see me, I suppose because she wanted to flaunt her newly acquired engagement ring. The first thing I knew, I had invited her to lunch. We took the bus to the Neu Bornholt, and on the way I outlined my adventures of the past year.

"Poor devil!" she said. "So what's happening now?"

"Looking for a cheap apartment," I said. "But I doubt that it's possible to get a decent place at a reasonable rate. The housing shortage and its partner, inflation, will be with us for a long time."

"That's a funny thing," Stampfert said. "You're the second . . . person . . . today who has said almost those exact words."

"And who was the first?"

"Someone who's just started a new professional career," Stampfert said. "He's having a hard go of it just now. He's looking for a roommate to share not only expenses but a partnership. Someone who's experienced in police work. You seem to fit the bill. The only thing is . . ."

She hesitated, and I said, "If he's easy to get along with, I'd be delighted to share the expenses with him. And work is something I need badly."

"Well, there's more to it than that, though he is easy to get along with. Lovable, in fact."

She hesitated, then said, "Are you allergic to animals?"

I stared at her and said, "Not at all. Why, does this man have pets?"

"Not exactly," Stampfert said, looking rather strange.

"Well, then, what is it?"

"There is a dog," she said. "A highly intelligent . . . police dog."

"Don't tell me this fellow is blind?" I said. "Not that it will matter, of course."

"Just color blind," she said. "His name is Ralph."

"Yes, go on," I said. "What about Herr Ralph?"

"That's his first name," Stampfert said. "His full name is Ralph von Wau Wau."

"What?" I said, and then I guffawed. "A man

whose last name is a dog's bark?" (In Germany "wau wau"—pronounced vau vau—corresponds to the English "bow wow.")

Suddenly, I said, "Ach!" I had just remembered where I had heard, or rather read, of von Wau Wau.

"What you're saying," I said slowly, "is that the dog is also the fellow who wants to share the apartment and is looking for a partner?"

Stampfert nodded.

Chapter II
The Science of Odorology

And so, fifteen minutes later, we entered the apartment building at 12 Bellener Street and took the elevator to the second story. Stampfert rang the bell at 2K, and a moment later the door swung in. This operation had been effected by an electrical motor controlled by an on-off button on a control panel set on the floor in a corner. This, it was obvious, had been pressed by the paw of the dog now trotting toward us. He was the largest police dog I've ever seen, weighing approximately one hundred and sixty pounds. He had keen eyes which were the deep lucid brown of a bottle of maple syrup at times and at other times the opaque rich brown of a frankfurter. His face was black, and his back bore a black saddlemark.

"Herr Doktor Weisstein, Herr Ralph von Wau Wau," said Stampfert.

He grinned, or at least opened his jaws, to reveal some very long and sharp teeth.

"Come in, please, and make yourself at home," he said.

Though I'd been warned, I was startled. His mouth did not move while the words came from his throat. The words were excellent standard High German. But the voice was that of a long-dead American movie actor.

Humphrey Bogart's, to be exact.

I would have picked Basil Rathbone's, but *de gustibus non est disputandum.* Especially someone with teeth like Ralph's. There was no mystery or magic about the voice, though the effect, even to the prepared, was weird. The voice, like his high intelligence, was a triumph of German science. A dog (or any animal) lacks the mouth structure and vocal cords to reproduce human sounds intelligibly. This deficiency had been overcome by implanting a small nuclear-powered voder in Ralph's throat. This was connected by an artificial-protein neural complex to the speech center of the dog's brain. Before he could activate the voder, Ralph had to think of three code words. This was necessary, since otherwise he would be speaking whenever he thought in verbal terms. Inflection of the spoken words was automatic, responding to the emotional tone of Ralph's thoughts.

"What about pouring us a drink, sweetheart?" he said to Stampfert. "Park it there, buddy," he said to me, indicating with a paw a large and comfortable easy chair. I did so, unsure whether or not I should resent his familiarity. I decided not to do so. After all, what could, or should, one expect from a dog who has by his own admission seen *The Maltese Falcon* forty-nine times? Of course, I found this out later, just as I discovered later that his manner of address varied bewilderingly, often in the middle of a sentence.

Stampfert prepared the drinks at a well-stocked bar in the corner of the rather large living room. She made herself a tequila with lemon and salt, gave me the requested double Duggan's Dew o' Kirkintilloch on the rocks, and poured out three shots of King's Ransom Scotch in a rock-crystal saucer on the floor. The dog began lapping it; then seeing me raise my eyebrows, he said, "I'm a private eye, Doc. It's in the best tradition that P.I.'s drink. I always try to follow human traditions—when it pleases me. And if my drinking from a saucer offends you, I *can* hold a glass between my paws. But why the hell should I?"

"No reason at all," I said hastily.

He ceased drinking and jumped up onto a sofa, where he sat down facing us. "You two have been drinking at the Kennzeichen," he said. "You are old customers there. And then, later, you had lunch at the Neu Bornholt. Doctor Stampfert said you were coming in the taxi, but you changed your mind and took the bus."

There was a silence which lasted until I understood that I was supposed to comment on this. I could only say, "Well?"

"The babe didn't tell me any of this," Ralph said somewhat testily. "I was just demonstrating something that a mere human being could not have known."

"Mere?" I said just as testily.

Ralph shrugged, which was quite an accomplishment when one considers that dogs don't really have shoulders.

"Sorry, Doc. Don't get your bowels in an uproar. No offense."

"Very well," I said. "How did you know all this?"

And now that I came to think about it, I did wonder how he knew.

"The Kennzeichen is the only restaurant in town which gives a stein of Lowenbrau to each habitue as he enters the bar," von Wau Wau said. "You two obviously prefer other drinks, but you could not turn down the free drink. If you had not been at the Kennzeichen, I would not have smelled Lowenbrau on your breath. You then went to the Neu Bornholt for lunch. It serves a salad with its house dressing, the peculiar ingredients of which I detected with my sense of smell. This, as you know, is a million times keener than a human's. If you had come in a taxi, as the dame said you meant to do, you would be stinking much more strongly of kerosene. Your clothes and hair have absorbed a certain amount of that from being on the streets, of course, along with the high-sulfur coal now burned in many automobiles. But I deduce—olfactorily—that you took instead one of the electrically operated, fuel-celled, relatively odorless buses. Am I correct?"

"I would have said that it was amazing, but of course your nose makes it easy for you," I said.

"An extremely distinguished colleague of mine," Ralph said, "undoubtedly the most distinguished, once said that it is the first quality of a criminal investigator to see through a disguise. I would modify that to the *second* quality. The first is that he should smell through a disguise."

Though he seemed somewhat nettled, he became more genial after a few more laps from the saucer. So did I after a few more sips from my glass. He even gave me permission to smoke, provided that I did it under a special vent placed over my easy chair.

"Cuban make," he said, sniffing after I had lit up. *"La Roja Paloma de la Revolucion."*

"Now that is astounding!" I said. I was also astounded to find Stampfert on my lap.

"It's nothing," he said. "I started to write a trifling little monograph on the subtle distinctions among cigar odors, but I realized that it would make a massive textbook before I was finished. And who could use it?"

"What are you doing here?" I said to Stampfert. "This is business. I don't want to give Herr von Wau Wau the wrong impression."

"You didn't used to mind," she said, giggling. "But I'm here because I want to smoke, too, and this is the only vent he has, and he told me not to smoke unless I sat under it."

Under the circumstances, it was not easy to carry on a coherent conversation with the dog, but we managed. I told him that I had read something of his life. I knew that his parents had been the property of the Hamburg Police Department. He was one of a litter of eight, all mutated to some degree since they and their parents had been subjected to scientific experiments. These had been conducted by the biologists of *das Institut und die Tankstelle fur Gehirntaschenspielerei.* But his high intelligence was the result of biosurgery. Although his brain was no larger than it should have been for a dog his size, its complexity was comparable to that of a human's. The scientists had used artificial protein to make billions of new nerve circuits in his cerebrum. This had been done, however, at the expense of his cerebellum or hindbrain. As a result, he had very little subconscious and hence could not dream.

As everybody now knows, failure to dream results in a progressive psychosis and eventual mental breakdown. To rectify this, Ralph created dreams during the day, recorded them audiovisually, and fed them into his brain at night. I don't have space to go into this in detail in this narrative, but a full description will be found in *The Case of the Stolen Dreams.* (Not yet published.)

When Ralph was still a young pup, an explosion had wrecked the Institute and killed his siblings and the scientists responsible for his sapiency. Ralph was taken over again by the Police Department and sent to school. He attended obedience school and the other courses requisite for a trained *Schutzhund* canine. But he was the only pup who also attended classes in reading, writing, and arithmetic.

Ralph was now twenty-eight years old but looked five. Some attributed this anomaly to the mutation experiments. Others claimed that the scientists had perfected an age-delaying elixir which had been administered to Ralph and his siblings. If the explosion had not destroyed the records, the world might now have the elixir at its disposal. (More of this in *A Short Case of Longevity,* n.y.p.)

Ralph's existence had been hidden for many years from all except a few policemen and officials sworn to silence. It was believed that publicity would reduce his effectiveness in his detective work. But recently the case had come to the attention of the public because of Ralph's own doing. Fed up with being a mere police dog, proud and ambitious, he had resigned to become a private investigator. His application for a license had, of course, resulted in an uproar. Mass mediapersons had descended on Hamburg in droves, herds, coveys, and gaggles. There was in fact litigation against him in the courts, but pending the result of this, Ralph von Wau Wau was proceeding as if he were a free agent. (For the conclusion of this famous case, see *The Caper of Kupper, the Copper's Keeper,* n.y.p.)

But whether or not he was the property of the police department, he was still very dependent upon human beings. Hence, his search for a roommate and a partner.

I told him something about myself. He listened quietly and then said, "I like your odor, buddy. It's an honest one and uncondescending. I'd like you to come in with me."

"I'd be delighted," I said. "But there is only one bedroom . . ."

"All yours," he said. "My tastes are Spartan. Or perhaps I should say canine. The other bedroom has been converted to a laboratory, as you have observed. But I sleep in it on a pile of blankets under a table. You may have all the privacy you need, bring all the women you want, as long as you're not noisy about it. I think we should get one thing straight though. I'm the senior partner here. If that offends your human chauvinism, then we'll call it quits before we start, amigo."

"I forsee no cause for friction," I replied, and I stood up to walk over to Ralph to shake hands. Unfortunately, I had forgotten that Stampfert was still on my lap. She thumped into the floor on her buttocks and yelled with pain and indignation. It was, I admit, stupid—well, at least an unwise, action. Stampfert, cursing, headed toward the door. Ralph looked at my outstretched hand and said, "Get this straight, mac. I never shake hands or sit up and beg."

I dropped my hand and said, "Of course."

The door opened. I turned to see Stampfert, still rubbing her fanny, going out the door.

"Auf Wiedersehen," I said.

"Not if I can help it, you jerk," she said.

"She always did take offense too easily," I said to Ralph.

I left a few minutes later to pick up my belongings from the hotel. When I re-entered his door with my suitcases in hand, I suddenly stopped. Ralph was sitting on the sofa, his eyes bright, his huge red tongue hanging out, and his breath coming in deep happy pants. Across from him sat one of the loveliest women I have ever seen. Evidently she had done something to change his mood because his manner of address was now quite different.

"Come in, my dear Weisstein," he said. "Your first case as my colleague is about to begin."

Chapter III
The Statement
of the Case

An optimist is one who ignores, or forgets, experience. I am an optimist. Which is another way of saying that I fell in love with Lisa Scarletin at once. As I stared at this striking yet petite woman with the curly chestnut hair and great lustrous brown eyes, I completely forgot that I was still holding the two heavy suitcases. Not until after we had been introduced, and she looked down amusedly, did I realize what a foolish figure I made. Red-faced, I eased them down and took her dainty hand in mine. As I kissed it, I smelled the subtle fragrance of a particularly delightful—and, I must confess, aphrodisiacal—perfume.

"No doubt you have read, or seen on TV, reports of Mrs. Scarletin's missing husband?" my partner said. "Even if you do not know of his disappearance, you surely have heard of such a famous artist?"

"My knowledge of art is not nil," I said coldly. The tone of my voice reflected my inward coldness, the dying glow of delight on first seeing her. So, she was married! I should have known on seeing her ring. But I had been too overcome for it to make an immediate impression.

Alfred Scarletin, as my reader must surely know, was a wealthy painter who had become very famous in the past decade. Personally, I consider the works of the so-called Fauve Mauve school to be outrageous nonsense, a thumbing of the nose at commonsense. I would sooner have the originals of the *Katzenjammer Kids* comic strip hung up in the museum than any of the maniac creations of Scarletin and his kind. But, whatever his failure of artistic taste, he certainly possessed a true eye for women. He had married the beautiful Lisa Maria Mohrstein only three years ago. And now there was speculation that she might be a widow.

At which thought, the warm glow returned.

A. Scarletin, as I remembered, had gone for a walk on a May evening two months ago and had failed to return home. At first, it was feared that he had been kidnapped. But, when no ransom was demanded, that theory was discarded.

When I had told Ralph what I knew of the case, he nodded.

"As of last night there has been a new development in the case," he said. "And Mrs. Scarletin has come to me because she is extremely dissatisfied with the progress—lack of it, rather—that the police have made. Mrs. Scarletin, please tell Doctor Weisstein what you have told me."

She fixed her bright but deep brown eyes upon me and in a voice as lovely as her eyes—not to mention her figure—sketched in the events of yesterday. Ralph, I noticed, sat with his head cocked and his ears pricked up. I did not know it then, but he had asked her to repeat the story because he wanted to listen to her inflections again. He could detect subtle tones that would escape the less sensitive ears of humans. As he was often to say, "I cannot only *smell* hidden emotions, my dear Weisstein, I can also *hear* them."

"At about seven last evening, as I was getting ready to go out . . ." she said.

With whom? I thought, feeling jealousy burn through my chest but knowing that I had no right to feel such.

"... Lieutenant Strasse of the Hamburg Metropolitan Police phoned me. He said that he had something important to show me and asked if I would come down to headquarters. I agreed, of course, and took a taxi down. There the sergeant took me into a room and showed me a painting. I was astounded. I had never seen it before, but I knew at once that it was my husband's work. I did not need his signature—in its usual place in the upper righthand corner—to know that. I told the sergeant that and then I said, 'This must mean that Alfred is still alive! But where in the world did you get it?'

"He replied that it had come to the attention of the police only that morning. A wealthy merchant, Herr Lausitz, had died a week before. The lawyer supervising the inventory of his estate found this painting in a locked room in Lausitz's mansion. It was only one of many valuable objets d'art which had been stolen. Lausitz was not suspected of being a thief except in the sense that he had undoubtedly purchased stolen goods or commissioned the thefts. The collection was valued at many millions of marks. The lawyer had notified the police, who identified the painting as my husband's because of the signature."

"You may be sure that Strasse would never have been able to identify a Scarletin by its style alone," Ralph said sarcastically.

Her delicate eyebrows arched. "Ach! So that's the way it is! The lieutenant did not take it kindly when I told him that I was thinking of consulting you. But that was later.

"Anyway, I told Strasse that this was evidence that Alfred was still alive. Or at least had been until very recently. I know that it would take my husband at least a month and a half to have painted it—if he were under pressure. Strasse said that it could be: one, a forgery; or, two, Alfred might have painted it before he disappeared. I told him that it was no forgery; I could tell at a glance. And what did he mean, it was painted some time ago? I knew exactly—from day to day—what my husband worked on."

She stopped, looked at me, and reddened slightly.

"That isn't true. My husband visited his mistress at least three times a week. I did not know about her until after he disappeared, when the police reported to me that he had been seeing her . . . Hilda Speck . . . for about two years. However, according to the police, Alfred had not been doing any painting in her apartment. Of course, she could have removed all evidence, though Strasse tells me that she would have been unable to get rid of all traces of pigments and hairs from brushes."

What a beast that Scarletin was! I thought, how could anybody married to this glorious woman pay any attention to another woman?

"I have made some inquiries about Hilda Speck," Ralph said. "First, she has an excellent alibi, what the English call ironclad. She was visiting friends in Bremen two days before Scarletin disappeared. She did not return to Hamburg until two days afterward. As for her background, she worked as a typist-clerk for an export firm until two years ago when Scarletin began supporting her. She has no criminal record, but her brother has been arrested several times for extortion and assault. He escaped conviction each time. He is a huge obese man, as ugly as his sister is beautiful. He is nicknamed, appropriately enough, *Flusspferd*. (Hippopotamus. Literally, river-horse.) His whereabouts have been unknown for about four months."

He sat silent for a moment, then he went to the telephone. This lay on the floor; beside it was a curious instrument. I saw its function the moment Ralph put one paw on its long, thin but blunt end and slipped the other paw snugly into a funnel-shaped cup at the opposite end. With the thin end he punched the buttons on the telephone.

A police officer answered over the loudspeaker. Ralph asked for Lt. Strasse. The officer said that he was not in the station. Ralph left a message, but when he turned off the phone, he said, "Strasse won't answer for a while, but eventually his curiosity will get the better of him."

It is difficult to tell when a dog is smiling, but I will swear that Ralph was doing more than just exposing his teeth. And his eyes seemed to twinkle.

Suddenly, he raised a paw and said, quietly, "No sound, please."

We stared at him. None of us heard anything, but it was evident he did. He jumped to the control panel on the floor and pushed the on button. Then he dashed toward the door, which swung inward. A man wearing a stethoscope stood looking stupidly at us. Seeing Ralph bounding at him, he yelled and turned to run. Ralph struck him on the back and sent him crashing against the opposite wall of the hallway. I ran to aid him, but to my surprise Ralph trotted back into the room. It was then that I saw the little device attached to the door. The man rose glaring and unsteadily to his feet. He was just above minimum height for a policeman and looked as if he were thirty-five years old. He had a narrow face with a long nose and small close-set black eyes.

"Doctor Weisstein," Ralph said. "Lieutenant Strasse."

Strasse did not acknowledge me. Instead, he tore off the device and put it with the stethoscope in his jacket pocket. Some of his paleness disappeared.

"That eavesdropper device is illegal in America and should be here," Ralph said.

"So should talking dogs," Strasse said. He bowed to Mrs. Scarletin and clicked his heels.

Ralph gave several short barks, which I found out later was his equivalent of laughter. He said, "No need to ask you why you were spying on us. You're stuck in this case, and you hoped to overhear me say something that would give you a clue. Really, my dear Lieutenant!"

Strasse turned red, but he spoke up bravely enough.

"Mrs. Scarletin, you can hire this . . . this . . . hairy four-footed Holmes . . ."

"I take that as a compliment," Ralph murmured.

". . . if you wish, but you cannot discharge the police. Moreover, there is grave doubt about the legality of his private investigator's license, and you might get into trouble if you persist in hiring him."

"Mrs. Scarletin is well aware of the legal ramifications, my dear Strasse," Ralph said coolly. "She is also confident that I will win my case. Meantime, the authorities have permitted me to practice. If you dispute this, you may phone the mayor himself."

"You . . . you!" Strasse sputtered. "Just because you once saved His Honor's child!"

"Let's drop all this time-wasting nonsense," Ralph said. "I would like to examine the painting myself. I believe that it may contain the key to Scarletin's whereabouts."

"That is police property," Strasse said. "As long as I have anything to say about it, you won't put your long nose into a police building. Not unless you do so as a prisoner."

I was astonished at the hatred that leaped and crackled between these two like discharges in a Van de Graaff generator. I did not learn until later that Strasse was the man to whom Ralph had been assigned when he started police work. At first they got along well, but as it became evident that Ralph was much the more intelligent, Strasse became jealous. He did not, however, ask for another dog. He was taking most of the credit for the cases cracked by Ralph, and he was rising rapidly in rank because of Ralph. By the time the dog resigned from the force, Strasse had become a lieutenant. Since then he had bungled two cases, and the person responsible for Strasse's rapid rise was now obvious to all.

"Pardon me," Ralph said. "The police may be holding the painting as evidence, but it is clearly Mrs. Scarletin's property. However, I think I'll cut through the red tape. I'll just make a complaint to His Honor."

"Very well," Strasse said, turning pale again.

"But I'll go with you to make sure that you don't tamper with the evidence."

"And to learn all you can," Ralph said, barking laughter. "Weisstein, would you bring along that little kit there? It contains the tools of my trade."

Chapter IV
Light in the Darkness, Courtesy of Von Wau Wau

On the way to the station in the taxi (Strasse having refused us use of a police vehicle), Ralph told me a little more of Alfred Scarletin.

"He is the son of an American teacher who became a German citizen and of a Hamburg woman. Naturally, he speaks English like a native of California. He became interested in painting at a very early age and since his early adolescence has tramped through Germany painting both urban and rural scenes. He is extremely handsome, hence, attracts women, has a photographic memory, and is an excellent draftsman. His paintings were quite conventional until the past ten years when he founded the Fauve Mauve school. He is learned in both German and English literature and has a fondness for the works of Frank Baum and Lewis Carroll. He often uses characters from them in his paintings. Both writers, by the way, were fond of puns."

"I am well aware of that," I said stiffly. After all, one does not like to be considered ignorant by a dog. "And all this means?"

"It may mean all or nothing."

About ten minutes later, we were in a large room

in which many articles, the jetsam and flotsam of crime, were displayed. Mrs. Scarletin led us to the painting (though we needed no leading), and we stood before it. Strasse, off to one side, regarded us suspiciously. I could make no sense out of the painting and said so even though I did not want to offend Mrs. Scarletin. She, however, laughed and said my reaction was that of many people.

Ralph studied it for a long time and then said, "It may be that my suspicions are correct. We shall see."

"About what?" Strasse said, coming closer and leaning forward to peer at the many figures on the canvas.

"We can presume that Mrs. Scarletin knows all her husband's works—until the time he disappeared. This appeared afterward, and so we can presume that he painted it within the last two months. It's evident that he was kidnapped not for ransom but for the money to be made from the sale of new paintings by Scarletin. They must have threatened him with death if he did not paint new works for them. He has done at least one for them and probably has done, or is doing, more for them.

"They can't sell Scarletins on the open market. But there are enough fanatical and unscrupulous collectors to pay very large sums for their private collections. Lausitz was one such. Scarletin is held prisoner and, we suppose, would like to escape. He can't do so, but he is an intelligent man, and he thinks of a way to get a message out. He knows his paintings are being sold, even if he isn't told so. Ergo, why not put a message in his painting?"

"How wonderful!" Mrs. Scarletin said and she

patted Ralph's head. Ralph wagged his tail, and I felt a thrust of jealousy.

"Nonsense!" Strasse growled. "He must have known that the painting would go to a private collector who could not reveal that Scarletin was a prisoner. One, he'd be put in jail himself for having taken part in an illegal transaction. Two, why should he suspect that the painting contained a message? Three, I don't believe there is any message there!"

"Scarletin would be desperate and so willing to take a long chance," Ralph said. "At least, it'd be better than doing nothing. He could hope that the collector might get an attack of conscience and tell the police. This is not very likely, I'll admit. He could hope that the collector would be unable to keep from showing the work off to a few close friends. Perhaps one of these might tell the police, and so the painting would come into the hands of the police. Among them might be an intelligent and well-educated person who would perceive the meaning of the painting. I'll admit, however, that neither of these theories is likely."

Strasse snorted.

"And then there was the very slight chance—which nevertheless occurred—that the collector would die. And so the legal inventory of his estate would turn up a Scarletin. And some person just might be able to read the meaning in this—if there is any."

"Just what I was going to say," Strasse said.

"Even if what you say happened did happen," he continued, "his kidnappers wouldn't pass on the painting without examining it. The first thing they'd suspect would be a hidden message. It's so obvious."

"You didn't think so a moment ago," Ralph said. "But you are right . . . in agreeing with me. Now, let us hypothesize. Scarletin, a work of art, but he wishes to embody in it a message. Probably a map of sorts which will lead the police—or someone else looking for him—directly to the place where he is kept prisoner.

"How is he to do this without detection by the kidnappers? He has to be subtle enough to escape their inspection. *How* subtle depends, I would imagine, on their education and perceptivity. But too subtle a message will go over everybody's head. And he is limited in his choice of symbols by the situation, by the names or professions of his kidnappers—if he knows them—and by the particular location of his prison—if he knows that."

"If, if, if!" Strasse said, throwing his hands up in the air.

"If me no ifs," Ralph said. "But first let us consider that Scarletin is equally at home in German or English. He loves the pun-loving Carroll and Baum. So, perhaps, due to the contingencies of the situation, he is forced to pun in both languages."

"It would be like him," Mrs. Scarletin said. "But is it likely that he would use this method when he would know that very few people would be capable of understanding him?"

"As I said, it was a long shot, madame. But better than nothing.

"Now, Weisstein, whatever else I am, I am a dog. Hence, I am color blind. (But not throughout his career. See *The Adventure of the Tired Color Man,* to be published.) Please describe the colors of each object on this canvas."

Strasse sniggered, but we ignored him. When I had finished, Ralph said, "Thank you, my dear Weisstein. Now, let us separate the significant from the insignificant. Though, as a matter of fact, in this case even the insignificant is significant. Notice the two painted walls which divide the painting into three parts—like Gaul. One starts from the middle of the left-hand side and curves up to the middle of the upper edge. The other starts in the middle of the right-hand side and curves down to the middle of the lower side. All three parts are filled with strange and seemingly unrelated—and often seemingly unintelligible—objects. The Fauve Mauve apologists, however, maintain that their creations come from the collective unconscious, not the individual or personal, and so are intelligible to everybody."

"Damned nonsense!" I said, forgetting Lisa in my indignation.

"Not in this case, I suspect," Ralph said. "Now, notice that the two walls, which look much like the Great Wall of China, bear many zeros on their tops. And that within the area these walls enclose, other zeros are scattered. Does this mean nothing to you?"

"Zero equals nothing," I said.

"A rudimentary observation, Doctor, but valid," Ralph said. "I would say that Scarletin is telling us that the objects within the walls mean nothing. It is the central portion that bears the message. There are no zeros there."

"Prove it," Strasse said.

"The first step first—if one can find it. Observe

in the upper right-hand corner the strange figure of a man. The upper half is, obviously, Sherlock Holmes, with his deerstalker hat, cloak, pipe—though whether his meditative brierroot or disputatious clay can't be determined—and his magnifying glass in hand. The lower half, with the lederhosen and so on, obviously indicates a Bavarian in particular and a German in general. The demi-figure of Holmes means two things to the earnest seeker after the truth. One, that we are to use detective methods on this painting. Two, that half of the puzzle is in English. The lower half means that half of the puzzle is in German. Which I anticipated."

"Preposterous!" Strasse said. "And just what does that next figure, the one in sixteenth-century costume, mean?"

"Ah, yes, the torso of a bald and bearded gentleman with an Elizabethan ruff around his neck. He is writing with a pen on a sheet of paper. There is a title on the upper part of the paper. Doctor, please look at it through the magnifying glass which you'll find in my kit."

Chapter V
More Dawning Light

I did so, and I said, "I can barely make it out. Scarletin must have used a glass to do it. It says *New Atlantis*."

"Does that suggest anything to anybody?" Ralph said.

Obviously it did to him, but he was enjoying the

sensation of being more intelligent than the humans around him. I resented his attitude somewhat, and yet I could understand it. He had been patronized by too many humans for too long a time.

"The great scholar and statesman Francis Bacon wrote the *New Atlantis*," I said suddenly. Ralph winked at me, and I cried, "Bacon! Scarletin's mistress is Hilda Speck!"

(*Speck* in German means *bacon*.)

"You have put one foot forward, my dear Weisstein," Ralph said. "Now let us see you bring up the other."

"The Bacon, with the next two figures, comprise a group separate from the others," I said. "Obviously, they are to be considered as closely related. But I confess that I cannot make much sense out of Bacon, a green horse, and a house with an attic window from which a woman with an owl on her shoulder leans. Nor do I know the significance of the tendril which connects all of them."

"Stuck in the mud, eh, kid?" Ralph said, startling me. But I was to get used to his swift transitions from the persona of Holmes to Spade and others and back again.

"Tell me, Doc, is the green of the oats-burner of any particular shade?"

"Hmm," I said.

"It's Nile green," Lisa said.

"You're certainly a model client, sweetheart," Ralph said. "Very well, my dear sawbones, does this mean nothing to you? Yes? What about you, Strasse?"

Strasse muttered something.

Lisa said, *"Nilpferd!"*

"Yes," Ralph said. *"Nilpferd.* (Nile-horse.) Another word for hippopotamus. And Hilda Speck's brother is nicknamed *Hippopotamus.* Now for the next figure, the house with the woman looking out the attic and bearing an owl on her shoulder. Tell me, Strasse, does the Hippo have any special pals? One who is perhaps, Greek? From the city of Athens?"

Strasse sputtered and said, "Somebody in the department has been feeding you information. I'll . . ."

"Not at all," Ralph said. "Obviously, the attic and the woman with, the owl are the significant parts of the image. *Dachstube* (attic) conveys no meaning in German, but if we use the English translation, we are on the way to light. The word has two meanings in English. If capitalized, Attic, it refers to the ancient Athenian language or culture and, in a broader sense, to Greece as a whole. Note that the German adjective *attisch* is similar to the English *Attic.* To clinch this, Scarletin painted a woman with an owl on her shoulder. Who else could this be but the goddess of wisdom, patron deity of Athens? Scarletin was taking a chance on using her, since his kidnappers, even if they did not get beyond high school, might have encountered Athena. But they might not remember her, and, anyway, Scarletin had to use some redundancy to make sure his message got across. I would not be surprised if we do not run across considerable redundancy here."

"And the tendrils?" I said.

"A pun in German, my dear Doctor. *Ranke* (tendril) is similar to *Ranke* (intrigues). The three figures are bound together by the tendril of intrigue."

Strasse coughed and said, "And the mirror beneath the house with the attic?"

"Observe that the yellow brick road starts from the mirror and curves to the left or westward. I suggest that Scarletin means here that the road actually goes to the right or eastward. Mirror images are in reverse, of course."

"What road?" Strasse said.

Ralph rolled his eyes and shook his head.

"Surely the kidnappers made my husband explain the symbolism?" Lisa said. "They would be very suspicious that he might do exactly what he did do."

"There would be nothing to keep him from a false explanation," Ralph said. "So far, it is obvious that Scarletin has named the criminals. How he was able to identify them or to locate his place of imprisonment, I don't know. Time and deduction—with a little luck—will reveal all. Could we have a road map of Germany, please?"

"I'm no dog to fetch and carry," Strasse grumbled, but he obtained a map nevertheless. This was the large Mair's, scale of 1:750,000, used primarily to indicate the autobahn system. Strasse unfolded it and pinned it to the wall with the upper part of Germany showing.

"If Scarletin had put, say, an American hamburger at the beginning of the brick road, its meaning would have been obvious even to the *dummkopf* kidnappers," Ralph said. "He credited his searchers—if any—with intelligence. They would realize the road has to start where the crime started—in Hamburg."

He was silent while comparing the map and the painting. After a while the fidgeting Strasse said, "Come, man! I mean, dog! You . . ."

"You mean Herr von Wau Wau, yes?" Ralph said.

Strasse became red-faced again, but after a struggle he said, "Of course. Herr von Wau Wau. How do you interpret this, this mess of a mystery?"

"You'll note that there are many figures along the yellow brick road until one gets to the large moon rising behind the castle. All these figures have halos over their heads. This puzzled me until I understood that the halos are also zeros. We are to pay no attention to the figures beneath them.

"But the moon behind the castle? Look at the map. Two of the roads running southeast out of Hamburg meet just above the city of Luneburg. A *burg* is a castle, but the *Lune* doesn't mean anything in German in this context. It is, however, similar to the English *lunar,* hence the moon. And the yellow brick road goes south from there.

"I must confess that I am now at a loss. So, we get in a car and travel to Luneburg and south of it while I study the map and the painting."

"We can't take the painting with us; it's too big!" Strasse said.

"I have it all in here," Ralph said, tapping his head with his paw. "But I suggest we take a color Polaroid shot of the painting for you who have weak memories," and he grinned at Strasse.

Chapter VI
Follow the Yellow
Brick Road

Strasse did not like it, but he could not proceed without Ralph, and Ralph insisted that Mrs. Scarletin and I be brought along. First, he sent two men to watch Hilda Speck and to make sure she did not try to leave town—as the Americans say. He had no evidence to arrest her as yet, nor did he really think—I believe—that he was going to have any.

The dog, Lisa, and I got into the rear of a large police limousine, steam-driven, of course. Strasse sat in the front with the driver. Another car, which kept in radio contact with us, was to follow us at a distance of a kilometer.

An hour later, we were just north of Luneburg. A half hour later, still going south, we were just north of the town of Uelzen. It was still daylight, and so I could easily see the photo of the painting which I held. The yellow road on it ran south of the moon rising behind the castle (Luneburg) and extended a little south of a group of three strange figures. These were a hornless sheep (probably a female), a section of an overhead railway, and an archer with a medieval Japanese coiffure and medieval clothes.

Below this group the road split. Two roads wound toward the walls in the upper and lower parts of the picture and eventually went through them. The other curved almost due south to the left and then went through or by some more puzzling figures.

The first was a representation of a man (he

looked like the risen Jesus) coming from a tomb
set in the middle of some trees. To its right and a
little lower was a waistcoat. Next was what looked
like William Penn, the Quaker. Following it was a
man in a leopard loincloth with two large apes at
his heels.

Next was a man dressed in clothes such as the
ancient Mesopotamian people wore. He was down
on all fours, his head bent close to the grass. Beside
him was a banana tree.

Across the road was a large hot-air balloon with
a bald-headed man in the wicker basket. On the
side of the bag in large letters were: O.Z.

Across the road from it were what looked like
two large Vikings wading through a sea. Behind
them was the outline of a fleet of dragon-prowed
longships and the silhouette of a horde of horn-
helmeted bearded men. The two leaders were ap-
proaching a body of naked warriors, colored blue,
standing in horse-drawn chariots.

South of these was a woman dressed in mid-
Victorian clothes, hoopskirts and all, and behind
her a mansion typical of the pre–Civil War American south. By it was a tavern, if the drunks lying
outside it and the board hanging over the doorway
meant anything. The sign was too small to contain
even letters written under a magnifying glass.

A little to the left, the road terminated in a pair
of hands tearing a package from another pair of
hands.

Just before we got to Uelzen, Strasse said, "How
do you know that we're on the right road?"

"Consider the sheep, the raised section of railway, and the Japanese archer," Ralph said. "In En-

glish, *U* is pronounced exactly like the word for the female sheep—*ewe.* An elevated railway is colloquially an *el.* The Japanese archer could be a Samurai, but I do not think so. He is a *Zen* archer. Thus, *U, el,* and *zen* or the German city of Uelzen."

"All of this seems so easy, so apparent, now that you've pointed it out," I said.

"Hindsight has twenty/twenty vision," he said somewhat bitterly.

"And the rest?" I said.

"The town of Esterholz is not so difficult. Would you care to try?"

"Another English-German hybrid pun," I said, with more confidence than I felt. "*Ester* sounds much like *Easter,* hence the risen Christ. And the wood is the *holz,* of course. *Holt,* archaic English for a small wood or copse, by the way, comes from the same Germanic root as *holz.*"

"And the Weste (waistcoat)?" Ralph said.

"I would guess that that means to take the road west of Esterholz," I said somewhat more confidently.

"Excellent, Doctor," he said. "And the Quaker?"

"I really don't know," I said, chagrined because Lisa had been looking admiringly at me.

He gave his short barking laughter and said, "And neither do I, my dear fellow! I am sure that some of these symbols, perhaps most, have a meaning which will not be apparent until we have studied the neighborhood."

Seven kilometers southeast of Uelzen, we turned into the village of Esterholz and then west onto the road to Wrestede. Looking at the hands tearing loose the package from the other pair, I suddenly cried out, "Of course! Wrestede! Suggesting the English, *wrested*! The hands are *wresting* the package away! Then that means that Scarletin is a prisoner somewhere between Esterholz and Wrestede!"

"Give that man the big stuffed teddy bear," Ralph said. "OK, toots, so where is Scarletin?"

I fell silent. The others said nothing, but the increasing tension was making us sweat. We all looked waxy and pale in the light of the sinking sun. In half an hour, night would be on us.

"Slow down so I can read the names on the gateways of the farms," Ralph said. The driver obeyed, and presently Ralph said, "Ach!"

I could see nothing which reminded me of a Quaker.

"The owner of that farm is named Fuchs (fox)," I said.

"Yes, and the founder of the Society of Friends, or The Quakers, was George Fox," he said.

He added a moment later, "As I remember it, it was in this area that some particularly bestial—or should I say human?—murders occurred in 1845. A man named Wilhelm Graustock was finally caught and convicted."

I had never heard of this case, but, as I was to find out, Ralph had an immense knowledge of sensational literature. He seemed to know the details of every horror committed in the last two centuries.

"What is the connection between Herr Graustock and this figure which is obviously Tarzan?" I said.

"Graustock is remarkably similar in sound to Greystoke," he said. "As you may or may not know, the lord of the jungle was also Lord

Greystoke of the British peerage. As a fact, Graustock and Greystoke both mean exactly the same thing, a gray stick or pole. They have common Germanic roots. Ach, there it is! The descendants of the infamous butcher still hold his property, but are, I believe, singularly peaceful farmers."

"And the man on all fours by a banana tree?" Strasse growled. It hurt him to ask, but he could not push back his curiosity.

Ralph burst out laughing again. "Another example of redundancy, I believe. And the most difficult to figure out. A tough one, sweetheart. Want to put in your two pfennigs' worth?"

"Aw, go find a fireplug," Strasse said, at which Ralph laughed even more loudly.

"Unless I'm mistaken," Ralph said, "the next two images stand for a word, not a thing. They symbolize *nebanan* (next door). The question is, next door to what? The Graustock farm or the places indicated by the balloon and the battle tableau and the antebellum scene? I see nothing as yet which indicates that we are on or about to hit the bull's-eye. Continue at the same speed, driver."

There was silence for a minute. I refused to speak because of my pride. Finally, Lisa said, "For heaven's sake, Herr von Wau Wau, I'm dying of curiosity! How did you ever get *nebanan*?"

"The man on all fours with his head close to the ground looks to me like ancient Nebuchadnezzar, the Babylonian king who went mad and ate grass. By him is the banana (Banane) tree. Collapse those two words into one, à la Lewis Carroll and his portmanteau words, and you have *nebanan* (next to)."

"This Scarletin is crazy," Strasse said.

"If he is, he has a utilitarian madness," Ralph said.

"You're out of your mind, too!" Strasse said triumphantly. "Look!" And he pointed at a name painted on the wall. Neb Bannons.

Ralph was silent for a few seconds while Strasse laughed, and then he said, quietly, "Well, I was wrong in the particular but right in the principle. Ach! Here we are! Maintain the same speed driver! The rest of you, look straight ahead, don't gawk! Someone may be watching from the house, but they won't think it suspicious if they see a dog looking out of the window!"

I did as he said, but I strained out of the corners of my eyes to see both sides of the road. On my right were some fields of barley. On my left I caught a glimpse of a gateway with a name over it in large white-painted letters: Schindeler. We went past that and by a field on my left in which two stallions stood by the fence looking at us. On my right was a sign against a stone wall which said: Bergmann.

Ralph said delightedly, "That's it!"

I felt even more stupid.

"Don't stop until we get around the curve ahead and out of sight of the Schindeler house," Ralph said.

A moment later, we were parked beyond the curve and pointed west. The car which had been trailing us by several kilometers reported by radio that it had stopped near the Graustock farm.

"All right!" Strasse said fiercely. "Things seem to have worked out! But before I move in, I want to make sure I'm not arresting the wrong people. Just how did you figure this one out?"

"Button your lip and flap your ears, sweetheart," Ralph said. "Take the balloon with O.Z. on it. That continues the yellow brick road motif. You noticed the name Bergmann (miner)? A Bergmann is a man who digs, right? Well, for those of you who may have forgotten, the natal or Nebraskan name of the Wizard of Oz was Diggs."

Strasse looked as if he were going to have an apoplectic fit. "And what about those ancient Teutonic warriors and those naked blue men in chariots across the road from the balloon?" he shouted.

"Those Teutonic warriors were Anglo-Saxons, and they were invading ancient Britain. The Britons were tattooed blue and often went into battle naked. As all educated persons know," he added, grinning. "As for the two leaders of the Anglo-Saxons, traditionally they were named Hengist and Horsa. Both names meant *horse*. In fact, as you know, *Hengst* is a German word for stallion, and *Ross* also means horse. Ross is cognate with the Old English *hrossa,* meaning horse."

"God preserve me from any case like this one in the future!" Strasse said. "Very well, we won't pause in this madness! What does this pre–Civil War house with the Southern belle before it and the tavern by it mean? How do you know that it means that Scarletin is prisoner there?"

"The tableau suggests, among other things, the book and the movie *Gone With the Wind*," Ralph said. "You probably haven't read the book, Strasse, but you surely must have seen the movie. The heroine's name is Scarlett O'Hara, right, pal? And a *tavern,* in English, is also an *inn.* Scarlett-inn, get it?"

A few minutes later, Ralph said, "If you don't control yourself, my dear Strasse, your men will have to put you in a strait jacket."

The policeman ceased his bellowing but not his trembling, took a few deep breaths, followed by a deep draught from a bottle in the glove compartment, breathed schnapps all over us, and said, "So! Life is not easy! And duty calls! Let us proceed to make the raid upon the farmhouse as agreed upon!"

Chapter VII
No Emerald City for Me

An hour after dark, policemen burst into the front and rear doors of the Schindeler house. By then it had been ascertained that the house had been rented by a man giving the name of Albert Habicht. This was Hilda Speck's brother, Albert Speck, the Hippopotamus. His companion was a Wilhelm Erlesohn, a tall skinny man nicknamed *die Giraffe.* A fine zoological pair, both now behind bars.

Hilda Speck was also convicted but managed to escape a year later. But we were to cross her path again. (*The Case of the Seeing Eye Man.*)

Alfred Scarletin was painting another canvas with the same message but different symbols when we collared his kidnappers. He threw down his brush and took his lovely wife into his arms, and my heart went into a decaying orbit around my hopes. Apparently, despite his infidelity, she still loved him.

Most of this case was explained, but there was

still an important question to be answered. How had Scarletin known where he was?

"The kidnaping took place in daylight in the midst of a large crowd," Scarletin said. "Erlesohn jammed a gun which he had in his coat pocket against my back. I did as he said and got into the back of a delivery van double-parked nearby. Erlesohn then rendered me unconscious with a drug injected by a hypodermic syringe. When I woke up, I was in this house. I have been confined to this room ever since, which, as you see, is large and has a southern exposure and a heavily barred skylight and large heavily barred windows. I was told that I would be held until I had painted twelve paintings. These would be sufficient for the two men to become quite wealthy through sales to rich but unscrupulous collectors. Then I would be released.

"I did not believe them of course. After the twelve paintings were done, they would kill me and bury me somewhere in the woods. I listened often at the door late at night and overheard the two men, who drank much, talking loudly. That is how I found out their names. I also discovered that Hilda was in on the plot, though I'd suspected that all along. You see, I had quit her only a few days before I was kidnapped, and she was desperate because she no longer had an income.

"As for how I knew where I was, that is not so remarkable. I have a photographic memory, and I have tramped up and down Germany painting in my youth and early middle age. I have been along this road a number of times on foot when I was a teen-ager. In fact, I once painted the Graustock farmhouse. It is true that I had forgotten this, but after a while the memory came back. After all, I looked out the window every day and saw the Graustock farm.

"And now, tell me, who is the man responsible for reading my message? He must be an extraordinary man."

"No man," I said, feeling like Ulysses in Polyphemus' cave.

"Ach, then, it was you, Lisa?" he cried.

"It's yours truly, sweetheart," the voice of Humphrey Bogart said.

Scarletin is a very composed man, but he has fainted at least once in his life.

Chapter VIII
The Conclusion

It was deep in winter with the fuel shortage most critical. We were sitting in our apartment trying to keep warm by the radiations from the TV set. The Scotch helped, and I was trying to forget our discomfort by glancing over my notes and listening to the records of our cases since the Scarletin case. Had Ralph and I, in that relatively short span of time, really experienced the affair of the aluminum creche, the adventures of the human camel and the Old-School Thai, and the distressing business with the terrible Venetian, Granelli? The latter, by the way, is being written up under the title: *The Doge Whose Barque Was Worse Than His Bight.*

At last, I put the notes and records to one side and picked up a book. Too many memories were making me uncomfortable. A long silence followed, broken when Ralph said, "You may not have lost her after all, my dear Weisstein."

I started, and I said, "How did you know I was thinking of *her*?"

Ralph grinned (at least, I think he was grinning). He said, "Even the lead-brained Strasse would know that you cannot forget her big brown eyes, her smiles, her deep rich tones, her figure, and her etcetera. What else these many months would evoke those sighs, those moping stares, those frequent attacks of insomnia and absent-mindedness? It is evident at this moment that you are not at all as deep in one of C. S. Forester's fine sea stories as you pretend.

"But cheer up! The fair Lisa may yet have good cause to divorce her artistic but philandering spouse. Or she may become a widow."

"What makes you say that?" I cried.

"I've been thinking that it might not be just a coincidence that old Lausitz died after he purchased Scarletin's painting. I've been sniffing around the painting—literally and figuratively—and I think there's one Hamburger that's gone rotten."

"You suspect Scarletin of murder!" I said. "But how could he have killed Lausitz?"

"I don't know yet, pal," he said. "But I will. You can bet your booties I will. Old murders are like old bones—I dig them up."

And he was right, but that adventure was not to happen for another six months.

The Winner

DONALD WESTLAKE

Donald Westlake is primarily known for his crime fiction. From the hard-edged world of the professional thief Parker to the inept criminal mastermind Dortmunder, he has examined man's evil side in many excellent novels and short stories. Of course, when he combines his passion for the world of crime with an examination of what the future may bring, the following story is the result.

Wordman stood at the window, looking out, and saw Revell walk away from the compound. "Come here," he said to the interviewer. "You'll see the Guardian in action."

The interviewer came around the desk and stood beside Wordman at the window. He said, "That's one of them?"

"Right." Wordman smiled, feeling pleasure. "You're lucky," he said. "It's rare when one of them even makes the attempt. Maybe he's doing it for your benefit."

The interviewer looked troubled. He said, "Doesn't he know what it will do?"

"Of course. Some of them don't believe it, not till they've tried it once. Watch."

They both watched. Revell walked without apparent haste, directly across the field toward the woods on the other side. After he'd gone about two hundred yards from the edge of the compound he began to bend forward slightly at the middle, and a few yards farther on he folded his arms across his stomach as though it ached him. He tottered, but kept moving forward, staggering more and more, appearing to be in great pain. He managed to stay on his feet nearly all the way to the trees, but finally crumpled to the ground, where he lay unmoving.

Wordman no longer felt pleasure. He liked the theory of the Guardian better than its application. Turning to his desk, he called the infirmary and said, "Send a stretcher out to the east, near the woods. Revell's out there."

The interviewer turned at the sound of the name, saying, "Revell? Is that who that is? The poet?"

"If you can call it poetry." Wordman's lips curled in disgust. He'd read some of Revell's so-called poems; garbage, garbage.

The interviewer looked back out the window. "I'd heard he was arrested," he said thoughtfully.

Looking over the interviewer's shoulder, Wordman saw that Revell had managed to get back up onto hands and knees, was now crawling slowly and painfully toward the woods. But a stretcher team was already trotting toward him and Wordman watched as they reached him, picked up the pain-weakened body, strapped it to the stretcher, and carried it back to the compound.

As they moved out of sight, the interviewer said, "Will he be all right?"

"After a few days in the infirmary. He'll have strained some muscles."

The interviewer turned away from the window. "That was very graphic," he said carefully.

"You're the first outsider to see it," Wordman told him, and smiled, feeling good again. "What do they call that? A scoop?"

"Yes," agreed the interviewer, sitting back down in his chair. "A scoop."

They returned to the interview, just the most recent of dozens Wordman had given in the year since this pilot project of the Guardian had been set up. For perhaps the fiftieth time he explained what the Guardian did and how it was of value to society.

The essence of the Guardian was the miniature black box, actually a tiny radio receiver, which was surgically inserted into the body of every prisoner. In the center of this prison compound was the Guardian transmitter, perpetually sending its message to these receivers. As long as a prisoner stayed within the hundred-and-fifty-yard range of that transmitter, all was well. Should he move beyond that range, the black box inside his skin would begin to send messages of pain throughout his nervous system. This pain increased as the prisoner moved farther from the transmitter, until at its peak it was totally immobilizing.

"The prisoner can't hide, you see," Wordman explained. "Even if Revell had reached the woods, we'd have found him. His screams would have led us to him."

The Guardian had been initially suggested by Wordman himself, at that time serving as assistant warden at a more ordinary penitentiary in the Federal system. Objections, mostly from sentimentalists, had delayed its acceptance for several years, but now at last this pilot project had been established, with a guaranteed five-year trial period, and Wordman had been placed in charge.

"If the results are as good as I'm sure they will be," Wordman said, "all prisons in the Federal system will be converted to the Guardian method."

The Guardian method had made jailbreaks impossible, riots easy to quell—by merely turning off the transmitter for a minute or two—and prisons simplicity to guard. "We have no guards here as such," Wordman pointed out. "Service employees only are needed here, people for the mess hall, infirmary and so on."

For the pilot project, prisoners were only those who had committed crimes against the State rather than against individuals. "You might say," Wordman said, smiling, "that here are gathered the Disloyal Opposition."

"You mean, political prisoners," suggested the interviewer.

"We don't like that phrase here," Wordman said, his manner suddenly icy. "It sounds Commie."

The interviewer apologized for his sloppy use of terminology, ended the interview shortly afterward, and Wordman, once again in a good mood, escorted him out of the building. "You see," he said, gesturing. "No walls. No machine guns in towers. Here at last is the model prison."

The interviewer thanked him again for his time, and went away to his car. Wordman watched him leave, then went over to the infirmary to see Revell. But he'd been given a shot, and was already asleep.

Revell lay flat on his back and stared at the ceiling. He kept thinking, over and over again, "I didn't know it would be as bad as that. I didn't know it would be as bad as that." Mentally, he took a big brush of black paint and wrote the words on the spotless white ceiling: *"I didn't know it would be as bad as that."*

"Revell."

He turned his head slightly and saw Wordman standing beside the bed. He watched Wordman, but made no sign.

Wordman said, "They told me you were awake."

Revell waited.

"I tried to tell you when you first came," Wordman reminded him. "I told you there was no point trying to get away."

Revell opened his mouth and said, "It's all right, don't feel bad. You do what you have to do, I do what I have to do."

"Don't *feel* bad!" Wordman stared at him. "What have *I* got to feel bad about?"

Revell looked up at the ceiling, and the words he had painted there just a minute ago were gone already. He wished he had paper and pencil. Words were leaking out of him like water through a sieve. He needed paper and pencil to catch them in. He said, "May I have paper and pencil?"

"To write more obscenity? Of course not."

"Of course not," echoed Revell. He closed his eyes and watched the words leaking away. A man doesn't have time both to invent and memorize, he has to choose, and long ago Revell had chosen invention. But now there was no way to put the inventions down on paper and they trickled through his mind like water and eroded away into the great outside world. "Twinkle, twinkle, little pain," Revell said softly, "in my groin and in my brain, down so low and up so high, will you live or will I die?"

"The pain goes away," said Wordman. "It's been three days, it should be gone already."

"It will come back," Revell said. He opened his eyes and wrote the words on the ceiling. "It will come back."

Wordman said, "Don't be silly. It's gone for good, unless you run away again."

Revell was silent.

Wordman waited, half-smiling, and then frowned. "You aren't," he said.

Revell looked at him in some surprise. "Of course I am," he said. "Didn't you know I would?"

"No one tries it twice."

"I'll never stop leaving. Don't you know that? I'll never stop leaving, I'll never stop being, I'll not stop believing I'm who I must be. You had to know that."

Wordman stared at him. "You'll go through it *again*?"

"Ever and ever," Revell said.

"It's a bluff." Wordman pointed an angry finger at Revell, saying, "If you want to die, I'll let you die. Do you know if we don't bring you back you'll die out there?"

"That's escape, too," Revell said.

"Is that what you want? All right. Go out there again, and I won't send anyone after you, that's a promise."

"Then you lose," Revell said. He looked at Wordman finally, seeing the blunt angry face. "They're your rules," Revell told him, "and by your own rules you're going to lose. You say your black box will make me stay, and that means the black box will make me stop being me. I say you're wrong. I say as long as I'm leaving you're losing, and if the black box kills me you've lost forever."

Spreading his arms, Wordman shouted, "Do you think this is a *game*?"

"Of course," said Revell. "That's why you invented it."

"You're insane," Wordman said. He started for the door. "You shouldn't be here, you should be in an asylum."

"That's losing, too," Revell shouted after him, but Wordman had slammed the door and gone.

Revell lay back on the pillow. Alone again, he could dwell once more on his terrors. He was afraid of the black box, much more now that he knew what it could do to him, afraid to the point where his fear made him sick to his stomach. But he was afraid of losing himself, too, this a more abstract and intellectual fear but just as strong. No, it was even stronger, because it was driving him to go out again.

"But I didn't know it would be as bad as that," he whispered. He painted it once more on the ceiling, this time in red.

*   *   *

Wordman had been told when Revell would be re-leased from the infirmary, and he made a point of being at the door when Revell came out. Revell seemed somewhat leaner, perhaps a little older. He shielded his eyes from the sun with his hand, looked at Wordman, and said, "Good-bye, Word-man." He started walking east.

Wordman didn't believe it. He said, "You're bluffing, Revell."

Revell kept walking.

Wordman couldn't remember when he'd ever felt such anger. He wanted to run after Revell and kill him with his bare hands. He clenched his hands into fists and told himself he was a reasonable man, a rational man, a merciful man. As the Guardian was reasonable, was rational, was merciful. It re-quired only obedience, and so did he. It punished only such purposeless defiance as Revell's, and so did he. Revell was antisocial, self-destructive, he had to learn. For his own sake, as well as for the sake of society, Revell had to be taught.

Wordman shouted, "What are you trying to *get* out of this?" He glared at Revell's moving back, listened to Revell's silence. He shouted, "I won't send anyone after you! You'll crawl back *yourself*!"

He kept watching until Revell was far out from the compound, staggering across the field toward the trees, his arms folded across his stomach, his legs stumbling, his head bent forward. Wordman watched, and then gritted his teeth, and turned his back, and returned to his office to work on the monthly report. Only two attempted escapes last month.

Two or three times in the course of the afternoon

he looked out the window. The first time, he saw Revell far across the field, on hands and knees, crawling toward the trees. The last time, Revell was out of sight, but he could be heard screaming. Wordman had a great deal of trouble concentrating his attention on the report.

Toward evening he went outside again. Revell's screams sounded from the woods, faint but continuous. Wordman stood listening, his fists clenching and relaxing at his sides. Grimly he forced himself not to feel pity. For Revell's own good he had to be taught.

A staff doctor came to him a while later and said, "Mr. Wordman, we've got to bring him in."

Wordman nodded. "I know. But I want to be sure he's learned."

"For God's sake," said the doctor, "*listen* to him."

Wordman looked bleak. "All right, bring him in."

As the doctor started away, the screaming stopped. Wordman and the doctor both turned their heads, listened—silence. The doctor ran for the infirmary.

Revell lay screaming. All he could think of was the pain, and the need to scream. But sometimes, when he managed a scream of the very loudest, it was possible for him to have a fraction of a second for himself, and in those fractions of seconds he still kept moving away from the prison, inching along the ground, so that in the last hour he had moved approximately seven feet. His head and right arm were now visible from the country road that passed through these woods.

On one level, he was conscious of nothing but the pain and his own screaming. On another level, he was totally, even insistently, aware of everything around him, the blades of grass near his eyes, the stillness of the woods, the tree branches high overhead. And the small pickup truck, when it stopped on the road beyond him.

The man who came over from the truck and squatted beside Revell had a lined and weathered face and the rough clothing of a farmer. He touched Revell's shoulder and said, "You hurt, fella?"

"Eeeeast!" screamed Revell. "Eeeeast!"

"Is it okay to move you?" asked the man.

"Yesssss!" shrieked Revell. "Eeeeast!"

"I'd best take you to a doctor."

There was no change in the pain when the man lifted him and carried him to the truck and lay him down on the floor in back. He was already at optimum distance from the transmitter; the pain now was as bad as it could get.

The farmer tucked a rolled-up wad of cloth into Revell's open mouth. "Bite on this," he said. "It'll make it easier."

It made nothing easier, but it muffled his screams. He was grateful for that; the screams embarrassed him.

He was aware of it all, the drive through increasing darkness, the farmer carrying him into a building that was of colonial design on the outside but looked like the infirmary on the inside, and a doctor who looked down at him and touched his forehead and then went to one side to thank the farmer for bringing him. They spoke briefly over there, and then the farmer went away and the doctor came back to look at Revell again. He was young, dressed in laboratory white, with a pudgy face and red hair. He seemed sick and angry. He said, "You're from that prison, aren't you?"

Revell was still screaming through the cloth. He managed a head-spasm which he meant to be a nod. His armpits felt as though they were being cut open with knives of ice. The sides of his neck were being scraped by sandpaper. All of his joints were being ground back and forth, back and forth, the way a man at dinner separates the bones of a chicken wing. The interior of his stomach was full of acid. His body was stuck with needles, sprayed with fire. His skin was being peeled off, his nerves cut with razor blades, his muscles pounded with hammers. Thumbs were pushing his eyes out from inside his head. And yet, the genius of this pain, the brilliance that had gone into its construction, it permitted his mind to work, to remain constantly aware. There was no unconsciousness for him, no oblivion.

The doctor said, "What beasts some men are. I'll try to get it out of you. I don't know what will happen, we aren't supposed to know how it works, but I'll try to take the box out of you."

He went away, and came back with a needle. "Here. This will put you to sleep."

Ahhhhh.

"He isn't there. He just isn't anywhere in the woods."

Wordman glared at the doctor, but knew he had

to accept what the man reported. "All right," he said. "Someone took him away. He had a confederate out there, someone who helped him get away."

"No one would dare," said the doctor. "Anyone who helped him would wind up here themselves."

"Nevertheless," said Wordman. "I'll call the State Police," he said, and went on into his office.

Two hours later the State Police called back. They'd checked the normal users of that road, local people who might have seen or heard something, and had found a farmer who'd picked up an injured man near the prison and taken him to a Dr. Allyn in Boonetown. The State Police were convinced the farmer had acted innocently.

"But not the doctor," Wordman said grimly. "He'd have to know the truth almost immediately."

"Yes, sir, I should think so."

"And he hasn't reported Revell."

"No, sir."

"Have you gone to pick him up yet?"

"Not yet. We just got the report."

"I'll want to come with you. Wait for me."

"Yes, sir."

Wordman traveled in the ambulance in which they'd bring Revell back. They arrived without siren at Dr. Allyn's with two cars of state troopers, marched into the tiny operating room, and found Allyn washing instruments at the sink.

Allyn looked at them all calmly and said, "I thought you might be along."

Wordman pointed at the man who lay, unconscious, on the table in the middle of the room. "There's Revell," he said.

Allyn glanced at the operating table in surprise. "Revell? The poet?"

"You didn't know? Then why help him?"

Instead of answering, Allyn studied his face and said, "Would you be Wordman himself?"

Wordman said, "Yes, I am."

"Then I believe this is yours," Allyn said, and put into Wordman's hands a small and bloody black box.

The ceiling was persistently bare. Revell's eyes wrote on it words that should have singed the paint away, but nothing ever happened. He shut his eyes against the white at last and wrote in spidery letters on the inside of his lids the single word *oblivion*.

He heard someone come into the room, but the effort of making a change was so great that for a moment longer he permitted his eyes to remain closed. When he did open them he saw Wordman there, standing grim and mundane at the foot of the bed.

Wordman said, "How are you, Revell?"

"I was thinking about oblivion," Revell told him. "Writing a poem on the subject." He looked up at the ceiling, but it was empty.

Wordman said, "You asked, one time, you asked for pencil and paper. We've decided you can have them."

Revell looked at him in sudden hope, but then understood. "Oh," he said. "Oh, *that*."

Wordman frowned and said, "What's wrong? I said you can have pencil and paper."

"If I promise not to leave anymore."

Wordman's hands gripped the foot of the bed.

He said, "What's the matter with you? You can't get away, you have to know that by now."

"You mean I can't win. But I won't lose. It's your game, your rules, your home ground, your equipment; if I can manage a stalemate, that's pretty good."

Wordman said, "You still think it's a game. You think none of it matters. Do you want to see what you've done?" He stepped back to the door, opened it, made a motion, and Dr. Allyn was led in. Wordman said to Revell, "You remember this man?"

"I remember," said Revell.

Wordman said, "He just arrived. They'll be putting the Guardian in him in about an hour. Does it make you proud, Revell?"

Looking at Allyn, Revell said, "I'm sorry."

Allyn smiled and shook his head. "Don't be. I had the idea the publicity of a trial might help rid the world of things like the Guardian." His smile turned sour. "There wasn't very much publicity."

Wordman said, "You two are cut out of the same cloth. The emotions of the mob, that's all you can think of. Revell in those so-called poems of his, and you in that speech you made in court."

Revell, smiling, said, "Oh? You made a speech? I'm sorry I didn't get to hear it."

"It wasn't very good," Allyn said. "I hadn't known the trial would only be one day long, so I didn't have much time to prepare it."

Wordman said, "All right, that's enough. You two can talk later, you'll have years."

At the door Allyn turned back and said, "Don't

go anywhere till I'm up and around, will you? After my operation."

Revell said, "You want to come along next time?"

"Naturally," said Allyn.

The Detweiler Boy

TOM REAMY

Tom Reamy (1935–1977) was just starting to enjoy a successful writing career when he passed away, leaving behind only one novel and a handful of short stories. These, however, had already attracted critical recognition and an interest in works to come. He excelled at providing grittily realistic characters and examined the links between love, need, and death. "The Detweiler Boy" combines his attention to detail with the hard-boiled detective story genre, resulting in one of his best works.

The room had been cleaned with pine oil disinfectant and smelled like a public toilet. Harry Spinner was on the floor behind the bed, scrunched down between it and the wall. The almost colorless chenille bedspread had been pulled askew exposing part of the clean, but dingy, sheet. All I could see of Harry was one leg poking over the edge of the bed. He wasn't wearing a shoe, only a faded brown and tan argyle sock with a hole in it. The sock, long bereft of any elasticity, was crumpled around his thin rusty ankle.

I closed the door quietly behind me and walked around the end of the bed so I could see all of him. He was huddled on his back with his elbows propped up by the wall and the bed. His throat had been cut. The blood hadn't spread very far. Most of it had been soaked up by the threadbare carpet under the bed. I looked around the grubby little room but didn't find anything. There were no signs of a struggle, no signs of forced entry—but then, my Bank-Americard hadn't left any signs either. The window was open, letting in the muffled roar of traffic on the Boulevard. I stuck my head out and looked, but it was three stories down to the neon-lit marquee of the movie house.

It had been nearly two hours since Harry called me. "Bertram, my boy, I've run across something very peculiar. I don't really know what to make of it."

I had put away the report I was writing on Lucas McGowan's hyperactive wife. (She had a definite predilection for gas-pump jockeys, car-wash boys, and parking-lot attendants. I guess it had something to do with the Age of the Automobile.) I propped my feet on my desk and leaned back until the old swivel chair groaned a protest.

"What did you find this time, Harry? A nest of international spies or an invasion from Mars?" I guess Harry Spinner wasn't much use to anyone, not even himself, but I liked him. He'd helped me in a couple of cases, nosing around in places only the Harry Spinners of the world can nose around in unnoticed. I was beginning to get the idea he was trying to play Doctor Watson to my Sherlock Holmes.

"Don't tease me, Bertram. There's a boy here in

the hotel. I saw something I don't think he wanted me to see. It's extremely odd."

Harry was also the only person in the world, except my mother, who called me Bertram. "What did you see?"

"I'd rather not talk about it over the phone. Can you come over?"

Harry saw too many old private-eye movies on the late show. "It'll be a while. I've got a client coming in in a few minutes to pick up the poop on his wandering wife."

"Bertram, you shouldn't waste your time and talent on divorce cases."

"It pays the bills, Harry. Besides, there aren't enough Maltese falcons to go around."

By the time I filled Lucas McGowan in on all the details (I got the impression he was less concerned with his wife's infidelity than with her taste; that it wouldn't have been so bad if she'd been shacking up with movie stars or international playboys), collected my fee, and grabbed a Thursday special at Colonel Sanders, almost two hours had passed. Harry hadn't answered my knock, and so I let myself in with a credit card.

Birdie Pawlowicz was a fat, slovenly old broad somewhere between forty and two hundred. She was blind in her right eye and wore a black felt patch over it. She claimed she had lost the eye in a fight with a Creole whore over a riverboat gambler. I believed her. She ran the Brewster Hotel the way Florence Nightingale must have run that stinking army hospital in the Crimea. Her tenants were the losers habitating that rotting section of the Boulevard east of the Hollywood Freeway. She bossed them, cursed them, loved them, and took care of them. And they loved her back. (Once, a couple of years ago, a young black buck thought an old fat lady with one eye would be easy pickings. The cops found him three days later, two blocks away, under some rubbish in an alley where he'd hidden. He had a broken arm, two cracked ribs, a busted nose, a few missing teeth, and was stone-dead from internal hemorrhaging.)

The Brewster ran heavily in the red, but Birdie didn't mind. She had quite a bit of property in Westwood which ran very, very heavily in the black. She gave me an obscene leer as I approached the desk, but her good eye twinkled.

"Hello, lover!" she brayed in a voice like a cracked boiler. "I've lowered my price to a quarter. Are you interested?" She saw my face and her expression shifted from lewd to wary. "What's wrong, Bert?"

"Harry Spinner. You'd better get the cops, Birdie. Somebody killed him."

She looked at me, not saying anything, her face slowly collapsing into an infinitely weary resignation. Then she turned and telephoned the police.

Because it was just Harry Spinner at the Brewster Hotel on the wrong end of Hollywood Boulevard, the cops took over half an hour to get there. While we waited I told Birdie everything I knew, about the phone call and what I'd found.

"He must have been talking about the Detweiler boy," she said, frowning. "Harry's been kinda friendly with him, felt sorry for him, I guess."

"What's his room? I'd like to talk to him."

"He checked out."

"When?"

"Just before you came down."

"Damn!"

She bit her lip. "I don't think the Detweiler boy killed him."

"Why?"

"I just don't think he could. He's such a gentle boy."

"Oh, Birdie," I groaned, "you know there's no such thing as a killer type. Almost anyone will kill with a good enough reason."

"I know," she sighed, "but I still can't believe it." She tapped her scarlet fingernails on the dulled Formica desk top. "How long had Harry been dead?"

He had phoned me about ten after five. I had found the body at seven. "A while," I said. "The blood was mostly dry."

"Before six-thirty?"

"Probably."

She sighed again, but this time with relief. "The Detweiler boy was down here with me until six thirty. He'd been here since about four fifteen. We were playing gin. He was having one of his spells and wanted company."

"What kind of spell? Tell me about him, Birdie."

"But he couldn't have killed Harry," she protested.

"Okay," I said, but I wasn't entirely convinced. Why would anyone deliberately and brutally murder inoffensive, invisible Harry Spinner right after he told me he had discovered something "peculiar" about the Detweiler boy? Except the Detweiler boy?

"Tell me anyway. If he and Harry were friendly, he might know something. Why do you keep calling him a boy; how old is he?"

She nodded and leaned her bulk on the registration desk. "Early twenties, twenty-two, twenty-three, maybe. Not very tall, about five five or six. Slim, dark curly hair, a real good-looking boy. Looks like a movie star except for his back."

"His back?"

"He has a hump. He's a hunchback."

That stopped me for a minute, but I'm not sure why. I must've had a mental picture of Charles Laughton riding those bells or Igor stealing that brain from the laboratory. "He's good-looking and he's a hunchback?"

"Sure." She raised her eyebrows. The one over the patch didn't go up as high as the other. "If you see him from the front, you can't even tell."

"What's his first name?"

"Andrew."

"How long has he been living here?"

She consulted a file card. "He checked in last Friday night. The 22nd. Six days."

"What's this spell he was having?"

"I don't know for sure. It was the second one he'd had. He would get pale and nervous. I think he was in a lot of pain. It would get worse and worse all day; then he'd be fine, all rosy and healthy-looking."

"Sounds to me like he was hurtin' for a fix."

"I thought so at first, but I changed my mind. I've seen enough of that and it wasn't the same.

Take my word. He was real bad this evening. He came down about four fifteen, like I said. He didn't complain, but I could tell he was wantin' company to take his mind off it. We played gin until six thirty. Then he went back upstairs. About twenty minutes later he came down with his old suitcase and checked out. He looked fine, all over his spell."

"Did he have a doctor?"

"I'm pretty sure he didn't. I asked him about it. He said there was nothing to worry about, it would pass. And it did."

"Did he say why he was leaving or where he was going?"

"No, just said he was restless and wanted to be movin' on. Sure hated to see him leave. A real nice kid."

When the cops finally got there, I told them all I knew—except I didn't mention the Detweiler boy. I hung around until I found out that Harry almost certainly wasn't killed after six thirty. They set the time somewhere between five ten, when he called me, and six. It looked like Andrew Detweiler was innocent, but what "peculiar" thing had Harry noticed about him, and why had he moved out right after Harry was killed? Birdie let me take a look at his room, but I didn't find a thing, not even an abandoned paperclip.

Friday morning I sat at my desk trying to put the pieces together. Trouble was, I only had two pieces and *they* didn't fit. The sun was coming in off the Boulevard, shining through the window, projecting the chipping letters painted on the glass against the wall in front of me. BERT MALLORY

Confidential Investigations. I got up and looked out. This section of the Boulevard wasn't rotting yet, but it wouldn't be long.

There's one sure gauge for judging a part of town: the movie theaters. It never fails. For instance, a new picture hadn't opened in downtown L.A. in a long, long time. The action ten years ago was on the Boulevard. Now it's in Westwood. The grand old Pantages, east of Vine and too near the freeway, used to be the site of the most glittering premieres. They even had the Oscar ceremonies there for a while. Now it shows exploitation and double-feature horror films. Only Grauman's Chinese and the once Paramount, once Loew's, now Downtown Cinema (or something) at the west end got good openings. The Nu-View, across the street and down, was showing an X-rated double feature. It was too depressing. So I closed the blind.

Miss Tremaine looked up from her typing at the rattle and frowned. Her desk was out in the small reception area, but I had arranged both desks so we could see each other and talk in normal voices when the door was open. It stayed open most of the time except when I had a client who felt secretaries shouldn't know his troubles. She had been transcribing the Lucas McGowan report for half an hour, *humphing* and *tsk-tsking* at thirty-second intervals. She was having a marvelous time. Miss Tremaine was about forty-five, looked like a constipated librarian, and was the best secretary I'd ever had. She'd been with me seven years. I'd tried a few young and sexy ones, but it hadn't worked out. Either they wouldn't play at all, or they wanted to play all the time. Both kinds were a pain in the ass to face first thing in the morning, every morning.

"Miss Tremaine, will you get Gus Verdugo on the phone, please?"

"Yes, Mr. Mallory." She dialed the phone nimbly, sitting as if she were wearing a back brace.

Gus Verdugo worked in R&I. I had done him a favor once, and he insisted on returning it tenfold. I gave him everything I had on Andrew Detweiler and asked him if he'd mind running it through the computer. He wouldn't mind. He called back in fifteen minutes. The computer had never heard of Andrew Detweiler and had only seven hunchbacks, none of them fitting Detweiler's description.

I was sitting there, wondering how in hell I would find him, when the phone rang again. Miss Tremaine stopped typing and lifted the receiver without breaking rhythm. "Mr. Mallory's office," she said crisply, really letting the caller know he'd hooked onto an efficient organization. She put her hand over the mouthpiece and looked at me. "It's for you—an obscene phone call." She didn't bat an eyelash or twitch a muscle.

"Thanks," I said and winked at her. She dropped the receiver back on the cradle from a height of three inches and went back to typing. Grinning, I picked up my phone. "Hello, Janice," I said.

"Just a minute till my ear stops ringing," the husky voice tickled my ear.

"What are you doing up this early?" I asked. Janice Fenwick was an exotic dancer at a club on the Strip nights and was working on her master's in oceanography at UCLA in the afternoons. In the year I'd known her I'd seldom seen her stick her nose into the sunlight before eleven.

"I had to catch you before you started following that tiresome woman with the car."

"I've finished that. She's picked up her last parking-lot attendant—at least with this husband," I chuckled.

"I'm glad to hear it."

"What's up?"

"I haven't had an indecent proposition from you in days. So I thought I'd make one of my own."

"I'm all ears."

"We're doing some diving off Catalina tomorrow. Want to come along?"

"Not much we can do in a wetsuit."

"The wetsuit comes off about four; then we'll have Saturday night and all of Sunday."

"Best indecent proposition I've had all week."

Miss Tremaine *humphed*. It might have been over something in the report, but I don't think it was.

I picked up Janice at her apartment in Westwood early Saturday morning. She was waiting for me and came striding out to the car all legs and healthy golden flesh. She was wearing white shorts, sneakers, and that damned Dallas Cowboys jersey. It was authentic. The name and number on it were quite well-known—even to nonfootball fans. She wouldn't tell me how she got it, just smirked and looked smug. She tossed her suitcase in the back seat and slid up against me. She smelled like sunshine.

We flew over and spent most of the day *glubbing*

around in the Pacific with a bunch of kids fifteen years younger than I and five years younger than Janice. I'd been on these jaunts with Janice before and enjoyed them so much I'd bought my own wetsuit. But I didn't enjoy it nearly as much as I did Saturday night and all of Sunday.

I got back to my apartment on Beachwood fairly late Sunday night and barely had time to get something to eat at the Mexican restaurant around the corner on Melrose. They have marvelous carne asada. I live right across the street from Paramount, right across from the door people go in to see them tape *The Odd Couple.* Every Friday night when I see them lining up out there, I think I might go someday, but I never seem to get around to it. (You might think I'd see a few movie stars living where I do, but I haven't. I did see Seymour occasionally when he worked at Channel 9, before he went to work for Gene Autry at Channel 5.)

I was so pleasantly pooped I completely forgot about Andrew Detweiler. Until Monday morning when I was sitting at my desk reading the *Times.*

It was a small story on page three, not very exciting or newsworthy. Last night a man named Maurice Milian, age 51, had fallen through the plate-glass doors leading onto the terrace of the high rise where he lived. He had been discovered about midnight when the people living below him had noticed dried blood on *their* terrace. The only thing to connect the deaths of Harry Spinner and Maurice Milian was a lot of blood flowing around. If Milian had been murdered, there *might* be a link, however tenuous. But Milian's death was accidental—a dumb, stupid accident. It niggled around in my brain for an hour before I gave in. There was only one way to get it out of my head.

"Miss Tremaine, I'll be back in an hour or so. If any slinky blondes come in wanting me to find their kid sisters, tell 'em to wait."

She *humphed* again and ignored me.

The Almsbury was half a dozen blocks away on Yucca. So I walked. It was a rectangular monolith about eight stories tall, not real new, not too old, but expensive-looking. The small terraces protruded in neat, orderly rows. The long, narrow grounds were immaculate with a lot of succulents that looked like they might have been imported from Mars. There were also the inevitable palm trees and clumps of bird of paradise. A small, discreet, polished placard dangled in a wrought-iron frame proclaiming, ever so softly, NO VACANCY.

Two willowy young men gave me appraising glances in the carpeted lobby as they exited into the sunlight like exotic jungle birds. It's one of those, I thought. My suspicions were confirmed when I looked over the tenant directory. All the names seemed to be male, but none of them was Andrew Detweiler.

Maurice Milian was still listed as 407. I took the elevator to four and rang the bell of 409. The bell played a few notes of Bach, or maybe Vivaldi or Telemann. All those old Baroques sound alike to me. The vision of loveliness who opened the door was about forty, almost as slim as Twiggy, but as tall as I. He wore a flowered silk shirt open to the waist, exposing his bony hairless chest, and tight white pants that might as well have been made of

Saran Wrap. He didn't say anything, just let his eyebrows rise inquiringly as his eyes flicked down, then up.

"Good morning," I said and showed him my ID. He blanched. His eyes became marbles brimming with terror. He was about to panic, tensing to slam the door. I smiled my friendly, disarming smile and went on as if I hadn't noticed. "I'm inquiring about a man named Andrew Detweiler." The terror trickled from his eyes, and I could see his thin chest throbbing. He gave me a blank look that meant he'd never heard the name.

"He's about twenty-two," I continued, "dark, curly hair, very good-looking."

He grinned wryly, calming down, trying to cover his panic. "Aren't they all?" he said.

"Detweiler is a hunchback."

His smile contracted suddenly. His eyebrows shot up. "Oh," he said. "Him."

Bingo!

Mallory, you've led a clean, wholesome life and it's paying off.

"Does he live in the building?" I swallowed to get my heart back in place and blinked a couple of times to clear away the skyrockets.

"No. He was . . . visiting."

"May I come in and talk to you about him?"

He was holding the door three quarters shut, and so I couldn't see anything in the room but an expensive-looking color TV. He glanced over his shoulder nervously at something behind him. The inner ends of his eyebrows drooped in a frown. He looked back at me and started to say something, then, with a small defiance, shrugged his eyebrows. "Sure, but there's not much I can tell you."

He pushed the door all the way open and stepped back. It was a good-sized living room come to life from the pages of a decorator magazine. A kitchen behind a half wall was on my right. A hallway led somewhere on my left. Directly in front of me were double sliding glass doors leading to the terrace. On the terrace was a bronzed hunk of beef stretched out nude trying to get bronzer. The hunk opened his eyes and looked at me. He apparently decided I wasn't competition and closed them again. Tall and lanky indicated one of two identical orange- and brown-striped couches facing each other across a football-field-size marble and glass cocktail table. He sat on the other one, took a cigarette from an alabaster box and lit it with an alabaster lighter. As an afterthought, he offered me one.

"Who was Detweiler visiting?" I asked as I lit the cigarette. The lighter felt cool and expensive in my hand.

"Maurice—next door." He inclined his head slightly toward 407.

"Isn't he the one who was killed in an accident last night?"

He blew a stream of smoke from pursed lips and tapped his cigarette on an alabaster ashtray. "Yes," he said.

"How long had Maurice and Detweiler known each other?"

"Not long."

"How long?"

He snuffed his cigarette out on pure-white alabaster and sat so prim and pristine I would have bet his feces came out wrapped in cellophane. He shrugged his eyebrows again. "Maurice picked him up somewhere the other night."

"Which night?"

He thought a moment. "Thursday, I think. Yes, Thursday."

"Was Detweiler a hustler?"

He crossed his legs like a Forties pin-up and dangled his Roman sandal. His lips twitched scornfully. "If he was, he would've starved. He was de-*formed*!"

"Maurice didn't seem to mind." He sniffed and lit another cigarette. "When did Detweiler leave?"

He shrugged. "I saw him yesterday afternoon. I was out last night . . . until quite late."

"How did they get along? Did they quarrel or fight?"

"I have no idea. I only saw them in the hall a couple of times. Maurice and I were . . . not close." He stood, fidgety. "There's really not anything I can tell you. Why don't you ask David and Murray. They and Maurice are . . . were thick as thieves."

"David and Murray?"

"Across the hall. 408."

I stood up. "I'll do that. Thank you very much." I looked at the plate-glass doors. I guess it would be pretty easy to walk through one of them if you thought it was open. "Are all the apartments alike? Those terrace doors?"

He nodded. "Ticky-tacky."

"Thanks again."

"Don't menton it." He opened the door for me

and then closed it behind me. I sighed and walked across to 408. I rang the bell. It didn't play anything, just went *bing-bong*.

David (or Murray) was about twenty-five, red-headed, and freckled. He had a slim, muscular body which was also freckled. I could tell because he was wearing only a pair of jeans, cut off very short, and split up the sides to the waistband. He was barefooted and had a smudge of green paint on his nose. He had an open, friendly face and gave me a neutral smile-for-a-stranger. "Yes?" he asked.

I showed him my ID. Instead of going pale he had only looked interested. "I was told by the man in 409 you might be able to tell me something about Andrew Detweiler."

"Andy?" He frowned slightly. "Come on in. I'm David Fowler." He held out his hand.

I shook it. "Bert Mallory." The apartment couldn't have been more different from the one across the hall. It was comfortable and cluttered, and dominated by a drafting table surrounded by jars of brushes and boxes of paint tubes. Architecturally, however, it was almost identical. The terrace was covered with potted plants rather than naked muscles. David Fowler sat on the stool at the drafting table and began cleaning brushes. When he sat, the split in his shorts opened and exposed half his butt, which was also freckled. But I got the impression he wasn't exhibiting himself; he was just completely indifferent.

"What do you want to know about Andy?"

"Everything."

He laughed. "That lets me out. Sit down. Move the stuff."

I cleared a space on the couch and sat. "How did Detweiler and Maurice get along?"

He gave me a knowing look. "Fine. As far as I know. Maurice liked to pick up stray puppies. Andy was a stray puppy."

"Was Detweiler a hustler?"

He laughed again. "No. I doubt if he knew what the word meant."

"Was he gay?"

"No."

"How do you know?"

He grinned. "Haven't you heard? We can spot each other a mile away. Would you like some coffee?"

"Yes, I would. Thank you."

He went to the half wall separating the kitchen and poured two cups from a pot that looked like it was kept hot and full all the time. "It's hard to describe Andy. There was something very little-boyish about him. A real innocent. Delighted with everything new. It's sad about his back. Real sad." He handed me the cup and returned to the stool. "There was something very secretive about him. Not about his feelings; he was very open about things like that."

"Did he and Maurice have sex together?"

"No. I told you it was a stray puppy relationship. I wish Murray were here. He's much better with words than I am. I'm visually oriented."

"Where is he?"

"At work. He's a lawyer."

"Do you think Detweiler could have killed Maurice?"

"No."

"Why?"

"He was here with us all evening. We had dinner and played Scrabble. I think he was real sick, but he tried to pretend he wasn't. Even if he hadn't been here I would not think so."

"When was the last time you saw him?"

"He left about half an hour before they found Maurice. I imagine he went over there, saw Maurice dead, and decided to disappear. Can't say as I blame him. The police might've gotten some funny ideas. We didn't mention him."

"Why not?"

"There was no point in getting him involved. It was just an accident."

"He couldn't have killed Maurice after he left here?"

"No. They said he'd been dead over an hour. What did Desmond tell you?"

"Desmond?"

"Across the hall. The one who looks like he smells something bad."

"How did you know I talked to him and not the side of beef?"

He laughed and almost dropped his coffee cup. "I don't think Roy *can* talk."

"He didn't know nothin' about nothin.' " I found myself laughing also. I got up and walked to the glass doors. I slid them open and then shut again. "Did you ever think one of these was open when it was really shut?"

"No. But I've heard of it happening."

I sighed. "So have I." I turned and looked at what he was working on at the drafting table. It was a small painting of a boy and girl, she in a soft white dress, and he in jeans and tee shirt. They looked about fifteen. They were embracing, about to kiss. It was quite obviously the first time for both of them. It was good. I told him so.

He grinned with pleasure. "Thanks. It's for a paperback cover."

"Whose idea was it that Detweiler have dinner and spend the evening with you?"

He thought for a moment. "Maurice." He looked up at me and grinned. "Do you know stamps?"

It took me a second to realize what he meant. "You mean stamp collecting? Not much."

"Maurice was a philatelist. He specialized in postwar Germany—locals and zones, things like that. He'd gotten a kilo of buildings and wanted to sort them undisturbed."

I shook my head. "You've lost me. A kilo of buildings?"

He laughed. "It's a set of twenty-eight stamps issued in the American Zone in 1948 showing famous German buildings. Conditions in Germany were still pretty chaotic at the time, and the stamps were printed under fairly makeshift circumstances. Consequently, there's an enormous variety of different perforations, watermarks, and engravings. Hundreds as a matter of fact. Maurice could spend hours and hours poring over them."

"Are they valuable?"

"No. Very common. Some of the varieties are hard to find, but they're not valuable." He gave me a knowing look. "Nothing was missing from Maurice's apartment."

I shrugged. "It had occurred to me to wonder where Detweiler got his money."

"I don't know. The subject never came up." He wasn't being defensive.

"You liked him, didn't you?"

There was weary sadness in his eyes. "Yes," he said.

That afternoon I picked up Birdie Pawlowicz at the Brewster Hotel and took her to Harry Spinner's funeral. I told her about Maurice Milian and Andrew Detweiler. We talked it around and around. The Detweiler boy obviously couldn't have killed Harry *or* Milian, but it was stretching coincidence a little bit far.

After the funeral I went to the Los Angeles Public Library and started checking back issues of the *Times*. I'd only made it back three weeks when the library closed. The LA *Times* is *thick,* and unless the death is sensational or the dead prominent, the story might be tucked in anywhere except the classifieds.

Last Tuesday, the 26th, a girl had cut her wrists with a razor blade in North Hollywood.

The day before, Monday, the 25th, a girl had miscarried and hemorrhaged. She had bled to death because she and her boy friend were stoned out of their heads. They lived a block off Western—very near the Brewster—and Detweiler was at the Brewster Monday.

Sunday, the 24th, a wino had been knifed in MacArthur Park.

Saturday, the 23rd, I had three. A knifing in a

bar on Pico, a shooting in a rooming house on Irolo, and a rape and knifing in an alley off La Brea. Only the gunshot victim had bled to death, but there had been a lot of blood in all three.

Friday, the 22nd, the same day Detweiler checked in the Brewster, a two-year-old boy had fallen on an upturned rake in his backyard on Larchemont—only eight or ten blocks from where I lived on Beachwood. And a couple of Chicano kids had had a knife fight behind Hollywood High. One was dead and the other was in jail. Ah, *machismo!*

The list went on and on, all the way back to Thursday, the 7th. On that day was another slashed-wrist suicide near Western and Wilshire.

The next morning, Tuesday, the 3rd, I called Miss Tremaine and told her I'd be late getting in but would check in every couple of hours to find out if the slinky blonde looking for her kid sister had shown up. She *humphed.*

Larchemont is a middle-class neighborhood huddled in between the old wealth around the country club and the blight spreading down Melrose from Western Avenue. It tries to give the impression of suburbia—and does a pretty good job of it—rather than just another nearly downtown shopping center. The area isn't big on apartments or rooming houses, but there are a few. I found the Detweiler boy at the third one I checked. It was a block and a half from where the little kid fell on the rake.

According to the landlord, at the time of the kid's death Detweiler was playing bridge with him and a couple of elderly old-maid sisters in number twelve. He hadn't been feeling well and had moved out later that evening—to catch a bus to San Diego, to visit his ailing mother. The landlord had felt sorry for him, so sorry he'd broken a steadfast rule and refunded most of the month's rent Detweiler had paid in advance. After all, he'd only been there three days. So sad about his back. Such a nice, gentle boy—a writer, you know.

No, I didn't know, but it explained how he could move around so much without seeming to work.

I called David Fowler: "Yes, Andy had a portable typewriter, but he hadn't mentioned being a writer."

And Birdie Pawlowicz: "Yeah, he typed a lot in his room."

I found the Detweiler boy again on the 16th and the 19th. He'd moved into a rooming house near Silver Lake Park on the night of the 13th and moved out again on the 19th. The landlady hadn't refunded his money, but she gave him an alibi for the knifing of an old man in the park on the 16th and the suicide of a girl in the same rooming house on the 19th. He'd been in the pink of health when he moved in, sick on the 16th, healthy the 17th, and sick again the 19th.

It was like a rerun. He lived a block away from where a man was mugged, knifed, and robbed in an alley on the 13th—though the details of the murder didn't seem to fit the pattern. But he was sick, had an alibi, and moved to Silver Lake.

Rerun it on the 10th: a woman slipped in the bathtub and fell through the glass shower doors, cutting herself to ribbons. Sick, alibi, moved.

It may be because I was always rotten in math, but it wasn't until right then that I figured out Detweiler's timetable. Milian died the 1st, Harry Spinner the 28th, the miscarriage was on the 25th, the little kid on the 22nd, Silver Lake on the 16th, and 19th, etc., etc., etc.

A bloody death occurred in Detweiler's general vicinity every third day.

But I couldn't figure out a pattern for the victims: male, female, little kids, old aunties, married, unmarried, rich, poor, young, old. No pattern of any kind, and there's *always* a pattern. I even checked to see if the names were in alphabetical order.

I got back to my office at six. Miss Tremaine sat primly at her desk, cleared of everything but her purse and a notepad. She reminded me quite a lot of Desmond. "What are you still doing here, Miss Tremaine? You should've left an hour ago." I sat at my desk, leaned back until the swivel chair groaned twice, and propped my feet up.

She picked up the pad. "I wanted to give you your calls."

"Can't they wait? I've been sleuthing all day and I'm bushed."

"No one is paying you to find this Detweiler person, are they?"

"No."

"Your bank statement came today."

"What's that supposed to mean?"

"Nothing. A good secretary keeps her employer informed. I was informing you."

"Okay. Who called?"

She consulted the pad, but I'd bet my last gumshoe she knew every word on it by heart. "A Mrs. Carmichael called. Her French poodle has been kidnaped. She wants you to find her."

"Ye Gods! Why doesn't she go to the police?"

"Because she's positive her ex-husband is the kidnaper. She doesn't want to get him in any trouble; she just wants Gwendolyn back."

"Gwendolyn?"

"Gwendolyn. A Mrs. Bushyager came by. She wants you to find her little sister."

I sat up so fast I almost fell out of the chair. I gave her a long, hard stare, but her neutral expression didn't flicker. "You're kidding." Her eyebrows rose a millimeter. "Was she a slinky blonde?"

"No. She was a dumpy brunette."

I settled back in the chair, trying not to laugh. "Why does Mrs. Bushyager want me to find her little sister?" I sputtered.

"Because Mrs. Bushyager thinks she's shacked up somewhere with *Mr.* Bushyager. She'd like you to call her tonight."

"Tomorrow. I've got a date with Janice tonight." She reached in her desk drawer and pulled out my bank statement. She dropped it on the desk with a papery plop. "Don't worry," I assured her, "I won't spend much money. Just a little spaghetti and wine tonight and ham and eggs in the morning." She *humphed.* My point. "Anything else?"

"A Mr. Bloomfeld called. He wants you to get the goods on Mrs. Bloomfeld so he can sue for divorce."

I sighed. Miss Tremaine closed the pad. "Okay. No to Mrs. Carmichael and make appointments for Bushyager and Bloomfeld." She lowered her eyelids at me. I spread my hands. "Would Sam Spade go looking for a French poodle named Gwendolyn?"

"He might if he had your bank statement. Mr. Bloomfeld will be in at two, Mrs. Bushyager at three."

"Miss Tremaine, you'd make somebody a wonderful mother." She didn't even *humph;* she just picked up her purse and stalked out. I swiveled the chair around and looked at the calendar. Tomorrow was the 4th.

Somebody would die tomorrow and Andrew Detweiler would be close by.

I scooted up in bed and leaned against the headboard. Janice snorted into the pillow and opened one eye, pinning me with it. "I didn't mean to wake you," I said.

"What's the matter," she muttered, "too much spaghetti?"

"No. Too much Andrew Detweiler."

She scooted up beside me, keeping the sheet over her breasts, and turned on the light. She rummaged around on the nightstand for a cigarette. "Who wants to divorce him?"

"That's mean, Janice," I groaned.

"You want a cigarette?"

"Yeah."

She put two cigarettes in her mouth and lit them both. She handed me one. "You don't look a bit like Paul Henreid," I said.

She grinned. "That's funny. You look like Bette Davis. Who's Andrew Detweiler?"

So I told her.

"It's elementary, my dear Sherlock," she said. "Andrew Detweiler is a vampire." I frowned at her. "Of course, he's a *clever* vampire. Vampires are usually stupid. They always give themselves away by leaving those two little teeth marks on people's jugulars."

"Darling, even vampires have to be at the scene of the crime."

"He always has an alibi, huh?"

I got out of bed and headed for the bathroom. "That's suspicious in itself."

When I came out she said, "Why?"

"Innocent people usually don't have alibis, especially not one every three days."

"Which is probably why innocent people get put in jail so often."

I chuckled and sat on the edge of the bed. "You may be right."

"Bert, do that again."

I looked at her over my shoulder. "Do what?"

"Go to the bathroom."

"I don't think I can. My bladder holds only so much."

"I don't mean that. Walk over to the bathroom door."

I gave her a suspicious frown, got up, and walked over to the bathroom door. I turned around, crossed my arms and leaned against the door frame. "Well?"

She grinned. "You've got a cute rear end. Almost as cute as Burt Reynolds'. Maybe he's twins."

"What?" I practically screamed.

"Maybe Andrew Detweiler is twins. One of them commits the murders and the other establishes the alibis."

"Twin vampires?"

She frowned. "That is a bit much, isn't it? Had

they discovered blood groups in Bram Stoker's day?"

I got back in bed and pulled the sheet up to my waist, leaning beside her against the headboard. "I haven't the foggiest idea."

"That's another way vampires are stupid. They never check the victim's blood group. The wrong blood group can kill you."

"Vampires don't exactly get transfusions."

"It all amounts to the same thing, doesn't it?" I shrugged. "Oh, well," she sighed, "vampires are stupid." She reached over and plucked at the hair on my chest. "I haven't had an indecent proposition in hours," she grinned.

So I made one.

Wednesday morning I made a dozen phone calls. Of the nine victims I knew about, I was able to find the information on six.

All six had the same blood group.

I lit a cigarette and leaned back in the swivel chair. The whole thing was spinning around in my head. I'd found *a* pattern for the victims, but I didn't know if it was *the* pattern. It just didn't make sense. Maybe Detweiler *was* a vampire.

"Mallory," I said out loud, "you're cracking up."

Miss Tremaine glanced up. "If I were you, I'd listen to you," she said poker-faced.

The next morning I staggered out of bed at six a.m. I took a cold shower, shaved, dressed, and put Murine in my eyes. They still felt like I'd washed them in rubber cement. Mrs. Bloomfeld had kept me up until two the night before, doing all the night spots in Santa Monica with some dude I hadn't identified yet. When they checked into a motel, I went home and went to bed.

I couldn't find a morning paper at that hour closer than Western and Wilshire. The story was on page seven. Fortunately they found the body in time for the early edition. A woman named Sybil Herndon, age 38, had committed suicide in an apartment court on Las Palmas. (Detweiler hadn't gone very far. The address was just around the corner from the Almsbury.) She had cut her wrists on a piece of broken mirror. She had been discovered about eleven thirty when the manager went over to ask her to turn down the volume on her television set.

It was too early to drop around, and so I ate breakfast, hoping this was one of the times Detweiler stuck around for more than three days. Not for a minute did I doubt he would be living at the apartment court on Las Palmas, or not far away.

The owner-manager of the court was one of those creatures peculiar to Hollywood. She must have been a starlet in the Twenties or Thirties, but success had eluded her. So she had tried to freeze herself in time. She still expected, at any moment, a call from The Studio. But her flesh hadn't cooperated. Her hair was the color of tarnished copper, and the fire-engine-red lipstick was painted far past her thin lips. Her watery eyes peered at me through a Lone Ranger mask of Maybelline on a plaster-white face. Her dress had obviously been copied from the wardrobe of Norma Shearer.

"Yes?" She had a breathy voice. Her eyes quickly traveled the length of my body. That happens often enough to keep me feeling good, but this time it gave me a queasy sensation, like I was being measured for a mummy case. I showed her my ID and asked if I could speak to her about one of the tenants.

"Of course. Come on in. I'm Lorraine Nesbitt." Was there a flicker of disappointment that I hadn't recognized the name? She stepped back holding the door for me. I could tell that detectives, private or otherwise, asking about her tenants wasn't a new thing. I walked into the doilied room, and she looked at me from a hundred directions. The faded photographs covered every level surface and clung to the walls like leeches. She had been quite a dish—forty years ago. She saw me looking at the photos and smiled. The make-up around her mouth cracked.

"Which one do you want to ask me about?" The smile vanished and the cracks closed.

"Andrew Detweiler." She looked blank. "Young, good-looking, with a hunchback."

The cracks opened. "Oh, yes. He's only been here a few days. The name had slipped my mind."

"He's still here?"

"Oh, yes." She sighed. "It's so unfair for such a beautiful young man to have a physical impairment."

"What can you tell me about him?"

"Not much. He's only been here since Sunday night. He's very handsome, like an angel, a dark angel. But it wasn't his handsomeness that attracted me." She smiled. "I've seen many handsome men in my day, you know. It's difficult to verbalize. He has such an incredible innocence. A lost, doomed look that Byron must have had. A vulnerability that makes you want to shield and protect him. I don't know for sure what it is, but it struck a chord in my soul. Soul," she mused. "Maybe that's it. He wears his soul on his face." She nodded, as if to herself. "A dangerous thing to do." She looked back up at me. "If that quality, whatever it is, would photograph, he would become a star over-night, whether he could act or not. Except—of course—for his infirmity."

Lorraine Nesbitt, I decided, was as nutty as a fruitcake.

Someone entered the room. He stood leaning against the door frame, looking at me with sleepy eyes. He was about twenty-five, wearing tight chi-nos without underwear and a tee shirt. His hair was tousled and cut unfashionably short. He had a good-looking Kansas face. The haircut made me think he was new in town, but the eyes said he wasn't. I guess the old broad liked his hair that way.

She simpered. "Oh, Johnny! Come on in. This detective was asking about Andrew Detweiler in number seven." She turned back to me. "This is my protege, Johnny Peacock—a very talented young man. I'm arranging for a screen test as soon as Mr. Goldwyn returns my calls." She lowered her eyelids demurely. "I was a Goldwyn Girl, you know."

Funny, I thought Goldwyn was dead. Maybe he wasn't.

Johnny took the news of his impending stardom with total unconcern. He moved to the couch and sat down, yawning. "Detweiler? Don't think I ever laid eyes on the man. What'd he do?"

"Nothing. Just routine." Obviously he thought I was a police detective. No point in changing his mind. "Where was he last night when the Herndon woman died?"

"In his room, I think. I heard his typewriter. He wasn't feeling well," Lorraine Nesbitt said. Then she sucked air through her teeth and clamped her fingers to her scarlet lips. "Do you think he had something to do with *that*?"

Detweiler had broken his pattern. He didn't have an alibi. I couldn't believe it.

"Oh, Lorraine," Johnny grumbled.

I turned to him. "Do you know where Detweiler was?"

He shrugged. "No idea."

"Then why are you so sure he had nothing to do with it?"

"She committed suicide."

"How do you know for sure?"

"The door was bolted from the inside. They had to break it down to get in."

"What about the window? Was it locked too?"

"No. The window was open. But it has bars on it. No way anybody could get in."

"When I couldn't get her to answer my knock last night, I went around to the window and looked in. She was lying there with blood all over." She began to sniffle. Johnny got up and put his arms around her. He looked at me, grinned, and shrugged.

"Do you have a vacancy?" I asked, getting a whiz-bang idea.

"Yes," she said, the sniffles disappearing instantly. "I have two. Actually three, but I can't rent Miss Herndon's room for a few days—until someone claims her things."

"I'd like to rent the one closest to number seven," I said.

I wasn't lucky enough to get number six or eight, but I did get five. Lorraine Nesbitt's nameless, dingy apartment court was a fleabag. Number five was one room with a closet, a tiny kitchen, and a tiny bath—identical with the other nine units she assured me. With a good deal of tugging and grunting the couch turned into a lumpy bed. The refrigerator looked as if someone had spilled a bottle of Br'er Rabbit back in 1938 and hadn't cleaned it up yet. The stove looked like a lube rack. Well, I sighed, it was only for three days. I had to pay a month's rent in advance anyway, but I put it down as a bribe to keep Lorraine's and Johnny's mouths shut about my being a detective.

I moved in enough clothes for three days, some sheets and pillows, took another look at the kitchen and decided to eat out. I took a jug of Lysol to the bathroom and crossed my fingers. Miss Tremaine brought up the bank statement and *humphed* a few times.

Number five had one door and four windows— identical to the other nine Lorraine assured me. The door had a heavy-duty bolt that couldn't be fastened or unfastened from the outside. The window beside the door didn't open at all and wasn't intended to. The bathroom and kitchen windows cranked out and were tall and skinny, about twenty-four by six. The other living room window, opposite the door, slid upward. The iron bars bolted to the frame were so rusted I doubted if they could be removed without ripping out the whole window. It appeared Andrew Detweiler had another perfect alibi after all—along with the rest of the world.

I stood outside number seven suddenly feeling like a teen-ager about to pick up his first date. I could hear Detweiler's typewriter *tickety-ticking* away inside. Okay, Mallory, this is what you've been breaking your neck on for a week.

I knocked on the door.

I heard the typewriter stop ticking and the scrape of a chair being scooted back. I didn't hear anything else for fifteen or twenty seconds, and I wondered what he was doing. Then the bolt was drawn and the door opened.

He was buttoning his shirt. That must have been the delay: he wouldn't want anyone to see him with his shirt off. Everything I'd been told about him was true. He wasn't very tall: the top of his head came to my nose. He was dark, though not as dark as I'd expected. I couldn't place his ancestry. It certainly wasn't Latin-American and I didn't think it was Slavic. His features were soft without the angularity usually found in the Mediterranean races. His hair wasn't quite black. It wasn't exactly long and it wasn't exactly short. His clothes were nondescript. Everything about him was neutral— except his face. It was just about the way Lorraine Nesbitt had described it. If you called central casting and asked for a male angel, you'd get Andrew Detweiler in a blond wig. His body was slim and well-formed—from where I was standing I couldn't see the hump and you'd never know there was one. I had a glimpse of his bare chest as he buttoned the shirt. It wasn't muscular but it was very well made. He was very healthy-looking—pink and flushed with health, though slightly pale as if he didn't get out in the sun much. His dark eyes were astounding. If you blocked out the rest of the face, leaving nothing but the eyes, you'd swear he was no more than four years old. You've seen little kids with those big, guileless, unguarded, inquiring eyes, haven't you?

"Yes?" he asked.

I smiled. "Hello, I'm Bert Mallory. I just moved in to number five. Miss Nesbitt tells me you like to play gin."

"Yes," he grinned. "Come on in."

He turned to move out of my way and I saw the hump. I don't know how to describe what I felt. I suddenly had a hurting in my gut. I felt the same unfairness and sadness the others had, the way you would feel about any beautiful thing with one over-whelming flaw.

"I'm not disturbing you, am I? I heard the type-writer." The room was indeed identical to mine, though it looked a hundred per cent more livable. I couldn't put my finger on what he had done to it to make it that way. Maybe it was just the semi-darkness. He had the curtains tightly closed and one lamp lit beside the typewriter.

"Yeah, I was working on a story, but I'd rather play gin." He grinned, open and artless. "If I could make money playing gin, I wouldn't write."

"Lots of people make money playing gin."

"Oh, I couldn't. I'm too unlucky."

He certainly had a right to say that, but there was no self-pity, just an observation. Then he looked at me with slightly distressed eyes. "You . . . ah . . . didn't want to play for money, did you?"

"Not at all," I said and his eyes cleared. "What kind of stories do you write?"

"Oh, all kinds." He shrugged. "Fantasy mostly."

"Do you sell them?"

"Most of 'em."

"I don't recall seeing your name anywhere. Miss Nesbitt said it was Andrew Detweiler?"

He nodded. "I use another name. You probably wouldn't know it either. It's not exactly a household word." His eyes said he'd really rather not tell me what it was. He had a slight accent, a sort of soft slowness, not exactly a drawl and not exactly Deep South. He shoved the typewriter over and pulled out a deck of cards.

"Where're you from?" I asked. "I don't place the accent."

He grinned and shuffled the cards. "North Carolina. Back in the Blue Ridge."

We cut and I dealt. "How long have you been in Hollywood?"

"About two months."

"How do you like it?"

He grinned his beguiling grin and picked up my discard. "It's very . . . unusual. Have you lived here long, Mr. Mallory?"

"Bert. All my life. I was born in Inglewood. My mother still lives there."

"It must be . . . unusual . . . to live in the same place all your life."

"You move around a lot?"

"Yeah. Gin."

I laughed. "I thought you were unlucky."

"If we were playing for money, I wouldn't be able to do anything right."

We played gin the rest of the afternoon and talked—talked a lot. Detweiler seemed eager to talk or, at least, eager to have someone to talk with. He never told me anything that would connect him to nine deaths, mostly about where he'd been, things he'd read. He read a lot, just about anything he could get his hands on. I got the impression he hadn't really *lived* life so much as he'd *read* it, that all the things he knew about had never physically affected him. He was like an insulated island. Life flowed around him but never touched him. I wondered if the hump on his back made that much difference, if it made him such a green monkey he'd had to retreat into his insular existence. Practically everyone I had talked to liked him, mixed with varying portions of pity, to be sure, but liking nevertheless. Harry Spinner liked him, but had discovered something "peculiar" about him. Birdie Pawlowicz, Maurice Milian, David Fowler, Lorraine Nesbitt, they all liked him.

And, God damn it, I liked him too.

At midnight I was still awake, sitting in number five in my jockey shorts with the light out and the door open. I listened to the ticking of the Detweiler boy's typewriter and the muffled roar of Los Angeles. And thought, and thought and thought. And got nowhere.

Someone walked by the door, quietly and carefully. I leaned my head out. It was Johnny Peacock. He moved down the line of bungalows silent as a shadow. He turned south when he reached the sidewalk. Going to Selma or the Boulevard to turn a trick and make a few extra bucks. Lorraine must keep tight purse strings. Better watch it, kid. If she finds out, you'll be back on the streets again. And you haven't got too many years left where you can make good money by just gettin' it up.

I dropped in at the office for a while Friday morning and checked the first-of-the-month bills. Miss Tremaine had a list of new prospective clients. "Tell everyone I can't get to anything till Monday."

She nodded in disapproval. "Mr. Bloomfeld called."

"Did he get my report?"

"Yes. He was very pleased, but he wants the man's name."

"Tell him I'll get back on it Monday."

"Mrs. Bushyager called. Her sister and Mr. Bushyager are still missing."

"Tell her I'll get on it Monday." She opened her mouth. "If you say anything about my bank account, I'll put Spanish fly in your Ovaltine." She didn't *humph,* she giggled. I wonder how many points *that* is?

That afternoon I played gin with the Detweiler boy. He was genuinely glad to see me, like a friendly puppy. I was beginning to feel like a son of a bitch.

He hadn't mentioned North Carolina except that once the day before, and I was extremely interested in all subjects he wanted to avoid. "What's it like in the Blue Ridge? Coon huntin' and moonshine?"

He grinned and blitzed me. "Yeah, I guess. Most of the things you read about it are pretty nearly true. It's really a different world back in there, with almost no contact with the outside."

"How far in did you live?"

"About as far as you can get without comin' out

the other side. Did you know most of the people never heard of television or movies and some of 'em don't even know the name of the President? Most of 'em never been more than thirty miles from the place they were born, never saw an electric light? You wouldn't believe it. But it's more than just *things* that're different. People are different, think different—like a foreign country." He shrugged. "I guess it'll all be gone before too long though. Things keep creepin' closer and closer. Did you know I never went to school?" he said grinning. "Not a day of my life. I didn't wear shoes till I was ten. You wouldn't believe it." He shook his head, remembering. "Always kinda wished I coulda gone to school," he murmured softly.

"Why did you leave?"

"No reason to stay. When I was eight, my parents were killed in a fire. Our house burned down. I was taken in by a balmy old woman who lived not far away. I had some kin, but they didn't want me." He looked at me, trusting me. "They're pretty superstitious back in there, you know. Thought I was . . . marked. Anyway, the old woman took me in. She was a midwife, but she fancied herself a witch or something. Always making me drink some mess she'd brewed up. She fed me, clothed me, educated me, after a fashion, tried to teach me all her conjures, but I never could take 'em seriously." He grinned sheepishly. "I did chores for her and eventually became a sort of assistant, I guess. I helped her birth babies . . . I mean, deliver babies a couple of times, but that didn't last long. The parents were afraid me bein' around might mark the baby. She taught me to read and I couldn't stop. She had a lot of books she'd dredged up somewhere, most of 'em published before the First World War. I read a complete set of encyclopedias—published in 1911."

I laughed.

His eyes clouded. "Then she . . . died. I was fifteen, so I left. I did odd jobs and kept reading. Then I wrote a story and sent it to a magazine. They bought it; paid me fifty dollars. Thought I was rich, so I wrote another one. Since then I've been traveling around and writing. I've got an agent who takes care of everything, and so all I do is just write."

Detweiler's flush of health was wearing off that afternoon. He wasn't ill, just beginning to feel like the rest of us mortals. And I was feeling my resolve begin to crumble. It was hard to believe this beguiling kid could possibly be involved in a string of bloody deaths. Maybe it was just a series of unbelievable coincidences. Yeah, "unbelievable" was the key word. He *had* to be involved unless the laws of probability had broken down completely. Yet I could swear Detweiler wasn't putting on an act. His guileless innocence was real, damn it, *real.*

Saturday morning, the third day since Miss Herndon died, I had a talk with Lorraine and Johnny. If Detweiler wanted to play cards or something that night, I wanted them to agree and suggest I be a fourth. If he didn't bring it up, I would, but I had a feeling he would want his usual alibi this time.

Detweiler left his room that afternoon for the first time since I'd been there. He went north on Las Palmas, dropped a large manila envelope in the mailbox (the story he'd been working on, I guess), and bought groceries at the supermarket on Highland. Did that mean he wasn't planning to move? I had a sudden pang in my belly. What if he was staying because of his friendship with *me*? I felt more like a son of a bitch every minute.

Johnny Peacock came by an hour later acting very conspiratorial. Detweiler had suggested a bridge game that night, but Johnny didn't play bridge, and so they settled on Scrabble.

I dropped by number seven. The typewriter had been put away, but the cards and score pad were still on the table. His suitcase was on the floor by the couch. It was riveted cowhide of a vintage I hadn't seen since I was a kid. Though it wore a mellow patina of age, it had been preserved with neat's-foot oil and loving care. I may have been mistaken about his not moving.

Detweiler wasn't feeling well at all. He was pale and drawn and fidgety. His eyelids were heavy and his speech was faintly slurred. I'm sure he was in pain, but he tried to act as if nothing were wrong.

"Are you sure you feel like playing Scrabble tonight?" I asked.

He gave me a cheerful, if slightly strained, smile. "Oh, sure. I'm all right. I'll be fine in the morning."

"Do you think you ought to play?"

"Yeah, it . . . takes my mind off my . . . ah . . . headache. Don't worry about it. I have these spells all the time. They always go away."

"How long have you had them?"

"Since . . . I was a kid." He grinned. "You think it was one of those brews the old witch-woman gave me caused it? Maybe I could sue for malpractice."

"Have you seen a doctor? A real one?"

"Once."

"What did he tell you?"

He shrugged. "Oh, nothing much. Take two aspirin, drink lots of liquids, get plenty of rest, that sort of thing." He didn't want to talk about it. "It always goes away."

"What if one time it doesn't?"

He looked at me with an expression I'd never seen before, and I knew why Lorraine said he had a lost, doomed look. "Well, we can't live forever, can we? Are you ready to go?"

The game started out like a Marx Brothers routine. Lorraine and Johnny acted like two canaries playing Scrabble with the cat, but Detweiler was so normal and unconcerned they soon settled down. Conversation was tense and ragged at first until Lorraine got off on her "career" and kept us entertained and laughing. She had known a lot of famous people and was a fountain of anecdotes, most of them funny and libelous. Detweiler proved quickly to be the best player, but Johnny, to my surprise, was no slouch. Lorraine played dismally but she didn't seem to mind.

I would have enjoyed the evening thoroughly if I hadn't known someone nearby was dead or dying.

After about two hours, in which Detweiler grew progressively more ill, I excused myself to go to the bathroom. While I was away from the table, I palmed Lorraine's master key.

In another half hour I said I had to call it a night. I had to get up early the next morning. I always spent Sunday with my mother in Inglewood. My mother was touring Yucatán at the time, but that was neither here nor there. I looked at Johnny. He nodded. He was to make sure Detweiler stayed at least another twenty minutes and then follow him when he did leave. If he went anywhere but his apartment, he was to come and let me know, quick.

I let myself into number seven with the master key. The drapes were closed, and so I took a chance and turned on the bathroom light. Detweiler's possessions were meager. Eight shirts, six pairs of pants, and a light jacket hung in the closet. The shirts and jacket had been altered to allow for the hump. Except for that, the closet was bare. The bathroom contained nothing out of the ordinary—just about the same as mine. The kitchen had one plastic plate, one plastic cup, one plastic glass, one plastic bowl, one small folding skillet, one small folding sauce pan, one metal spoon, one metal fork, and a medium-sized kitchen knife. All of it together would barely fill a shoebox.

The suitcase, still beside the couch, hadn't been unpacked—except for the clothes hanging in the closet and the kitchen utensils. There was underwear, socks, an extra pair of shoes, an unopened ream of paper, a bunch of other stuff necessary for his writing, and a dozen or so paperbacks. The books were rubber-stamped with the name of a used-book store on Santa Monica Boulevard. They were a mixture: science fiction, mysteries, biographies, philosophy, several by Colin Wilson.

There was also a carbon copy of the story he'd just finished. The return address on the first page was a box number at the Hollywood post office. The title of the story was "Deathsong." I wish I'd had time to read it.

All in all, I didn't find anything. Except for the

books and the deck of cards there was nothing of
Andrew Detweiler personally in the whole apartment. I hadn't thought it possible for anyone to
lead such a turnip existence.

I looked around to make sure I hadn't disturbed
anything, turned off the bathroom light, and got in
the closet, leaving the door open a crack. It was
the only possible place to hide. I sincerely hoped
Detweiler wouldn't need anything out of it before
I found out what was going on. If he did, the only
thing I could do was confront him with what I'd
found out. And then what, Mallory, a big guilty
confession? With what you've found out he could
laugh in your face and have you arrested for illegal entry.

And what about this, Mallory. What if someone
died nearby tonight while you were with Detweiler;
what if he comes straight to his apartment and goes
to bed; what if he wakes up in the morning feeling
fine; what if nothing is going on, you son of a bitch?

It was so dark in there with the curtains drawn
that I couldn't see a thing. I left the closet and
opened them a little on the front window. It didn't
let in a lot of light, but it was enough. Maybe Detweiler wouldn't notice. I went back to the closet
and waited.

Half an hour later the curtains over the barred
open window moved. I had squatted down in the
closet and wasn't looking in that direction, but the
movement caught my eye. Something hopped in
the window and scooted across the floor and went
behind the couch. I only got a glimpse of it, but it
might have been a cat. It was probably a stray looking for food or hiding from a dog. Okay, cat, you

don't bother me and I won't bother you. I kept my eye on the couch, but it didn't show itself again.

Detweiler didn't show for another hour. By that time I was sitting flat on the floor trying to keep my legs from cramping. My position wasn't too graceful if he happened to look in the closet, but it was too late to get up.

He came in quickly and bolted the door behind him. He didn't notice the open curtain. He glanced around, clicking his tongue softly. His eyes caught on something at the end of the couch. He smiled. At the *cat*? He began unfastening his shirt, fumbling at the buttons in his haste. He slipped off the shirt and tossed it on the back of a chair.

There were straps across his chest.

He turned toward the suitcase, his back to me. The hump was artificial, made of something like foam rubber. He unhooked the straps, opened the suitcase, and tossed the hump in. He said something, too soft for me to catch, and lay face down on the couch with his feet toward me. The light from the opened curtain fell on him. His back was scarred, little white lines like scratches grouped around a hole.

He had a hole in his back, between his shoulder blades, an unhealed wound big enough to stick your finger in.

Something came around the end of the couch. It wasn't a cat. I thought it was a monkey, and then a frog, but it was neither. It was human. It waddled on all fours like an enormous toad.

Then it stood erect. It was about the size of a cat. It was pink and moist and hairless and naked. Its very human hands and feet and male genitals were too large for its tiny body. Its belly was swollen, turgid and distended like an obscene tick. Its head was flat. Its jaw protruded like an ape's. It too had a scar, a big, white, puckered scar between its shoulder blades, at the top of its jutting backbone.

It reached its too-large hand up and caught hold of Detweiler's belt. It pulled its bloated body up with the nimbleness of a monkey and crawled onto the boy's back. Detweiler was breathing heavily, clasping and unclasping his fingers on the arm of the couch.

The thing crouched on Detweiler's back and placed its lips against the wound.

I felt my throat burning and my stomach turning over, but I watched in petrified fascination.

Detweiler's breathing grew slower and quieter, more relaxed. He lay with his eyes closed and an expression of almost sexual pleasure on his face. The thing's body got smaller and smaller, the skin on its belly growing wrinkled and flaccid. A trickle of blood crawled from the wound, making an erratic line across the Detweiler boy's back. The thing reached out its hand and wiped the drop back with a finger.

It took about ten minutes. The thing raised its mouth and crawled over beside the boy's face. It sat on the arm of the couch like a little gnome and smiled. It ran its fingers down the side of Detweiler's cheek and pushed his damp hair back out of his eyes. Detweiler's expression was euphoric. He sighed softly and opened his eyes sleepily. After a while he sat up.

He was flushed with health, rosy and clear and shining.

He stood up and went in the bathroom. The light came on and I heard water running. The thing sat in the same place watching him. Detweiler came out of the bathroom and sat back on the couch. The thing climbed onto his back, huddling between his shoulder blades, its hands on his shoulders. Detweiler stood up, the thing hanging onto him, retrieved the shirt, and put it on. He wrapped the straps neatly around the artificial hump and stowed it in the suitcase. He closed the lid and locked it.

I had seen enough, more than enough. I opened the door and stepped out of the closet.

Detweiler whirled, his eyes bulging. A groan rattled in his throat. He raised his hands as if fending me off. The groan rose in pitch, becoming an hysterical keening. The expression on his face was too horrible to watch. He stepped backward and tripped over the suitcase.

He lost his balance and toppled over. His arms flailed for equilibrium, but never found it. He struck the edge of the table. It caught him square across the hump on his back. He bounced and fell forward on his hands. He stood up agonizingly, like a slow motion movie, arching his spine backward, his face contorted in pain.

There were shrill, staccato shrieks of mindless torment, but they didn't come from Detweiler.

He fell again, forward onto the couch, blacking out from pain. The back of his shirt was churning. The scream continued, hurting my ears. Rips appeared in the shirt and a small misshapen arm poked out briefly. I could only stare, frozen. The shirt was ripped to shreds. Two arms, a head, a torso came through. The whole thing ripped its way out and fell onto the couch beside the boy. Its face was twisted, tortured, and its mouth kept opening and closing with the screams. Its eyes looked uncomprehendingly about. It pulled itself along with its arms, dragging its useless legs, its spine obviously broken. It fell off the couch and flailed about on the floor.

Detweiler moaned and came to. He rose from the couch, still groggy. He saw the thing, and a look of absolute grief appeared on his face.

The thing's eyes focused for a moment on Detweiler. It looked at him, beseeching, held out one hand, pleading. Its screams continued, that one monotonous, hopeless note repeated over and over. It lowered its arm and kept crawling about mindlessly, growing weaker.

Detweiler stepped toward it, ignoring me, tears pouring down his face. The thing's struggles grew weaker, the scream became a breathless rasping. I couldn't stand it any longer. I picked up a chair and smashed it down on the thing. I dropped the chair and leaned against the wall and heaved.

I heard the door open. I turned and saw Detweiler run out.

I charged after him. My legs felt rubbery but I caught him at the street. He didn't struggle. He just stood there, his eyes vacant, trembling. I saw people sticking their heads out of doors and Johnny Peacock coming toward me. My car was right there. I pushed Detweiler into it and drove away. He sat hunched in the seat, his hands hanging limply, staring into space. He was trembling uncontrollably and his teeth chattered.

I drove, not paying any attention to where I was going, almost as deeply in shock as he was. I finally started looking at the street signs. I was on Mullholland. I kept going west for a long time, crossed the San Diego Freeway, into the Santa Monica Mountains. The pavement ends a couple of miles past the freeway, and there's ten or fifteen miles of dirt road before the pavement picks up again nearly to Topanga. The road isn't traveled much, there are no houses on it, and people don't like to get their cars dusty. I was about in the middle of the unpaved section when Detweiler seemed to calm down. I pulled over to the side of the road and cut the engine. The San Fernando Valley was spread like a carpet of lights below us. The ocean was on the other side of the mountains.

I sat and watched Detweiler. The trembling had stopped. He was asleep or unconscious. I reached over and touched his arm. He stirred and clutched at my hand. I looked at his sleeping face and didn't have the heart to pull my hand away.

The sun was poking over the mountains when he woke up. He roused and was momentarily unaware of where he was; then memory flooded back. He turned to me. The pain and hysteria were gone from his eyes. They were oddly peaceful.

"Did you hear him?" he said softly. "Did you hear him die?"

"Are you feeling better?"

"Yes. It's all over."

"Do you want to talk about it?"

His eyes dropped and he was silent for a moment. "I want to tell you. But I don't know how without you thinking I'm a monster."

I didn't say anything.

"He . . . was my brother. We were twins. Siamese twins. All those people died so I could stay alive." There was no emotion in his voice. He was detached, talking about someone else. "He kept me alive. I'll die without him." His eyes met mine again. "He was insane, I think. I thought that first I'd go mad too, but I didn't. I think I didn't. I never knew what he was going to do, who he would kill. I didn't want to know. He was very clever. He always made it look like an accident or suicide when he could. I didn't interfere. I didn't want to die. We had to have blood. He always did it so there was lots of blood, so no one would miss what he took." His eyes were going empty again.

"Why did you need the blood?"

"We were never suspected before."

"Why did you need the blood?" I repeated.

"When we were born," he said, and his eyes focused again, "we were joined at the back. But I grew and he didn't. He stayed little bitty, like a baby riding around on my back. People didn't like me . . . us. They were afraid. My father and mother too. The old witch-woman I told you about, she birthed us. She seemed always to be hanging around. When I was eight, my parents died in a fire. I think the witch-woman did it. After that I lived with her. She was demented, but she knew medicine and healing. When we were fifteen she decided to separate us. I don't know why. I think she wanted him without me. I'm sure she thought he was an imp from hell. I almost died. I'm not sure what was wrong. Apart, we weren't whole. I wasn't whole. He had something I didn't have, something we'd been sharing. She would've let me die, but he knew and got blood for me. Hers." He sat staring at me blankly, his mind living the past.

"Why didn't you go to a hospital or something?" I asked, feeling enormous pity for the wretched boy.

He smiled faintly. "I didn't know much about anything then. Too many people were already dead. If I'd gone to a hospital, they'd have wanted to know how I'd stayed alive so far. Sometimes I'm glad it's over, and, then, the next minute I'm terrified of dying."

"How long?"

"I'm not sure. I've never been more than three days. I can't stand it any longer than that. He knew. He always knew when I had to have it. And he got it for me. I never helped him."

"Can you stay alive if you get regular transfusions?"

He looked at me sharply, fear creeping back. "Please. No!"

"But you'll stay alive."

"In a cage! Like a freak! I don't want to be a freak anymore. It's over. I want it to be over. Please."

"What do you want me to do?"

"I don't know. I don't want you to get in trouble."

I looked at him, at his face, at his eyes, at his soul. "There's a gun in the glove compartment," I said.

He sat for a moment, then solemnly held out his

hand. I took it. He shook my hand, then opened
the glove compartment. He removed the gun and
slipped out of the car. He went down the hill into
the brush.

I waited and waited and never did hear a shot.

Time Exposures

WILSON TUCKER

Wilson Tucker writes quiet, understated science fiction which can leave an impact so subtle it sometimes isn't realized at first. His books such as *The Year of the Quiet Sun* and *The Lincoln Hunters* are full of attention to historical detail combined with an extrapolation of what the future may hold. In "Time Exposures" he draws on another aspect of his life to detail the story, his forty-year career as a film projectionist.

Sergeant Tabbot climbed the stairs to the woman's third-floor apartment. The heavy camera case banged against his leg as he climbed and threatened collision with his bad knee. He shifted the case to his left hand and muttered under his breath: the woman *could* have been gracious enough to die on the first floor.

A patrolman loafed on the landing, casually guarding the stairway and the third floor corridor.

Tabbot showed surprise. "No keeper? Are they still working in there? Which apartment is it?"

The patrolman said: "Somebody forgot the keeper, Sergeant—somebody went after it. There's a crowd in there, the coroner ain't done yet. Number 33." He glanced down at the bulky case. "She's pretty naked."

"Shall I make you a nice print?"

"No, *sir,* not this one! I mean, she's naked but she ain't pretty anymore."

Tabbot said: "Murder victims usually lose their good looks." He walked down the corridor to number 33 and found the door ajar. A rumbling voice was audible. Tabbot swung the door open and stepped into the woman's apartment. A small place: probably only two rooms.

The first thing he saw was a finger man working over a glass-topped coffee table with an aerosol can and a portable blacklight; the sour expression on the man's face revealed a notable lack of fingerprints. A precinct Lieutenant stood just beyond the end of the coffee table, watching the roving blacklight with an air of unruffled patience; his glance flickered at Tabbot, at the camera case, and dropped again to the table. A plainclothesman waited behind the door, doing nothing. Two men with a wicker basket sat on either arm of an overstuffed chair, peering over the back of the chair at something on the floor. One of them swung his head to stare at the newcomer and then turned his attention back to the floor. Well beyond the chair a bald-headed man wearing too much fat under his clothing was brushing dust from the knees of his trousers. He had just climbed to his feet and the exertion caused a dry, wheezy breathing through an open mouth.

Tabbot knew the Lieutenant and the coroner.

The coroner looked at the heavy black case Tabbot put down just inside the door and asked: "Pictures?"

"Yes, sir. Time exposures."

"I'd like to have prints, then. Haven't seen a shooting in eight or nine years. Damned rare anymore." He pointed a fat index finger at the thing on the floor. "*She* was shot to death. Can you imagine that? Shot to death in *this* day and age! I'd like to have prints. Want to see a man with the gall to carry a gun."

"Yes, sir." Tabbot swung his attention to the precinct Lieutenant. "Can you give me an idea?"

"It's still hazy, Sergeant," the officer answered. "The victim knew her assailant; I think she let him in the door and then walked away from him. He stood where you're standing. Maybe an argument, but no fighting—nothing broken, nothing disturbed, no fingerprints. That knob behind you was wiped clean. She was standing behind that chair when she was shot, and she fell there. Can you catch it all?"

"Yes, sir, I think so. I'll set up in that other room—in the doorway. A kitchen?"

"Kitchen and shower. This one is a combination living room and bedroom."

"I'll start in the doorway and then move in close. Nothing in the kitchen?"

"Only dirty dishes. No floorstains, but I would appreciate prints just the same. The floors are clean everywhere except behind *that* chair."

Sergeant Tabbot looked at the window across the room and looked back to the Lieutenant.

"No fire escape," the officer said. "But cover it anyway, cover everything. Your routine."

Tabbot nodded easily, then took a strong grip on

his stomach muscles. He moved across the room to the overstuffed chair and peered carefully over the back of it. The two wicker basket men turned their heads in unison to watch him, sharing some macabre joke between them. It would be at his expense. His stomach plunged despite the rigid effort to control it.

She was a sandy blonde and had been about thirty years old; her face had been reasonably attractive but was not likely to have won a beauty contest; it was scrubbed clean, and free of makeup. There was no jewelry on her fingers, wrists, or about her neck; she was literally naked. Her chest had been blown away. Tabbot blinked his shocked surprise and looked down her stomach toward her legs simply to move his gaze away from the hideous sight. He thought for a moment he'd lose his breakfast. His eyes closed while he fought for iron control, and when they opened again he was looking at old abdominal scars from a long ago pregnancy.

Sergeant Tabbot backed off rapidly from the chair and bumped into the coroner. He blurted: "She was shot in the back!"

"Well, of course." The wheezing fat man stepped around him with annoyance. "There's a *little* hole in the spine. Little going in and big—bigod it was big—coming out. Destroyed the rib cage coming out. That's natural. Heavy caliber pistol, I think." He stared down at the naked feet protruding from behind the chair. "*First* shooting I've seen in eight or nine years. Can you imagine that? Somebody carrying a gun." He paused for a wheezing breath and then pointed the same fat finger at the basket men. "Pick it up and run, boys. We'll do an autopsy."

Tabbot walked out to the kitchen.

The kitchen table showed him a dirty plate, coffee cup, fork and spoon, and toast crumbs. A sugar bowl without a lid and a small jar of powdered coffee creamer completed the setting. He looked under the table for the missing knife and butter.

"It's not there," the Lieutenant said. "She liked her toast dry."

Tabbot turned. "How long ago was breakfast? How long has she been dead?"

"We'll have to wait on the coroner's opinion for that but I would guess three, maybe four hours ago. The coffee pot was cold, the body was cold, the egg stains were dry—oh, say three hours plus."

"That gives me a good margin," Tabbot said. "If it happened last night, yesterday, I'd just pick up my camera and go home." He glanced through the doorway at a movement caught in the corner of the eye and found the wicker basket men carrying their load through the front door into the corridor. His glance quickly swung back to the kitchen table. "Eggs and dry toast, sugar in white coffee. That doesn't give you much."

The Lieutenant shook his head. "I'm not worried about *her;* I don't give a damn what she ate. Let the coroner worry about her breakfast; he'll tell us how long ago she ate it and we'll take it from there. Your prints are more important. I want to see pictures of the assailant."

Tabbot said: "Let's hope for daylight, and let's hope it was *this* morning. Are you sure that isn't yesterday's breakfast? There's no point in setting up the camera if it happened yesterday morning, or last night. My exposure limit is between ten and fourteen hours—and you know how poor fourteen-hour prints are."

"This morning," the officer assured him. "She went in to work yesterday morning but when she failed to check in this morning, when she didn't answer the phone, somebody from the shop came around to ask why."

"Did the somebody have a key?"

"No, and that eliminated the first suspect. The janitor let him in. Will you make a print of the door to corroborate their story? A few minutes after nine o'clock; they can't remember the exact time now."

"Will do. What kind of a shop? What did she do?"

"Toy shop. She made Christmas dolls."

Sergeant Tabbot considered that. After a moment he said: "The first thing that comes to mind is toy guns."

The Lieutenant gave him a tight, humorless grin. "We had the same thing in mind and sent men over there to comb the shop. Black market things, you know, toys or the real article. But no luck. They haven't made anything resembling a gun since the Dean Act was passed. That shop was clean."

"You've got a tough job, Lieutenant."

"I'm waiting on your prints, Sergeant."

Tabbot thought that a fair hint. He went back to the outer room and found everyone gone but the silent plainclothesman. The detective sat down on the sofa behind the coffee table and watched him unpack the case. A tripod was set up about five feet from the door. The camera itself was a heavy, unwieldy instrument and was lifted onto the tripod with a certain amount of hard grunting and a muttered curse because of a nipped finger. When it was solidly battened to the tripod, Tabbot picked a film magazine out of the supply case and fixed it to the rear of the camera. A lens and the timing instrument was the last to be fitted into place. He looked to make sure the lens was clean.

Tabbot focused on the front door, and reached into a pocket for his slide rule. He checked the time *now* and then calculated backward to obtain four exposures at nine o'clock, nine-five, nine-ten, and nine-fifteen, which should pretty well bracket the arrival of the janitor and the toy shop employee. He cocked and tripped the timer, and then checked to make sure the nylon film was feeding properly after each exposure. The data for each exposure was jotted down in a notebook, making the later identification of the prints more certain.

The plainclothesman broke his stony silence. "I've never seen one of those things work before."

Tabbot said easily: "I'm taking pictures from nine o'clock to nine-fifteen this morning; if I'm in luck I'll catch the janitor opening the door. If I'm not in luck I'll catch only a blurred movement—or nothing at all—and then I'll have to go back and make an exposure for each minute after nine until I find him. A blurred image of the moving door will pinpoint him."

"*Good* pictures?" He seemed skeptical.

"At nine o'clock? Yes. There was sufficient light coming in that window at nine and not too much time has elapsed. Satisfactory conditions. Things get sticky when I try for night exposures with no more than one or two lamps lit; that simply isn't enough light. I wish *everything* would happen outdoors at noon on a bright day—and not more than an hour ago!"

The detective grunted and inspected the ticking camera. "I took some of your pictures into court once. Bank robbery case, last year. The pictures were bad and the judge threw them out and the case collapsed."

"I remember them," Tabbot told him. "And I apologize for the poor job. Those prints were made right at the time limit; fourteen hours, perhaps a little more. The camera and the film are almost useless beyond ten or twelve hours—that is simply too *much* elapsed time. I use the very best film available but it can't find or make a decent image more than twelve hours in the past. Your bank prints were nothing more than grainy shadows; that's all I can get from twelve to fourteen hours."

"Nothing over fourteen hours?"

"Absolutely nothing. I've tried, but nothing." The camera stopped ticking and shut itself off. Tabbot turned it on the tripod and aimed at the sofa. The detective jumped up.

The sergeant protested. "Don't get up—you won't be in the way. The lens won't see you *now*."

"I've got work to do," the detective muttered. He flipped a dour farewell gesture at the Lieutenant and left the apartment, slamming the door behind him.

"He's still sore about those bank pictures," the officer said.

Tabbot nodded agreement and made a single adjustment on the timing mechanism. He tripped the shutter for one exposure and then grinned at the Lieutenant.

"I'll send him a picture of himself sitting there three minutes ago. Maybe that will cheer him up."

"Or make him mad enough to fire you."

The sergeant began another set of calculations on the slide rule and settled himself down to the routine coverage of the room from six to nine o'clock in the morning. He angled the heavy camera at the coffee table, the kitchen doorway, the overstuffed chair, the window behind the chair, a smaller chair and a bookcase in the room, the floor, a vase of artificial flowers resting on a tiny shelf above a radiator, a floor lamp, a ceiling light, and eventually worked around the room in a circle before coming back to the front door. Tabbot rechecked his calculations and then lavished a careful attention on the door and the space beside it where *he* had stood when he first entered.

The camera poked and pried and peered into the recent past, into the naked blonde's last morning alive, recording on nylon film those images now three or four hours gone. During the circle coverage—between the bookcase and the vase of artificial flowers—a signal light indicated an empty film magazine, and the camera paused in its work until a new magazine was fixed in place. Tabbot made a small adjustment on the timer to compensate for lost time. He numbered the old and the new film magazines, and continued his detailed notes for each angle and series of exposures. The camera ignored the present and probed into the past.

The Lieutenant asked: "How much longer?"

"Another hour for the preliminaries; I can do the kitchen in another hour. And, say, two or three hours for the retakes after something is pinned down."

"I've got work piling up." The officer scratched the back of his neck and then bent down to peer into the lens. "I guess you can find me at the precinct house. Make extra copies of the key prints."

"Yes, sir."

The Lieutenant turned away from his inspection of the lens and gave the room a final, sweeping glance. He did not slam the door behind him as the detective had done.

The full routine of photographing went on.

Tabbot moved the camera backward into the kitchen doorway to gain a broader coverage of the outer room; he angled at the sofa, the overstuffed chair, and again the door. He wanted the vital few moments when the door was opened and the murderer stepped through it to fire the prohibited pistol. Changing to a wide-angle lens, he caught the entire room in a series of ten-minute takes over a period of three hours. The scene was thoroughly documented.

He changed magazines to prepare for the kitchen.

A wild notion stopped his hand, stopped him in the act of swiveling the camera. He walked over to the heavy chair, walked around behind it, side-stepped the spilled blood, and found himself in direct line between door and window. Tabbot looked out of the window—imagining a gun at his back—and pivoted slowly to stare at the door: early sunlight coming in the window should have limned the man's face. The camera placed *here* should photograph the assailant's face and record the gun blast as well.

Tabbot hauled tripod and camera across the room and set up in position behind the chair, aiming at the door. The lens was changed again. Another calculation was made. If he was *really* lucky on this series the murderer would fire at the camera.

Kitchen coverage was a near repetition of the first room. It required a little less time.

Tabbot photographed the table and two chairs, the dirty dishes, the toast crumbs, the tiny stove, the aged refrigerator, the tacked-on dish cupboards above the sink and drain board, the sink itself, a cramped water closet masquerading as a broom closet behind a narrow door, and the stained folding door of the shower stall. The stall had leaked.

He opened the refrigerator door and found a half bottle of red wine alongside the foodstuff: two takes an hour apart. He peered into the cramped confines of the water closet: a few desultory exposures, and a hope that the blonde wasn't sitting in there. The shower stall was lined with an artificial white tile now marred by rust stains below a leaky showerhead: two exposures by way of an experiment, because the stall also contained a miniature wash basin, a mirror, and a moisture-proof light fixture. He noted with an absent approval that the fixture lacked a receptacle for plugging in razors.

Tabbot changed to the wide-angle lens for the wrap-up. There was no window in the kitchen, and he made a mental note of the absence of an escape door—a sad violation of the fire laws.

That exhausted the preliminary takes.

Tabbot fished his I.D. card out of his pocket, gathered up the exposed film magazines and walked out of the apartment. There was no keeper blocking passage through the doorway, and he stared with surprise at the patrolman still lounging in the corridor.

The patrolman read his expression.

"It's coming, Sergeant, it's coming. By this time I guess that Lieutenant has chewed somebody out good, so you can bet it's coming in a hurry."

Tabbot put the I.D. card in his pocket.

The patrolman asked: "*Was* she shot up, like they said? Back to front, right out the belly?"

Tabbot nodded uneasily, "Back to front, but out through the rib cage—not the belly. Somebody used a very heavy gun on her. *Do* you want a print? You could paste it up on your locker."

"Oh, hell no!" The man glanced down the corridor and came back to the sergeant. "I heard the coroner say it was a professional job; only the pro's are crazy enough to tote guns anymore. The risk and everything."

"I suppose so; I haven't heard of an amateur carrying one for years. That mandatory jail sentence for possession scares the hell out of them." Tabbot shifted the magazines to his other hand to keep them away from his bad knee going down the stairs.

The street was bright with sunlight—the kind of brilliant scene which Sergeant Tabbot wanted everything to happen in for better results. Given a bright sun he could reproduce images a little better than grainy shadows, right up to that fourteen-hour stopping point.

His truck was the only police vehicle parked at the curb.

Tabbot climbed into the back and closed the door behind him. He switched on the developing and drying machine in total darkness, and began feeding the film from the first magazine down into the tanks. When the tail of that film slipped out of the magazine and vanished, the leader of the second film was fed into the slot. The third followed when its time came. The sergeant sat down on a stool, waiting in the darkness until the developer and dryer had completed their cycles and delivered the nylon negatives into his hands. After a while he reached out to switch on the printer, and then did nothing more than sit and wait.

The woman's exploded breast hung before his eyes; it was more vivid in the darkness of the truck than in bright daylight. This time his stomach failed to churn, and he supposed he was getting used to the memory. Or the sight-memory was safely in his past. A few of the coming prints *could* resurrect that nightmare image.

The coroner believed some hood had murdered the woman who made Christmas dolls—some professional thug who paid as little heed to the gun law as he did to a hundred and one other laws. Perhaps—and perhaps not. Discharged servicemen were still smuggling weapons into the country, when coming in from overseas posts; he'd heard of that happening often enough, and he'd seen a few of the foolhardy characters in jails. For some reason he didn't understand, ex-Marines who'd served in China were the most flagrant offenders: they outnumbered smugglers from the other services three or four to one and the harsh penalties spelled out in the Dean Act didn't deter *them* worth a damn. Congress in its wisdom had proclaimed that only peace officers, and military personnel on active duty, had the privilege of carrying firearms; all other weapons must under the law be surrendered and destroyed.

Tabbot didn't own a gun; he had no use for one. That patrolman on the third floor carried a weapon, and the Lieutenant, and the plainclothesman—but he didn't think the coroner would have one. Nor the basket men. The Dean Act made stiff prison sentences mandatory for possession among the citizenry, but the Marines kept on carrying them and now and then some civilian died under gunfire. Like the woman who made Christmas dolls.

A soft buzzer signaled the end of the developer's job. Tabbot removed the three reels of nylon negative from the drying rack and fed them through the printer. The waiting time was appreciably shorter. Three long strips of printed pictures rolled out of the printer into his hands. Tabbot didn't waste time cutting the prints into individual frames. Draping two of the strips over a shoulder, he carried the third to the door of the truck and flung it open. Bright sunlight made him squint, causing his eyes to water.

Aloud: "Oh, what the hell! What went wrong?"

The prints were dark, much darker than they had any right to be. He *knew* without rechecking the figures in his notebook that the exposures had been made after sunrise, but still the prints were dark. Tabbot stared up the front of the building, trying to pick out the proper window, then brought his puzzled gaze back to the strip prints. The bedroom-living room was dark.

Peering closer, squinting against the bright light of the sun: four timed exposures of the front door, with the dim figures of the janitor and another man standing open-mouth on the third exposure. Ten minutes after nine. The fifth frame: a bright clear picture of the plainclothesman sitting on the sofa, talking up to Tabbot. The sixth frame and onward: dark images of the sofa opened out into a bed— coffee table missing—the kitchen doorway barely discernible, the overstuffed chair (and *there* was the coffee table beside it), the window— He stared with dismay at the window. The goddam drapes were drawn, shutting out the early light!

Tabbot hurriedly checked the second strip hanging on his shoulder: equally dark. The floor lamp and the ceiling light were both unlit. The drapes had been closed all night and the room was in cloudy darkness. He could just identify the radiator, the vase of flowers, the bookcase, the smaller chair, and the numerous exposures of the closed door. The floor frames were nearly black. Now the camera changed position, moving to the kitchen doorway and shooting back into the bedroom with a wide-angle lens. Dark frustration.

The bed was folded way into an ordinary sofa, the coffee table had moved back to its rightful position, the remaining pieces of furniture were undisturbed, the drapes covered the only window, the lights were not lit. He squinted at the final frames and caught his breath. A figure—a dim and indistinct somebody of a figure—stood at the far corner of the coffee table looking at the closed door.

Tabbot grabbed up the third strip of prints.

Four frames gave him nothing but a closed door. The fifth frame exploded in a bright halo of flash: the gun was fired into the waiting lens.

Sergeant Tabbot jumped out of the truck, slammed shut the door behind him and climbed the stairs to the third floor. His bad knee begged for an easier pace. The young patrolman was gone from his post upstairs.

A keeper blocked the door to the apartment.

Tabbot approached it cautiously while he fished in his pockets for the I.D. card. At a distance of only two feet he detected the uneasy squirmings of pain in his groin; if he attempted to squeeze past the machine into the apartment the damned thing would do its utmost to tear his guts apart. The testicles were most vulnerable. A keeper always reminded him of a second generation fire hydrant— but if he was grilled at one of the precinct houses he would never be able to describe a second generation fire hydrant to anyone's satisfaction. His interrogator would insist it was only a phallic symbol.

The keeper was fashioned of stainless steel and colorless plastic: it stood waist high with a slot and a glowing bullseye in its pointed head, and it generated a controlled fulguration emission—a high-frequency radiation capable of destroying animal tissue. The machines were remarkably useful for keeping prisoners *in* and inquisitive citizenry *out.*

Tabbot inserted his I.D. into the slot and waited for the glow to fade out of the bullseye.

A telephone rested on the floor at the far end of the sofa, half hidden behind a stack of dusty books: the woman had read Western novels. He dialed the precinct house and waited while an operator located the officer.

Impatiently: "Tabbot here. Who opened the drapes?"

"What the hell are you— What drapes?"

"The drapes covering the window, the only window in the room. Who opened them this morning? When?"

There was a speculative silence. "Sergeant, are those prints worthless?"

"Yes, sir—nearly so. I've got one beautiful shot of that detective sitting on the sofa *after* the drapes were opened." He hesitated for a moment while he consulted the notebook. "The shot was fired at six forty-five this morning; the janitor opened the door at ten minutes after nine. And I really have a nice print of the plainclothesman."

"Is that *all*?"

"All that will help you. I have one dim and dirty print of a somebody looking at the door, but I can't tell you if that somebody is man or woman, red or green."

The Lieutenant said: "Oh, shit!"

"Yes, sir."

"The coroner opened those drapes—he wanted more light to look at his corpse."

Wistfully: "I wish he'd opened them last night before she was a corpse."

"Are you *sure* they're worthless?"

"Well, sir, if you took them into court and drew that same judge, he'd throw you out."

"Damn it! What are you going to do now?"

"I'll go back to six forty-five and work around that gunshot. I should be able to follow the some-body to the door at the same time—I suppose it was the woman going over to let the murderer in. But don't get your hopes up, Lieutenant. This is a lost cause."

Another silence, and then: "All right, do what you can. A hell of a note, Sergeant."

"Yes, sir." He rang off.

Tabbot hauled the bulky camera into position at one end of the coffee table and angled at the door; he thought the set-up would encompass the woman walking to the door, opening it, turning to walk away, and the assailant coming in. All in murky darkness. He fitted a fresh magazine to the camera, inspected the lens for non-existent dirt, and began the timing calculations. The camera began ticking off the exposures bracketing the point of gunfire.

Tabbot went over to the window to finish his inspection of the third strip of prints: the kitchen. The greater bulk of them were as dark as the bedroom.

The strip of prints suddenly brightened just after that point at which he'd changed to a wide-angle lens, just after he'd begun the final wrap-up. A ceil-ing light had been turned on in the kitchen.

Tabbot stared at a naked woman seated at the table.

She held both hands folded over her stomach, as though pressing in a roll of flesh. Behind her the narrow door of the water closet stood ajar. The table was bare. Tabbot frowned at the woman, at the pose, and then rummaged through his notes for the retroactive exposure time: five minutes past six. The woman who made Christmas dolls was sitting at a bare table at five minutes past six in the morning, looking off to her left, and holding her hand over her stomach. Tabbot wondered if she was hungry—wondered if she waited on some imaginary maid to prepare and serve breakfast. Eggs, coffee, dry toast.

He searched for a frame of the stove: there was a low gas flame beneath the coffee pot. No eggs frying. Well . . . they were probably three-minute eggs, and these frames had been exposed five or ten minutes apart.

He looked again at the woman and apologized for the poor joke: she would be dead in forty minutes.

The only other item of interest on the third strip was a thin ribbon of light under the shower curtain. Tabbot skipped backward along the strip seeking the two exposures angled into the shower stall, but found them dark and the stall empty. The wrong hour.

Behind him the camera shut itself off and called for attention.

Tabbot carried the instrument across the room to an advantageous position beside an arm of the chair and again angled toward the door. The timer was reset for a duplicate coverage of the scenes just completed, but he expected no more than a shadowy figure entering, firing, leaving—a murky figure in a darkened room. A new series was started with that one flash frame as the centerpiece.

His attention went back to the woman at the

table. She sat with her hands clasped over her stomach, looking off to her left. Looking at what?

On impulse, Tabbot walked into the kitchen and sat down in her chair. Same position, same angle. Tabbot pressed his hands to his stomach and looked off to his left. Identical line of sight. He was looking at the shower stall.

One print had given him a ribbon of light under the stained curtain—no, stained folding door. The barrier had leaked water.

He said aloud: "Well, I'll be damned!"

The printed strips were stretched across the table to free his hands and then he examined his notebook item by item. Each of the prints had peered into the past at five minutes after six in the morning. Someone took a shower while the woman sat by the table.

Back to the last few frames of the second strip taken from the second magazine: a figure—a dim and indistinct somebody of a figure—stood at the far corner of the coffee table looking at the closed door. Time: six-forty. Five minutes before the shot was fired.

Did the woman simply stand there and wait a full five minutes for a knock on the door? Or did she open it only a moment after the exposure was made, let the man in, argue with him, and die five minutes later behind the chair? Five minutes was time enough for an argument, a heated exchange, a threat, a shot.

Tabbot braced his hand on the table edge.

What happened to the man in the shower? Was he still there—soaking himself for forty minutes— while the woman was gunned down? Or had he come out, dried himself, gulped down breakfast and quit the apartment minutes before the assailant arrived?

Tabbot supplied answers: no, no, no, and maybe.

He jumped up from the chair so quickly it fell over. The telephone was behind the stack of Western novels.

The man answering his call may have been one of the wicker basket men.

"County morgue."

"Sergeant Tabbot here, Photo Section. I've got preliminary prints on that woman in the apartment. She was seated at the breakfast table between six o'clock and six-fifteen. How does that square with the autopsy?"

The voice said cheerfully: "Right on the button, Sergeant. The toast was still there, know what I mean?"

Weakly: "I know what you mean. I'll send over the prints."

"Hey, wait—wait, there's more. She was just a little bit pregnant. Two months, maybe."

Tabbot swallowed. An unwanted image tried to form in his imagination: the autopsy table, a stroke or two of the blade, an inventory of the contents of the stomach— He thrust the image away and set down the telephone.

Aloud, in dismay: "I thought the man in the shower ate breakfast! But he didn't—he didn't." The inoperative phone gave him no answer.

The camera stopped peering into the past.

Tabbot hauled the instrument into the kitchen and set up a new position behind the woman's chair to take the table, stove, and shower stall. The angle

would be right over her head. A series of exposures
two minutes apart was programmed into the timer
with the first frame calculated at six o'clock. The
probe began. Tabbot reached around the camera
and gathered up the printed strips from the table.
The light was better at the window and he quit the
kitchen for yet another inspection of the dismal
preliminaries.

The front door, the janitor and a second man in
the doorway, the bright beauty of a frame with the
detective sitting on the sofa, the darkened frames
of the sofa pulled out to make a bed—Tabbot
paused and peered. Were there one or *two* figures
sprawled in the bed? Next: the kitchen doorway,
the overstuffed chair, the misplaced coffee table,
the window with the closed drapes— All of that.
On and on. Dark. But were there one or *two* people in the bed?

And now consider this frame: a dim and indistinct somebody looking at the closed door. Was
that somebody actually walking to the door, caught
in mid-stride? Was that somebody the man from
the shower?

Tabbot dropped the strips and sprinted for the
kitchen.

The camera hadn't finished its programmed series but Tabbot yanked it from position and
dragged it over the kitchen floor. The tripod left
marks. The table was pushed aside. He stopped the
timer and jerked aside the folding door to thrust
the lens into the shower stall. Angle at the tiny
wash basin and the mirror hanging above it; hope
for sufficient reflected light from the white tiles.
Strap on a fresh magazine. Work feverishly with

the slide rule. Check and check again the notes to be certain of times. Set the timer and start the camera. Stand back and wait.

The Lieutenant had been wrong.

The woman who made Christmas dolls did *not* walk to the door and admit a man at about six-forty in the morning; she didn't go to the door at all. She died behind the chair, as she was walking toward the window to pull the drapes. Her assailant had stayed the night, had slept with her in the unfolded bed until sometime shortly before six o'clock. They got up and one of them used the toilet, one of them put away the bed. *He* stepped into the shower while *she* sat down at the table. In that interval she held her belly, and later had breakfast. An argument started—or perhaps was carried over from the night before—and when the man emerged into a now *darkened* kitchen he dressed and made to leave without eating.

The argument continued into the living room; the woman went to the window to admit the morning sun while the professional gunman hesitated between the coffee table and the door. He half turned, fired, and made his escape.

"There's a *little* hole in the spine . . ."

Tabbot thought the Lieutenant was very wrong. In less than an hour he would have the prints to prove him wrong.

To save a few minutes' time he carried the exposed magazine down to the truck and fed the film into the developing tank. It was a nuisance to bother with the keeper each time he went in and out, and he violated regulations by leaving it inert. A police cruiser went by as he climbed down from the truck but he got nothing more than a vacant nod from the man riding alongside the driver. Tabbot's knee began to hurt as he climbed the steps to the third floor for what seemed the hundredth time that day.

The camera had completed the scene and stopped. Tabbot made ready to leave.

He carried his equipment outside into the corridor and shot three exposures of the apartment door. The process of packing everything back into the bulky case took longer than the unpacking. The tripod stubbornly refused to telescope properly and fit into the case. And the citizens' privacy law stubbornly refused to let him shoot the corridor: no crime there.

A final look at the unoccupied apartment: he could see through into the kitchen and his imagination could see the woman seated at the table, holding her stomach. When he craned his neck to peer around the door he could see the window limned in bright sunshine. Tabbot decided to leave the drapes open. If someone else were killed here today or tomorrow he wanted the drapes open.

He closed the apartment door and thrust his I.D. card into the keeper's slot to activate it. There was no rewarding stir of machinery, no theatrical buzzing of high-frequency pulsing but his guts began growling when the red bullseye glowed. He went down the stairs carefully because his knee warned against a fast pace. The camera case banged his other leg.

Tabbot removed the reel of film from the developing tanks and started it through the printer. The second magazine was fed into the developer. He closed the back door of the truck, went around to the driver's door and fished for the ignition key in his trouser pocket. It wasn't there. He'd left the key hanging in the ignition, another violation of the law. Tabbot got up in the cab and started the motor, briefly thankful the men in the police cruiser hadn't spotted the key—they would have given him a citation and counted him as guilty as any other citizen.

The lab truck moved out into traffic.

The printing of the two reels of nylon film was completed in the parking lot alongside the precinct house. He parked in a visitor's slot. Not knowing who might be watching from a window, Tabbot removed the key from the ignition and pocketed it before going around to the back to finish the morning's work.

The strip results from the first magazine were professionally insulting: dark and dismal prints he didn't really want to show anyone. There were two fine frames of gun flash, and two others of the dim and indistinct somebody making for the door. About the only satisfaction Tabbot could find in these last two was the dark coloring: a man dressed in dark clothing, moving through a darkened room. The naked woman would have been revealed as a pale whitish figure.

Tabbot scanned the prints on the second strip with a keen and professional eye. The white tile lining the shower stall had reflected light in a most satisfying manner: he thought it one of the best jobs of back-lighting he'd ever photographed. He watched the woman's overnight visitor shower, shave, brush his teeth and comb his hair. At one point—perhaps in the middle of that heated argument—he had nicked himself on the neck just above his Adam's apple. It had done nothing to improve the fellow's mood.

One exposure made outside the apartment door—the very last frame—was both rewarding and disappointing: the indistinct somebody was shown leaving the scene but he was bent over, head down, looking at his own feet. Tabbot supposed the man was too shy to be photographed coming out of a woman's room. He would be indignant when he learned that a camera had watched him in the little mirror above the wash basin. Indignant, and rather furious at this newest invasion of privacy.

Tabbot carried the prints into the precinct house. Another sergeant was on duty behind the desk, a man who recognized him by uniform if not by face or name.

"Who do you want?"

Tabbot said: "The Lieutenant. What's-his-name?"

The desk man jerked a thumb behind him. "In the squad room."

Tabbot walked around the desk and found his way to the squad room at the end of the building. It was a large room with desks, and four or five men working or loafing behind the desks. Most of them seemed to be loafing. All of them looked up at the photographer.

"Over here, Sergeant. Did you finish the job?"

"Yes, sir."

Tabbot turned and made his way to the Lieutenant's desk. He spread out the first strip of dark prints.

"Well, you don't seem too happy about it."

"No, sir."

The second strip was placed beside the first.

"They're all dark except those down at the bottom. It was brighter in the shower stall. That's you in the shower, Lieutenant. The backlighting gave me the only decent prints in the lot."

Getting Across

ROBERT SILVERBERG

> Robert Silverberg is a science-fiction writer and
> editor with few peers. His dozens of novels have
> addressed such social issues as overpopulation,
> war, drug abuse, man's use of technology, and
> other themes. He has also created many worlds
> of wonder with fantastic, detailed alien races and
> societies, garnering him four Hugo awards and
> five Nebula awards. His most recent creation is
> the planet of Majipoor, a world with over twenty
> million human and alien beings. Here, he looks at
> one way society might cripple itself under the
> guise of advancement.

I

On the first day of summer my month-wife, Silena
Ruiz, filched our district's master program from the
Ganfield Hold computer center and disappeared
with it. A guard at the Hold has confessed that she
won admittance by seducing him, then gave him a
drug. Some say she is in Conning Town now; others
have heard rumors that she has been seen in Morton Court; still others maintain her destination was
The Mill. I suppose it does not matter where she
has gone. What matters is that we are without our

program. We have lived without it for eleven days and things are starting to break down. The heat is abominable, but we must switch every thermostat to manual override before we can use our cooling system; I think we will boil in our skins before the job is done. A malfunction of the scanners that control our refuse compactor has stilled the garbage collectors, which will not go forth unless they have a place to dump what they collect. Since no one knows the proper command to give the compactor, rubbish accumulates, forming pestilential hills on every street, and dense swarms of flies or worse hover over the sprawling mounds. Beginning on the fourth day our police also began to go immobile—who can say why?—and by now all of them stand halted in their tracks. Some are already starting to rust, since the maintenance schedules are out of phase. Word has gone out that we are without protection, and outlanders cross into the district with impunity, molesting our women, stealing our children, raiding our stocks of foodstuffs. In Ganfield Hold, platoons of weary, sweating technicians toil constantly to replace the missing program, but it might be months, even years, before they will be able to devise a new one.

In theory, duplicate programs are stored in several places within the community against just such a calamity. In fact, we have none. The one kept in the district captain's office turned out to be some twenty years obsolete; the one in the care of the soul father's house had been devoured by rats; the program held in the vaults of the tax collectors appeared to be intact, but when it was placed in the input slot it mysteriously failed to activate the computers. So we are helpless: an entire district, hundreds of thousands of human beings, cut loose to drift on the tides of chance. Silena, Silena, Silena! To disable all of Ganfield, to make our already burdensome lives more difficult, to expose me to the hatred of my neighbors . . . Why, Silena? Why?

People glare at me on the streets. They hold me responsible, in a way, for all this. They point and mutter; in another few days they will be spitting and cursing; and if no relief comes soon, they may be throwing stones. Look, I want to shout, she was only my month-wife and she acted entirely on her own. I assure you I had no idea she would do such a thing. And yet they blame me. At the wealthy houses of Morton Court they will dine tonight on babies stolen in Ganfield this day, and I am held accountable.

What will I do? Where can I turn?

I may have to flee. The thought of crossing district lines chills me. Is it the peril of death I fear or only the loss of all that is familiar? Probably both: I have no hunger for dying and no wish to leave Ganfield. Yet I will go, no matter how difficult it will be to find sanctuary if I get safely across the line. If they continue to hold me tainted by Silena's crime, I will have no choice. I think I would rather die at the hands of strangers than perish at those of my own people.

II

This weltering night I find myself atop Ganfield Tower, seeking cool breezes and the shelter of darkness. Half the district has had the idea of escaping the heat by coming up here tonight, it

seems; to get away from the angry eyes and tightened lips, I have climbed to the fifth parapet, where
only the bold and the foolish ordinarily go. I am
neither, yet here I am.

As I move slowly around the tower's rim, warily
clinging to the old and eroded guardrail, I have a
view of our entire district. Ganfield is like a shallow
basin in form, gently sloping upward from the central spike that is the tower to a rise on the district
perimeter. They say that a broad lake once occupied the site where Ganfield now stands; it was
drained and covered over, centuries ago, when the
need for new living space became extreme. Yesterday I heard that great pumps are used to keep the
ancient lake from breaking through into our cellars,
and that before very long the pumps will fail or
shut themselves down for maintenance, and we will
be flooded. Perhaps so. Ganfield once devoured the
lake; will the lake now have Ganfield? Will we tum-
ble into the dark waters and be swallowed, with no
one to mourn us?

I look out over Ganfield. These tall brick boxes
are our dwellings, twenty stories high but dwarfed
from my vantage point far above. This sliver of
land, black in the smoky moonlight, is our pitiful
scrap of community park. These low flat-topped
buildings are our shops, a helter-skelter cluster.
This is our industrial zone, such that it is. That
squat shadow-cloaked bulk just north of the tower
is Ganfield Hold, where our crippled computers slip
one by one into idleness. I have spent nearly my
whole life within this one narrow swing of the com-
pass that is Ganfield. When I was a boy and affairs
were not nearly so harsh between one district and

its neighbor, my father took me on holiday to Morton Court, and another time to The Mill. When I was a young man I was sent on business across three districts to Parley Close. I remember those journeys as clearly and vividly as though I had dreamed them. But everything is quite different now and it is twenty years since I last left Ganfield. I am not one of your privileged commuters, gaily making transit from zone to zone. All the world is one great city, so it is said, with the deserts settled and the rivers bridged and all the open places filled, a universal city that has abolished the old boundaries, and yet it is twenty years since I passed from one district to the next. I wonder: Are we one city, then, or merely thousands of contentious, fragmented, tiny states?

Look here, along the perimeter. There are no more boundaries, but what is this? This is our boundary, Ganfield Crescent, that wide, curving boulevard surrounding the district. Are you a man of some other zone? Then cross the Crescent at risk of life. Do you see our police machines, blunt-snouted, glossy, formidably powerful, strewn like boulders in the broad avenue? They will interrogate you, and if your answers are uneasy, they may destroy you. Of course they can do no one any harm tonight.

Look outward now, at our hordes of brawling neighbors. I see beyond the Crescent to the east the gaunt spires of Conning Town, and on the west, descending stepwise into the jumbled valley, the shabby dark-walled buildings of The Mill, with happy Morton Court on the far side, and somewhere in the smoky distance other places, Folkstone and Budleigh and Hawk Nest and Parley Close and Kingston and Old Grove and all the rest, the districts, the myriad districts, part of the chain that stretches from sea to sea, from shore to shore, spanning our continent border to border, the districts, the chips of gaudy glass making up the global mosaic, the infinitely numerous communities that are the segments of the all-encompassing world-city. Tonight at the capital they are planning next month's rainfall patterns for districts that the planners have never seen. District food allocations—inadequate, always inadequate—are being devised by men to whom our appetites are purely abstract entities. Do they believe in our existence, at the capital? Do they really think there is such a place as Ganfield? What if we sent them a delegation of notable citizens to ask for help in replacing our lost program? Would they care? Would they even listen? For that matter, is there a capital at all? How can I, who have never seen nearby Old Grove, accept, on faith alone, the existence of a far-off governing center, aloof, inaccessible, shrouded in myth? Maybe it is only a construct of some cunning subterranean machine that is our real ruler. That would not surprise me. Nothing surprises me. There is no capital. There are no central planners. Beyond the horizon everything is mist.

III

In the office, at least, no one dares show hostility to me. There are no scowls, no glares, no snide references to the missing program. I am, after all, chief deputy to the District Commissioner of Nutrition, and since the commissioner is usually absent,

I am, in effect, in charge of the department. If Silena's crime does not destroy my career, it might prove to have been unwise for my subordinates to treat me with disdain. In any case we are so busy that there is no time for such gambits. We are responsible for keeping the community properly fed; our tasks have been greatly complicated by the loss of the program, for there is no reliable way now of processing our allocation sheets, and we must requisition and distribute food by guesswork and memory. How many bales of plankton cubes do we consume each week? How many pounds of proteoid mix? How much bread for the shops of Lower Ganfield? What fads of diet are likely to sweep the district this month? If demand and supply fall into imbalance as a result of our miscalculations, there could be widespread acts of violence, forays into neighboring districts, even renewed outbreaks of cannibalism within Ganfield itself. So we must draw up our estimates with the greatest precision. What a terrible spiritual isolation we feel deciding such things with no computers to guide us!

IV

On the fourteenth day of the crisis the district captain summons me. His message comes in late afternoon, when we all are dizzy with fatigue, choked by humidity. For several hours I have been tangled in complex dealings with a high official of the Marine Nutrients Board; this is an arm of the central city government, and I must therefore show the greatest tact, lest Ganfield's plankton quotas be arbitrarily lowered by a bureaucrat's sudden pique. Telephone contact is uncertain—the Marine Nutri-

ents Board has its headquarters in Melrose New
Port, half a continent away on the southeastern
coast—and the line sputters and blurs with distor-
tions that our computers, if the master program
were in operation, would normally erase. As we
reach a crisis in the negotiation my subdeputy gives
me a note: "District captain wants to see you."
"Not now," I say in silent lip talk. The haggling
proceeds. A few minutes later comes another note:
"It's urgent." I shake my head, brush the note from
my desk. The subdeputy retreats to the outer office,
where I see him engaged in frantic discussion with
a man in the gray-and-green uniform of the district
captain's staff. The messenger points vehemently at
me. Just then the phone line goes dead. I slam the
instrument down and call to the messenger, "What
is it?"

"The captain, sir. To his office at once, please."

"Impossible."

He displays a warrant bearing the captain's seal.
"He requires your immediate presence."

"Tell him I have delicate business to complete,"
I reply. "Another fifteen minutes, maybe."

He shakes his head. "I am not empowered to
allow a delay."

"Is this an arrest, then?"

"A summons."

"But with the force of an arrest?"

"With the force of an arrest, yes," he tells me.

I shrug and yield. All burdens drop from me.
Let the subdeputy deal with the Marine Nutrients
Board; let the clerk in the outer office do it, or no
one at all; let the whole district starve. I no longer
care. I am summoned. My responsibilities are dis-

charged. I give over my desk to the subdeputy and summarize for him, in perhaps a hundred words, my intricate hours of negotiation. All that is someone else's problem now.

The messenger leads me from the building into the hot, dank street. The sky is dark and heavy with rain, and evidently it has been raining some while, for the sewers are backing up and angry swirls of muddy water run shin-deep through the gutters. The drainage system, too, is controlled from Ganfield Hold, and must now be failing. We hurry across the narrow plaza fronting my office, skirt a gush of sewage-laden outflow, push into a close-packed crowd of irritable workers heading for home. The messenger's uniform creates an invisible sphere of untouchability for us; the throngs part readily and close again behind us. Wordlessly I am conducted to the stone-faced building of the district captain, and quickly to his office. It is no unfamiliar place to me, but coming here as a prisoner is quite different from attending a meeting of the district council. My shoulders are slumped, my eyes look toward the threadbare carpeting.

The district captain appears. He is a man of sixty, silver-haired, upright, his eyes frank and direct, his features reflecting little of the strain his position must impose. He has governed our district ten years. He greets me by name, but without warmth, and says, "You've heard nothing from your woman?"

"I would have reported it if I had."

"Perhaps. Perhaps. Have you any idea where she is?"

"I know only the common rumors," I say. "Conning Town, Morton Court, The Mill."

"She is in none of those places."

"Are you sure?"

"I have consulted the captains of those districts," he says. "They deny any knowledge of her. Of course, one has no reason to trust their word, but on the other hand why would they bother to deceive me?" His eyes fasten on mine. "What part did you play in the stealing of the program?"

"None, sir."

"She never spoke to you of treasonable things?"

"Never."

"There is strong feeling in Ganfield that a conspiracy existed."

"If so I knew nothing of it."

He judges me with a piercing look. After a long pause he says heavily, "She has destroyed us, you know. We can function at the present level of order for another six weeks, possibly, without the program—if there is no plague, if we are not flooded, if we are not overrun with bandits from outside. After that the accumulated effects of many minor breakdowns will paralyze us. We will fall into chaos. We will strangle on our own wastes, starve, suffocate, revert to savagery, live like beasts until the end—who knows? Without the master program we are lost. Why did she do this to us?"

"I have no theories," I say. "She kept her own counsel. Her independence of soul is what attracted me to her."

"Very well. Let her independence of soul be what attracts you to her now. Find her and bring back the program."

"Find her? Where?"

"That is for you to discover."

"I know nothing of the world outside Ganfield!"

"You will learn," the captain says coolly. "There are those here who would indict you for treason. I see no value in this. How does it help us to punish you? But we can *use* you. You are a clever and resourceful man; you can make your way through the hostile districts, and you can gather information, and you could well succeed in tracking her. If anyone has influence over her, you do; if you find her, you perhaps can induce her to surrender the program. No one else could hope to accomplish that. Go. We offer you immunity from prosecution in return for your cooperation."

The world spins wildly about me. My skin burns with shock. "Will I have safe-conduct through the neighboring districts?" I ask.

"To whatever extent we can arrange. That will not be much, I fear."

"You'll give me an escort, then? Two or three men?"

"We feel you will travel more effectively alone. A party of several men takes on the character of an invading force; you would be met with suspicion and worse."

"Diplomatic credentials, at least?"

"A letter of identification, calling on all captains to honor your mission and treat you with courtesy."

I know how much value such a letter will have in Hawk Nest or Folkstone.

"This frightens me," I say.

He nods, not unkindly. "I understand that. Yet someone must seek her, and who else is there but you? We grant you a day to make your preparations. You will depart on the morning after next, and God hasten your return."

V

Preparations. How can I prepare myself? What maps should I collect, when my destination is unknown? Returning to the office is unthinkable; I go straight home, and for hours I wander from one room to the other as if I face execution at dawn. At last I gather myself and fix a small meal, but most of it remains on my plate. No friends call; I call no one. Since Silena's disappearance my friends have fallen away from me. I sleep poorly. During the night there are hoarse shouts and shrill alarms in the street; I learn from the morning newscast that five men of Conning Town, here to loot, had been seized by one of the new vigilante groups that have replaced the police machines and were summarily put to death. I find no cheer in that, thinking that I might be in Conning Town in a day or so.

What clues to Silena's route? I ask to speak with the guard from whom she wangled entry into Ganfield Hold. He has been a prisoner ever since; the captain is too busy to decide his fate, and he languishes meanwhile. He is a small, thick-bodied man with stubbly red hair and a sweaty forehead; his eyes are bright with anger and his nostrils quiver. "What is there to say?" he demands. "I was on duty at the Hold. She came in. I had never seen her before, though I knew she must be high caste. Her cloak was open. She seemed naked beneath it. She was in a state of excitement."

"What did she tell you?"

"That she desired me. Those were her first

words." Yes. I could see Silena doing that, though
I had difficulty in imagining her long, slender form
enfolded in this squat little man's embrace. "She
said she knew of me and was eager for me to
have her."

"And then?"

"I sealed the gate. We went to an inner room
where there is a cot. It was a quiet time of day; I
thought no harm would come. She dropped her
cloak. Her body—"

"Never mind her body." I could see it all too
well in the eye of my mind, the sleek thighs, the
taut belly, the small high breasts, the cascade of choc-
olate hair falling to her shoulders. "What did you
talk about? Did she say anything of a political
kind? Some slogan, some words against the
government?"

"Nothing. We lay together naked a while, only
fondling each other. Then she said she had a drug
with her, one that would enhance the sensations of
love tenfold. It was a dark powder. I drank it in
water; she drank it also, or seemed to. Instantly I
was asleep. When I awoke the Hold was in uproar
and I was a prisoner." He glowers at me. "I should
have suspected a trick from the start. Such women
do not hunger for men like me. How did I ever
injure you? Why did you choose me to be the victim of your scheme?"

"Her scheme," I say. "Not mine. I had no part
in it. Her motive is a mystery to me. If I could
discover where she has gone, I would seek her and
wring answers from her. Any help you could give
me might earn you a pardon and your freedom."

"I know nothing," he says sullenly. "She came

in, she snared me, she drugged me, she stole the program."

"Think. Not a word? Possibly she mentioned the name of some other district."

"Nothing."

A pawn is all he is, innocent, useless. As I leave he cries out to me to intercede for him, but what can I do? "Your woman ruined me!" he roars.

"She may have ruined us all," I reply.

At my request a district prosecutor accompanies me to Silena's apartment, which has been under official seal since her disappearance. Its contents have been thoroughly examined, but maybe there is some clue I alone would notice. Entering, I feel a sharp pang of loss, for the sight of Silena's possessions reminds me of happier times. These things are painfully familiar to me: her neat array of books, her clothing, her furnishings, her bed. I knew her only eleven weeks, she was my month-wife for only two; I had not realized she had come to mean so much to me so quickly. We look around, the prosecutor and I. The books testify to the agility of her restless mind: little light fiction, mainly works of serious history, analyses of social problems, forecasts of conditions to come. Holman, *The Era of the World City*. Sawtelle, *Megalopolis Triumphant*. Doxiadis, *The New World of Urban Man*. Heggebend, *Fifty Billion Lives*. Marks, *Calcutta Is Everywhere*. Chasin, *The New Community*. I take a few of the books down, fondling them as though they were Silena. Many times when I had spent an evening here she reached for one of those books, Sawtelle or Heggebend or Marks or Chasin, to read me a passage that amplified some point she

was making. Idly I turn pages. Dozens of para-
graphs are underscored with fine, precise lines, and
lengthy marginal comments are abundant. "We've
analyzed all of that for possible significance," the
prosecutor remarks. "The only thing we've concluded is that she thinks the world is too crowded
for comfort." A ratcheting laugh. "As who doesn't?"
He points to a stack of green-bound pamphlets at
the end of the lower shelf. "These, on the other
hand, may be useful in your search. Do you know
anything about them?"

The stack consists of nine copies of something
called *Walden Three*: a Utopian fantasy, apparently,
set in an idyllic land of streams and forests. The
booklets are unfamiliar to me; Silena must have
obtained them recently. Why nine copies? Was she
acting as a distributor? They bear the imprint of a
publishing house in Kingston. Ganfield and Kingston severed trade relations long ago; material published there is uncommon here. "I've never seen
them," I say. "Where do you think she got them?"

"There are three main routes for subversive literature originating in Kingston. One is—"

"Is this pamphlet subversive, then?"

"Oh, very much so. It argues for complete rever-
sal of the social trends of the last hundred years.
As I was saying, there are three main routes for
subversive literature originating in Kingston. We
have traced one chain of distribution running by
way of Wisleigh and Cedar Mall, another through
Old Grove, Hawk Nest, and Conning Town, and
the third via Parley Close and The Mill. It is plausi-
ble that your woman is in Kingston now, having
traveled along one of these underground distribu-

tion routes, sheltered by her fellow subversives all the way. But we have no way of confirming this." He smiles emptily. "She could be in any of the other communities along the three routes. Or in none of them."

"I should think of Kingston, though, as my ultimate goal, until I learn anything to the contrary. Is that right?"

"What else can you do?"

What else, indeed? I must search at random through an unknown number of hostile districts, having no clue other than the vague one implicit in the place of origin of these nine booklets, while time ticks on and Ganfield slips deeper day by day into confusion.

The prosecutor's office supplies me with useful things: maps, letters of introduction, a commuter's passport that should enable me to cross at least some district lines unmolested, and an assortment of local currencies as well as bank notes issued by the central bank and therefore valid in most districts. Against my wishes I am given also a weapon—a small heat-pistol—and in addition a capsule that I can swallow in the event that a quick and easy death becomes desirable. As the final stage of my preparation I spend an hour conferring with a secret agent, now retired, whose career of espionage took him safely into hundreds of communities as far away as Threadmuir and Reed Meadow. What advice does he give someone about to try to get across? "Maintain your poise," he says. "Be confident and self-assured, as though you belong in whatever place you find yourself. Never slink. Look all men in the eye. However, say no more than is necessary. Be watchful at all times. Don't relax your guard." Such precepts I could have evolved without his aid. He has nothing in the nature of specific hints for survival. Each district, he says, presents unique problems, constantly changing; nothing can be anticipated, everything must be met as it arises. How comforting!

At nightfall I go to the soul father's house, in the shadow of Ganfield Tower. To leave without a blessing seems unwise. But there is something stagy and unspontaneous about my visit, and my faith flees as I enter. In the dim antechamber I light the nine candles, I pluck the five blades of grass from the ceremonial vase, I do the other proper ritual things, but my spirit remains chilled and hollow, and I am unable to pray. The soul father himself, having been told of my mission, grants me audience—gaunt old man with impenetrable eyes set in deep bony rims—and favors me with a gentle feather-light embrace. "Go in safety," he murmurs. "God watches over you." I wish I felt sure of that. Going home, I take the most roundabout possible route, as if trying to drink in as much of Ganfield as I can on my last night. The diminishing past flows through me like a river running dry. My birthplace, my school, the streets where I played, the dormitory where I spent my adolescence, the home of my first month-wife. Farewell. Farewell. Tomorrow I go across. I return to my apartment alone; once more my sleep is fitful. An hour after dawn I find myself, astonished by it, waiting in line among the commuters at the mouth of the transit tube, bound for Conning Town. And so my crossing begins.

VI

Aboard the tube-train no one speaks. Faces are tense; bodies are held rigid in the plastic seats. Occasionally someone on the other side of the aisle glances at me as though wondering who this newcomer to the commuter group may be, but his eyes quickly slide away as I take notice. I know none of these commuters, though they must have dwelt in Ganfield as long as I; their lives have never intersected mine before. Engineers, merchants, diplomats, whatever—their careers are tied to districts other than their own. It is one of the anomalies of our ever more fragmented and stratified society that some regular contact still survives between community and community; a certain number of people must journey each day to outlying districts, where they work encapsulated, isolated, among unfriendly strangers.

We plunge eastward at unimaginable speed. Surely we are past the boundaries of Ganfield by now and under alien territory. A glowing sign on the wall of the car announces our route: CONNING TOWN—HAWK NEST—OLD GROVE—KINGSTON—FOLKSTONE—PARLEY CLOSE—BUDLEIGH—CEDAR MALL—THE MILL—MORTON COURT—GANFIELD, a wide loop through our most immediate neighbors. I try to visualize the separate links in this chain of districts, each a community of three or four hundred thousand loyal and patriotic citizens, each with its own special tone, its flavor, its distinctive quality, its apparatus of government, its customs and rituals. But I can imagine them merely as a cluster of Ganfields, every place very much like the one I have just left.

I know this is not so. The world-city is no homogeneous collection of uniformities, a global bundle of indistinguishable suburbs. No, there is incredible diversity, a host of unique urban cores bound by common need into a fragile unity. No master plan brought them into being; each evolved at a separate point in time to serve the necessities of a particular purpose. This community sprawls gracefully along a curving river, that one boldly mounts the slopes of stark hills; here the prevailing architecture reflects an easy, gentle climate, there it wars with unfriendly nature; form follows topography and local function, creating individuality. The world is a richness—why then do I see only ten thousand Ganfields?

Of course it is not so simple. We are caught in the tension between forces that encourage distinctiveness and forces that compel all communities toward identicality. Centrifugal forces broke down the huge ancient cities, the Londons and Tokyos and New Yorks, into neighborhood communities that seized quasi-autonomous powers. Those giant cities were too unwieldy to survive; density of population, making long-distance transport unfeasible and communication difficult, shattered the urban fabric, destroyed the authority of the central government, and left the closely knit small-scale subcity as the only viable unit. Two dynamic and contradictory processes now asserted themselves. Pride and the quest for local advantage led each community toward specialization: this one a center primarily of industrial production, this one devoted to advanced education, this to finance, this to the processing of raw materials, this to wholesale marketing of commodities, this to retail distribution, and so on, the shape and texture of each district defined by its chosen function. And yet the new decentralization required a high degree of redundancy, duplication of governmental structures, of utilities, of community services; for its own safety each district felt the need to transform itself into a microcosm of the former full city. Ideally we should have hovered in perfect balance between specialization and redundancy, all communities striving to fulfill the needs of all other communities with the least possible overlap and waste of resources; in fact our human frailty has brought into being these irreversible trends of rivalry and irrational fear, dividing district from district, so that against our own self-interest we sever year after year our bonds of interdependence and stubbornly seek self-sufficiency at the district level. Since this is impossible, our lives grow constantly more impoverished. In the end, all districts will be the same and we will have created a world of pathetic, limping Ganfields, devoid of grace, lacking in variety.

So. The tube-train halts. This is Conning Town. I am across the first district line. I make my exit in a file of solemn-faced commuters. Imitating them, I approach a colossal Cyclopean scanning machine and present my passport. It is unmarked by visas; theirs are gaudy with scores of them. I tremble, but the machine accepts me and slams down a stamp that fluoresces a brilliant shimmering crimson against the pale-lavender page:

•DISTRICT OF CONNING TOWN•
•ENTRY VISA•
•24-HOUR VALIDITY•

Dated to the hour, minute, second. Welcome, stranger, but get out of town before sunrise!

Up the purring ramp, into the street. Bright morning sunlight pries apart the slim, sooty, close-ranked towers of Conning Town. The air is cool and sweet, strange to me after so many sweltering days in programless, demechanized Ganfield. Does our foul air drift across the border and offend them? Sullen eyes study me; those about me know me for an outsider. Their clothing is alien in style, pinched in at the shoulders, flaring at the waist. I find myself adopting an inane smile in response to their dour glares.

For an hour I walk aimlessly through the downtown section until my first fears melt and a comic cockiness takes possession of me: I pretend to myself that I am a native, and enjoy the flimsy imposture. This place is not much unlike Ganfield, yet nothing is quite the same. The sidewalks are wider; the street lamps have slender arching necks instead of angular ones; the fire hydrants are green and gold, not blue and orange. The police machines have flatter domes than ours, ringed with ten or twelve spy-eyes where ours have six or eight. Different, different, all different.

Three times I am halted by police machines. I produce my passport, display my visa, am allowed to continue. So far getting across has been easier than I imagined. No one molests me here. I suppose I look harmless. Why did I think my foreignness alone would lead these people to attack me? Ganfield is not at war with its neighbors, after all.

Drifting eastward in search of a bookstore, I pass through a shabby residential neighborhood and through a zone of dismal factories before I reach an area of small shops. Then in late afternoon I discover three bookstores on the same block, but they are antiseptic places, not the sort that might carry subversive propaganda like *Walden Three*. The first two are wholly automated, blank-walled charge-plate-and-scanner operations. The third has a human clerk, a man of about thirty, with drooping yellow moustachios and alert blue eyes. He recognizes the style of my clothing and says, "Ganfield, eh? Lot of trouble over there."

"You've heard?"

"Just stories. Computer breakdown, isn't it?"

I nod. "Something like that."

"No police, no garbage removal, no weather control, hardly anything working—that's what they say." He seems neither surprised nor disturbed to have an outlander in his shop. His manner is amiable and relaxed. Is he fishing for data about our vulnerability, though? I must be careful not to tell him anything that might be used against us. But evidently they already know everything here. He says, "It's a little like dropping back into the Stone Age for you people, I guess. It must be a real traumatic thing."

"We're coping," I say, stiffly casual.

"How did it happen, anyway?"

I give him a wary shrug. "I'm not sure about that." Still revealing nothing. But then something in his tone of a moment before catches me belatedly and neutralizes some of the reflexive automatic suspicion with which I have met his questions. I glance around. No one else in the shop.

I let something conspiratorial creep into my voice and say, "It might not even be so traumatic, actually, once we get used to it. I mean, there once was a time when we didn't rely so heavily on machines to do our thinking for us, and we survived, and even managed pretty well. I was reading a little book last week that seemed to be saying we might profit by trying to return to the old way of life. Book published in Kingston."

"Walden Three." Not a question but a statement.

"That's it." My eyes query his. "You've read it?"

"Seen it."

"A lot of sense in that book, I think."

He smiles warmly. "I think so too. You get much Kingston stuff over in Ganfield?"

"Very little, actually."

"Not much here, either."

"But there's some."

"Some, yes," he says.

Have I stumbled upon a member of Silena's underground movement? I say eagerly, "You know, maybe you could help me meet some people who—"

"No."

"No?"

"No." His eyes are still friendly but his face is tense. "There's nothing like that around here," he says, his voice suddenly flat and remote. "You'd have to go over into Hawk Nest."

"I'm told that that's a nasty place."

"Nevertheless, Hawk Nest is where you want to go. Nate and Holly Borden's shop, just off Box Street." Abruptly his manner shifts to one of exaggerated bland clerkishness. "Anything else I can do for you, sir? If you're interested in supernovels we've got a couple of good new double-amplified cassettes, just in. Perhaps I can show you—"

"Thank you, no." I smile, shake my head, leave the store. A police machine waits outside. Its dome rotates; eye after eye scans me intently; finally its resonant voice says, "Your passport, please." This routine is familiar by now. I produce the document. Through the bookshop window I see the clerk bleakly watching. The police machine says, "What is your place of residence in Conning Town?"

"I have none. I'm here on a twenty-four-hour visa."

"Where will you spend the night?"

"In a hotel, I suppose."

"Please show your room confirmation."

"I haven't made arrangements yet," I tell it.

A long moment of silence; the machine is conferring with its central, no doubt, keying into the master program of Conning Town for instructions. At length it says, "You are advised to obtain a legitimate reservation and display it to a monitor at the earliest opportunity within the next four hours. Failure to do so will result in cancellation of your visa and immediate expulsion from Conning Town." Some ominous clicks come from the depths of the machine. "You are now under formal surveillance," it announces.

Brimming with questions, I return hastily to the bookshop. The clerk is displeased to see me. Anyone who attracts monitors to his shop—"monitors" is what they call police machines here, it seems—

is unwelcome. "Can you tell me how to reach the nearest decent hotel?" I ask.

"You won't find one."

"No decent hotels?"

"No hotels. None where you could get a room, anyway. We have only two or three transient houses and accommodations are allocated months in advance to regular commuters."

"Does the monitor know that?"

"Of course."

"Where are strangers supposed to stay, then?"

The clerk shrugs. "There's no structural program here for strangers as such. The regular commuters have regular arrangements. Unauthorized intruders don't belong here at all. You fall somewhere in between, I imagine. There's no legal way for you to spend the night in Conning Town."

"But my visa—"

"Even so."

"I'd better go on into Hawk Nest, I suppose."

"It's late. You've missed the last tube-train. You've got no choice but to stay, unless you want to try a border crossing on foot in the dark. I wouldn't recommend that."

"Stay? But where?"

"Sleep in the street. If you're lucky the monitors will leave you alone."

"Some quiet back alley, I suppose."

"No," he says. "You sleep in an out-of-the-way place and you'll surely get sliced up by night bandits. Go to one of the designated sleeping streets. In the middle of a big crowd you might just go unnoticed, even though you're under surveillance." As he speaks he moves about the shop, closing it down for the night. He looks restless and uncomfortable. I take out my map of Conning Town and he shows me where to go. The map is some years out of date, apparently; he corrects it with irritable swipes of his pencil. We leave the shop together. I invite him to come with me to some restaurant as my guest, but he looks at me as if I carry plague. "Good-by," he says. "Good luck."

VII

Alone, apart from the handful of other diners, I take my evening meal at a squalid, dimly lit automated cafeteria at the edge of downtown. Silent machines offer me thin acrid soup, pale spongy bread, and a leaden stew containing lumpy ingredients of undeterminable origin, for which I pay with yellow plastic counters of Conning Town currency. Emerging undelighted, I observe a reddish glow in the western sky. It may be a lovely sunset or, for all I know, it may be a sign that Ganfield is burning. I look about for monitors. My four-hour grace period has nearly expired. I must disappear shortly into a throng. It seems too early for sleep, but I am only a few blocks from the place where the bookshop clerk suggested I should pass the night, and I go to it. Just as well; when I reach it—a wide plaza bordered by gray buildings of ornate facade— I find it already filling up with street-sleepers. There must be eight hundred of them, men, women, family groups, settling down in little squares of cobbled territory that are obviously claimed night after night under some system of squatters' rights. Others constantly arrive, flowing inward from the plaza's three entrances, finding

their places, laying out foam cushions or mounds
of clothing as their mattresses. It is a friendly
crowd; these people are linked by bonds of neigh-
borliness, a common poverty. They laugh, embrace,
play games of chance, exchange whispered confi-
dences, bicker, transact business, and join together
in the rites of the local religion, performing a routine that involves six people clasping hands and
chanting. Privacy seems obsolete here. They un-
dress freely before one another and there are in-
stances of open coupling. The gaiety of the scene—
a medieval carnival is what it suggests to me, a
Brueghelesque romp—is marred only by my awareness that this horde of revelers is homeless under
the inhospitable skies, vulnerable to rain, sleet,
damp fog, snow, and the other unkindnesses of winter and summer in these latitudes. In Ganfield we
have just a scattering of street-sleepers, those who
have lost their residential licenses and are tempo-
rarily forced into the open, but here it seems to be
an established institution, as though Conning Town
declared a moratorium some years ago on new residential construction without at the same time
checking the increase of population.

Stepping over and around and between people,
I reach the center of the plaza and select an unoccupied bit of pavement. But in a moment a little
ruddy-faced woman arrives, excited and animated,
and with a Conning Town accent so thick I can
barely understand her, she tells me she holds claim
here. Her eyes are bright with menace; her hands
are not far from becoming claws; several nearby
squatters sit up and regard me threateningly. I
apologize for my error and withdraw, stumbling

over a child and narrowly missing overturning a bubbling cooking pot. Onward. Not here. Not here. A hand emerges from a pile of blankets and strokes my leg as I look around in perplexity. Not here. A man with a painted face rises out of a miniature green tent and speaks to me in a language I do not understand. Not here. I move on again and again, thinking that I will be jostled out of the plaza entirely, excluded, disqualified even to sleep in this district's streets, but finally I find a cramped corner where the occupants indicate I am welcome. "Yes?" I say. They grin and gesture. Gratefully I seize the spot.

Darkness has come. The plaza continues to fill; at least a thousand people have arrived after me, cramming into every vacancy, and the flow does not abate. I hear booming laughter, idle chatter, earnest romantic persuasion, the brittle sound of domestic quarreling. Someone passes a jug of wine around, even to me; bitter stuff, fermented clam juice its probable base, but I appreciate the gesture. The night is warm, almost sticky. The scent of unfamiliar food drifts on the air—something sharp, spicy, a heavy, pungent smell. Curry? Is this then truly Calcutta? I close my eyes and huddle into myself. The hard cobblestones are cold beneath me. I have no mattress and I feel unable to remove my clothes before so many strangers. It will be hard for me to sleep in this madhouse, I think. But gradually the hubbub diminishes and—exhausted, drained—I slide into a deep, troubled sleep.

Ugly dreams. The asphyxiating pressure of a surging mob. Rivers leaping their channels. Towers toppling. Fountains of mud bursting from a thousand lofty windows. Bands of steel encircling my thighs; my legs, useless, withering away. A torrent of lice sweeping over me. A frosty hand touching me. Touching me. Touching me. Pulling me up from sleep.

Harsh white light drenches me. I blink, cringe, cover my eyes. Shortly I perceive that a monitor stands over me. About me the sleepers are awake, backing away, murmuring, pointing.

"Your street-sleeping permit, please."

Caught. I mumble excuses, plead ignorance of the law, beg forgiveness. But a police machine is neither malevolent nor merciful; it merely follows its program. It demands my passport and scans my visa. Then it reminds me I have been under surveillance. Having failed to obtain a hotel room as ordered, having neglected to report to a monitor within the prescribed interval, I am subject to expulsion.

"Very well," I say. "Conduct me to the border of Hawk Nest."

"You will return at once to Ganfield."

"I have business in Hawk Nest."

"Illegal entrants are returned to their district of origin."

"What does it matter to you where I go, so long as I get out of Conning Town?"

"Illegal entrants are returned to their district of origin," the machine tells me inexorably.

I dare not go back with so little accomplished. Still arguing with the monitor, I am led from the plaza through dark cavernous streets toward the mouth of a transit tube. On the station level a second monitor is given charge of me. "In three hours," the monitor that apprehended me informs me, "the Ganfield-bound train will arrive."

The first monitor rolls away.

Too late I realize that the machine has neglected to return my passport.

VIII

Monitor number two shows little interest in me. Patrolling the tube station, it swings in a wide arc around me, keeping a scanner perfunctorily trained on me but making no attempt to interfere with what I do. If I try to flee, of course, it will destroy me. Fretfully I study my maps. Hawk Nest lies to the northeast of Conning Town; if this is the tube station that I think it is, the border is not far. Five minutes' walk, perhaps. Passportless, there is no place I can go except Ganfield; my commuter status is revoked. But legalities count for little in Hawk Nest.

How to escape?

I concoct a plan. Its simplicity seems absurd, yet absurdity is often useful when dealing with machines. The monitor is instructed to put me aboard the train for Ganfield, yes. But not necessarily to keep me there.

I wait out the weary hours to dawn. I hear the crash of compressed air far up the tunnel. Snub-nosed, silken-smooth, the train slides into the station. The monitor orders me aboard. I walk into the car, cross it quickly, and exit by the open door on the far side of the platform. Even if the monitor has observed this maneuver, it can hardly fire across a crowded train. As I leave the car I break into a trot, darting past startled travelers, and sprint upstairs into the misty morning. At street level, running is unwise. I drop back to a rapid walking pace and melt into the throngs of early workers. The street is Crystal Boulevard. Good. I have memorized a route: Crystal Boulevard to Flagstone Square, thence via Mechanic Street to the border.

Presumably all monitors, linked to whatever central nervous system the machines of the district of Conning Town utilize, have instantaneously been apprised of my disappearance. But that is not the same as knowing where to find me. I head northward on Crystal Boulevard—its name shows a dark sense of irony, or else the severe transformations time can work—and, borne by the flow of pedestrian traffic, enter Flagstone Square, a grimy, lopsided plaza out of which, on the left, snakes curving Mechanic Street. I go unintercepted on this thoroughfare of small shops. The place to anticipate trouble is at the border.

I am there in a few minutes. It is a wide, dusty street, silent and empty, lined on the Conning Town side by a row of blocky brick warehouses, on the Hawk Nest side by a string of low, ragged buildings, some in ruins, the best of them defiantly slatternly. There is no barrier. To fence a district border is unlawful except in time of war, and I have heard of no war between Conning Town and Hawk Nest.

Dare I cross? Police machines of two species patrol the street: flat-domed ones of Conning Town and black hexagon-headed ones of Hawk Nest. Surely one or the other will gun me down in the no man's land between districts. But I have no choice. I must keep going forward.

I run out into the street at a moment when two police machines, passing each other on opposite or-bits, have left an unpatrolled space perhaps a block long. Midway in my crossing the Conning Town monitor spies me and blares a command. The words are unintelligible to me and I keep running, zigzagging in the hope of avoiding the bolt that very likely will follow. But the machine does not shoot; I must already be on the Hawk Nest side of the line and Conning Town no longer cares what becomes of me.

The Hawk Nest machine has noticed me. It rolls toward me as I stumble, breathless and gasping, onto the curb. "Halt!" it cries. "Present your docu-ments!" At that moment a red-bearded man, fierce-eyed, wide-shouldered, steps out of a decaying building close by me. A scheme assembles itself in my mind. Do the customs of sponsorship and sanctuary hold good in this harsh district?

"Brother!" I cry. "What luck!" I embrace him, and before he can fling me off I murmur, "I am from Ganfield. I seek sanctuary here. Help me!"

The machine has reached me. It goes into an interrogatory stance and I say, "This is my brother who offers me the privilege of sanctuary. Ask him! Ask him!"

"Is this true?" the machine inquires.

Redbeard, unsmiling, spits and mutters, "My brother, yes. A political refugee. I'll stand sponsor to him. I vouch for him. Let him be."

The machine clicks, hums, assimilates. To me it

says, "You will register as a sponsored refugee within twelve hours or leave Hawk Nest." Without another word it rolls away.

I offer my sudden savior warm thanks. He scowls, shakes his head, spits once again. "We owe each other nothing," he says brusquely, and goes striding down the street.

IX

In Hawk Nest nature has followed art. The name, I have heard, once had purely neutral connotations: some real-estate developer's high-flown metaphor, nothing more. Yet it determined the district's character, for gradually Hawk Nest became the home of predators that it is today, where all men are strangers, where every man is his brother's enemy.

Other districts have their slums. Hawk Nest *is* a slum. I am told they live here by looting, cheating, extorting, and manipulating. An odd economic base for an entire community, but maybe it works for them. The atmosphere is menacing. The only police machines seem to be those that patrol the border. I sense emanations of violence just beyond the corner of my eye: rapes and garrotings in shadowy byways, flashing knives and muffled groans, covert cannibal feasts. Perhaps my imagination works too hard. Certainly I have gone unthreatened so far; those I meet on the streets pay no heed to me, indeed will not even return my glance. Still, I keep my heat-pistol close by my hand as I walk through these shabby, deteriorating outskirts. Sinister faces peer at me through cracked, dirt-veiled windows. If I am attacked, will I have to fire in order to defend myself? God spare me from having to answer that.

X

Why is there a bookshop in this town of murder and rubble and decay? Here is Box Street, and here, in an oily pocket of spare-parts depots and flyspecked quick-lunch counters, is Nate and Holly Borden's place. Five times as deep as it is broad, dusty, dimly lit, shelves overflowing with old books and pamphlets, an improbable outpost of the nineteenth century, somehow displaced in time. There is no one in it but a large, impassive woman seated at the counter, fleshy, puffy-faced, motionless. Her eyes, oddly intense, glitter like glass disks set in a mound of dough. She regards me without curiosity.

I say, "I'm looking for Holly Borden."

"You've found her," she replies, deep in the baritone range.

"I've come across from Ganfield by way of Conning Town."

No response from her to this.

I continue, "I'm traveling without a passport. They confiscated it in Conning Town and I ran the border."

She nods. And waits. No show of interest.

"I wonder if you could sell me a copy of *Walden Three*," I say.

Now she stirs a little. "Why do you want one?"

"I'm curious about it. It's not available in Ganfield."

"How do you know I have one?"

"Is anything illegal in Hawk Nest?"

She seems annoyed that I have answered a question with a question. "How do you know *I* have a copy of that book?"

"A bookshop clerk in Conning Town said you might."

A pause. "All right. Suppose I do. Did you come all the way from Ganfield just to buy a book?" Suddenly she leans forward and smiles—a warm, keen, penetrating smile that wholly transforms her face: now she is keyed-up, alert, responsive, shrewd, commanding. "What's your game?" she asks.

"My game?"

"What are you playing? What are you up to here?"

It is the moment for total honesty. "I'm looking for a woman named Silena Ruiz, from Ganfield. Have you heard of her?"

"Yes. She's not in Hawk Nest."

"I think she's in Kingston. I'd like to find her."

"Why? To arrest her?"

"Just to talk to her. I have plenty to discuss with her. She was my month-wife when she left Ganfield."

"The month must be nearly up," Holly Borden says.

"Even so," I reply. "Can you help me reach her?"

"Why should I trust you?"

"Why not?"

She ponders that briefly. She studies my face. I feel the heat of her scrutiny. At length she says, "I expect to be making a journey to Kingston soon. I suppose I could take you with me."

XI

She opens a trap door; I descend into a room beneath the bookshop. After a good many hours a thin, gray-haired man brings me a tray of food. "Call me Nate," he says. Overhead I hear indistinct conversations, laughter, the thumping of boots on the wooden floor. In Ganfield, famine may be setting in by now. Rats will be dancing around Ganfield Hold. How long will they keep me here? Am I a prisoner? Two days. Three. Nate will answer no questions. I have books, a cot, a sink, a drinking glass. On the third day the trap door opens. Holly Borden peers down. "We're ready to leave," she says.

The expedition consists of just the two of us. She is going to Kingston to buy books and travels on a commercial passport that allows for one helper. Nate drives us to the tube-mouth in midafternoon. It no longer seems unusual to me to be passing from district to district; they are not such alien and hostile places, merely different from the place I know. I see myself bound on an odyssey that carries me across hundreds of districts, even thousands, the whole patchwork frenzy of our world. Why return to Ganfield? Why not go on, ever eastward, to the great ocean and beyond, to the unimaginable strangenesses on the far side?

Here we are in Kingston. An old district, one of the oldest. We are the only ones who journey hither today from Hawk Nest. There is only a perfunctory inspection of passports. The police machines of Kingston are tall, long-armed, with fluted bodies ornamented in stripes of red and green: quite a gay effect. I am becoming an expert in local

variations of police-machine design. Kingston itself
is a district of low pastel buildings arranged in
spokelike boulevards radiating from the famed university that is its chief enterprise. No one from
Ganfield has been admitted to the university in
my memory.

Holly is expecting friends to meet her, but they
have not come. We wait fifteen minutes. "Never
mind," she says. "We'll walk." I carry the luggage.
The air is soft and mild; the sun, sloping toward
Folkstone and Budleigh, is still high. I feel oddly
serene. It is as if I have perceived a divine purpose,
an overriding plan, in the structure of our society,
in our sprawling city of many cities, our network
of steel and concrete clinging like an armor of
scales to the skin of our planet. But what is that
purpose? What is that plan? The essence of it
eludes me; I am aware only that it must exist. A
cheery delusion.

Fifty paces from the station we are abruptly surrounded by a dozen or more buoyant young men
who emerge from an intersecting street. They are
naked but for green loincloths; their hair and
beards are untrimmed and unkempt; they have a
fierce and barbaric look. Several carry long un-
sheathed knives strapped to their waists. They circle wildly around us, laughing, jabbing at us with
their fingertips. "This is a holy district!" they cry.
"We need no blasphemous strangers here! Why
must you intrude on us?"

"What do they want?" I whisper. "Are we in
danger?"

"They are a band of priests," Holly replies. "Do
as they say and we will come to no harm."

They press close. Leaping, dancing, they shower us with sprays of perspiration. "Where are you from?" they demand. "Ganfield," I say. "Hawk Nest," says Holly. They seem playful yet dangerous. Surging about me, they empty my pockets in a series of quick, jostling forays: I lose my heat-pistol, my maps, my useless letters of introduction, my various currencies, everything, even my suicide capsule. These things they pass among themselves, exclaiming over them; then the heat-pistol and some of the currency are returned to me. "Ganfield," they murmur. "Hawk Nest!" There is distaste in their voices. "Filthy places," they say. "Places scorned by God," they say. They seize our hands and haul us about, making us spin. Heavy-bodied Holly is surprisingly graceful, breaking into a serene lumbering dance that makes them applaud in wonder.

One, the tallest of the group, catches our wrists and says, "What is your business in Kingston?"

"I come to purchase books," Holly declares.

"I come to find my month-wife Silena," say I.

"Silena! Silena! Silena!" Her name becomes a jubilant incantation on their lips. "His month-wife! Silena! His month-wife! Silena! Silena! Silena!"

The tall one thrusts his face against mine and says, "We offer you a choice. Come and make prayer with us or die on the spot."

"We choose to pray," I tell him.

They tug at our arms, urging us impatiently onward. Down street after street until at last we arrive at holy ground: a garden plot, insignificant in area, planted with unfamiliar bushes and flowers, tended with evident care. They push us aside.

"Kneel," they say.

"Kiss the sacred earth."

"Adore the things that grow in it, strangers."

"Give thanks to God for the breath you have just drawn."

"And for the breath you are about to draw."

"Sing!"

"Weep!"

"Laugh!"

"Touch the soil!"

"Worship!"

XII

Silena's room is cool and quiet, in the upper story of a residence overlooking the university grounds. She wears a soft green robe of coarse texture, no jewelry, no face paint. Her demeanor is calm and self-assured. I had forgotten the delicacy of her features, the cool, malicious sparkle of her dark eyes.

"The master program?" she says, smiling. "I destroyed it!"

The depth of my love for her unnerves me. Standing before her, I feel my knees turning to water. In my eyes she is bathed in a glittering aura of sensuality. I struggle to control myself. "You destroyed nothing," I say. "Your voice betrays the lie."

"You think I still have the program?"

"I know you do."

"Well, yes," she admits coolly. "I do."

My fingers tremble. My throat parches. An adolescent foolishness seeks to engulf me.

"Why did you steal it?" I ask.

"Out of love of mischief."

"I see the lie in your smile. What was the true reason?"

"Does it matter?"

"The district is paralyzed, Silena. Thousands of people suffer. We are at the mercy of raiders from adjoining districts. Many have already died of the heat, the stink of garbage, the failure of the hospital equipment. Why did you take the program?"

"Perhaps I had political reasons."

"Which were?"

"To demonstrate to the people of Ganfield how utterly dependent on these machines they have allowed themselves to become."

"We knew that already," I say. "If you meant only to dramatize our weaknesses, you were pressing the obvious. What was the point of crippling us? What could you gain from it?"

"Amusement?"

"Something more than that. You're not that shallow, Silena."

"Something more than that, then. By crippling Ganfield I help to change things. That's the purpose of any political act. To display the need for change, so that change may come about."

"Simply displaying the need is not enough."

"It's a place to begin."

"Do you think stealing our program was a rational way to bring change, Selena?"

"Are you happy?" she retorts. "Is this the kind of world you want?"

"It's the world we have to live in, whether we like it or not. And we need that program in order to go on coping. Without it we are plunged into chaos."

"Fine. Let chaos come. Let everything fall apart so we can rebuild it."

"Easy enough to say, Silena. What about the innocent victims of your revolutionary zeal, though?"

She shrugs. "There are always innocent victims in any revolution." In a sinuous movement she rises and approaches me. The closeness of her body is dazzling and maddening. With exaggerated voluptuousness she croons, "Stay here. Forget Ganfield. Life is good here. These people are building something worth having."

"Let me have the program," I say.

"They must have replaced it by now."

"Replacing it is impossible. The program is vital to Ganfield, Silena. Let me have it."

She emits an icy laugh.

"I beg you, Silena."

"How boring you are!"

"I love you."

"You love nothing but the status quo. The shape of things as they are gives you great joy. You have the soul of a bureaucrat."

"If you have always had such contempt for me, why did you become my month-wife?"

She laughs again. "For sport, perhaps."

Her words are like knives. Suddenly, to my own astonishment, I am brandishing the heat-pistol. "Give me the program or I'll kill you!" I cry.

She is amused. "Go. Shoot. Can you get the program from a dead Silena?"

"Give it to me."

"How silly you look holding that gun!"

"I don't have to kill you," I tell her. "I can merely wound you. This pistol is capable of inflicting light burns that scar the skin. Shall I give you blemishes, Silena?"

"Whatever you wish. I'm at your mercy."

I aim the pistol at her thigh. Silena's face remains expressionless. My arm stiffens and begins to quiver. I struggle with the rebellious muscles, but I succeed in steadying my aim only for a moment before the tremors return. An exultant gleam enters her eyes. A flush of excitement spreads over her face. "Shoot," she says defiantly. "Why don't you shoot me?"

She knows me too well. We stand in a frozen tableau for an endless moment outside time—a minute, an hour, a second?—and then my arm sags to my side. I put the pistol away. It never would have been possible for me to fire it. A powerful feeling assails me of having passed through some subtle climax; it will all be downhill from here for me, and we both know it. Sweat drenches me. I feel defeated, broken.

Silena's features reveal intense scorn. She has attained some exalted level of consciousness in these past few months where all acts become gratuitous, where love and hate and revolution and betrayal and loyalty are indistinguishable from one another. She smiles the smile of someone who has scored the winning point in a game the rules of which will never be explained to me.

"You little bureaucrat," she says calmly. "Here!"

From a closet she brings forth a small parcel which she tosses disdainfully to me. It contains a drum of computer film. "The program?" I ask.

"This must be some joke. You wouldn't actually give it to me, Silena."

"You hold the master program of Ganfield in your hand,"

"Really, now?"

"Really really," she says. "The authentic item. Go on. Go. Get out. Save your stinking Ganfield."

"Silena—"

"Go."

XIII

The rest is tedious but simple. I locate Holly Borden, who has purchased a load of books. I help her with them, and we return via tube to Hawk Nest. There I take refuge beneath the bookshop once more while a call is routed through Old Grove, Parley Close, The Mill, and possibly some other districts to the district captain of Ganfield. It takes two days to complete the circuit, since district rivalries make a roundabout relay necessary. Ultimately I am connected and convey my happy news: I have the program, though I have lost my passport and am forbidden to cross Conning Town. Through diplomatic channels a new passport is conveyed to me a few days later, and I take the tube home the long way, via Budleigh, Cedar Mall, and Morton Court. Ganfield is hideous, all filth and disarray, close to the point of irreversible collapse; its citizens have lapsed into a deadly stasis and await their doom placidly. But I have returned with the program.

The captain praises my heroism. I will be rewarded, he says. I will have promotion to the highest ranks of the civil service, with hope of ascent to the district council.

But I take pale pleasure from his words. Silena's contempt still governs my thoughts. *Bureaucrat. Bureaucrat.*

XIV

Still, Ganfield is saved. The police machines have begun to move again.

War Game

PHILIP K. DICK

Philip K. Dick (1928–1982) wrote novels and stories which examined "reality" in all of its myriad forms, letting his protagonists, along with his readers, try to sort out what was real and what wasn't. His novel *The Man in the High Castle* won the Hugo award in 1962, and he also received the John W. Campbell Memorial award. His work has also inspired films, most notably the Ridley Scott-directed *Blade Runner*.

In his office at the Terran Import Bureau of Standards, the tall man gathered up the morning's memos from their wire basket, and, seating himself at his desk, arranged them for reading. He put on his iris lenses, lit a cigarette.

"Good morning," the first memo said in its tinny, chattery voice, as Wiseman ran his thumb along the line of pasted tape. Staring off through the open window at the parking lot, he listened to it idly. "Say look, what's wrong with you people down there? We sent that lot of—" a pause as the speaker, the sales manager of a chain of New York department stores, found his records—"those Ganymedean toys. You realize we have to get them approved in time for the autumn buying plan, so we can get them stocked for Christmas." Grumbling, the sales manager concluded, "War games are going to be an important item again this year. We intend to buy big."

Wiseman ran his thumb down to the speaker's name and title.

"Joe Hauck," the memo-voice chattered. "Appeley's Children's Store."

To himself, Wiseman said, "Ah." He put down the memo, got a blank and prepared to reply. And then he said, half-aloud, "Yes, what about that lot of Ganymedean toys?"

It seemed like a long time that the testing labs had been on them. At least two weeks.

Of course, any Ganymedean products got special attention these days; the Moons had, during the last year, gotten beyond their usual state of economic greed and had begun—according to intelligence circles—mulling overt military action against competitive interests, of which the Inner Three planets could be called the foremost element. But so far nothing had shown up. Exports remained of adequate quality, with no special jokers, no toxic paint to be licked off, no capsules of bacteria.

And yet . . .

Any group of people as inventive as the Ganymedeans could be expected to show creativity in whatever field they entered. Subversion would be tackled like any other venture—with imagination and a flair for wit.

Wiseman got to his feet and left his office, in the direction of the separate building in which the testing labs operated.

*　　*　　*

Surrounded by half-disassembled consumers' products, Pinario looked up to see his boss, Leon Wiseman, shutting the final door of the lab.

"I'm glad you came down," Pinario said, although actually he was stalling; he knew that he was at least five days behind in his work, and this session was going to mean trouble. "Better put on a prophylaxis suit—don't want to take risks." He spoke pleasantly, but Wiseman's expression remained dour.

"I'm here about those inner-citadel-storming shock troops at six dollars a set," Wiseman said, strolling among the stacks of many-sized unopened products waiting to be tested and released.

"Oh, that set of Ganymedean toy soldiers," Pinario said with relief. His conscience was clear on that item; every tester in the labs knew the special instructions handed down by the Cheyenne Government on the Dangers of Contamination from Culture Particles Hostile to Innocent Urban Populations, a typically muddy ukase from officialdom. He could always—legitimately—fall back and cite the number of that directive. "I've got them off by themselves," he said, walking over to accompany Wiseman, "due to the special danger involved."

"Let's have a look," Wiseman said. "Do you believe there's anything in this caution, or is it more paranoia about 'alien milieux'?"

Pinario said, "It's justified, especially where children's artifacts are concerned."

A few hand-signals, and a slab of wall exposed a side room.

Propped up in the center was a sight that caused

Wiseman to halt. A plastic life-size dummy of a child, perhaps five years in appearance, wearing ordinary clothes, sat surrounded by toys. At this moment, the dummy was saying, "I'm tired of that. Do something else." It paused a short time, and then repeated, "I'm tired of that. Do something else."

The toys on the floor, triggered to respond to oral instructions, gave up their various occupations and started afresh.

"It saves on labor costs," Pinario explained. "This is a crop of junk that's got an entire repertoire to go through, before the buyer has his money's worth. If we stuck around to keep them active, we'd be in here all the time."

Directly before the dummy was the group of Ganymedean soldiers, plus the citadel which they had been built to storm. They had been sneaking up on it in an elaborate pattern, but, at the dummy's utterance, they had halted. Now they were regrouping.

"You're getting this all on tape?" Wiseman asked.

"Oh, yes," Pinario said.

The model soldiers stood approximately six inches high, made from the almost indestructible thermoplastic compounds that the Ganymedean manufacturers were famous for. Their uniforms were synthetic, a hodgepodge of various military costumes from the Moons and nearby planets. The citadel itself, a block of ominous dark metal-like stuff, resembled a legendary fort; peep-holes dotted its upper surfaces, a drawbridge had been drawn up out of sight, and from the top turret a gaudy flag waved.

With a whistling pop, the citadel fired a projectile at its attackers. The projectile exploded in a cloud of harmless smoke and noise, among a cluster of soldiers.

"It fights back," Wiseman observed.

"But ultimately it loses," Pinario said. "It has to. Psychologically speaking, it symbolizes the external reality. The dozen soldiers, of course, represent to the child his own efforts to cope. By participating in the storming of the citadel, the child undergoes a sense of adequacy in dealing with the harsh world. Eventually he prevails, but only after a painstaking period of effort and patience." He added, "Anyhow, that's what the instruction booklet says." He handed Wiseman the booklet.

Glancing over the booklet, Wiseman asked, "And their pattern of assault varies each time?"

"We've had it running for eight days now. The same pattern hasn't cropped up twice. Well, you've got quite a few units involved."

The soldiers were sneaking around, gradually nearing the citadel. On the walls, a number of monitoring devices appeared and began tracking the soldiers. Utilizing other toys being tested, the soldiers concealed themselves.

"They can incorporate accidental configurations of terrain," Pinario explained. "They're object-tropic; when they see, for example, a dollhouse here for testing, they climb into it like mice. They'll be all through it." To prove his point, he picked up a large toy spaceship manufactured by a Uranian company; shaking it, he spilled two soldiers from it.

"How many times do they take the citadel," Wiseman asked, "on a percentage basis?"

"So far, they've been successful one out of nine tries. There's an adjustment in the back of the citadel. You can set it for a higher yield of successful tries."

He threaded a path through the advancing soldiers; Wiseman accompanied him, and they bent down to inspect the citadel.

"This is actually the power supply," Pinario said. "Cunning. Also, the instructions to the soldiers emanate from it. High-frequency transmission, from a shot-box."

Opening the back of the citadel, he showed his boss the container of shot. Each shot was an instruction iota. For an assault pattern, the shot were tossed up, vibrated, allowed to settle in a new sequence. Randomness was thereby achieved. But since there was a finite number of shot, there had to be a finite number of patterns.

"We're trying them all," Pinario said.

"And there's no way to speed it up?"

"It'll just have to take time. It may run through a thousand patterns and then—"

"The next one," Wiseman finished, "may have them make a ninety-degree turn and start firing at the nearest human being."

Pinario said somberly, "Or worse. There're a good deal of ergs in that power pack. It's made to put out for five years. But if it all went into something simultaneously—"

"Keep testing," Wiseman said.

They looked at each other and then at the citadel. The soldiers had by now almost reached it.

Suddenly one wall of the citadel flapped down; a gun-muzzle appeared, and the soldiers had been flattened.

"I never saw that before," Pinario murmured.

For a moment, nothing stirred. And then the lab's child-dummy, seated among its toys, said, "I'm tired of that. Do something else."

With a tremor of uneasiness, the two men watched the soldiers pick themselves up and regroup.

Two days later, Wiseman's superior, a heavy-set, short, angry man with popping eyes, appeared in his office. "Listen," Fowler said, "you get those damn toys out of testing. I'll give you until tomorrow." He started back out, but Wiseman stopped him.

"This is too serious," he said. "Come down to the lab and I'll show you."

Arguing all the way, Fowler accompanied him to the lab. "You have no concept of the capital some of these firms have invested in this stuff!" he was saying as they entered. "For every product you've got represented here, there's a ship or a warehouse full on Luna, waiting for official clearance so it can come in!"

Pinario was nowhere in sight. So Wiseman used his key, bypassing the hand-signals that opened up the testing room.

There, surrounded by toys, sat the dummy that the lab men had built. Around it the numerous toys went through their cycles. The racket made Fowler wince.

"This is the item in particular," Wiseman said,

bending down by the citadel. A soldier was in the process of squirming on his belly toward it. "As you can see, there are a dozen soldiers. Given that many, and the energy available to them, plus the complex instruction data—"

Fowler interrupted. "I see only eleven."

"One's probably hiding," Wiseman said.

From behind them, a voice said, "No, he's right." Pinario, a rigid expression on his face, appeared. "I've been having a search made. One is gone."

The three men were silent.

"Maybe the citadel destroyed him," Wiseman finally suggested.

Pinario said, "There's a law of matter dealing with that. If it 'destroyed' him—*what did it do with the remains*?"

"Possibly converted him into energy," Fowler said, examining the citadel and the remaining soldiers.

"We did something ingenious," Pinario said, "when we realized that a soldier was gone. We weighed the remaining eleven plus the citadel. Their combined weight is exactly equal to that of the original set—the original dozen soldiers and the citadel. So he's in there somewhere." He pointed at the citadel, which at the moment was pinpointing the soldiers advancing toward it.

Studying the citadel, Wiseman had a deep intuitive feeling. It had changed. It was, in some manner, different.

"Run your tapes," Wiseman said.

"What?" asked Pinario, and then he flushed. "Of course." Going to the child-dummy, he shut it off, opened it, and removed the drum of video recording tape. Shakily, he carried it to the projector.

They sat watching the recording sequences flash by: one assault after another, until the three of them were bleary-eyed. The soldiers advanced, retreated, were fired on, picked themselves up, advanced again . . .

"Stop the transport," Wiseman said suddenly.

The last sequence was re-run.

A soldier moved steadily toward the base of the citadel. A missile, fired at him, exploded and for a time obscured him. Meanwhile, the other eleven soldiers scurried in a wild attempt to mount the walls. The soldier emerged from the cloud of dust and continued. He reached the wall. A section slid back.

The soldier, blending with the dingy wall of the citadel, used the end of his rifle as a screwdriver to remove his head, then one arm, then both legs. The disassembled pieces were passed into the aperture of the citadel. When only the arm and rifle remained, that, too, crawled into the citadel, worming blindly, and vanished. The aperture slid out of existence.

After a long time, Fowler said in a hoarse voice, "The presumption by the parent would be that the child had lost or destroyed one of the soldiers. Gradually the set would dwindle—with the child getting the blame."

Pinario said, "What do you recommend?"

"Keep it in action," Fowler said, with a nod from Wiseman. "Let it work out its cycle. But don't leave it alone."

"I'll have somebody in the room with it from now on," Pinario agreed.

"Better yet, stay with it yourself," Fowler said.

To himself, Wiseman thought: Maybe we all better stay with it. At least two of us, Pinario and myself.

I wonder what it did with the pieces, he thought. What did it make?

By the end of the week, the citadel had absorbed four more of the soldiers.

Watching it through a monitor, Wiseman could see in it no visible change. Naturally. The growth would be strictly internal, down out of sight.

On and on the eternal assaults, the soldiers wriggling up, the citadel firing in defense. Meanwhile, he had before him a new series of Ganymedean products. More recent children's toys to be inspected.

"Now what?" he asked himself.

The first was an apparently simple item: a cowboy costume from the ancient American West. At least, so it was described. But he paid only cursory attention to the brochure: the hell with what the Ganymedeans had to say about it.

Opening the box, he laid out the costume. The fabric had a gray, amorphous quality. What a miserably bad job, he thought. It only vaguely resembled a cowboy suit; the lines seemed unformed, hesitant. And the material stretched out of shape as he handled it. He found that he had pulled an entire section of it into a pocket that hung down.

"I don't get it," he said to Pinario. "This won't sell."

"Put it on," Pinario said. "You'll see."

With effort, Wiseman managed to squeeze himself into the suit. "Is it safe?" he asked.

"Yes," Pinario said. "I had it on earlier. This is a more benign idea, but it could be effective. To start it into action, you fantasize."

"Along what lines?"

"Any lines."

The suit made Wiseman think of cowboys, and so he imagined to himself that he was back at the ranch, trudging along the gravel road by the field in which black-faced sheep munched hay with that odd, rapid grinding motion of their lower jaws. He had stopped at the fence—barbed wire and occasional upright posts—and watched the sheep. Then, without warning, the sheep lined up and headed off, in the direction of a shaded hillside beyond his range of vision.

He saw trees, cypress growing against the skyline. A chicken hawk, far up, flapped its wings in a pumping action . . . as if, he thought, it's filling itself with more air, to rise higher. The hawk glided energetically off, then sailed at a leisurely pace. Wiseman looked for a sign of its prey. Nothing but the dry mid-summer fields munched flat by the sheep. Frequent grasshoppers. And, on the road itself, a toad. The toad had burrowed into the loose dirt; only its top part was visible.

As he bent down, trying to get up enough courage to touch the warty top of the toad's head, a man's voice said nearby him, "How do you like it?"

"Fine," Wiseman said. He took a deep breath of the dry grass smell; he filled his lungs. "Hey, how do you tell a female toad from a male toad? By the spots, or what?"

"Why?" asked the man, standing behind him slightly out of sight.

"I've got a toad here."

"Just for the record," the man said, "can I ask you a couple of questions?"

"Sure," Wiseman said.

"How old are you?"

That was easy. "Ten years and four months," he said, with pride.

"Where exactly are you, at this moment?"

"Out in the country, Mr. Gaylord's ranch, where my dad takes me and my mother every weekend when we can."

"Turn around and look at me," the man said. "And tell me if you know me."

With reluctance, he turned from the half-buried toad to look. He saw an adult with a thin face and a long, somewhat irregular nose. "You're the man who delivers the butane gas," he said. "For the butane company." He glanced around, and sure enough, there was the truck, parked by the butane gate. "My dad says butane is expensive, but there's no other—"

The man broke in, "Just for the sake of curiosity, what's the name of the butane company?"

"It's right on the truck," Wiseman said, reading the large painted letters. "Pinario Butane Distributors, Petaluma, California. You're Mr. Pinario."

"Would you be willing to swear that you're ten years old, standing in a field near Petaluma, California?" Mr. Pinario asked.

"Sure." He could see, beyond the field, a range

of wooded hills. Now he wanted to investigate them; he was tired of standing around gabbing. "I'll see you," he said, starting off. "I have to go get some hiking done."

He started running, away from Mr. Pinario, down the gravel road. Grasshoppers leaped away, ahead of him. Gasping, he ran faster and faster.

"Leon!" Mr. Pinario called after him. "You might as well give up! Stop running!"

"I've got business in those hills," Wiseman panted, still jogging along. Suddenly something struck him full force; he sprawled on his hands, tried to get back up. In the dry midday air, something shimmered; he felt fear and pulled away from it. A shape formed, a flat wall . . .

"You won't get to those hills," Mr. Pinario said, from behind him. "Better stay in roughly one place. Otherwise you collide with things."

Wiseman's hands were damp with blood; he had cut himself falling. In bewilderment, he stared down at the blood . . .

Pinario helped him out of the cowboy suit, saying, "It's as unwholesome a toy as you could want. A short period with it on, and the child would be unable to face contemporary reality. Look at you."

Standing with difficulty, Wiseman inspected the suit; Pinario had forcibly taken it from him.

"Not bad," he said in a trembling voice. "It obviously stimulates the withdrawal tendencies already present. I know I've always had a latent retreat fantasy toward my childhood. That particular period, when we lived in the country."

"Notice how you incorporated real elements into

it," Pinario said, "to keep the fantasy going as long as possible. If you'd had time, you would have figured a way of incorporating the lab wall into it, possibly as the side of a barn."

Wiseman admitted, "I—already had started to see the old dairy building, where the farmers brought their market milk."

"In time," Pinario said, "it would have been next to impossible to get you out of it."

To himself, Wiseman thought, If it could do that to an adult, just imagine the effect on a child.

"That other thing you have there," Pinario said, "that game, it's a screwball notion. You feel like looking at it now? It can wait."

"I'm okay," Wiseman said. He picked up the third item and began to open it.

"A lot like the old game of Monopoly," Pinario said. "It's called Syndrome."

The game consisted of a board, plus play money, dice, pieces to represent the players. And stock certificates.

"You acquire stock," Pinario said, "same as in all this kind, obviously." He didn't even bother to look at the instructions. "Let's get Fowler down here and play a hand; it takes at least three."

Shortly, they had the Division Director with them. The three men seated themselves at a table, the game of Syndrome in the center.

"Each player starts out equal with the others," Pinario explained, "same as all this type, and during the play, their statuses change according to the worth of the stock they acquire in various economic syndromes."

The syndromes were represented by small, bright

plastic objects, much like the archaic hotels and houses of Monopoly.

They threw the dice, moved their counters along the board, bid for and acquired property, paid fines, collected fines, went to the "decontamination chamber" for a period. Meanwhile, behind them, the seven model soldiers crept up on the citadel again and again.

"I'm tired of that," the child-dummy said. "Do something else."

The soldiers regrouped. Once more they started out, getting nearer and nearer the citadel.

Restless and irritable, Wiseman said, "I wonder how long that damn thing has to go on before we find out what it's for."

"No telling." Pinario eyed a purple-and-gold share of stock that Fowler had acquired. "I can use that," he said. "That's a heavy uranium mine stock on Pluto. What do you want for it?"

"Valuable property," Fowler murmured, consulting his other stocks. "I might make a trade, though."

How can I concentrate on a game, Wiseman asked himself, when that thing is getting closer and nearer to—God knows what? To whatever it was built to reach. Its critical mass, he thought.

"Just a second," he said in a slow, careful voice. He put down his hand of stocks. "Could that citadel be a pile?"

"Pile of what?" Fowler asked, concerned with his hand.

Wiseman said loudly, "Forget this game."

"An interesting idea," Pinario said, also putting

down his hand. "It's constructing itself into an atomic bomb, piece by piece. Adding until—" He broke off. "No, we thought of that. There're no heavy elements present in it. It's simply a five-year battery, plus a number of small machines controlled by instructions broadcast from the battery itself. You can't make an atomic pile out of that."

"In my opinion," Wiseman said, "we'd be safer getting it out of here." His experience with the cowboy suit had given him a great deal more respect for the Ganymedean artificers. And if the suit was the benign one . . .

Fowler, looking past his shoulder, said, "There are only six soldiers now."

Both Wiseman and Pinario got up instantly. Fowler was right. Only half of the set of soldiers remained. One more had reached the citadel and been incorporated.

"Let's get a bomb expert from the Military Services in here," Wiseman said, "and let him check it. This is out of our department." He turned to his boss, Fowler. "Don't you agree?"

Fowler said, "Let's finish this game first."

"Why?"

"Because we want to be certain about it," Fowler said. But his rapt interest showed that he had gotten emotionally involved and wanted to play to the end of the game. "What will you give me for this share of Pluto stock? I'm open to offers."

He and Pinario negotiated a trade. The game continued for another hour. At last, all three of them could see that Fowler was gaining control of the various stocks. He had five mining syndromes, plus two plastics firms, an algae monopoly, and all seven of the retail trading syndromes. Due to his control of the stock, he had, as a by-product, gotten most of the money.

"I'm out," Pinario said. All he had left were minor shares which controlled nothing. "Anybody want to buy these?"

With his last remaining money, Wiseman bid for the shares. He got them and resumed playing, this time against Fowler alone.

"It's clear that this game is a replica of typical interculture economic ventures," Wiseman said. "The retail trading syndromes are obviously Ganymedean holdings."

A flicker of excitement stirred in him; he had gotten a couple of good throws with the dice and was in a position to add a share to his meager holdings. "Children playing this would acquire a healthy attitude toward economic realities. It would prepare them for the adult world."

But a few minutes later, he landed on an enormous tract of Fowler holdings, and the fine wiped out his resources. He had to give up two shares of stock; the end was in sight.

Pinario, watching the soldiers advance toward the citadel, said, "You know, Leon, I'm inclined to agree with you. This thing may be one terminal of a bomb. A receiving station of some kind. When it's completely wired up, it might bring in a surge of power transmitted from Ganymede."

"Is such a thing possible?" Fowler asked, stacking his play money into the different denominations.

"Who knows what they can do?" Pinario said,

wandering around with his hands in his pockets. "Are you almost finished playing?"

"Just about," Wiseman said.

"The reason I say that," Pinario said, "is that now there're only five soldiers. It's speeding up. It took a week for the first one, and only an hour for the seventh. I wouldn't be surprised if the rest go within the next two hours, all five of them."

"We're finished," Fowler said. He had acquired the last share of stock and the last dollar.

Wiseman arose from the table, leaving Fowler. "I'll call Military Services to check the citadel. About this game, though, it's nothing but a steal from our Terran game Monopoly."

"Possibly they don't realize that we have the game already," Fowler said, "under another name."

A stamp of admissibility was placed on the game of Syndrome and the importer was informed. In his office, Wiseman called Military Services and told them what he wanted.

"A bomb expert will be right over," the unhurried voice at the other end of the line said. "Probably you should leave the object alone until he arrives."

Feeling somewhat useless, Wiseman thanked the clerk and hung up. They had failed to dope out the soldiers-and-the citadel war game; now it was out of their hands.

The bomb expert was a young man, with close-cropped hair, who smiled friendlily at them as he set down his equipment. He wore ordinary coveralls, with no protective devices.

"My first advice," he said, after he had looked the citadel over, "is to disconnect the leads from the battery. Or, if you want, we can let the cycle finish out, and then disconnect the leads before any reaction takes place. In other words, allow the last mobile elements to enter the citadel. Then, as soon as they're inside, we disconnect the leads and open her up and see what's been taking place."

"Is it safe?" Wiseman asked.

"I think so," the bomb expert said. "I don't detect any sign of radioactivity in it." He seated himself on the floor, by the rear of the citadel, with a pair of cutting pliers in his hand.

Now only three soldiers remained.

"It shouldn't be long," the young man said cheerfully.

Fifteen minutes later, one of the three soldiers crept up to the base of the citadel, removed his head, arm, legs, body, and disappeared piecemeal into the opening provided for him.

"That leaves two," Fowler said.

Ten minutes later, one of the two remaining soldiers followed the one ahead of him.

The four men looked at each other. "This is almost it," Pinario said huskily.

The last remaining soldier wove his way toward the citadel. Guns within the citadel fired at him, but he continued to make progress.

"Statistically speaking," Wiseman said aloud, to break some of the tension, "it should take longer each time, because there are fewer men for it to concentrate on. It should have started out fast, then got more infrequent until finally this last soldier should put in at least a month trying to—"

"Pipe down," the young bomb expert said in a quiet, reasonable voice. "If you don't mind."

The last of the twelve soldiers reached the base of the citadel. Like those before him, he began to disassemble himself.

"Get those pliers ready," Pinario grated.

The parts of the soldier traveled into the citadel. The opening began to close. From within, a humming became audible, a rising pitch of activity.

"Now, for God's sake!" Fowler cried.

The young bomb expert reached down his pliers and cut into the positive lead of the battery. A spark flashed from the pliers and the young bomb expert jumped reflexively; the pliers flew from his hands and skidded across the floor. "Jeez!" he said. "I must have been grounded." Groggily, he groped about for the pliers.

"You were touching the frame of the thing," Pinario said excitedly. He grabbed the pliers himself and crouched down, fumbling for the lead. "Maybe if I wrap a handkerchief around it," he muttered, withdrawing the pliers and fishing in his pocket for a handkerchief. "Anybody got any thing I can wrap around this? I don't want to get knocked flat. No telling how many—"

"Give it to me," Wiseman demanded, snatching the pliers from him. He shoved Pinario aside and closed the jaws of the pliers about the lead.

Fowler said calmly, "Too late."

Wiseman hardly heard his superior's voice; he heard the constant tone within his head, and he put up his hands to his ears, futilely, trying to shut it out. Now it seemed to pass directly from the citadel through his skull, transmitted by the bone. *We stalled around too long,* he thought. *Now it has us.* It won out because there are too many of us; we got to squabbling . . .

Within his mind, a voice said, "Congratulations. By your fortitude, you have been successful."

A vast feeling pervaded him then, a sense of accomplishment.

"The odds against you were tremendous," the voice inside his mind continued. "Anyone else would have failed."

He knew then that everything was all right. They had been wrong.

"What you have done here," the voice declared, "you can continue to do all your life. You can always triumph over adversaries. By patience and persistence, you can win out. The universe isn't such an overwhelming place, after all . . ."

No, he realized with irony, it wasn't.

"They are just ordinary persons," the voice soothed. "So even though you're only one, an individual against many, you have nothing to fear. Give it time—and don't worry."

"I won't," he said aloud.

The humming receded. The voice was gone.

After a long pause, Fowler said, "It's over."

"I don't get it," Pinario said.

"That was what it was supposed to do," Wiseman said. "It's a therapeutic toy. Helps give the child confidence. The disassembling of the soldiers"—he grinned—"ends the separation between him and the world. He becomes one with it. And, in doing so, conquers it."

"Then it's harmless," Fowler said.

"All this work for nothing," Pinario groused. To the bomb expert, he said, "I'm sorry we got you up here for nothing."

The citadel had now opened its gates wide. Twelve soldiers, once more intact, issued forth. The cycle was complete; the assault could begin again.

Suddenly Wiseman said, "I'm not going to release it."

"What?" Pinario said. "Why not?"

"I don't trust it," Wiseman said. "It's too complicated for what it actually does."

"Explain," Fowler demanded.

"There's nothing to explain," Wiseman said. "Here's this immensely intricate gadget, and all it does is take itself apart and then reassemble itself. There *must* be more, even if we can't—"

"It's therapeutic," Pinario put in.

Fowler said, "I'll leave it up to you, Leon. If you have doubts, then don't release it. We can't be too careful."

"Maybe I'm wrong," Wiseman said, "but I keep thinking to myself: *What did they actually build this for*? I feel we still don't know."

"And the American Cowboy Suit," Pinario added. "You don't want to release that either."

"Only the game," Wiseman said. "Syndrome, or whatever it's called." Bending down, he watched the soldiers as they hustled toward the citadel. Bursts of smoke, again . . . activity, feigned attacks, careful withdrawals . . .

"What are you thinking?" Pinario asked, scrutinizing him.

"Maybe it's a diversion," Wiseman said. "To keep our minds involved. So we won't notice something else." That was his intuition, but he couldn't pin it down. "A red herring," he said. "While something else takes place. That's why it's so complicated. We were *supposed* to suspect it. That's why they built it."

Baffled, he put his foot down in front of a soldier. The soldier took refuge behind his shoe, hiding from the monitors of the citadel.

"There must be something right before our eyes," Fowler said, "that we're not noticing."

"Yes." Wiseman wondered if they would ever find it. "Anyhow," he said, "we're keeping it here, where we can observe it."

Seating himself nearby, he prepared to watch the soldiers. He made himself comfortable for a long, long wait.

At six o'clock that evening, Joe Hauck, the sales manager for Appeley's Children's Store, parked his car before his house, got out, and strode up the stairs.

Under his arm he carried a large flat package, a "sample" that he had appropriated.

"Hey!" his two kids, Bobby and Lora, squealed as he let himself in. "You got something for us, Dad?" They crowded around him, blocking his path. In the kitchen, his wife looked up from the table and put down her magazine.

"A new game I picked up for you," Hauck said. He unwrapped the package, feeling genial. There was no reason why he shouldn't help himself to one of the new games; he had been on the phone for weeks, getting the stuff through Import Standards—and after all was said and done, only one of the three items had been cleared.

As the kids went off with the game, his wife said in a low voice, "More corruption in high places." She had always disapproved of his bringing home items from the store's stock.

"We've got thousands of them," Hauck said. "A warehouse full. Nobody'll notice one missing."

At the dinner table, during the meal, the kids scrupulously studied every word of the instructions that accompanied the game. They were aware of nothing else.

"Don't read at the table," Mrs. Hauck said reprovingly.

Leaning back in his chair, Joe Hauck continued his account of the day. "And after all that time, what did they release? One lousy item. We'll be lucky if we can push enough to make a profit. It was that Shock Troop gimmick that would really have paid off. And that's tied up indefinitely."

He lit a cigarette and relaxed, feeling the peacefulness of his home, the presence of his wife and children.

His daughter said, "Dad, do you want to play? It says the more who play, the better."

"Sure," Joe Hauck said.

While his wife cleared the table, he and his children spread out the board, counters, dice and paper money and shares of stock. Almost at once he was deep in the game, totally involved; his childhood memories of game-playing swam back, and he acquired shares of stock with cunning and originality, until, toward the conclusion of the game, he had cornered most of the syndromes.

He settled back with a sigh of contentment. "That's that," he declared to his children. "Afraid I had a head start. After all, I'm not new to this type of game." Getting hold of the valuable holdings on the board filled him with a powerful sense of satisfaction. "Sorry to have to win, kids."

His daughter said, "You didn't win."

"You lost," his son said.

"What?" Joe Hauck exclaimed.

"The person who winds up with the most stock *loses*," Lora said.

She showed him the instructions. "See? The idea is to get rid of your stocks. Dad, you're out of the game."

"The heck with that," Hauck said, disappointed. "That's no kind of game." His satisfaction vanished. "That's no fun."

"Now we two have to play out the game," Bobby said, "to see who finally wins."

As he got up from the board, Joe Hauck grumbled, "I don't get it. What would anybody see in a game where the winner winds up with nothing at all?"

Behind him, his two children continued to play. As stock and money changed hands, the children became more and more animated. When the game entered its final stages, the children were in a state of ecstatic concentration.

"They don't know Monopoly," Hauck said to himself, "so this screwball game doesn't seem strange to them."

Anyhow, the important thing was that the kids enjoyed playing Syndrome; evidently it would sell, and that was what mattered. Already the two youngsters were learning the naturalness of surrendering their holdings. They gave up their stocks and money avidly, with a kind of trembling abandon.

Glancing up, her eyes bright, Lora said, "It's the best educational toy you ever brought home, Dad!"

ARM

LARRY NIVEN

Larry Niven has received the Hugo award four
times for his short fiction, and a Hugo and Nebula
award for his novel *Ringworld.* From his first story,
"The Coldest Place," published in *If* in 1964, he
has carved a wide niche for himself in the field of
hard science fiction. Primarily working in his own
universe called Known Space, his fictional future
involves mankind's first contact with aliens who
are actually fully evolved humans, and the compli-
cations and triumphs that arise from this. Look for
more exciting Gil Hamilton stories in *Flatlander*
(Del Ray Books) as well as a new novel, *The
Ringworld Throne* (Del Ray Books).

The ARM building had been abnormally quiet for
some months now.

We'd needed the rest—at first. But these last few
mornings the silence had had an edgy quality. We
waved at each other on our paths to our respective
desks, but our heads were elsewhere. Some of us
had a restless look. Others were visibly, deter-
minedly busy.

Nobody wanted to join a mother hunt.

This past year we'd managed to cut deep into

the organlegging activities in the West Coast area. Pats on the back all around, but the results were predictable: other activities were going to increase. Sooner or later the newstapers would start screaming about stricter enforcement of the Fertility Laws, and then we'd all be out hunting down illegitimate parents . . . all of us who were not involved in something else.

It was high time I got involved in something else.

This morning I walked to my office through the usual edgy silence. I ran coffee from the spigot, carried it to my desk, punched for messages at the computer terminal. A slender file slid from the slot. A hopeful sign. I picked it up—one-handed, so that I could sip coffee as I went through it—and let it fall open in the middle.

Color holographs jumped out at me. I was looking down through a pair of windows over two morgue tables.

Stomach to brain: LURCH! What a hell of an hour to be looking at people with their faces burnt off! Get eyes to look somewhere else, and don't try to swallow that coffee. Why don't you change jobs?

They were hideous. Two of them, a man and a woman. Something had burnt their faces away down to the skulls and beyond: bones and teeth charred, brain tissue cooked.

I swallowed and kept looking. I'd seen the dead before. These had just hit me at the wrong time.

Not a laser weapon, I thought . . . though that was chancy. There are thousands of jobs for lasers, and thousands of varieties to do the jobs. Not a hand laser, anyway. The pencil-thin beam of a hand laser would have chewed channels in the flesh. This had been a wide, steady beam of some kind.

I flipped back to the beginning and skimmed.

Details: They'd been found on the Wilshire slidewalk in West Los Angeles around 4:30 A.M. People don't use the slidewalks that late. They're afraid of organleggers. The bodies could have traveled up to a couple of miles before anyone saw them.

Preliminary autopsy: They'd been dead three or four days. No signs of drugs or poisons or puncture marks. Apparently the burns had been the only cause of death.

It must have been quick, then: a single flash of energy. Otherwise they'd have tried to dodge, and there'd be burns elsewhere. There were none. Just the faces, and char marks around the collars.

There was a memo from Bates, the coroner. From the looks of them, they might have been killed by some new weapon. So he'd sent the file over to us. Could we find anything in the ARM files that would fire a blast of heat or light a foot across?

I sat back and stared into the holos and thought about it.

A light weapon with a beam a foot across? They make lasers in that size, but as war weapons, used from orbit. One of those would have vaporized the heads, not charred them.

There were other possibilities. Death by torture, with the heads held in clamps in the blast from a commercial attitude jet. Or some kind of weird industrial accident: a flash explosion that had caught them both looking over a desk or something. Or even a laser beam reflected from a convex mirror.

Forget about its being an accident. The way the bodies were abandoned reeked of guilt, of something to be covered up. Maybe Bates was right. A new, illegal weapon.

And I could be deeply involved in searching for it when the mother hunt started.

The ARM has three basic functions. We hunt organleggers. We monitor world technology: new developments that might create new weapons, or that might affect the world economy or the balance of power among nations. And we enforce the Fertility Laws.

Come, let us be honest with ourselves. Of the three, protecting the Fertility Laws is probably the most important.

Organleggers don't aggravate the population problem.

Monitoring of technology is necessary enough, but it may have happened too late. There are enough fusion power plants and fusion rocket motors and fusion crematoria and fusion seawater distilleries around to let any madman or group thereof blow up the Earth or any selected part of it.

But if a lot of people in one region started having illegal babies, the rest of the world would scream. Some nations might even get mad enough to abandon population control. Then what? We've got eighteen billion on Earth now. We couldn't handle more.

So the mother hunts are necessary. But I hate them. It's no fun hunting down some poor sick woman so desperate to have children that she'll go through hell to avoid her six-month contraceptive shots. I'll get out of it if I can.

I did some obvious things. I sent a note to Bates at the coroner's office. *Send all further details on the autopsies, and let me know if the corpses are identified.* Retinal prints and brain-wave patterns were obviously out, but they might get something on gene patterns and fingerprints.

I spent some time wondering where two bodies had been kept for three to four days, and why, before being abandoned in a way that could have been used three days earlier. But that was a problem for the LAPD detectives. Our concern was with the weapon.

So I started writing a search pattern for the computer: find me a widget that will fire a beam of a given description. From the pattern of penetration into skin and bone and brain tissue, there was probably a way to express the frequency of the light as a function of the duration of the blast, but I didn't fool with that. I'd pay for my laziness later, when the computer handed me a foot-thick list of light-emitting machinery and I had to wade through it.

I had punched in the instructions, and was relaxing with more coffee and a cigarette, when Ordaz called.

Detective-Inspector Julio Ordaz was a slender, dark-skinned man with straight black hair and soft black eyes. The first time I saw him in a phone screen, he had been telling me of a good friend's murder. Two years later I still flinched when I saw him.

"Hello, Julio. Business or pleasure?"

"Business, Gil. It is to be regretted."

"Yours or mine?"

"Both. There is murder involved, but there is also a machine . . . Look, can you see it behind me?" Ordaz stepped out of the field of view, then reached invisibly to turn the phone camera.

I looked into somebody's living room. There was a wide circle of discoloration in the green indoor grass rug. In the center of the circle, a machine and a man's body.

Was Julio putting me on? The body was old, half mummified. The machine was big and cryptic in shape, and it glowed with a subdued, eery blue light.

Ordaz sounded serious enough. "Have you ever seen anything like this?"

"No. That's some machine." Unmistakably an experimental device: no neat plastic case, no compactness, no assembly-line welding. Too complex to examine through a phone camera, I decided. "Yah, that looks like something for us. Can you send it over?"

Ordaz came back on. He was smiling, barely. "I'm afraid we cannot do that. Perhaps you should send someone here to look at it."

"Where are you now?"

"In Raymond Sinclair's apartment on the top floor of the Rodewald Building in Santa Monica."

"I'll come myself," I said. My tongue suddenly felt thick.

"Please land on the roof. We are holding the elevator for examination."

"Sure." I hung up.

Raymond Sinclair!

I'd never met Raymond Sinclair. He was something of a recluse. But the ARM had dealt with him once, in connection with one of his inventions, the FyreStop device. And everyone knew that he had lately been working on an interstellar drive. It was only a rumor, of course . . . but if someone had killed the brain that held that secret . . .

I went.

The Rodewald Building was forty stories of triangular prism with a row of triangular balconies going up each side. The balconies stopped at the thirty-eighth floor.

The roof was a garden. There were rose bushes in bloom along one edge, full-grown elms nestled in ivy along another, and a miniature forest of Bonsai trees along the third. The landing pad and carport were in the center. A squad car was floating down ahead of my taxi. It landed, then slid under the carport to give me room to land.

A cop in vivid orange uniform came out to watch me come down. I couldn't tell what he was carrying until I had stepped out. It was a deep-sea fishing pole, still in its kit.

He said, "May I see some ID, please?"

I had my ARM ident in my hand. He checked it in the console in the squad car, then handed it back. "The Inspector's waiting downstairs," he said.

"What's the pole for?"

He smiled suddenly, almost secretively. "You'll see."

We left the garden smells via a flight of concrete stairs. They led down into a small room half full of gardening tools, and a heavy door with a spy-eye in it. Ordaz opened the door for us. He shook my hand briskly, glanced at the cop. "You found something? Good."

The cop said, "There's a sporting goods store six blocks from here. The manager let me borrow it. He made sure I knew the name of the store."

"Yes, there will certainly be publicity on this matter. Come, Gil—" Ordaz took my arm. "You should examine this before we turn it off."

No garden smells here, but there was something—a whiff of something long dead, that the air conditioning hadn't quite cleared away. Ordaz walked me into the living room.

It looked like somebody's idea of a practical joke.

The indoor grass covered Sinclair's living room floor, wall to wall. In a perfect fourteen-foot circle between the sofa and the fireplace, the rug was brown and dead. Elsewhere it was green and thriving.

A man's mummy, dressed in stained slacks and turtleneck, lay on its back in the center of the circle. At a guess it had been about six months dead. It wore a big wristwatch with extra dials on the face and a fine-mesh platinum band, loose now around a wrist of bones and brown skin. The back of the skull had been smashed open, possibly by the classic blunt instrument lying next to it.

If the fireplace was false—it almost had to be; nobody burns wood—the fireplace instruments were genuine nineteenth or twentieth century antiques. The rack was missing a poker. A poker lay inside the circle, in the dead grass next to the disintegrating mummy.

The glowing goldberg device sat just in the center of the magic circle.

I stepped forward, and a man's voice spoke sharply. "Don't go inside that circle of rug. It's more dangerous than it looks."

It was a man I knew: Officer-One Valpredo, a tall man with a small, straight mouth and a long, narrow Italian face.

"Looks dangerous enough to me," I said.

"It is. I reached in there myself," Valpredo told me, "right after we got here. I thought I could flip the switch off. My whole arm went numb. Instantly. No feeling at all. I yanked it away fast, but for a minute or so after that my whole arm was dead meat. I thought I'd lost it. Then it was all pins and needles, like I'd slept on it."

The cop who had brought me in had almost finished assembling the deep-sea fishing pole.

Ordaz waved into the circle. "Well? Have you ever seen anything like this?"

I shook my head, studying the violet-glowing machinery. "Whatever it is, it's brand new. Sinclair's really done it this time."

An uneven line of solenoids was attached to a plastic frame with homemade joins. Blistered spots of the plastic showed where other objects had been attached and later removed. A breadboard bore masses of heavy wiring. There were six big batteries hooked in parallel, and a strange, heavy piece of sculpture in what we later discovered was pure silver, with wiring attached at three curving points.

The silver was tarnished almost black and there were old file marks at the edges.

Near the center of the arrangement, just in front of the silver sculpture, were two concentric solenoids embedded in a block of clear plastic. They glowed blue shading to violet. So did the batteries. A less perceptible violet glow radiated from everywhere on the machine, more intensely in the interior parts.

That glow bothered me more than anything else. It was too theatrical. It was like something a special effects man might add to a cheap late-night thriller, to suggest a mad scientist's laboratory.

I moved around to get a closer look at the dead man's watch.

"Keep your head out of the field!" Valpredo said sharply.

I nodded. I squatted on my heels outside the borderline of dead grass.

The dead man's watch was going like crazy. The minute hand was circling the dial every seven seconds or so. I couldn't find the second hand at all.

I backed away from the arc of dead grass and stood up. Interstellar drive, hell. This blue-glowing monstrosity looked more like a time machine gone wrong.

I studied the single-throw switch welded to the plastic frame next to the batteries. A length of nylon line dangled from the horizontal handle. It looked like someone had tugged the switch *on* from outside the field by using the line; but he'd have had to hang from the ceiling to tug it *off* that way.

"I see why you couldn't send it over to ARM headquarters. You can't even touch it. You stick your arm or your head in there for a second, and that's ten minutes without a blood supply."

Ordaz said, "Exactly."

"It looks like you could reach in there with a stick and flip that switch off."

"Perhaps. We are about to try that." He waved at the man with the fishing pole. "There was nothing in this room long enough to reach the switch. We had to send—"

"Wait a minute. There's a problem."

He looked at me. So did the cop with the fishing pole.

"That switch could be a self-destruct. Sinclair was supposed to be a secretive bastard. Or the—field might hold considerable potential energy. Something might go blooey."

Ordaz sighed. "We must risk it. Gil, we have measured the rotation of the dead man's wristwatch. One hour per seven seconds. Fingerprints, footprints, laundry marks, residual body odor, stray eyelashes, all disappearing at an hour per seven seconds." He gestured, and the cop moved in and began trying to hook the switch.

"Already we may never know just when he was killed," said Ordaz.

· The tip of the pole wobbled in large circles, steadied beneath the switch, made contact. I held my breath. The pole bowed. The switch snapped up, and suddenly the violet glow was gone. Valpredo reached into the field, warily, as if the air might be red hot. Nothing happened, and he relaxed.

Then Ordaz began giving orders, and quite a lot happened. Two men in lab coats drew a chalk outline around the mummy and the poker. They moved the mummy onto a stretcher, put the poker in a plastic bag and put it next to the mummy.

I said, "Have you identified that?"

"I'm afraid so," said Ordaz. "Raymond Sinclair had his own autodoc—"

"*Did* he. Those things are expensive."

"Yes. Raymond Sinclair was a wealthy man. He owned the top two floors of this building, and the roof. According to records in his 'doc, he had a new set of bud teeth implanted two months ago." Ordaz pointed to the mummy, to the skinned-back dry lips and the buds of new teeth that were just coming in.

Right. That was Sinclair.

That brain had made miracles, and someone had smashed it with a wrought-iron rod. The interstellar drive . . . that glowing goldberg device? Or had it been still inside his head?

I said, "We'll have to get whoever did it. We'll *have* to. Even so . . ." Even so. No more miracles.

"We may have her already," Julio said.

I looked at him.

"There is a girl in the autodoc. We think she is Dr. Sinclair's great-niece, Janice Sinclair."

It was a standard drugstore autodoc, a thing like a giant coffin with walls a foot thick and a headboard covered with dials and red and green lights. The girl lay face up, her face calm, her breathing shallow. Sleeping Beauty. Her arms were in the guts of the 'doc, hidden by bulky rubbery sleeves.

She was lovely enough to stop my breath. Soft brown hair showing around the electrode cap;

small, perfect nose and mouth; smooth pale blue
skin shot with silver threads . . .

That last was an evening dye job. Without it the
impact of her would have been much lessened. The
blue shade varied slightly to emphasize the shape
of her body and the curve of her cheekbones. The
silver lines varied too, being denser in certain areas,
guiding the eye in certain directions: to the tips of
her breasts, or across the slight swell of abdominal
muscle to a lovely oval navel.

She'd paid high for that dye job. But she would
be beautiful without it.

Some of the headboard lights were red. I
punched for a readout, and was jolted. The 'doc
had been forced to amputate her right arm.
Gangrene.

She was in for a hell of a shock when she
woke up.

"All right," I said. "She's lost her arm. That
doesn't make her a killer."

Ordaz asked, "If she were homely, would it
help?"

I laughed. "You question my dispassionate judgment? Men have died for less!" Even so, I thought
he could be right. There was good reason to think
that the killer was now missing an arm.

"What do you think happened here, Gil?"

"Well . . . any way you look at it, the killer had
to want to take Sinclair's, ah, time machine with
him. It's priceless, for one thing. For another, it
looks like he tried to set it up as an alibi. Which
means that he knew about it before he came here."
I'd been thinking this through. "Say he made sure
some people knew where he was a few hours be-

fore he got here. He killed Sinclair within range of the . . . call it a generator. Turned it on. He figured Sinclair's own watch would tell him how much time he was gaining. Afterward he could set the watch back and leave with the generator. There'd be no way the police could tell he wasn't killed six hours earlier, or any number you like."

"Yes. But he did not do that."

"There was that line hanging from the switch. He must have turned it on from outside the field . . . probably because he didn't want to sit with the body for six hours. If he tried to step outside the field after he'd turned it on, he'd bump his nose. It'd be like trying to walk through a wall, going from field time to normal time. So he turned it off, stepped out of range and used that nylon line to turn it on again. He probably made the same mistake Valpredo did: he thought he could step back in and turn it off."

Ordaz nodded in satisfaction. "Exactly. It was very important for him—or her—to do that. Otherwise he would have no alibi and no profit. If he continued to try to reach into the field—"

"Yah, he could lose the arm to gangrene. That'd be convenient for us, wouldn't it? He'd be easy to find. But, look, Julio: the girl could have done the same thing to herself trying to *help* Sinclair." He might not have been that obviously dead when she got home."

"He might even have been alive," Ordaz pointed out.

I shrugged.

"In point of fact, she came home at one ten, in her own car, which is still in the carport. There are cameras mounted to cover the landing pad and carport. Doctor Sinclair's security was thorough. This girl was the only arrival last night. There were no departures."

"From the roof, you mean."

"Gil, there are only two ways to leave these apartments. One is from the roof, and the other is by elevator, from the lobby. The elevator is on this floor, and it was turned off. It was that way when we arrived. There is no way to override that control from elsewhere in this building."

"So someone could have taken it up here and turned it off afterward . . . or Sinclair could have turned it off before he was killed . . . I see what you mean. Either way, the killer has to be still here." I thought about that. I didn't like its taste. "No, it doesn't fit. How could she be bright enough to work out that alibi, then dumb enough to lock herself in with the body?"

Ordaz shrugged. "She locked the elevator before killing her uncle. She did not want to be interrupted. Surely that was sensible? After she hurt her arm she must have been in a great hurry to reach the 'doc."

One of the red lights turned green. I was glad for that. She didn't look like a killer. I said, half to myself, "Nobody looks like a killer when he's asleep."

"No. But she is where a killer ought to be *Qué lástima.*"

We went back to the living room. I called ARM Headquarters and had them send a truck.

The machine hadn't been touched. While we waited I borrowed a camera from Valpredo and took pictures of the setup *in situ*. Relative positions of the components might be important.

The lab men were in the brown grass using aerosol sprays to turn fingerprints white and give a vivid yellow glow to faint traces of blood. They got plenty of fingerprints on the machine, none at all on the poker. There was a puddle of yellow in the grass where the mummy's head had been, and a long yellow snail track ending at the business end of the poker. It looked like someone had tried to drag the poker out of the field after it had fallen.

Sinclair's apartments were roomy and comfortable and occupied the entire top floor. The lower floor was the laboratory where Sinclair had produced his miracles. I went through it with Valpredo. It wasn't that impressive. It looked like an expensive hobby setup. These tools would assemble components already fabricated, but they would not build anything complex.

—Except for the computer terminal. That was like a little womb, with a recline chair inside a three-hundred-and-sixty-degree wrap-around holovision screen and enough banked controls to fly the damn thing to Alpha Centauris.

The secrets there must be in that computer! But I didn't try to use it. We'd have to send an ARM programmer to break whatever failsafe codes Sinclair had put in the memory banks.

The truck arrived. We dragged Sinclair's legacy up the stairs to the roof in one piece. The parts were sturdily mounted on their frame, and the stairs were wide and not too steep.

I rode home in the back of the truck. Studying the generator. That massive piece of silver had

something of the look of *Bird In Flight:* a triangle
operated on by a topology student, with wires at
what were still the corners. I wondered if it was
the heart of the machine, or just a piece of misdi-
rection. Was I really riding with an interstellar
drive? Sinclair could have started that rumor himself, to cover whatever this was. Or . . . there was
a law against his working two projects simultaneously?

I was looking forward to Bera's reaction.

Jackson Bera came upon us moving it through
the halls of ARM Headquarters. He trailed along
behind us. Nonchalant. We pulled the machine into
the main laboratory and started checking it against
the holos I'd taken, in case something had been
jarred loose. Bera leaned against the door jamb,
watching us, his eyes gradually losing interest until
he seemed about to go to sleep.

I'd met him three years ago, when I returned
from the asteroids and joined the ARM. He'd been
twenty then, and two years an ARM; but his father
and grandfather had both been ARMs. Much of
my training had come from Bera. And as I learned
to hunt men who hunt other men, I had watched
what it was doing to him.

An ARM needs empathy. He needs the ability
to piece together a picture of the mind of his prey.
But Bera had too much empathy. I remember his
reaction when Kenneth Graham killed himself: a
single surge of current through the plug in his skull
and down the wire to the pleasure center of his
brain. Bera had been twitchy for weeks. And the
Anubis case early last year. When we realized what

the man had done, Bera had been close to killing him on the spot. I wouldn't have blamed him.

Last year Bera had had enough. He'd gone into the technical end of the business. His days of hunting organleggers were finished. He was now running the ARM laboratory.

He *had* to want to know what this oddball contraption was. I kept waiting for him to ask . . . and he watched, faintly smiling. Finally it dawned on me. He thought it was a practical joke, something I'd cobbled together for his own discomfiture.

I said, "Bera—"

And he looked at me brightly and said, "Hey, man, what is it?"

"You ask the most embarrassing questions."

"Right, I can understand your feeling that way, but what *is* it? I love it, it's neat, but what is this that you have brought me?"

I told him all I knew, such as it was. When I finished he said, "It doesn't sound much like a new space drive."

"Oho, you heard that too, did you? No, it doesn't. Unless—" I'd been wondering since I first saw it. "Maybe it's supposed to accelerate a fusion explosion. You'd get greater efficiency in a fusion drive."

"Nope. They get better than ninety percent now, and that widget looks *heavy.*" He reached to touch the bent silver triangle, gently, with long, tapering fingers. "Huh. Well, we'll dig out the answers."

"Good luck. I'm going back to Sinclair's place."

"Why? The action is here." Often enough he'd heard me talking wistfully of joining an interstellar colony. He must know how I'd feel about a better drive for the interstellar slowboats.

"It's like this," I said. "We've got the generator, but we don't know anything about it. We might wreck it. I'm going to have a whack at finding someone who knows something about Sinclair's generator."

"Meaning?"

"Whoever tried to steal it. Sinclair's killer."

"If you say so." But he looked dubious. He knew me too well. He said, "I understand there's a mother hunt in the offing."

"Oh?"

He smiled. "Just a rumor. You guys are lucky. When my dad first joined, the business of the ARM was *mostly* mother hunts. The organleggers hadn't really got organized yet, and the Fertility Laws were new. If we hadn't enforced them nobody would have obeyed them at all."

"Sure, and people threw rocks at your father. Bera, those days are *gone*."

"They could come back. Having children is basic."

"Bera, I did not join the ARM to hunt unlicensed parents." I waved and left before he could answer. I could do without the call to duty from Bera, who had done with hunting men and mothers.

I'd had a good view of the Rodewald Building, dropping toward the roof this morning. I had a good view now from my commandeered taxi. This time I was looking for escape paths.

There were no balconies on Sinclair's floors, and

the windows were flush to the side of the building.
A cat burglar would have trouble with them. They
didn't look like they'd open.

I tried to spot the cameras Ordaz had mentioned
as the taxi dropped toward the roof. I couldn't find
them. Maybe they were mounted in the elms.

Why was I bothering? I hadn't joined the ARM
to chase mothers or machinery or common murder-
ers. I'd joined to pay for my arm. My new arm
had reached the World Organ Bank Facility via a
captured organlegger's cache. Some honest citizen
had died unwillingly on a city slidewalk, and now
his arm was part of me.

I'd joined the ARM to hunt organleggers.

The ARM doesn't deal in murder *per se*. The
machine was out of my hands now. A murder investigation wouldn't keep me out of a mother hunt.
And I'd never met the girl. I knew nothing of her,
beyond the fact that she was where a killer ought
to be.

Was it just that she was pretty?

Poor Janice. When she woke up . . . For a solid
month I'd wakened to that same stunning shock,
the knowledge that my right arm was gone.

The taxi settled. Valpredo was waiting below.

I speculated . . . Cars weren't the only things that
flew. But anyone flying one of those tricky ducted-
fan flycycles over a city, where he could fall on a
pedestrian, wouldn't have to worry about a murder
charge. They'd feed him to the organ banks regardless. And anything that flew would have to have
left traces anywhere but on the landing pad itself.
It would crush a rose bush or a Bonsai tree or be
flipped over by an elm.

The taxi took off in a whisper of air.

Valpredo was grinning at me. "The Thinker. What's on your mind?"

"I was wondering if the killer could have come down on the carport roof."

He turned to study the situation. "There are two cameras mounted on the edge of the roof. If his vehicle was light enough, sure, he could land there, and the cameras wouldn't spot him. Roof wouldn't hold a car, though. Anyway, nobody did it."

"How do you know?"

"I'll show you. By the way, we inspected the camera system. We're pretty sure the cameras weren't tampered with."

"And nobody came down from the roof last night except the girl?"

"Nobody. Nobody even landed here until seven this morning. Look here." We had reached the concrete stairs that led down into Sinclair's apartments. Valpredo pointed at a glint of light in the sloping ceiling, at heart level. "This is the only way down. The camera would get anyone coming in or out. It might not catch his face, but it'd show if someone had passed. It takes sixty frames a minute."

I went on down. A cop let me in.

Ordaz was on the phone. The screen showed a young man with a deep tan and shock showing through the tan. Ordaz waved at me, a shushing motion, and went on talking. "Then you'll be here in fifteen minutes? That will be a great help to us. Please land on the roof. We are still working on the elevator."

He hung up and turned to me. "That was Andrew Porter, Janice Sinclair's lover. He tells us that he and Janice spent the evening at a party. She dropped him off at his home around one o'clock."

"Then she came straight home, if that's her in the 'doc."

"I think it must be. Mr. Porter says she was wearing a blue skin-dye job." Ordaz was frowning. "He put on a most convincing act, if it was that. I think he really was not expecting any kind of trouble. He was surprised that a stranger answered, shocked when he learned of Dr. Sinclair's death, and horrified when he learned that Janice had been hurt."

With the mummy and the generator removed, the murder scene had become an empty circle of brown grass marked with random streaks of yellow chemical and outlines of white chalk.

"We had some luck," said Ordaz. "Today's date is June 4, 2124. Dr. Sinclair was wearing a calendar watch. It registered January 17, 2125. If we switched the machine off at ten minutes to ten—which we did—and if it was registering an hour for every seven seconds that passed outside the field, then the field must have gone on around one o'clock last night, give or take a margin of error."

"Then if the girl didn't do it, she must have just missed the killer."

"Exactly."

"What about the elevator? Could it have been jiggered?"

"No. We took the workings apart. It was on this floor, and locked by hand. Nobody could have left by elevator . . ."

"Why did you trail off like that?"

Ordaz shrugged, embarrassed. "This peculiar machine really does bother me, Gil. I found myself thinking, suppose it can reverse time? Then the killer could have gone down in an elevator that was going up."

He laughed with me. I said, "In the first place, I don't believe a word of it. In the second place, he didn't have the machine to do it with. Unless . . . he made his escape before the murder. Dammit, now you've got me doing it."

"I would like to know more about the machine."

"Bera's investigating it now. I'll let you know as soon as we learn anything. And *I'd* like to know more about how the killer couldn't possibly have left."

He looked at me. "Details?"

"Could someone have opened a window?"

"No. These apartments are forty years old. The smog was still bad when they were built. Dr. Sinclair apparently preferred to depend on his air conditioning."

"How about the apartment below? I presume it has a different set of elevators—"

"Yes, of course. It belongs to Howard Rodewald, the owner of this building—of this chain of buildings, in fact. At the moment he is in Europe. His apartment has been loaned to friends."

"There are no stairs down to there?"

"No. We searched these apartments thoroughly."

"All right. We know the killer had a nylon line, because he left a strand of it on the generator. Could he have climbed down to Rodewald's balcony from the roof?"

"Thirty feet? Yes, I suppose so." Ordaz' eyes sparked. "We must look into that. There is still the matter of how he got past the camera, and whether he could have gotten inside once he was on the balcony."

"Yah."

"Try this, Gil. Another question. How did he *expect* to get away?" He watched for my reaction, which must have been satisfying, because it *was* a damn good question. "You see, if Janice Sinclair murdered her great-uncle, then neither question applies. If we are looking for someone else, we have to assume that his plans misfired. He had to improvise."

"Uh huh. He could still have been planning to use Rodewald's balcony. And that would mean he had a way past the camera . . ."

"Of course he did. The generator."

Right. If he came to steal the generator . . . and he'd have to steal it regardless, because if we found it here it would shoot his alibi sky high. So he'd leave it on while he trundled it up the stairs. Say it took him a minute; that's only an eighth of a second of normal time. One chance in eight that the camera would fire, and it would catch nothing but a streak . . . "Uh oh."

"What is it?"

"He had to be planning to steal the machine. Is he really going to lower it to Rodewald's balcony by *rope*?"

"I think it unlikely," said Ordaz. "It weighed more than fifty pounds. He could have moved it upstairs. The frame would make it portable. But to lower it by rope . . ."

"We'd be looking for one hell of an athlete."

"At least you will not have to search far to find

him. We assume that your hypothetical killer came
by elevator, do we not?"

"Yah." Nobody but Janice Sinclair had arrived
by the roof last night.

"The elevator was programed to allow a number
of people to enter it, and to turn away all others.
The list is short. Dr. Sinclair was not a gregarious
man."

"You're checking them out? Whereabouts, alibis
and so forth?"

"Of course."

"There's something else you might check on,"
I said. But Andrew Porter came in and I had to
postpone it.

Porter came casual, in a well-worn translucent
one-piece jump suit he must have pulled on while
running for a taxi. The muscles rolled like boulders
beneath the loose fabric, and his belly muscles
showed like the plates on an armadillo. Surfing
muscles. The sun had bleached his hair nearly white
and burned him as brown as Jackson Bera. You'd
think a tan that dark would cover for blood drain-
ing out of a face, but it doesn't.

"Where is she?" he demanded. He didn't wait
for an answer. He knew where the 'doc was, and
he went there. We trailed in his wake.

Ordaz didn't push. He waited while Porter
looked down at Janice, then punched for a readout
and went through it in detail. Porter seemed calmer
then, and his color was back. He turned to Ordaz
and said, "What happened?"

"Mr. Porter, did you know anything of Dr. Sinclair's latest project?"

"The time compressor thing? Yah. He had it set

up in the living room when I got here yesterday evening—right in the middle of that circle of dead grass. Any connection?"

"When did you arrive?"

"Oh, about . . . six. We had some drinks, and Uncle Ray showed off his machine. He didn't tell us much about it. Just showed what it could do." Porter showed us flashing white teeth. "It *worked.* That thing can compress time! You could live your whole life in there in two months! Watching him move around inside the field was like trying to keep track of a hummingbird. Worse. He struck a match—"

"When did you leave?"

"About eight. We had dinner at Cziller's House of Irish Coffee, and— Listen, what *happened* here?"

"There are some things we need to know first, Mr. Porter. Were you and Janice together for all of last evening? Were there others with you?"

"Sure. We had dinner alone, but afterward we went to a kind of party. On the beach at Santa Monica. Friend of mine has a house there. I'll give you the address. Some of us wound up back at Cziller's around midnight. Then Janice flew me home."

"You have said that you are Janice's lover. Doesn't she live with you?"

"No. I'm her steady lover, you might say, but I don't have any strings on her." He seemed embarrassed. "She lives here with Uncle Ray. Lived. Oh, *hell.*" He glanced into the 'doc. "Look, the readout said she'll be waking up any minute. Can I get her a robe?"

"Of course."

We followed Porter to Janice's bedroom, where he picked out a peach-colored negligée for her. I was beginning to like the guy. He had good instincts. An evening dye job was not the thing to wear on the morning of a murder. And he'd picked one with long, loose sleeves. Her missing arm wouldn't show so much.

"You call him Uncle Ray," said Ordaz.

"Yah. Because Janice did."

"He did not object? Was he gregarious?"

"Gregarious? Well, no, but *we* liked each other. We both liked puzzles, you understand? We traded murder mysteries and jigsaw puzzles. Listen, this may sound silly, but are you sure he's dead?"

"Regrettably, yes. He is dead, and murdered. Was he expecting someone to arrive after you left?"

"Yes."

"He said so?"

"No. But he was wearing a shirt and pants. When it was just us he usually went naked."

"Ah."

"Older people don't do that much," Porter said. "But Uncle Ray was in good shape. He took care of himself."

"Have you any idea whom he might have been expecting?"

"No. Not a woman; not a date, I mean. Maybe someone in the same business."

Behind him, Janice moaned.

Porter was hovering over her in a flash. He put a hand on her shoulder and urged her back. "Lie still, love. We'll have you out of there in a jiffy."

She waited while he disconnected the sleeves and other paraphernalia. She said, "What happened?"

"They haven't told me yet," Porter said with a flash of anger. "Be careful sitting up. You've had an accident."

"What kind of—? *Oh!*"

"It'll be all right."

"My *arm!*"

Porter helped her out of the 'doc. Her arm ended in pink flesh two inches below the shoulder. She let Porter drape the robe around her. She tried to fasten the sash, quit when she realized she was trying to do it with one hand.

I said, "Listen, I lost my arm once."

She looked at me. So did Porter.

"I'm Gil Hamilton. With the UN Police. You really don't have anything to worry about. See?" I raised my right arm, opened and closed the fingers. "The organ banks don't get much call for arms, as compared to kidneys, for instance. You probably won't even have to wait. I didn't. It feels just like the arm I was born with, and it works just as well."

"How did you lose it?" she asked.

"Ripped away by a meteor," I said, not without pride. "While I was asteroid mining in the Belt." I didn't have to tell her that we'd caused the meteor cluster ourselves, by setting the bomb wrong on an asteroid we wanted to move.

Ordaz said to her, "Do you remember how you lost your own arm?"

"Yes." She shivered. "Could we go somewhere where I could sit down? I feel a bit weak."

We moved to the living room. Janice dropped onto the couch a bit too hard. It might have been shock, or the missing arm might be throwing her balance off. I remembered. She said, "Uncle Ray's dead, isn't he?"

"Yes."

"I came home and found him that way. Lying next to that time machine of his, and the back of his head all bloody. I thought maybe he was still alive, but I could see the machine was going; it had that violet glow. I tried to get hold of the poker. I wanted to use it to switch the machine off, but I couldn't get a grip. My arm wasn't just numb, it wouldn't move. You know, you can try to wiggle your toes when your foot's asleep, but . . . I could get my hands on the handle of the damn poker, but when I tried to pull it just slid off."

"You kept trying?"

"For a while. Then . . . I backed away to think it over. I wasn't about to waste any time, with Uncle Ray maybe dying in there. My arm felt stone dead . . . I guess it was, wasn't it?" She shuddered. "Rotting meat. It smelled that way. And all of a sudden I felt so weak and dizzy, like I was dying myself. I barely made it into the 'doc."

"Good thing you did," I said. The blood was leaving Porter's face again as he realized what a close thing it had been.

Ordaz said, "Was your great-uncle expecting visitors last night?"

"I think so."

"Why do you think so?"

"I don't know. He just—acted that way."

"We are told that you and some friends reached Cziller's House of Irish Coffee around midnight. Is that true?"

"I guess so. We had some drinks, then I took Drew home and came home myself."

"Straight home?"

"Yes." She shivered. "I put the car away and went downstairs. I knew something was wrong. The door was open. Then there was Uncle Ray lying next to that machine! I knew better than to just run up to him. He'd told us not to step into the field."

"Oh? Then you should have known better than to reach for the poker."

"Well, yes. I could have used the tongs," she said as if the idea had just occurred to her. "It's just as long. I didn't think of it. There wasn't *time*. Don't you understand, he was dying in there, or dead!"

"Yes, of course. Did you interfere with the murder scene in any way?"

She laughed bitterly. "I suppose I moved the poker about two inches. Then when I felt what was happening to me I just ran for the 'doc. It was awful. Like dying."

"Instant gangrene," said Porter.

Ordaz said, "You did not, for example, lock the elevator?"

Damn! I should have thought of that.

"No. We usually do, when we lock up for the night, but I didn't have time."

Porter said, "Why?"

"The elevator was locked when we arrived," Ordaz told him.

Porter ruminated on that. "Then the killer must have left by the roof. You'll have pictures of him."

Ordaz smiled apologetically. "That is our problem. No cars left the roof last night. Only one car arrived. That was yours, Miss Sinclair."

"But," said Porter, and he stopped. He thought it through again. "Did the police turn on the elevator again after they got here?"

"No. The killer could not have left after we got here."

"Oh."

"What happened was this," said Ordaz. "Around five thirty this morning, the tenants in—" He stopped to remember. "In 36A called the building maintenance man about a smell as of rotting meat coming through the air conditioning system. He spent some time looking for the source, but once he reached the roof it was obvious. He—"

Porter pounced. "He reached the roof in what kind of vehicle?"

"Mr. Steeves says that he took a taxi from the street. There is no other way to reach Dr. Sinclair's private landing pad, is there?"

"No. But why would he do that?"

"Perhaps there have been other times when strange smells came from Dr. Sinclair's laboratory. We will ask him."

"Do that."

"Mr. Steeves followed the smell through the doctor's open door. He called us. He waited for us on the roof."

"What about his taxi?" Porter was hot on the scent. "Maybe the killer just waited till that taxi got here, then took it somewhere else when Steeves finished with it."

"It left immediately after Steeves had stepped out. He had a taxi clicker if he wanted another. The cameras were on it the entire time it was on the roof." Ordaz paused. "You see the problem?"

Apparently Porter did. He ran both hands through his white-blond hair. "I think we ought to put off discussing it until we know more."

He meant Janice. Janice looked puzzled; she hadn't caught on. But Ordaz nodded at once and stood up. "Very well. There is no reason Miss Sinclair cannot go on living here. We may have to bother you again," he told her. "For now, our condolences."

He made his exit. I trailed along. So, unexpectedly, did Drew Porter. At the top of the stairs he stopped Ordaz with a big hand around the Inspector's upper arm. "You're thinking Janice did it, aren't you?"

Ordaz sighed. "What choice have I? I must consider the possibility."

"She didn't have any reason. She loved Uncle Ray. She's lived with him on and off these past twelve years. She hasn't got the slightest reason to kill him."

"Is there no inheritance?"

His expression went sour. "All right, *yes*, she'll have some money coming. But Janice wouldn't care about anything like that!"

"Ye-es. Still, what choice have I? Everything we now know tells us that the killer could not have left the scene of the killing. We searched the premises immediately. There was only Janice Sinclair and her murdered uncle."

Porter bit back an answer, chewed it . . . He must have been tempted. Amateur detective, one step ahead of the police all the way. Yes, Watson, these *gendarmes* have a talent for missing the obvious . . . But he had too much to lose. Porter said, "And the maintenance man. Steeves."

Ordaz lifted one eyebrow. "Yes, of course. We shall have to investigate Mr. Steeves."

"How did he get that call from uh, 36A? Bedside phone or pocket phone? Maybe he was already on the roof."

"I don't remember that he said. But we have pictures of his taxi landing."

"He had a taxi clicker. He could have just called it down."

"One more thing," I said, and Porter looked at me hopefully. "Porter, what about the elevator? It had a brain in it, didn't it? It wouldn't take anyone up unless they were on its list."

"Or unless Uncle Ray buzzed down. There's an intercom in the lobby. But at that time of night he probably wouldn't let anyone up unless he was expecting him."

"So if Sinclair was expecting a business associate, he or she was probably in the tape. How about going down? Would the elevator take you down to the lobby if you weren't in the tape?"

"I'd . . . think so."

"It would," said Ordaz. "The elevator screens entrances, not departures."

"Then why didn't the killer use it? I don't mean Steeves, necessarily. I mean *anyone*, whoever it might have been. Why didn't he just go down in the elevator? Whatever he did do, that had to be easier."

They looked at each other, but they didn't say anything.

"Okay." I turned to Ordaz. "When you check

out the people in the tape, see if any of them shows a damaged arm. The killer might have pulled the same stunt Janice did: ruined her arm trying to turn off the generator. And I'd like a look at who's in that tape."

"Very well," said Ordaz, and we moved toward the squad car under the carport. We were out of earshot when he added, "How does the ARM come into this, Mr. Hamilton? Why your interest in the murder aspect of this case?"

I told him what I'd told Bera: that Sinclair's killer might be the only living expert on Sinclair's time machine. Ordaz nodded. What he'd really wanted to know was: could I justify giving orders to the Los Angeles Police Department in a local matter? And I had answered: yes.

The rather simple-minded security system in Sinclair's elevator had been built to remember the thumbprints and the facial bone structures (which it scanned by deep-radar, thus avoiding the problems raised by changing beard styles and masquerade parties) of up to one hundred people. Most people know about a hundred people, plus or minus ten or so. But Sinclair had only listed a dozen, including himself.

RAYMOND SINCLAIR
ANDREW PORTER
JANICE SINCLAIR
EDWARD SINCLAIR SR.
EDWARD SINCLAIR III
HANS DRUCKER
GEORGE STEEVES
PAULINE URTHIEL

BERNATH PETERFI
LAWRENCE MUHAMMAD ECKS
BERTHA HALL
MURIEL SANDUSKY

Valpredo had been busy. He'd been using the police car and its phone setup as an office while he guarded the roof. "We know who some of these are," he said. "Edward Sinclair Third, for instance, is Edward Senior's grandson, Janice's brother. He's in the Belt, in Ceres, making something of a name for himself as an industrial designer. Edward Senior is Raymond's brother. He lives in Kansas City. Hans Drucker and Bertha Hall and Muriel Sandusky all live in the Greater Los Angeles area; we don't know what their connection with Sinclair is. Pauline Urthiel and Bernath Peterfi are technicians of sorts. Ecks is Sinclair's patent attorney."

"I suppose we can interview Edward Third by phone." Ordaz made a face. A phone call to the Belt wasn't cheap. "These others—"

I said, "May I make a suggestion?"

"Of course."

"Send me along with whoever interviews Ecks and Peterfi and Urthiel. They probably knew Sinclair in a business sense, and having an ARM along will give you a little clout to ask a little more detailed questions."

"I could take those assignments," Valpredo volunteered.

"Very well." Ordaz still looked unhappy. "If this list were exhaustive I would be grateful. Unfortunately we must consider the risk that Dr. Sinclair's visitor simply used the intercom in the lobby and asked to be let in."

Bernath Peterfi wasn't answering his phone.

We got Pauline Urthiel via her pocket phone. A brusque contralto voice, no picture. We'd like to talk to her in connection with a murder investigation; would she be at home this afternoon? No. She was lecturing that afternoon, but would be home around six.

Ecks answered dripping wet and not smiling. So sorry to get you out of a shower, Mr. Ecks. We'd like to talk to you in connection with a murder investigation—

"Sure, come on over. Who's dead?"

Valpredo told him.

"Sinclair? *Ray* Sinclair? You're sure?"

We were.

"Oh, lord. Listen, he was working on something important. An interstellar drive, if it works out. If there's any possibility of salvaging the hardware—"

I reassured him and hung up. If Sinclair's patent attorney thought it was a star drive . . . maybe it was.

"Doesn't sound like he's trying to steal it," said Valpredo.

"No. And even if he'd got the thing, he couldn't have claimed it was his. If he's the killer, that's not what he was after."

We were moving at high speed, police-car speed. The car was on automatic, of course, but it could need manual override at any instant. Valpredo concentrated on the passing scenery and spoke without looking at me.

"You know, you and the Detective-Inspector aren't looking for the same thing."

"I know. I'm looking for a hypothetical killer. Julio's looking for a hypothetical visit. It could be tough to prove there wasn't one, but if Porter and the girl were telling the truth, maybe Julio can prove the visitor didn't do it."

"Which would leave the girl," he said.

"Whose side are you on?"

"Nobody's. All I've got is interesting questions." He looked at me sideways. "But you're pretty sure the girl didn't do it."

"Yah."

"Why?"

"I don't know. Maybe because I don't think she's got the brains. It wasn't a simple killing."

"She's Sinclair's niece. She can't be a complete idiot."

"Heredity doesn't work that way. Maybe I'm kidding myself. Maybe it's her arm. She's lost an arm; she's got enough to worry about." And I borrowed the car phone to dig into records in the ARM computer.

PAULINE URTHIEL. Born Paul Urthiel. Ph.D. in plasma physics, University of California at Ervine. Sex change and legal name change, 2111. Six years ago she'd been in competition for a Nobel prize, for research into the charge suppression effect in the Slaver disintegrator. Height: 5' 9". Weight: 135. Married Lawrence Muhammad Ecks, 2117. Had kept her (loosely speaking) maiden name. Separate residences.

BERNATH PETERFI. Ph.D. in subatomics and related fields, MIT. Diabetic. Height: 5' 8". Weight:

145. Application for exemption to the Fertility Laws denied, 2119. Married 2118, divorced 2122. Lived alone.

LAWRENCE MUHAMMAD ECKS. Masters degree in physics. Member of the bar. Height: 6' 1". Weight: 190. Artificial left arm. Vice President, CET (Committee to End Transplants).

Valpredo said. "Funny how the human arm keeps cropping up in this case."

"Yah." Including one human ARM who didn't really belong there. "Ecks has a masters. Maybe he could have talked people into thinking the generator was his. Or maybe he thought he could."

"He didn't try to snow *us*."

"Suppose he blew it last night? He wouldn't necessarily want the generator lost to humanity, now would he?"

"How did he get out?"

I didn't answer.

Ecks lived in a tapering tower almost a mile high. At one time Lindstetter's Needle must have been the biggest thing ever built, before they started with the arcologies. We landed on a pad a third of the way up, then took a drop shaft ten floors down.

He was dressed when he answered the door, in blazing yellow pants and a net shirt. His skin was very dark, and his hair was a puffy black dandelion with threads of grey in it. On the phone screen I hadn't been able to tell which arm was which, and I couldn't now. He invited us in, sat down and waited for the questions.

Where was he last night? Could he produce an alibi? It would help us considerably.

"Sorry, nope. I spent the night going through a rather tricky case. You wouldn't appreciate the details."

I told him I would. He said, "Actually, it involves Edward Sinclair—Ray's great-nephew. He's a Belt immigrant, and he's done an industrial design that could be adapted to Earth. Swivel for a chemical rocket motor. The trouble is it's not *that* different from existing designs, it's just *better*. His Belt patent is good, but the UN laws are different. You wouldn't believe the legal tangles."

"Is he likely to lose out?"

"No, it just might get sticky if a firm called Fire-Storm decides to fight the case. I want to be ready for that. In a pinch I might even have to call the kid back to Earth. I'd hate to do that, though. He's got a heart condition."

Had he made any phone calls, say to a computer, during his night of research?

Ecks brightened instantly. "Oh, sure. Constantly, all night. Okay, I've got an alibi."

No point in telling him that such calls could have been made from anywhere. Valpredo asked, "Do you have any idea where your wife was last night?"

"No, we don't live together. She lives three hundred stories over my head. We've got an open marriage . . . maybe too open," he added wistfully.

There seemed a good chance that Raymond Sinclair was expecting a visitor last night. Did Ecks have any idea—?

"He knew a couple of women," said Ecks. "You might ask them. Bertha Hall is about eighty, about Ray's age. She's not too bright, not by Ray's standards, but she's as much of a physical fitness nut as he is. They go backpacking, play tennis, maybe sleep together, maybe not. I can give you her address. Then there's Muriel something. He had a crush on her a few years ago. She'd be thirty now. I don't know if they still see each other or not."

Did Sinclair know other women?

Ecks shrugged.

Who did he know professionally?

"Oh, lord, that's an endless list. Do you know anything about the way Ray worked?" He didn't wait for an answer. "He used computer setups mostly. Any experiment in his field was likely to cost millions, or more. What he was good at was setting up a computer analogue of an experiment that would tell him what he wanted to know. Take, oh . . . I'm sure you've heard of the Sinclair molecule chain."

Hell, yes. We'd used it for towing in the Belt; nothing else was light enough and strong enough. A loop of it was nearly invisibly fine, but it would cut steel.

"He didn't start working with chemicals until he was practically finished. He told me he spent four years doing molecular designs by computer analogue. The tough part was the ends of the molecule chain. Until he got that the chain would start disintegrating from the endpoints the minute you finished making it. When he finally had what he wanted, he hired an industrial chemical lab to make it for him.

"That's what I'm getting at," Ecks continued. "He hired other people to do the concrete stuff, once he knew what he had. And the people he hired had to know what they were doing. He knew the top physicists and chemists and field theorists everywhere on Earth and in the Belt."

Like Pauline? Like Bernath Peterfi?

"Yah, Pauline did some work for him once. I don't think she'd do it again. She didn't like having to give him all the credit. She'd rather work for herself. I don't blame her."

Could he think of anyone who might want to murder Raymond Sinclair?

Ecks shrugged. "I'd say that was your job. Ray never liked splitting the credit with anyone. Maybe someone he worked with nursed a grudge. Or maybe someone was trying to steal this latest project of his. Mind you, I don't know much about what he was trying to do, but if it worked it would have been fantastically valuable, and not just in money."

Valpredo was making noises like he was about finished. I said, "Do you mind if I ask a personal question?"

"Go ahead."

"Your arm. How'd you lose it?"

"Born without it. Nothing in my genes, just a bad prenatal situation. I came out with an arm and a turkey wishbone. By the time I was old enough for a transplant, I knew I didn't want one. You want the standard speech?"

"No, thanks, but I'm wondering how good your artificial arm is. I'm carrying a transplant myself."

Ecks looked me over carefully for signs of moral degeneration. "I suppose you're also one of those people who keep voting the death penalty for more and more trivial offenses?"

"No, I—"

"After all, if the organ banks ran out of criminals you'd be in trouble. You might have to live with your mistakes."

"No, I'm one of those people who blocked the second corpsicle law, kept that group from going into the organ banks. And I hunt organleggers for a living. But I don't have an artificial arm, and I suppose the reason is that I'm squeamish."

"Squeamish about being part mechanical? I've heard of that," Ecks said. "But you can be squeamish the other way, too. What there is of me is all me, not part of a dead man. I'll admit the sense of touch isn't quite the same, but it's just as good. And—look."

He put a hand on my upper forearm and squeezed.

It felt like the bones were about to give. I didn't scream, but it took an effort. "That isn't all my strength," he said. "And I could keep it up all day. This arm doesn't get tired."

He let go.

I asked if he would mind my examining his arms. He didn't. But then, Ecks didn't know about my imaginary hand.

I probed the advanced plastics of Ecks' false arm, the bone and muscle structure of the other. It was the real arm I was interested in.

When we were back in the car Valpredo said, "Well?"

"Nothing wrong with his real arm," I said. "No scars."

Valpredo nodded.

But the bubble of accelerated time wouldn't hurt plastic and batteries, I thought. And if he'd been planning to lower fifty pounds of generator two stories down on a nylon line, his artificial arm had the strength for it.

We called Peterfi from the car. He was in. He was a small man, dark complected, mild of face, his hair straight and shiny black around a receding hairline. His eyes blinked and squinted as if the light were too bright, and he had the scruffy look of a man who has slept in his clothes. I wondered if we had interrupted an afternoon nap.

Yes, he would be glad to help the police in a murder investigation.

Peterfi's condominium was a slab of glass and concrete set on a Santa Monica cliff face. His apartment faced the sea. "Expensive, but worth it for the view," he said, showing us to chairs in the living room. The drapes were closed against the afternoon sun. Peterfi had changed clothes. I noticed the bulge in his upper left sleeve, where an insulin capsule and automatic feeder had been anchored to the bone of the arm.

"Well, what can I do for you? I don't believe you mentioned who had been murdered."

Valpredo told him.

He was shocked. "Oh, my. Ray Sinclair. But there's no telling how this will affect—" and he stopped suddenly.

"Please go on," said Valpredo.

"We were working on something together. Something—revolutionary."

An interstellar drive?

He was startled. He debated with himself, then, "Yes. It was supposed to be secret."

We admitted having seen the machine in action. How did a time compression field serve as an interstellar drive?

"That's not exactly what it is," Peterfi said. Again he debated with himself. Then, "There have always been a few optimists around who thought that just because mass and inertia have always been associated in human experience, it need not be a universal law. What Ray and I have done is to create a condition of low inertia. You see—"

"An inertialess drive!"

Peterfi nodded vigorously at me. "Essentially yes. Is the machine intact? If not—"

I reassured him on that point.

"That's good. I was about to say that if it had been destroyed, I could recreate it. I did most of the work of building it. Ray preferred to work with his mind, not with his hands."

Had Peterfi visited Sinclair last night?

"No. I had dinner at a restaurant down the coast, then came home and watched the holo wall. What times do I need alibis for?" he asked jokingly.

Valpredo told him. The joking look turned into a nervous grimace. No, he'd left the Mail Shirt just after nine; he couldn't prove his whereabouts after that time.

Had he any idea who might have wanted to murder Raymond Sinclair?

Peterfi was reluctant to make outright accusations. Surely we understood. It might be someone he had worked with in the past, or someone he'd insulted. Ray thought most of humanity were fools. Or—we might look into the matter of Ray's brother's exemption.

Valpredo said, "Edward Sinclair's exemption? What about it?"

"I'd really prefer that you get the story from someone else. You may know that Edward Sinclair was refused the right to have children because of an inherited heart condition. His grandson has it too. There is some question as to whether he really did the work that earned him the exemption."

"But that must have been forty to fifty years ago. How could it figure in a murder now?"

Peterfi explained patiently. "Edward had a child by virtue of an exemption to the Fertility Laws. Now there are two grandchildren. Suppose the matter came up for review? His grandchildren would lose the right to have children. They'd be illegitimate. They might even lose the right to inherit."

Valpredo was nodding. "Yah. We'll look into that, all right."

I said, "You applied for an exemption yourself not long ago. I suppose your, uh—"

"Yes, my diabetes. It doesn't interfere with my life at all. Do you know how long we've been using insulin to handle diabetes? Almost two hundred years! What does it matter if I'm a diabetic? If my children are?"

He glared at us, demanding an answer. He got none.

"But the Fertility Laws refuse me children. Do you know that I lost my wife because the Board refused me an exemption? I deserved it. My work on plasma flow in the solar photosphere— Well, I'd hardly lecture you on the subject, would I? But my work can be used to predict the patterns of proton storms near any G-type star. Every colony world owes something to my work!"

That was an exaggeration, I thought. Proton storms affected mainly asteroidal mining operations . . . "Why don't you move to the Belt?" I asked. "They'd honor you for your work, and they don't have Fertility Laws."

"I get sick off Earth. It's biorhythms; it has nothing to do with diabetes. Half of humanity suffers from biorhythm upset."

I felt sorry for the guy. "You could still get the exemption. For your work on the inertialess drive. Wouldn't that get you your wife back?"

"I . . . don't know. I doubt it. It's been two years. In any case, there's no telling which way the Board will jump. I thought I'd have the exemption last time."

"Do you mind if I examine your arms?"

He looked at me. "What?"

"I'd like to examine your arms."

"That seems a most curious request. Why?"

"There seems a good chance that Sinclair's killer damaged his arm last night. Now, I'll remind you that I'm acting in the name of the UN Police. If you've been hurt by the side effects of a possible space drive, one that might be used by human colonists, then you're concealing evidence in a—" I stopped, because Peterfi had stood up and was taking off his tunic.

He wasn't happy, but he stood still for it. His arms looked all right. I ran my hands along each arm, bent the joints, massaged the knuckles. Inside the flesh I ran my imaginary fingertips along the bones.

Three inches below the shoulder joint the bone was knotted. I probed the muscles and tendons . . .

"Your right arm is a transplant," I said. "It must have happened about six months ago."

He bridled. "You may not be aware of it, but surgery to re-attach my own arm would show the same scars."

"Is that what happened?"

Anger made his speech more precise. "Yes. I was performing an experiment, and there was an explosion. The arm was nearly severed. I tied a tourniquet and got to a 'doc before I collapsed."

"Any proof of this?"

"I doubt it. I never told anyone of this accident, and the 'doc wouldn't keep records. In any case, I think the burden of proof would be on you."

"Uh huh."

Peterfi was putting his tunic back on. "Are you quite finished here? I'm deeply sorry for Ray Sinclair's death, but I don't see what it could possibly have to do with my stupidity of six months ago."

I didn't either. We left.

Back in the car. It was seventeen twenty; we could pick up a snack on the way to Pauline Urthiel's place. I told Valpredo, "I think it was a transplant. And he didn't want to admit it. He must have gone to an organlegger."

"Why would he do that? It's not that tough to get an arm from the public organ banks."

I chewed that. "You're right. But if it was a normal transplant, there'll be a record. Well, it could have happened the way he said it did."

"Uh huh."

"How about this? He was doing an experiment,

and it was illegal. Something that might cause pollution in a city, or even something to do with radiation. He picked up radiation burns in his arm. If he'd gone to the public organ banks he'd have been arrested."

"That would fit too. Can we prove it on him?"

"I don't know. I'd like to. He might tell us how to find whoever he dealt with. Let's do some digging: maybe we can find out what he was working on six months ago."

Pauline Urthiel opened the door the instant we rang. "Hi! I just got in myself. Can I make you drinks?"

We refused. She ushered us into a smallish apartment with a lot of fold-into-the-ceiling furniture. A sofa and coffee table were showing now; the rest existed as outlines on the ceiling. The view through the picture window was breathtaking. She lived near the top of Lindstetter's Needle, some three hundred stories up from her husband.

She was tall and slender, with a facial structure that would have been effeminate on a man. On a woman it was a touch masculine. The well-formed breasts might be flesh or plastic, but surgically implanted in either case.

She finished making a large drink and joined us on the couch. And the questions started.

Had she any idea who might have wanted Raymond Sinclair dead?

"Not really. How did he die?"

"Someone smashed in his skull with a poker," Valpredo said. If he wasn't going to mention the generator, neither was I.

"How quaint." Her contralto turned acid. "His own poker, too, I presume. Out of his own fireplace rack. What you're looking for is a traditionalist." She peered at us over the rim of her glass. Her eyes were large, the lids decorated in semi-permanent tattoo as a pair of flapping UN flags. "That doesn't help much, does it? You might try whoever was working with him on whatever his latest project was."

That sounded like Peterfi, I thought. But Valpredo said, "Would he necessarily have a collaborator?"

"He generally works alone at the beginning. But somewhere along the line he brings in people to figure out how to make the hardware, and make it. He never made anything real by himself. It was all just something in a computer bank. It took someone else to make it real. And he never gave credit to anyone."

Then his hypothetical collaborator might have found out how little credit he was getting for his work, and— But Urthiel was shaking her head. "I'm talking about a psychotic, not someone who's really been cheated. Sinclair never *offered* anyone a share in anything he did. He always made it damn plain what was happening. I knew what I was doing when I set up the FyreStop prototype for him, and I knew what I was doing when I quit. It was all him. He was using my training, not my brain. I wanted to do something original, something *me*."

Did she have any idea what Sinclair's present project was?

"My husband would know. Larry Ecks, lives in this same building. He's been dropping cryptic hints, and when I want more details he has this grin—" She grinned herself, suddenly. "You'll gather I'm interested. But he won't say."

Time for me to take over, or we'd never get certain questions asked. "I'm an ARM. What I'm about to tell you is secret," I said. And I told her what we knew of Sinclair's generator. Maybe Valpredo was looking at me disapprovingly; maybe not.

"We know that the field can damage a human arm in a few seconds. What we want to know," I said, "is whether the killer is now wandering around with a half-decayed hand or arm—or foot, for that—"

She stood and pulled the upper half of her body stocking down around her waist.

She looked very much a real woman. If I hadn't known—and why would it matter? These days the sex change operation is elaborate and perfect. Hell with it; I was on duty. Valpredo was looking nonchalant, waiting for me.

I examined both her arms with my eyes and my three hands. There was nothing. Not even a bruise.

"My legs too?"

I said, "Not if you can stand on them."

Next question. Could an artificial arm operate within the field?

"Larry? You mean *Larry*? You're out of your teeny mind."

"Take it as a hypothetical question."

She shrugged. "Your guess is as good as mine. There aren't any experts on inertialess fields."

"There was one. He's dead," I reminded her.

"All I know is what I learned watching the Gray

Lensman show in the holo wall when I was a kid."
She smiled suddenly. "That old space opera—"

Valpredo laughed. "You too? I used to watch
that show in study hall on a little pocket phone.
One day the Principal caught me at it."

"Sure. And then we outgrew it. Too bad. Those
inertialess ships . . . I'm sure an inertialess ship
wouldn't behave like those did. You couldn't possibly get rid of the time compression effect." She
took a long pull on her drink, set it down and said,
"Yes and no. He could reach in, but—you see the
problem? The nerve impulses that move the motors
in Larry's arm, they're coming into the field too
slowly."

"Sure."

"But if Larry closed his fist on something, say,
and reached into the field with it, it would probably
stay closed. He could have brained Ray with—no,
he couldn't. The poker wouldn't be moving any
faster than a glacier. Ray would just dodge."

And he couldn't pull a poker out of the field,
either. His fist wouldn't close on it after it was inside. But he could have tried, and still left with his
arm intact, I thought.

Did Urthiel know anything of the circumstances
surrounding Edward Sinclair's exemption?

"Oh, that's an old story," she said. "Sure, I heard
about it. How could it possibly have anything to
do with, with Ray's murder?"

"I don't know," I confessed. "I'm just thrashing around."

"Well, you'll probably get it more accurately
from the UN files. Edward Sinclair did some math-
ematics on the fields that scoop up interstellar hy-

drogen for the cargo ramrobots. He was a shoo-in
for the exemption. That's the surest way of getting
it: make a breakthrough in anything that has anything to do with the interstellar colonies. Every
time you move one man away from Earth, the population drops by one."

"What was wrong with it?"

"Nothing anyone could prove. Remember, the
Fertility Restriction Laws were new then. They
couldn't stand a real test. But Edward Sinclair's a
pure math man. He works with number theory, not
practical applications. I've seen Edward's equations, and they're closer to something Ray would
come up with. And Ray didn't need the exemption.
He never wanted children."

"So you think—"

"I don't *care* which of them redesigned the ram-
scoops. Diddling the Fertility Board like that, that
takes *brains.*" She swallowed the rest of her drink,
set the glass down. "Breeding for brains is never a
mistake. It's no challenge to the Fertility Board
either. The people who do the damage are the ones
who go into hiding when their shots come due,
have their babies, then scream to high heaven when
the Board has to sterilize them. Too many of those
and we won't have Fertility Laws any more. And
that—" She didn't have to finish.

Had Sinclair known that Pauline Urthiel was
once Paul?

She stared. "Now just what the bleep has that
got to do with anything?"

I'd been toying with the idea that Sinclair might
have been blackmailing Urthiel with that information. Not for money, but for credit in some discov-

ery they'd made together. "Just thrashing around," I said.

"Well . . . all right. I don't know if Ray knew or not. He never raised the subject, but he never made a pass either, and he must have researched me before he hired me. And, say, listen: Larry doesn't know. I'd appreciate it if you wouldn't blurt it out."

"Okay."

"See, he had his children by his first wife. I'm not denying him children . . . Maybe he married me because I had a touch of, um, masculine insight. Maybe. But he doesn't know it, and he doesn't want to. I don't know whether he'd laugh it off or kill me."

I had Valpredo drop me off at ARM Headquarters.

This peculiar machine really does bother me, Gil . . . Well it should, Julio. The Los Angeles Police were not trained to deal with a mad scientist's nightmare running quietly in the middle of a murder scene.

Granted that Janice wasn't the type. Not for this murder. But Drew Porter was precisely the type to evolve a perfect murder around Sinclair's generator, purely as an intellectual exercise. He might have guided her through it; he might even have been there, and used the elevator before she shut it off. It was the one thing he forgot to tell her: not to shut off the elevator.

Or: he outlined a perfect murder to her, purely as a puzzle, never dreaming she'd go through with it—badly.

Or: one of them had killed Janice's uncle on impulse. No telling what he'd said that one of them couldn't tolerate. But the machine had been right there in the living room, and Drew had wrapped his big arm around Janice and said, *Wait, don't do anything yet, let's think this out . . .*

Take any of these as the true state of affairs, and a prosecutor could have a hell of a time proving it. He could show that no killer could possibly have left the scene of the crime without Janice Sinclair's help, and therefore . . . But what about that glowing thing, that time machine built by the dead man? *Could* it have freed a killer from an effectively locked room? How could a judge know its power?

Well, could it?

Bera might know.

The machine was running. I caught the faint violet glow as I stepped into the laboratory, and a flickering next to it . . . and then it was off, and Jackson Bera stood suddenly beside it, grinning, silent, waiting.

I wasn't about to spoil his fun. I said, "Well? Is it an interstellar drive?"

"Yes!"

A warm glow spread through me. I said, "Okay."

"It's a low inertia field," said Bera. "Things inside lose most of their inertia . . . not their mass, just the resistance to movement. Ratio of about five hundred to one. The interface is sharp as a razor. We think there are quantum levels involved."

"Uh huh. The field doesn't affect time directly?"

"No, it . . . I shouldn't say that. Who the hell knows what time really is? It affects chemical and nuclear reactions, energy release of all kinds . . . but it doesn't affect the speed of light. You know, it's kind of kicky to be measuring the speed of light at three hundred and seventy miles per second with honest instruments."

Dammit. I'd been half-hoping it was an FTL drive. I said, "Did you ever find out what was causing that blue glow?"

Bera laughed at me. "Watch." He'd rigged a remote switch to turn the machine on. He used it, then struck a match and flipped it toward the blue glow. As it crossed an invisible barrier the match flared violet-white for something less than an eyeblink. I blinked. It had been like a flashbulb going off.

I said, "Oh, *sure*. The machinery's warm."

"Right. The blue glow is just infrared radiation being boosted to violet when it enters normal time."

Bera shouldn't have had to tell me that. Embarrassed, I changed the subject. "But you said it was an interstellar drive."

"Yah. It's got drawbacks," said Bera. "We can't just put a field around a whole starship. The crew would think they'd lowered the speed of light, but so what? A slowboat doesn't get that close to lightspeed anyway. They'd save a little trip time, but they'd have to live through it five hundred times as fast."

"How about if you just put the field around your fuel tanks?"

Bera nodded. "That's what they'll probably do. Leave the motor and the life support system outside. You could carry a godawful amount of fuel that way . . . Well, it's not our department. Someone else'll be designing the starships," he said a bit wistfully.

"Have you thought of this thing in relation to robbing banks? or espionage?"

"If a gang could afford to build one of these jobs, they wouldn't need to rob banks." He ruminated. "I hate making anything this big a UN secret. But I guess you're right. The average government could afford a whole stable of the things."

"Thus combining James Bond and the Flash."

He rapped on the plastic frame. "Want to try it?"

"Sure," I said.

Heart to brain: THUD! What're you doing? You'll get us all killed! I knew we should never have put you in charge of things . . . I stepped up to the generator, waited for Bera to scamper beyond range, then pulled the switch.

Everything turned deep red. Bera became as a statue.

Well, here I was. The second hand on the wall clock had stopped moving. I took two steps forward and rapped with my knuckles. Rapped, hell: it was like rapping on contact cement. The invisible wall was tacky.

I tried leaning on it for a minute or so. That worked fine until I tried to pull away, and then I knew I'd done something stupid. I was embedded in the interface. It took me another minute to pull loose, and then I went sprawling backward; I'd picked up too much inward velocity, and it all came into the field with me.

At that I'd been lucky. If I'd leaned there a little longer I'd have lost my leverage. I'd have been sinking deeper and deeper into the interface, unable to yell to Bera, building up more and more velocity outside the field.

I picked myself up and tried something safer. I took out my pen and dropped it. It fell normally: thirty-two feet per second, field time. Which scratched one theory as to how the killer had thought he would be leaving.

I switched the machine off. "Something I'd like to try," I told Bera. "Can you hang the machine in the air, say by a cable around the frame?"

"What have you got in mind?"

"I want to try standing on the bottom of the field."

Bera looked dubious.

It took us twenty minutes to set it up. Bera took no chances. He lifted the generator about five feet. Since the field seemed to center on that oddly shaped piece of silver, that put the bottom of the field just a foot in the air. We moved a stepladder into range, and I stood on the stepladder and turned on the generator.

I stepped off.

Walking down the side of the field was like walking in progressively stickier taffy. When I stood on the bottom I could just reach the switch.

My shoes were stuck solid. I could pull my feet out of them, but there was no place to stand except in my own shoes. A minute later my feet were stuck too: I could pull one loose, but only by fixing the other ever more deeply in the interface. I sank deeper, and all sensation left the soles of my feet. It was scary, though I knew nothing terrible could happen to me. My feet wouldn't die out there: they wouldn't have time.

But the interface was up to my ankles now, and I started to wonder what kind of velocity they were building up out there. I pushed the switch up. The lights flashed bright, and my feet slapped the floor hard.

Bera said, "Well? Learn anything?"

"Yah. I don't want to try a real test: I might wreck the machine."

"What kind of real test—?"

"Dropping it forty stories with the field on. Quit worrying, I'm not going to do it."

"Right. You aren't."

"You know, this time compression effect would work for more than just spacecraft. After you're on the colony world you could raise full grown cattle from frozen fertilized eggs in just a few minutes."

"Mmm . . . Yah." The happy smile flashing white against darkness, the infinity look in Bera's eyes . . . Bera liked playing with ideas. "Think of one of these mounted on a truck, say on Jinx. You could explore the shoreline regions without ever worrying about the bandersnatchi attacking. They'd never move fast enough. You could drive across any alien world and catch the whole ecology laid out around you, none of it running from the truck. Predators in mid-leap, birds in mid-flight, couples in courtship."

"Or larger groups."

"I . . . think that habit is unique to humans." He looked at me sideways. "You wouldn't spy on *people*, would you? Or shouldn't I ask?"

"That five-hundred-to-one ratio. Is that constant?"

He came back to here and now. "We don't know.

Our theory hasn't caught up to the hardware it's supposed to fit. I wish to hell we had Sinclair's notes."

"You were supposed to send a programmer out there—"

"He came back," Bera said viciously. "Clayton Wolfe. Clay says the tapes in Sinclair's computer were all wiped before he got there. I don't know whether to believe him or not. Sinclair was a secretive bastard, wasn't he?"

"Yah. One false move on Clay's part and the computer might have wiped everything. But he says different, hmmm?"

"He says the computer was blank, a newborn mind all ready to be taught. Gil, is that possible? Could whoever killed Sinclair have wiped the tapes?"

"Sure, why not? what he couldn't have done is left afterward." I told him a little about the problem. "It's even worse than that, because as Ordaz keeps pointing out, he thought he'd be leaving with the machine. I thought he might have been planning to roll the generator off the roof, step off with it and float down. But that wouldn't work. Not if it falls five hundred times as fast. He'd have been killed."

"Losing the machine maybe saved his life."

"But *how did he get out*?"

Bera laughed at my frustration. "Couldn't his niece be the one?"

"Sure, she could have killed her uncle for the money. But I can't see how she'd have a motive to wipe the computer. Unless—"

"Something?"

"Maybe. Never mind." Did Bera ever miss this kind of manhunting? But I wasn't ready to discuss this yet; I didn't know enough. "Tell me more about the machine. Can you vary that five-hundred-to-one ratio?"

He shrugged. "We tried adding more batteries. We thought it might boost the field strength. We were wrong; it just expanded the boundary a little. And using one less battery turns it off completely. So the ratio seems to be constant, and there do seem to be quantum levels involved. We'll know better when we build another machine."

"How so?"

"Well, there are all kinds of good questions," said Bera. "What happens when the fields of two generators intersect? They might just add, but maybe not. That quantum effect . . . And what happens if the generators are right next to each other, operating in each other's accelerated time? The speed of light could drop to a few feet per second. Throw a punch and your hand gets shorter!"

"That'd be kicky, all right."

"Dangerous, too. Man, we'd better try that one on the Moon!"

"I don't see that."

"Look, with one machine going, infrared light comes out violet. If two machines were boosting each other's performance, what kind of radiation would they put out? Anything from X-rays to anti-matter particles."

"An expensive way to build a bomb."

"Well, but it's a bomb you can use over and over again."

I laughed. "We did find you an expert," I said. "You may not need Sinclair's tapes. Bernath Peterfi says he was working with Sinclair. He could be lying—more likely he was working *for* him, under contract—but at least he knows what the machine does."

Bera seemed relieved at that. He took down Peterfi's address. I left him there in the laboratory, playing with his new toy.

The file from City morgue was sitting on my desk, open, waiting for me since this morning. Two dead ones looked up at me through sockets of blackened bone; but not accusingly. They had patience. They could wait.

The computer had processed my search pattern. I braced myself with a cup of coffee, then started leafing through the thick stack of printout. When I knew what had burned away two human faces, I'd be close to knowing who. Find the tool, find the killer. And the tool must be unique, or close to it.

Lasers, lasers—more than half the machine's suggestions seemed to be lasers. Incredible, the way lasers seemed to breed and mutate throughout human industry. Laser radar. The laser guidance system on a tunneling machine. Some suggestions were obviously unworkable . . . and one was a lot too workable.

A standard hunting laser fires in pulses. But it can be jiggered for a much longer pulse or even a continuous burst.

Set a hunting laser for a long pulse, and put a grid over the lens. The mesh has to be optically fine, on the order of angstroms. Now the beam will spread as it leaves the grid. A second of pulse will vaporize the grid, leaving no evidence. The grid would be no bigger than a contact lens; if you didn't trust your aim you could carry a pocketful of them.

The grid-equipped laser would be less efficient, as a rifle with a silencer is less efficient. But the grid would make the murder weapon impossible to identify.

I thought about it and got cold chills. Assassination is already a recognized branch of politics. If this got out—but that was the trouble; someone seemed to have thought of it already. If not, someone would. Someone always did.

I wrote up a memo for Lucas Garner. I couldn't think of anyone better qualified to deal with this kind of sociological problem.

Nothing else in the stack of printout caught my eye. Later I'd have to go through it in detail. For now, I pushed it aside and punched for messages.

Bates, the coroner, had sent me another report. They'd finished the autopsies on the two charred corpses. Nothing new. But Records had identified the fingerprints. Two missing persons, disappeared six and eight months ago. Ah HA!

I knew that pattern. I didn't even look at the names; I just skipped on to the gene coding.

Right. The fingerprints did not match the genes. All twenty fingertips must be transplants. And the man's scalp was a transplant; his own hair had been blond.

I leaned back in my chair, gazing fondly down at holographs of charred skulls.

You evil sons of bitches. Organleggers, both of

you. With all that raw material available, most organleggers change their fingerprints constantly—and their retina prints; but we'd never get prints from those charred eyeballs. So: weird weapon or no, they were ARM business. My business.

And we still didn't know what had killed them, or who.

It could hardly have been a rival gang. For one thing, there was no competition. There must be plenty of business for every organlegger left alive after the ARM had swept through them last year. For another, why had they been dumped on a city slidewalk? Rival organleggers would have taken them apart for their own organ banks. Waste not, want not.

On that same philosophy, I had something to be deeply involved in when the mother hunt broke. Sinclair's death wasn't ARM business, and his time compression field wasn't in my field. This was both.

I wondered what end of the business the dead ones had been in. The file gave their estimated ages: forty for the man, forty-three for the woman, give or take three years each. Too old to be raiding the city street for donors. That takes youth and muscle. I billed them as doctors, culturing the transplants and doing the operations; or sales persons, charged with quietly letting prospective clients know where they could get an operation without waiting two years for the public organ banks to come up with material.

So: they'd tried to sell someone a new kidney and been killed for their impudence. That would make the killer a hero.

So why hide them for three days, then drag them out onto a city slidewalk in the dead of night?

Because they'd been killed with a fearsome new weapon?

I looked at the burnt faces and thought: fearsome, right. Whatever did that *had* to be strictly a murder weapon. As the optical grid over a laser lens would be strictly a murder technique.

So: a secretive scientist and his deformed assistant, fearful of rousing the wrath of the villagers, had dithered over the bodies for three days, then disposed of them in that clumsy fashion because they panicked when the bodies started to smell. Maybe.

But a prospective client needn't have used his shiny new terror weapon. He had only to call the cops after they were gone. It read better if the killer was a prospective *donor*; he'd fight with anything he could get his hands on.

I flipped back to full shots of the bodies. They looked to be in good condition. Not much flab. You don't collect a donor by putting an armlock on him; you use a needle gun. But you still need muscle to pick up the body and move it to your car, and you have to do that damn quick. Hmmm . . .

Someone knocked at my door.

I shouted, "Come on in!"

Drew Porter came in. He was big enough to fill the office, and he moved with a grace he must have learned on a board. "Mr. Hamilton? I'd like to talk to you."

"Sure. What about?"

He didn't seem to know what to do with his hands. He looked grimly determined. "You're an

ARM," he said. "You're not actually investigating Uncle Ray's murder. That's right, isn't it?"

"That's right. Our concern is with the generator. Coffee?"

"Yes, thanks. But you know all about the killing. I thought I'd like to talk to you, straighten out some of my own ideas."

"Go ahead." I punched for two coffees.

"Ordaz thinks Janice did it, doesn't he?"

"Probably. I'm not good at reading Ordaz' mind. But it seems to narrow down to two distinct groups of possible killers. Janice and everyone else. Here's your coffee."

"Janice didn't do it." He took the cup from me, gulped at it, set it down on my desk and forgot about it.

"Janice and X," I said. "But X couldn't have left. In fact, X couldn't have left even if he'd had the machine he came for. And we still don't know why he didn't just take the elevator."

He scowled as he thought that through. "Say he had a way to leave," he said. "He wanted to take the machine—he *had* to want that, because he tried to use the machine to set up an alibi. But even if he couldn't take the machine, he'd still use his alternate way out."

"Why?"

"It'd leave Janice holding the bag, if he knew Janice was coming home. If he didn't, he'd be leaving the police with a locked room mystery."

"Locked room mysteries are good clean fun, but I never heard of one happening in real life. In fiction they usually happen by accident." I waved aside his protest. "Never mind. You argue well. But what was his alternate escape route?"

Porter didn't answer.

"Would you care to look at the case against Janice Sinclair?"

"She's the only one who could have done it," he said bitterly. "But she didn't. She couldn't kill anyone, not that cold-blooded, pre-packaged way, with an alibi all set up and a weird machine at the heart of it. Look, that machine is too *complicated* for Janice."

"No, she isn't the type. But—no offense intended—you are."

He grinned at that. "Me? Well, maybe I am. But why would I want to?"

"You're in love with her. I think you'd do anything for her. Aside from that, you might enjoy setting up a perfect murder. And there's the money."

"You've got a funny idea of a perfect murder."

"Say I was being tactful."

He laughed at that. "All right. Say I set up a murder for the love of Janice. Damn it, if she had that much hate in her I wouldn't love her! Why would she want to kill Uncle Ray?"

I dithered as to whether to drop that on him. Decided *yes*. "Do you know anything about Edward Sinclair's exemption?"

"Yah, Janice told me something about . . ." He trailed off.

"Just what did she tell you?"

"I don't have to say."

That was probably intelligent. "All right," I said. "For the sake of argument, let's assume it was Ray-

mond Sinclair who worked out the math for the
new ramrobot scoops, and Edward took the credit,
with Raymond's connivance. It was probably Raymond's idea. How would that sit with Edward?"

"I'd think he'd be grateful forever," said Porter.
"Janice says he is."

"Maybe. But people are funny, aren't they?
Being grateful for fifty years could get on a man's
nerves. It's not a natural emotion."

"You're so young to be so cynical," Porter said
pityingly.

"I'm trying to think this out like a prosecution
lawyer. If these brothers saw each other too often
Edward might get to feeling embarrassed around
Raymond. He'd have a hard time relaxing with
him. The rumors wouldn't help . . . oh, yes, there
are rumors. I've been told that Edward couldn't
have worked out those equations because he
doesn't have the ability. If that kind of thing got
back to Edward, how would he like it? He might
even start avoiding his brother. Then Ray might
remind brother Edward of just how much he owed
him . . . and that's the kiss of death."

"Janice says no."

"Janice could have picked up the hate from her
father. Or she might have started worrying about
what would happen if Uncle Ray changed his mind
one day. It could happen any time, if things were
getting strained between the elder Sinclairs. So one
day she shut his mouth—"

Porter growled in his throat.

"I'm just trying to show you what you're up
against. One more thing: the killer may have wiped
the tapes in Sinclair's computer."

"Oh?" Porter thought that over. "Yah. Janice could have done that just in case there were some notes in there, notes on Ed Sinclair's ramscoop field equations. But, look: X could have wiped those tapes too. Stealing the generator doesn't do him any good unless he wipes it out of Uncle Ray's computer."

"True enough. Shall we get back to the case against X?"

"With pleasure." He dropped into a chair. Watching his face smooth out, I added, *and with great relief.*

I said, "Let's not call him X. Call him K for killer." We already had an Ecks involved . . . and his family name probably *had* been X, once upon a time. "We've been assuming K set up Sinclair's time compression effect as an alibi."

Porter smiled. "It's a lovely idea. *Elegant,* as a mathematician would say. Remember, I never saw the actual murder scene. Just chalk marks."

"It was—macabre. Like a piece of surrealism. A very bloody practical joke. K could have deliberately set it up that way, if his mind is twisted enough."

"If he's that twisted, he probably escaped by running himself down the garbage disposal."

"Pauline Urthiel thought he might be a psychotic. Someone who worked with Sinclair, who thought he wasn't getting enough credit." Like Peterfi, I thought, or Pauline herself.

"I like the alibi theory."

"It bothers me. Too many people knew about the machine. How did he expect to get away with it? Lawrence Ecks knew about it. Peterfi knew enough about the machine to rebuild it from scratch. Or so he says. You and Janice saw it in action."

"Say he's crazy then. Say he hated Uncle Ray enough to kill him and then set him up in a make-shift Dali painting. He'd still have to get *out*." Porter was working his hands together. The muscles bulged and rippled in his arms. "This whole thing depends on the elevator, doesn't it? If the elevator hadn't been locked and on Uncle Ray's floor, there wouldn't be a problem."

"So?"

"So. Say he did leave by elevator. Then Janice came home, and she automatically called the elevator up and locked it. She does that without thinking. She had a bad shock last night. This morning she didn't remember."

"And this evening it could come back to her."

Porter looked up sharply. "I wouldn't—"

"You'd better think long and hard before you do. If Ordaz is sixty percent sure of her now, he'll be a hundred percent sure when she lays that on him."

Porter was working his muscles again. In a low voice he said, "It's possible, isn't it?"

"Sure. It makes things a lot simpler, too. But if Janice said it now, she'd sound like a liar."

"But it's *possible*."

"I give up. Sure, it's possible."

"Then who's our killer?"

There wasn't any reason I shouldn't consider the question. It wasn't my case at all. I did, and presently I laughed. "Did I say it'd make things simpler? Man, it throws the case *wide open! Anyone* could have done it. Uh, anyone but Steeves. Steeves wouldn't have had any reason to come back this morning."

Porter looked glum. "Steeves wouldn't have done it anyway."

"He was your suggestion."

"Oh, in pure mechanical terms, he's the only one who didn't need a way out. But—you don't know Steeves. He's a big, brawny guy with a beer belly and no brains. A nice guy, you understand. I *like* him, but if he ever killed anyone it'd be with a beer bottle. And he was proud of Uncle Ray. He liked having Raymond Sinclair in his building."

"Okay, forget Steeves. Is there anyone you'd particularly like to pin it on? Bearing in mind that now *anyone* could get in to do it."

"Not anyone. Anyone in the elevator computer, plus anyone Uncle Ray might have let up."

"Well?"

He shook his head.

"You make a hell of an amateur detective. You're afraid to accuse anyone."

He shrugged, smiling, embarrassed.

"What about Peterfi? Now that Sinclair's dead, he can claim they were equal partners in the, uh, time machine. And he tumbled to it awfully fast. The moment Valpredo told him Sinclair was dead, Peterfi was his partner."

"Sounds typical."

"Could he be telling the truth?"

"I'd say he's lying. Doesn't make him a killer, though."

"No. What about Ecks? if he didn't know Peterfi

was involved, he might have tried the same thing. Does he need money?"

"Not hardly. And he's been with Uncle Ray for longer than I've been alive."

"Maybe he was after the Immunity. He's had kids, but not by his present wife. He may not know she can't have children."

"Pauline *likes* children. I've seen her with them." Porter looked at me curiously. "I don't see having children as that big a motive."

"You're young. Then there's Pauline herself. Sinclair knew something about her. Or Sinclair might have told Ecks, and Ecks blew up and killed him for it."

Porter shook his head. "In red rage? I can't think of anything that'd make Larry do that. Pauline, maybe. Larry, no."

But, I thought, there are men who would kill if they learned that their wives had gone through a sex change. I said, "Whoever killed Sinclair, if he wasn't crazy, he had to want to take the machine. One way might have been to lower it by rope . . ." I trailed off. Fifty pounds or so, lowered two stories by nylon line. Ecks' steel and plastic arm . . . or the muscles now rolling like boulders in Porter's arms. I thought Porter could have managed it.

Or maybe he'd thought he could. He hadn't actually had to go through with it.

My phone rang.

It was Ordaz. "Have you made any progress on the time machine? I'm told that Dr. Sinclair's computer—"

"Was wiped, yah. But that's all right. We're learning quite a lot about it. If we run into trouble,

Bernath Peterfi can help us. He helped build it. Where are you now?"

"At Dr. Sinclair's apartment. We had some further questions for Janice Sinclair."

Porter twitched. I said, "All right, we'll be right over. Andrew Porter's with me." I hung up and turned to Porter. "Does Janice know she's a suspect?"

"No. Please don't tell her unless you have to. I'm not sure she could take it."

I had the taxi drop us at the lobby level of the Rodewald Building. When I told Porter I wanted a ride in the elevator, he just nodded.

The elevator to Raymond Sinclair's penthouse was a box with a seat in it. It would have been comfortable for one, cozy for two good friends. With me and Porter in it it was crowded. Porter hunched his knees and tried to fold into himself. He seemed used to it.

He probably was. Most apartment elevators are like that. Why waste room on an elevator shaft when the same space can go into apartments?

It was a fast ride. The seat was necessary; it was two gee going up and a longer period at half a gee slowing down, while lighted numbers flickered past. Numbers, but no doors.

"Hey, Porter. If this elevator jammed, would there be a door to let us out?"

He gave me a funny look and said he didn't know. "Why worry about it? If it jammed at this speed it'd come apart like a handful of shredded lettuce."

It was just claustrophobic enough to make me

wonder. K hadn't left by elevator. Why not? Because the ride up had terrified him? *Brain to memory: dig into the medical records of that list of suspects. See if any of them have records of claustrophobia.* Too bad the elevator brain didn't keep records. We could find out which of them had used the boxlike elevator once or not at all.

In which case we'd be looking for K_2. By now I was thinking in terms of three groups. K_1 had killed Sinclair, then tried to use the low-inertia field as both loot and alibi. K_2 was crazy; he hadn't wanted the generator at all, except as a way to set up his macabre tableau. K_3 was Janice and Drew Porter.

Janice was there when the doors slid open. She was wan and her shoulders slumped. But when she saw Porter she smiled like sunlight and ran to him. Her run was wobbly, thrown off by the missing weight of her arm.

The wide brown circle was still there in the grass, marked with white chalk and the yellow chemical that picks up bloodstains. White outlines to mark the vanished body, the generator, the poker.

Something knocked at the back door of my mind. I looked from the chalk outlines, to the open elevator, to the chalk . . . and a third of the puzzle fell into place.

So simple. We were looking for K_1 . . . and I had a pretty good idea who he was.

Ordaz was asking me, "How did you happen to arrive with Mr. Porter?"

"He came to my office. We were talking about a hypothetical killer"—I lowered my voice slightly—"a killer who isn't Janice."

"Very good. Did you reason out how he must have left?"

"Not yet. But play the game with me. Say there was a way."

Porter and Janice joined us, their arms about each other's waists. Ordaz said, "Very well. We assume there was a way out. Did he improvise it? And why did he not use the elevator?"

"He must have had it in mind when he got here. He didn't use the elevator because he was planning to take the machine. It wouldn't have fit."

They all stared at the chalk outline of the generator. So simple. Porter said, "Yah! Then he used it anyway, and left you a locked room mystery!"

"That may have been his mistake," Ordaz said grimly. "When we know his escape route we may find that only one man could have used it. But of course we do not even know that the route exists."

I changed the subject. "Have you got everyone on the elevator tape identified?"

Valpredo dug out his spiral notebook and flipped to the jotted names of those people permitted to use Sinclair's elevator. He showed it to Porter. "Have you seen this?"

Porter studied it. "No, but I can guess what it is. Let's see . . . Hans Drucker was Janice's lover before I came along. We still see him. In fact, he was at that beach party last night at the Randalls'."

"He flopped on the Randalls' rug last night," said Valpredo. "Him and four others. One of the better alibis."

"Oh, *Hans* wouldn't have anything to do with this!" Janice exclaimed. The idea horrified her.

Porter was still looking at the list. "You know

about most of these people already. Bertha Hall and Muriel Sandusky were lady friends of Uncle Ray's. Bertha goes backpacking with him."

"We interviewed them too," Valpredo told me. "You can hear the tapes if you like."

"No, just give me the gist. I already know who the killer is."

Ordaz raised his eyebrows at that, and Janice said, "Oh, good! Who?" which question I answered with a secretive smile. Nobody actually called me a liar.

Valpredo said, "Muriel Sandusky's been living in England for almost a year. Married. Hasn't seen Sinclair in years. Big, beautiful redhead."

"She had a crush on Uncle Ray once," said Janice. "And vice versa. I think his lasted longer."

"Bertha Hall is something else again," Valpredo continued. "Sinclair's age, and in good shape. Wiry. She says that when Sinclair was on the home stretch on a project he gave up everything: friends, social life, exercise. Afterward he'd call Bertha and go backpacking with her to catch up with himself. He called her two nights ago and set a date for next Monday."

I said, "Alibi?"

"Nope."

"Really!" Janice said indignantly. "Why, we've known Bertha since I was that high! If you know who killed Uncle Ray, why don't you just say so?"

"Out of this list, I sure do, given certain assumptions. But I don't know how he got out, or how he expected to, or whether we can prove it on him. I can't accuse anyone *now*. It's a damn shame he didn't lose his arm reaching for that poker."

Porter looked frustrated. So did Janice.

"You would not want to face a lawsuit," Ordaz suggested delicately. "What of Sinclair's machine?"

"It's an inertialess drive, sort of. Lower the inertia, time speeds up. Bera's already learned a lot about it, but it'll be awhile before he can really . . ."

"You were saying?" Ordaz asked when I trailed off.

"Sinclair was *finished* with the damn thing."

"Sure he was," said Porter. "He wouldn't have been showing it around otherwise."

"Or calling Bertha for a backpacking expedition. Or spreading rumors about what he had. Yeah. Sure, he knew everything he could learn about that machine. Julio, you were cheated. It all depends on the machine. And the bastard did wrack up his arm, and we can prove it on him."

We were piled into Ordaz' commandeered taxi: me and Ordaz and Valpredo and Porter. Valpredo had set the thing for conventional speeds so he wouldn't have to worry about driving. We'd turned the interior chairs to face each other.

"This is the part I won't guarantee," I said, sketching rapidly in Valpredo's borrowed notebook. "But remember, he had a length of line with him. He must have expected to use it. Here's how he planned to get out."

I sketched in a box to represent Sinclair's generator, a stick-figure clinging to the frame. A circle around them to represent the field. A bow knot tied to the machine, with one end trailing up through the field.

"See it? He goes up the stairs with the field on. The camera has about one chance in eight of catching him while he's moving at that speed. He wheels the machine to the edge of the roof, ties the line a good distance away, pushes the generator off the roof and steps off with it. The line falls at thirty-two feet per second squared, normal time, plus a little more because the machine and the killer are tugging down on it. Not hard, because they're in a low-inertia field. By the time the killer reaches ground he's moving at something more than, uh, twelve hundred feet per second over five hundred . . . uh, say three feet per second internal time, and he's got to pull the machine out of the way fast, because the rope is going to hit like a bomb."

"It looks like it would work," said Porter.

"Yah. I thought for a while that he could just stand on the bottom of the field. A little fooling with the machine cured me of that. He'd smash both legs. But he could hang onto the frame; it's strong enough."

"But he didn't have the machine," Valpredo pointed out.

"That's where you got cheated. What happens when two fields intersect?"

They looked blank.

"It's not a trivial question. Nobody knows the answer yet. *But Sinclair did.* He had to, he was *finished.* He must have had two machines. The killer took the second machine."

Ordaz said, "Ahh."

Porter said, "Who's K?"

We were settling on the carport. Valpredo knew where we were, but he didn't say anything. We left the taxi and headed for the elevators.

"That's a lot easier," I said. "He expected to use the machine as an alibi. That's silly, considering how many people knew it existed. But if he didn't know that Sinclair was ready to start showing it to people—specifically to you and Janice—who's left? Ecks only knew it was some kind of interstellar drive."

The elevator was uncommonly large. We piled into it.

"And," said Valpredo, "there's the matter of the arm. I think I've got that figured too."

"I gave you enough clues," I told him.

Peterfi was a long time answering our buzz. He may have studied us through the door camera, wondering why a parade was marching through his hallway. Then he spoke through the grid. "Yes? What is it?"

"Police. Open up," said Valpredo.

"Do you have a warrant?"

I stepped forward and showed my ident to the camera. "I'm an ARM. I don't need a warrant. Open up. We won't keep you long." *One way or another.*

He opened the door. He looked neater now than he had this afternoon, despite informal brown indoor pajamas. "Just you," he said. He let me in, then started to close the door on the others.

Valpredo put his hand against the door. "Hey—"

"It's okay," I said. Peterfi was smaller than I was, and I had a needle gun. Valpredo shrugged and let him close the door.

My mistake. I had two-thirds of the puzzle, and I thought I had it all.

Peterfi folded his arms and said, "Well? What is it you want to search this time? Would you like to examine my legs?"

"No, let's start with the insulin feeder on your upper arm."

"Certainly," he said, and startled hell out of me.

I waited while he took off his shirt—unnecessary, but he needn't know that—then ran my imaginary fingers through the insulin feed. The reserve was nearly full. "I should have known," I said. "Dammit. You got six months' worth of insulin from the organlegger."

His eyebrows went up. "Organlegger?" He pulled loose. "Is this an accusation, Mr. Hamilton? I'm taping this for my attorney."

And I was setting myself up for a lawsuit. The hell with it. "Yah, it's an accusation. You killed Sinclair. Nobody else could have tried that alibi stunt."

He looked puzzled—honestly, I thought. "Why not?"

"If anyone else had tried to set up an alibi with Sinclair's generator, Bernath Peterfi would have told the police all about what it was and how it worked. But you were the only one who knew that, until last night, when he started showing it around."

There was only one thing he could say to that kind of logic, and he said it. "Still recording, Mr. Hamilton."

"Record and be damned. There are other things we can check. Your grocery delivery service. Your water bill."

He didn't flinch. He was smiling. Was it a bluff? I sniffed the air. Six months' worth of body odor emitted in one night? By a man who hadn't taken more than four or five baths in six months? But his air conditioning was too good.

The curtains were open now to the night and the ocean. They'd been closed this afternoon, and he'd been squinting. But it wasn't evidence. The lights: he only had one light burning now, and so what?

The big, powerful campout flashlight sitting on a small table against a wall. I hadn't even noticed it this afternoon. Now I was sure I knew what he'd used it for . . . but how to prove it?

Groceries . . . "If you didn't buy six months' worth of groceries last night, you must have stolen them. Sinclair's generator is perfect for thefts. We'll check the local supermarkets."

"And link the thefts to me? How?"

He was too bright to have kept the generator. But come to think of it, where could he abandon it? He was *guilty*. He couldn't have covered *all* his tracks—

"Peterfi? I've got it."

He believed me. I saw it in the way he braced himself. Maybe he'd worked it out before I did. I said, "Your contraceptive shots must have worn off six months early. Your organlegger couldn't get you that; he's got no reason to keep contraceptives around. You're dead, Peterfi."

"I might as well be. Damn you, Hamilton! You've cost me the exemption!"

"They won't try you right away. We can't afford to lose what's in your head. You know too much about Sinclair's generator."

"Our generator! We built it together!"

"Yah."

"You won't try me at all," he said more calmly. "Are you going to tell a court how the killer left Ray's apartment?"

I dug out my sketch and handed it to him. While he was studying it I said, "How did you like going off the roof? You couldn't have *known* it would work."

He looked up. His words came slowly, reluctantly. I guess he had to tell someone, and it didn't matter now. "By then I didn't care. My arm hung like a dead rabbit, and it stank. It took me three minutes to reach the ground. I thought I'd die on the way."

"Where'd you dig up an organlegger that fast?"

His eyes called me a fool. "Can't you guess? Three years ago. I was hoping diabetes could be cured by a transplant. When the government hospitals couldn't help me I went to an organlegger. I was lucky he was still in business last night."

He drooped. It seemed all the anger went out of him. "Then it was six months in the field, waiting for the scars to heal. In the dark. I tried taking that big campout flashlight in with me." He laughed bitterly. "I gave that up after I noticed the walls were smoldering."

The wall above that little table had a scorched look. I should have wondered about that earlier.

"No baths," he was saying. "I was afraid to use up that much water. No exercise, practically. But I had to eat, didn't I? And all for nothing."

"Will you tell us how to find the organlegger you dealt with?"

"This is your big day, isn't it, Hamilton? All right, why not. It won't do you any good."

"Why not?"

He looked up at me very strangely.

Then he spun about and ran.

He caught me flatfooted. I jumped after him. I didn't know what he had in mind; there was only one exit to the apartment, excluding the balcony, and he wasn't headed there. He seemed to be trying to reach a blank wall . . . with a small table set against it, and a camp flashlight on it and a drawer in it. I saw the drawer and thought, *gun!* And I surged after him and got him by the wrist just as he reached the wall switch above the table.

I threw my weight backward and yanked him away from there . . . and then the field came on.

I held a hand and arm up to the elbow. Beyond was a fluttering of violet light: Peterfi thrashing frantically in a low-inertia field. I hung on while I tried to figure out what was happening.

The second generator was here somewhere. In the wall? The switch seemed to have been recently plastered in, now that I saw it close. Figure a closet on the other side, and the generator in it. Peterfi must have drilled through the wall and fixed that switch. Sure, what else did he have to do with six months of spare time?

No point in yelling for help. Peterfi's soundproofing was too modern. And if I didn't let go Peterfi would die of thirst in a few minutes.

Peterfi's feet came straight at my jaw. I threw myself down, and the edge of a boot sole nearly tore my ear off. I rolled forward in time to grab his ankle. There was more violet fluttering, and his other leg thrashed wildly outside the field. Too many conflicting nerve impulses were pouring into the muscles. The leg flopped about like something dying. If I didn't let go he'd break it in a dozen places.

He'd knocked the table over. I didn't see it fall, but suddenly it was lying on its side. The top, drawer included, must have been well beyond the field. The flashlight lay just beyond the violet fluttering of his hand.

Okay. He couldn't reach the drawer; his hand wouldn't get coherent signals if it left the field. I could let go of his ankle. He'd turn off the field when he got thirsty enough.

And if I didn't let go, he'd die in there.

It was like wrestling a dolphin one-handed. I hung on anyway, looking for a flaw in my reasoning. Peterfi's free leg seemed broken in at least two places . . . I was about to let go when something must have jarred together in my head.

Faces of charred bone grinned derisively at me. *Brain to hand: HANG ON! Don't you understand? He's trying to reach the flashlight!*

I hung on.

Presently Peterfi stopped thrashing. He lay on his side, his face and hands glowing blue. I was trying to decide whether he was playing possum when the blue light behind his face quietly went out.

I let them in. They looked it over. Valpredo went off to search for a pole to reach the light switch. Ordaz asked, "Was it necessary to kill him?"

I pointed to the flashlight. He didn't get it.

"I was overconfident," I said. "I shouldn't have come in alone. He's already killed two people with that flashlight. The organleggers who gave him his new arm. He didn't want them talking, so he burned their faces off and then dragged them out onto a slidewalk. He probably tied them to the generator and then used the line to pull it. With the field on the whole setup wouldn't weigh more than a couple of pounds."

"With a flashlight?" Ordaz pondered. "Of course. It would have been putting out five hundred times as much light. A good thing you thought of that in time."

"Well, I do spend more time dealing with these oddball science fiction devices than you do."

"And welcome to them," said Ordaz.

THRILLING SCI-FI NOVELS

☐ **EXILE by Al Sarrantonio.** It is the end of the 25th century. Human civilization has expanded into the Four Worlds of Earth, Mars, Titan, and Pluto. Recent progress in terraforming promises to turn Venus into the Fifth. But for Prime Cornelian, usurper of Martian rule, there will be no rest until all planets bow before him. "A very talented writer."—*Washington Post Book World*   (455215—$5.99)

☐ **FLIES FROM THE AMBER by Wil McCarthy.** An Unuan mining expedition has discovered an alien mineral they name centrokrist—a stone of incomparable beauty. Yet when the Earth scientists at last arrive to investigate, they find a phenomenon eclipsing the centrokrist crystals. For this double-sunned solar system is nestled right next to a black hole.   (454065—$4.99)

☐ **BEYOND THIS HORIZON by Robert A. Heinlein.** This classic tale portrays a utopian Earth of the future, in a time when humanity is free of illness and imperfection. Yet even in paradise there are some like the privileged Hamilton Felix who harbor deep doubts about the very point of human existence.   (166760—$5.99)

Prices slightly higher in Canada.

TERRIFYING TALES

☐ **THE GALLERY OF HORROR 20 chilling tales by the modern masters of dread. Stephen King, Eric Van Lustbader, Ramsey Campbell and 17 others. Edited by Charles L. Grant.** Some galleries specialize in the arts of painting, or sculpture, or crafts. But the gallery you are about to visit specializes in the most irresistibly riveting art of all—the art of horror. For connoisseurs of classic chills for whom no leap into unknown evil is too bold or too scary.
(454618—$21.95)

☐ **NIGHT SCREAMS Edited by Ed Gorman and Martin H. Greenberg.** Let Clive Barker, Lawrence Block, David Morrell, Ray Bradbury, and 19 other of today's greatest terror writers take you on a guided tour into the realms of horror . . . where sex and slaying make strange bedfellows . . . and where there is nowhere to run and no place to hide from an imagination that leaps at you from the darkest depths and will not let go.
(455126—$5.99)

☐ **THE MISTS FROM BEYOND** *20 Ghost Stories & Tales From the Other Side* **by Peter Straub, Clive Baker, Joyce Carol Oates and 17 others. Edited by Robert Weinberg, Stefan R. Dziemianowicz, and Martin H. Greenberg.** Twenty of the most haunting ghost tales ever created . . . all of them certain to transport you, if only for a brief time, from our everyday world to one in which even the faintest of shadows takes on a ghostly life of its own.
(452399—$20.00)

☐ **BETWEEN TIME AND TERROR 17 Tales by such masters of suspense as Dean Koontz, Isaac Asimov, Arthur C. Clarke, Robert A. Heinlein, Clive Baker and 12 others. Edited by Bob Weinberg, Stefan Dziemianowicz, and Martin H. Greenberg.** Take a terror-laden trip to a dark, hidden place where fear feeds on the mind and science devours the soul. With contributions from acclaimed science fiction, fantasy and suspense writers, this riveting collection is a free fall of fright that speeds you through one magnificent story after another.
(454529—$4.99)

☐ **CONFEDERACY OF THE DEAD All-original Civil War stories by such masters of fantasy and horror as Anne McCaffrey, Michael Moorcook, William S. Burroughs, Kristine Kathryn Rusch, and 21 others. Edited by Martin H. Greenberg, Richard Gilliam, and Ed Kramer.** Now these original and evocative tales bring to life that tumultuous and troubled time when "patriots" fought for glory, honor, and sometimes for greed. An age when the demands of love, duty, or vengeance could make brave soldiers heed the call to battle—even from beyond the grave. . . .
(454774—$5.99)

*Prices slightly higher in Canada

Buy them at your local bookstore or use this convenient coupon for ordering.

PENGUIN USA
P.O. Box 999 — Dept. #17109
Bergenfield, New Jersey 07621

Please send me the books I have checked above.
I am enclosing $_____ (please add $2.00 to cover postage and handling). Send check or money order (no cash or C.O.D.'s) or charge by Mastercard or VISA (with a $15.00 minimum). Prices and numbers are subject to change without notice.

Card #_____ Exp. Date _____
Signature_____
Name_____
Address_____
City _____ State _____ Zip Code _____

For faster service when ordering by credit card call **1-800-253-6476**

Allow a minimum of 4-6 weeks for delivery. This offer is subject to change without notice.